DUE NORTH

BOOK 1 OF THE KARA MASON STORY

JILL N DAVIES

JILL N DAVIES PUBLISHING

DUE NORTH

Cover design by Jeff Brown

Edited by Stephen Parolini

Copyedited by Jess Reynolds

Author photo by A Piece of Time Photography

For information about the author please go to www.jillndavies.com

❀ Created with Vellum

To everyone who took the hard path to get here,

I see you

KARA MASON

AUTHOR'S NOTE

Thank you for diving into Kara's story. Please note the content warnings and read at your own discretion.

To my mother, who hates zombies and "all that stuff," you're right. This book contains a disease that makes people present as zombies, but there is so much more to the story. Due North is about people. It's about overcoming insurmountable odds. The zombies, much like the sterile laboratory environment, are just the setting.

Content warning:
Depictions of trauma, violence, gore, blood, vomiting, character death, family loss, manipulation, power imbalance, sexual harassment, and PTSD.

CONTENTS

PART ONE
THE TEST

THE DOOR SNICKS shut behind me, cutting off the black-suited test administrator before he can finish his instructions. *I know how to exit a building.* I roll my eyes as I walk away from the room, grateful to be free from the bizarre situation. I've never taken a test like that before. *Hooked up to a machine…* It was a hard test, but I'm pretty sure I aced it.

I can't wait to throw it in Hank's face.

A fragment of a laugh escapes before I can stop it. My hand flies to my mouth, too late to stifle the noise before it echoes through the empty hall of the government building. I glance over my shoulder to see if anyone heard the ill-timed sound, but there's no one there. The hallway is empty, which seems strange considering how many doors there are.

I look around again as the test fades into the background. The walls are a stark white interrupted by mahogany-trimmed doors and black-rimmed photographs of stern-looking government officials in slim-fitting black suits. *They heard me,* I think, glancing down so that none of them can make eye contact with me. That's when I realize that the floor is purple.

Bruce told me that the floors in the government building were purple, but I didn't believe him. I told him there's no such thing as purple wood. I look up to make sure it's not just a trick of the light. But it's just regular light, which means that the floors are actually purple. I study them as I continue down the corridor, noting my expression staring back at me as if I were staring into a mirror. A purple, wooden mirror. I'm suddenly overcome with the urge to take off my shoes and slide across the polished surface on socked feet.

The thought brings a smile to my lips. Then I remember the people watching from the walls. They are far too serious to tolerate such a carefree act. They probably don't even approve of the smile. I make certain to keep my lips just as straight as theirs, casting my eyebrows down so that I appear downright austere. I check the mirror underfoot to make sure I've got it just right. All I'm missing is the trim, black suit.

Hank finds me the second I burst through the glass doors onto the pale stone steps that raise the government building above the others.

"Kara! What took you so long?" Hank throws his arm around my shoulder so we descend together.

"Aw! I thought I finished first." I try to pry his arm off, but his grip is a vice.

"No way. You know I always win." He smiles, pulling me in for a sickly-sweet side embrace.

"Yeah, well, I'm sure I beat you this time. I wasn't even testing for the last part. The administrator made me stay longer because he said he had to take some extra readings," I boast.

Hank loosens his grip, and I break free at the bottom of the steps, scanning the passing bodies for Bruce. He had a test today too, so he should be in front of the government building somewhere.

"That was weird, wasn't it?" Hank asks, rubbing his hand through his unkempt mop of reddish-blond hair.

"Yeah." I agree absently, locking in on Bruce's lanky frame leaning against the gate that separates the towering school building from the government grounds. I call out to his back, "Bruce!"

"There's no way you beat me," Hank presses, unwilling to let the matter drop.

Bruce turns around after the second time I call his name. He strides toward us, looking confused by our appearance at the base of the stairs. He waits for a woman toting two young children to pass us before asking, "What are you two doing in the government building?"

"Me? I was just beating Hank on a test." I smile, knowing Hank won't be able to let the statement stand.

"As if! I always get better grades," Hank protests.

"So far. But a day will come. And that day, my brother, is today. Just you wait." I bite my lip to keep from ruining my seriousness. It doesn't work, and soon I'm overcome with fits of giggles as we begin to move away from the center of the city.

Bruce stops suddenly in front of the animated billboards that dot the walkway, his body partially blocking the woman in the white lab coat standing against a pristine blue sky dotted with fluffy white clouds. Concern washes over his face. He looks way too serious and grown up. "Wait," he says. "What do you mean, you took a test?"

"It was just some random test. What's the big deal?" Hank shrugs.

The clouds fade away to a clip of a man with a scrunched-up forehead peering down at his arm and shaking his head. The voice-over contrasts the image with a tinny cheerfulness that wafts through the air like a gentle breeze. "Worried about that scratch? Don't leave anything to chance! Get looked at by an expert today in one of our five convenient clinic locations." The image shifts again to show the clinics as glowing blue squares on the city map as the three-note tune signifies the end of the message. Wordlessly, we move away from the sensor so that the message won't play again.

Bruce shakes his head as if to rid it of the artificial voice. Hank leads the way past towering buildings and fast-moving people who won't look at us toward the edge of the city, where the tunnel offers passage through the force field.

"You took a test today too, didn't you?" I ask, taking big strides to try and catch up with Hank.

"No. Ours got bumped to next week for some reason," Bruce responds. His face is pinched so that he looks like the man on the billboard. Not like Hank, who looks like he's on the verge of some great discovery.

"Ha! They bumped your class so we could test first!" Hank whirls around so he's walking backward, looking triumphant.

"You didn't take *the* test. That's next year. You two are only fourteen!" Bruce brushes his hand across his troubled face.

"It sure seemed like *the* test. We took it in the capitol building with a government administrator. What other test could it have been?" I ask, trying to shrug off his seriousness. Two more steps and I'm parallel with Hank again. I spin around to match his backward progress, offering Bruce a smile and a shrug.

The furrows in his brow only deepen, making him look older. *Making him look like Dad*. I glance over at Hank to catch his reaction to Bruce. Hank raises an eyebrow before blowing air through his pursed lips, making a dismissive, farty noise at Bruce, then turns around again. I follow suit so that we turn as if there were only one mind controlling the both of us. It always aggravates Bruce when we do things like this.

"Maybe they decided they just couldn't wait to test a couple of geniuses. It's not like you're going to ever pass," Hank teases Bruce. I lift my hand with his for effect.

"Yeah, well, that's on purpose!" Bruce blurts. His eyes go wide and he looks around. When he sees that there isn't anyone else on this block, he relaxes, but his face is still pinched.

"What do you mean 'on purpose'?" I demand, reeling around without Hank, forgetting the twins act.

Bruce shakes his head, his dark brown hair flopping to one side before his hand jumps up and shoves it back. The motion is meant to tell me *not here*. Another secret we have to wait until we get home for Dad to spell out for us. I roll my eyes.

"Why does everything have to be a—what's the word?"

"Conspiracy?" Hank offers.

"Yeah. Conspiracy." I agree, liking the sound of conspiracy better than collusion.

"You two have no idea," Bruce says, urging us around another corner onto a quiet side street with towering housing buildings. I glance up briefly at the drab brown siding dotted with square, dirty windows shut tight against the outside. No one is home. It makes the street feel lonely. I like it better when we follow the main street past the factories and catch the tram to the city's edge.

"Then enlighten us, oh big brother!" Hank throws his hands up in exasperation.

"If you took *the* test—and I said *if*." He points his finger at Hank, then swings it over to me as I refocus, trying not to think about the empty buildings. He brushes his hand through his hair again. I wonder if our lodging coordinator will make him cut it when we check back in next week. He starts again, keeping his voice low so that no one will accidentally hear him. "If you took the test, then it's a problem." He gets even quieter. "You aren't supposed to pass it."

"What?" Hank asks.

"Why not?" My voice overlaps with Hank's.

Bruce puts his hand up to stop our protests. "Dad will explain when we get home. We should probably drop it for now."

"Conspiracy," Hank mumbles, turning away from Bruce and racing toward the next street.

"Intrigue," I add, running off to catch Hank. We might as well hurry up if we're walking all the way to the tunnel. I imagine Bruce burying his face in his hands before taking off to catch us.

I catch Hank right as he dodges around the crowd gathering at the tram stop in front of the hospital.

"What's his problem?" I puff, trying to sound nonchalant, but sneaking a glance at his reaction when I think he won't notice.

"Who knows. It's like he doesn't want us to have good prospects for our future or something." Hank shrugs. Bruce's quick footsteps announce his approach.

"My administrator said that passing the test opens up our career path to more possibilities. Even the people in the hallway were scientists first," I say.

"The people in the hallway?" Hank asks, running his hand across the waxy green leaves of the hedge that separates the walkway from the hospital grounds.

"You know—the pictures," I tell him.

"Did your administrator also tell you that if you pass the test you'll probably never set foot in a city again?" Bruce asks.

"That can't be true!" Hank protests.

"What about the hallway people?"

"If you pass the test, you go to the Institute. If you're lucky, your picture will come back, but you never will," Bruce confirms.

I pluck one of the leaves from the hedge, rubbing the smooth surface between my thumb and finger, thinking about how certain Bruce sounds.

"How would you know?" Hank challenges him.

"Dad told me," Bruce says.

"That's not what our instructor says. Maybe things are different now," I say.

"Yeah. If we pass the test, we can join an elite team dedicated to ridding the world of disease," Hank adds.

"Doesn't that sound cool?" I flash an excited smile toward Bruce.

Hank doesn't miss a beat. "We'll be on the front line. Agents of prevention!"

"Heroes of medicine!" I recite the speech our instructor gave us before the class filed into the testing area.

"Face to face with the near-dead," Bruce says, spoiling my enthusiasm. I hadn't given that eventuality much thought.

"Bring 'em on," Hank says.

"Yeah," I agree, loaded with false confidence.

Hank turns toward me, his tongue lolling out of the side of his mouth with his teeth bared. He lets out a low moan and throws his arms up in front of me, opening and closing his hands as he reaches for me. I lift my finger and point it at him, pulling the trigger to my imaginary gun. "Eat cure and die, you disease-riddled monster!"

Hank recoils, shrieking and laughing at the same time. I step forward, pulling the trigger a few more times for good measure, laughing. "Die!"

Bruce grabs both of us by our collars, pulling us apart and giving us a hard shake. "Knock it off!"

"What gives? We're just having a little fun. Is that not allowed either?" Hank whines.

Bruce jerks his head to the side to indicate the reason for his censure. I follow his gaze through the gap in the bushes to see a line of people in front of a large transport vehicle. A woman in a crisp white shirt brushes a wisp of hair from her face, which is red and splotchy. A tall, gaunt man turns his head, coughing into his sleeve before excusing himself. We watch in silence as half a dozen people load onto the transport. The door hisses shut behind them.

As the vehicle pulls out of the back lot of the hospital grounds, Bruce gives us yet another stern look. "This isn't a joke, okay? So don't act like it is when you tell Dad about the test tonight."

I swallow hard. "Do you think they're all infected?" I whisper.

"I don't know," Bruce admits.

Hank shakes his head as though he's torn between seriousness and incredulity. "Why would anyone leave if they don't have to?"

"Dad says it's not that simple." Bruce says.

CHAPTER
TWO

THE IMAGE of the transport vehicle pulling away from the hospital lot replays again in my mind, leaving me unsettled and more than a little apprehensive. *There were so many people on board.* I picture their faces as I peer down the dark tunnel. LED lights line either side of the passageway, and the ceiling is dotted with hanging flood lights. Still, nothing can drive away the darkness.

"What's the hold up?" Hank chides, nudging me forward.

"Nothing. It just always seems so dark," I say.

"You want us to go first?" Hank teases.

"Sure, be my guest. If you go first, then it proves I'm smarter than you." I smirk.

Bruce rolls his eyes. "Oh, come on. We *always* go first. You're too old to still be scared of the dark. Hank isn't."

"Yeah, Hank isn't," Hank chides.

"It's not that I'm *scared*…" I begin. "Actually, it's just that I'm *smart*. Never be the first to enter a passageway." I triumph in my concise explanation.

"You've got to be kidding me! We do this every week! That's just advice for stupid city kids. Are you a city kid all of a sudden?" Hank retorts.

"No," I grumble, still looking down the dark pathway. "But why should that mean that I go first?"

Bruce puts his hand on my shoulder and leans forward so that he's eye level with me. His hair flops over his forehead again. Up close, I can see the spindly hairs on his unshaven face. "Kara," he says in his most adult voice.

"Why don't you shave, Bruce? You look goofy like that!" I giggle.

He rubs his face self-consciously. "I like my beard!"

"Takes more than six hairs to make a beard!" Hank chides.

"Give it time," Bruce says, sounding hurt.

I duck behind him, thinking I've dodged the situation, but Bruce grabs my arm before I can escape. "Come on, Kara. There's nothing to be afraid of. Just do it or I won't stop Hank from making fun of you all weekend."

I let out a heavy sigh. "Okay."

"We'll be right behind you," Bruce says in his most supportive, adult voice.

"Yeah, hot on your heels like a pack of near-dead!" Hank says, making another mock-gurgle noise like the creatures in the video clips.

"Shut up!" I smack him hard, just above his kidney, making him grunt. While he's busy smarting from the blow, I close my eyes and force the image of the long dark tunnel out of my imagination. Instead I picture the other side—the open field with wildflowers and the force field hidden by the ferns and rhododendron.

"Mark, set, go!" I say, just like Bruce, before setting off as fast as I can run into the tunnel. I listen to the echo of my feet as each step impacts the asphalt. It doesn't seem so dark now that we're in it.

"Echo!" Hank hollers out behind me.

"Echo!" Bruce and I call back.

Hank comes up on my left, clearly intent on passing. I cut him off, banking into the tunnel's curve and running as fast as I can around the bend until I see the daylight beckoning us from the other end. I speed on, giddy to reach that light before my brothers for the first time. We burst into the open with thunderous energy and laughter, the late evening sunlight making us squint in the open field.

"Ha! I beat you!" I gasp, pointing my finger at Hank's flushed face.

"I let you," Hank grumbles, holding his chest high and trying to act like he's not out of breath.

"Like hell you did," Bruce laughs, nudging him and knocking him off balance.

"She had a head start," Hank protests, kicking at the tall grass.

I ignore the bickering. We're home—one hundred acres of freedom from the regiment of school and congestion of the city. For three whole days we have nothing better to do but help Dad on the power generator and monitor our security systems—granted we finish all our homework and follow instructions completely. Hank will likely spend the bulk of his time shut away in our room and tinkering on his projects, but I suspect Bruce will be up to some sort of adventure.

It's nearly dusk when we first catch sight of our house. The power cells tower high above it like a homing beacon, but the house itself is mostly obscured by foliage. A small creek makes its way through the field, resulting in a gradient of greenery, from rich and dark by the water source to pale and then wheat blond dotted with yellow and purple wildflowers in the farthest corners. The land is wild—not a single soul besides my family ever sets foot around here. We're the keepers of this power generator.

We clamber onto the porch, stomping our feet and stripping off our boots before pouring through the door. "Dad! We're home!" I call out.

"Dad?" Bruce calls out behind me. "Where are you?"

"Long time no see!" Dad bursts into the kitchen from the back of the house with a huge smile plastered across his sun-kissed cheeks.

I throw myself at him, ignoring Hank's *we're too old for that stuff* decree and wrapping my arms around his slender waist. Hank's arm brushes against me as he joins in the reunion.

"I missed you!" I say.

He wraps his arms around us. "I missed my little monsters too. Tell me about your week."

Hank releases him first. "We took a test today." His voice is bright and positive.

I watch for Dad's reaction. It's much more measured than Bruce's, but I catch the edge of alarm that momentarily brightens his dark eyes. "A test?" There's forced humor in his voice. He looks at Bruce.

"They were in the capitol building," Bruce says.

Their eyes exchange a private conversation before Dad pulls away to reach for the kitchen data port. "What was the test like?" He's not trying to sound light anymore.

"Really hard!" I say, even though it might prompt Hank to boast the opposite.

He doesn't. He can see the tension pulling Dad's face tight as he cues up our academic portfolios on the screen.

"Why would they do it early?" Bruce asks, stepping up to look over Dad's shoulder.

"I don't know, son."

The screen flickers red before displaying our names. Mine is on top. I beat Hank, and from the looks of it, I beat him by a lot. Next to both of our names in bold text is one word. *Pass.*

"No." It's barely a whisper, but Dad's voice sends a chill through my whole body. He brings his fingers up to his lips, then covers his whole mouth with his hand as though he's stifling a sob.

"Dad?" Hank tries, sounding as bewildered as I feel.

He repeats his objection, louder this time. The word is laced with anger. His hand shoots out and slams against the side of the data port, knocking it from the counter. The glass crunches and shatters from the impact, making me wince in the silence that follows. I want to put my hands over my ears to drown out the strange tension that fills the room and demand an explanation, but I'm paralyzed.

Dad looks at us, his eyes watery and red. I haven't seen him cry since Mom died. Hank looks away, embarrassed. Bruce puts his hands on each of our shoulders, protectively. He always tries to be more grown up than he is.

"They didn't know," Bruce says, as if to shield us.

"It's my fault," Dad says, letting a tear fall freely down the side of his face.

Hank scuffs his feet together, fussing at a knot in the floor with great interest.

"It'll be okay, Dad. They won't take them until they're—what? Maybe seventeen? We have time to figure something out." He sounds so smart, so grown up.

I look over my shoulder at him, then at Dad as he processes Bruce's proposition. *Did your administrator also tell you that if you pass the test, you'll probably never set foot in a city again?*

"No," Dad says, wiping his eyes and finding his resolve. "I won't give them a chance to take my babies."

Hank crinkles his nose at being called a baby. He whips his head up and looks at Dad. "What's the big deal? So we go to the Institute? *You* went!"

"Exactly! And that's why I won't let them take you! I'm not sending you off to your deaths!" He snaps.

"How can you say that when you and Mom made it out just fine?" Hank retorts, his reddening face contorting with defiance.

"Do you think it was easy? Do you think there weren't consequences? That we didn't have to pay for it?" Dad snaps again. His words make my stomach flip. Hank's face turns white. This isn't how he usually talks to us. *What's going on?*

"What are you going to do, Dad?" Bruce asks.

"We have to go," he says.

"Go?" I ask, my voice much higher and squeakier than usual.

"Yes. Go. Run away," Dad confirms.

Hank recovers at this. Where I prefer the comfort of home and routine, Hank always romanticizes extreme situations. "Sure, that's a good plan. We can build some weapons and plan an escape—" Hank is a builder. He can create from nothing.

"No," Dad interrupts. "I mean now. We need to go right now."

Hank opens his mouth to protest, but Dad lifts his finger to stop him. He looks at us all with fire in his eyes. "Get your things—only what you need to survive, like when we used to pretend. You have ten minutes to meet me back here. We're going in ten minutes."

I stand rigid next to Hank in disbelief—there's no way Dad is serious. There's no way this is actually happening.

"I mean it!" He almost yells before raising his voice again. "Go! Now!"

Bruce nods, almost like he expected this. His action stirs me into motion. I scurry after Hank, shutting the door behind us before looking around the bedroom, terrified to leave anything behind but mostly just terrified. Hank grabs his pack and begins dumping the contents of his desk drawers into it. For Hank, creation is a necessity.

"Are we really running away?" I ask, watching Hank shove a tiny tool kit into the side pocket.

"I guess so. Sure wish they'd let us in on it," Hank mutters, holding up a pack of diodes to count the remaining tiny tubes.

I grab my own pack and start shoving things into it: my multitools, an extra sweater, a sleep-sack, water canteen, a headlamp, my fire starter… I pick up my school data tablet, considering its value.

"Dad said nothing that uses energy," Hank reminds me.

"Everything you packed uses energy," I protest, clinging to the smooth, comforting edges.

"It's different and you know it," he says, grabbing his sleep sack.

The ache of leaving something so precious behind numbs some of the fear.

We're both still rifling through our things when I hear Dad calling for us. Reluctantly, I set the tablet back on the desk before shuffling out of the bedroom with Hank, dragging my pack behind me. Dad's got more supplies on the kitchen table. Nutrition, iodine drops, paper maps I've never seen before, first aid, emergency flares… I'm overwhelmed by the number of things he has lined up.

"How long have you been planning this?" I ask, heaving my pack to the ground.

He ignores my question, pushing us to stay on task. "Everyone take your portion. It's going to be heavy, but this is what we need to survive," he explains.

We shove the supplies into our packs silently. I watch Bruce trade out a notebook to make room for more nutrition packs. Hank moves the tool kit from his pack to his jacket pocket. Within minutes, our packs are so full the zippers threaten to burst. I glance out the window to see that it's dark. I hate the dark. Dad reemerges from the back room holding something I've never seen before—four long poles with loose wires dangling from the ends.

"Kids," Dad explains. "These are called lashing poles. They're weapons."

He hands us each a pole. I turn mine over in my hands. It's surprisingly light for a weapon. I smack it against the table, unimpressed and afraid for why Dad thinks we might need weapons.

"No," Dad corrects, "Like this." He flicks the pole out in front of him and presses a button. The wire at the end crackles with electricity and wraps around the headrest of the chair.

"The electric current generates a magnetic field that holds the wire in place around whatever you've lashed. Try it."

The three of us flick our poles at the chair. Our weapons respond with the same electric crackle as Dad's did, but with a lot less finesse. If we need weapons, we should be using something we have some experience with…

"Good!" he exclaims, oblivious to our apprehension.

"What do we need weapons for?" Hank asks, releasing the button and trying again. His brow furrows as he considers his clumsy aim.

"It's best to be prepared," Dad says.

"These aren't very good weapons," Hanks says, trying for a third time.

"Prepared for what, Dad? Where are we going?" I ask, my finger still compressing the electromagnetic button and my mind dancing between disbelief and horror.

"I'll explain everything, I promise, but right now we need to hurry," Dad says.

"Why? Why do we need weapons? Why do we need to hurry?" I demand, succumbing to the rising panic.

"Because I said so!" Dad yells, whirling around to face me. His face is contorted with… anger? Fear? *Dad isn't afraid of anything.*

Hank's at my side in the same instant. He puts a reassuring hand on my shoulder. "You know that's a lousy answer," he says.

Dad thrusts his hand into his face and lets out a strained sigh. "I know. I'm sorry. I need to get my thoughts together, and then I'll share them with you, but please trust me?"

I *do* trust him.

"Okay. But just this one more time," Hank says.

"Okay." Dad nods, and his body relaxes. He looks at the lashing pole wound around the chair and says, "One last thing. If you need to kill whatever you've lashed, twist your pole like this."

He twists his left hand over his right and the pole responds. A sharp blade protrudes from the edge of the pole like a bayonet. The blade pierces through the chair head, splintering the wood.

"Everyone understand?" Dad asks, releasing the chair and turning to us.

We each release the charge on our poles and look toward Dad. We nod dutifully, and Bruce turns to the door. Hank moves to follow him, but Dad stops him. "The perpetual motion device you created?"

Hank looks back at him, confused. "What about it?"

"I need you to stop it. Can you do that remotely?"

"Yeah, of course I can, but Dad… without coolant, the reactor will melt and the whole place will go down," Hank protests.

"That's exactly what I want to happen," Dad says.

Hank looks like he wants to argue, but instead he just says, "Alright, but not here. Right before we leave, just in case."

"Alright. Let's go."

We march out the back door. I take one last look at our home. The power generator blinks like a lighthouse as we move away. At the border of the property where the ferns grow thick, there's a shimmer. We're at the force field now. Dad stops. I catch my breath. My pack is so heavy. I console myself that Hank's face looks as flushed as mine.

Dad looks at Hank, who looks back at him, admiration masking anxiety. "Do it now," he says.

"What if the force field isn't strong enough?" he protests, hands shoved deep into his pockets.

"The force field will hold. I'm not going to let anything happen to any of you," Dad says, urging him on.

Hank pulls the device from his pocket. He steps into the open and squints back at our place, pointing the small electronic pack. There's a tiny click, then nothing. He turns back to Dad.

"It's done."

Dad turns to the force field and puts something small and round up against it. There's an electric crackle, then a small circle barely large enough to crawl through appears. Bruce goes first, then reaches back for my hands. Hank crawls through right after me, then Dad. The other side looks exactly the same. I don't know what I expected it to look like, but it's the same. Same fern, same trees, same grass and wildflowers. Summer is approaching. Dad touches the circle and it begins to disappear, erasing the hole we just traveled through.

There's a low rumble in the ground, and the scream of an alarm carries on the breeze.

"They'll think we're dead," Dad explains.

We turn and start to run again. There is no path. The brush is thick and the ground is damp. The smell of dirt and rotten earth fills my nostrils.

Everything shakes when the fusion reactor blows. The impact of the burst forces us to the ground. With my head buried in the dirt, I imagine the force field lighting up with a golden glow, absorbing the energy of the blast and protecting us. No one on the inside could have survived.

We're a dead family as we run into the night.

CHAPTER
THREE

MILES of uncharted forest and one sleepless night later, we're navigating the thick wooded area that stretches outward from the west side of the City State as the sun races across the sky. I picture the location in my head as it appears on my data tablet—shades of textured green with a thin vein of blackish-blue that opens into the gaping maw of a river racing toward the sea. It's nothing like that up close. I lift my head to take in the moss-covered branches hanging over us like suspended green rain. The earth squishes underfoot, revealing spindly roots from the surrounding greenery and making each step unsure. *There's even more texture up close.* It's quiet and wild. I pause long enough to watch a butterfly light on the narrow petals of a small purple flower growing above the ferns.

"That's a Woodland Skipper," I say, matching the brown and orange pattern on the frayed wings to the archive of insects that's taken residence in my memory.

"What?" Dad stops to look back at me.

"Woodland Skipper," I repeat, pointing at it. "They're supposed to be extinct."

"It's probably just an Angelwing," Hank says, stomping over and disrupting the butterfly's place of rest.

I shake my head at him before turning to catch up to Dad and Bruce. "No. It was a Woodland Skipper. I'm sure."

"How can you be sure you saw an extinct bug?" Hank asks.

"Because I don't spend my time bent over a pile of wires. I'm *sure*," I insist.

"Somebody give Kara a medal. She brought a butterfly back from the dead," Hank patronizes.

"She's probably right. She spent all last summer cataloging the bugs at home," Bruce offers. His hands are resting against the taught straps of his overloaded pack.

"Yeah, but those weren't extinct," Hank argues.

"I've already seen six insects that should be extinct—the firefly beetle, a larder, a cranefly—"

"Who cares?" Hank moans.

I give him a nasty side glance before returning my eyes to the crumpled ferns and torn moss that mark our passage. "And it's not just the insects. Did you see that Merlin this morning?"

"No, I didn't see the Merlin." Hank crinkles his nose, nearly tripping on a root from not paying attention.

"How can there be so many species that are supposed to be extinct? We're not even far from home yet. Why hasn't anyone noticed?" I ask, easily missing Hank's tripping point.

"Because nobody is supposed to see them," Dad answers. He stops to look around where the trees bunch up against a dirty slope. He heads uphill in a way that suggests he knows exactly where he's going without even stopping to look at the map. The loose-packed dirt slides back under his feet. He leans forward to grip the branch of a fallen tree and hoists himself upward.

"Why not?" Hank asks.

"Because it means the world is coming back to life," Dad says simply. His feet skid on the packed earth.

"Where are we going?" I ask, watching him traverse the steep terrain.

"South," Dad says, dodging trees and continuing his climb.

Bruce boosts me so that I can grab the tree and follow.

"We're going up," I mumble, brushing my dirty hands against my pants.

"To another city?" Hank asks. We can't be headed to another city— we would have to register, and we're supposed to be dead now.

"No, south of the cities. We're going to the uninhabited region." Even breathless, Dad sounds confident.

"To the Deadlands? We'll die!" I protest.

"No, we won't die. There are safe places to live. We just need a little bit of help getting there."

"Who's going to help us?" I ask. I don't want to live in the Deadlands.

"A group of people called dissenters who live outside the City States," he says.

The way ahead is steep again. I look back to note that we're leaving the trees behind. The thought makes me nervous.

"How do you know them?"

"Why do they want to help us?"

Hank's question and mine overlap, creating the sound that Bruce calls twinterference.

"I told you I'm going to explain everything. But right now, we need to get to the descent point," Dad says, huffing out a breath that sounds a little bit like his normal laugh.

Always later.

"Time's up. Tell us now." Hank whines as the same demand forms in my head.

"Lay off him, yeah? He'll answer all your questions when we get to the bottom," Bruce scolds.

A cool breeze pulls at the sweat beading on my forehead, sending a chill down my arms. "We're going up, not down."

"We *will* be going down," Bruce says.

"How do you know?" I ask, daring to look back at him again. The trees wave at me from behind him.

Hank stops in front of me, looking ahead at Dad, then back at Bruce before settling on me. "Isn't it obvious? He knows where we're going. Dad told him."

"Did he?" I demand, wounded from being left out of another grand scheme.

"Of course he did. Just like he told *him* about the test we shouldn't have passed. He probably even knows why that's such a bad thing," Hank butts in before Bruce can answer.

I can tell by the look on Bruce's face that Hank is right. His reaction fills me with a buzzing, hot energy that makes me want to run the rest of the way to the top of the hill. He isn't supposed to keep secrets from us.

"It's not his fault. I told him to keep it from you until we were ready," Dad says. He takes careful steps back down the granite until we're standing in a lopsided circle.

"Which part?" Hank's words are laced with hurt from the betrayal.

"The test. The plan. The dissenters. All of it." Dad wipes a sleeve across his forehead, smearing sweat and dirt.

"Why?" I demand.

"Because I thought we had more time. Because I wanted to protect you from… from everything!" He says. His voice is tense and breathy from the climb. He looks away from both of us and shakes his head. "I'm sorry. I'm *going* to tell you everything. No more secrets."

"Why not now?" I ask.

"Because Bruce is right. We've got a big descent ahead of us, and we need to hurry or we'll be doing it in the dark," Dad says. He puts his hand on my shoulder and urges me forward. After a moment of hesitation, I press on as if there were a way to outrun the sinking sun. Explanations are just as easy in the dark.

We reach the edge of a steep cliff after an hour of silence broken only by our heavy breaths. I look down and the world spins as I take in the treetops so far below. Up here they look like the satellite images on my data tablet. Further out from the base of the streaked granite structure, the greenery is separated by the line of a river. I look up to see if the clouds are as close as they should be this high up. They remain out of reach in the crisp, thin air. I back up from the edge, taking care with each step. Though there is plenty of space at the top, the vastness of what's below us makes it seem like we're straddling a flimsy ledge.

Dad takes off his pack and pulls out a long rope and some climbing gear. He's got a large tool that looks like a hooked ax and pegs.

"Are we going to climb down this?" Hank asks, balancing one foot on a protruding rock speckled with sparkling black. Watching him makes my stomach do flips, even though I know he's safe.

"It's the fastest way south," Dad insists.

"Will we make it before dark?" I ask.

Dad studies the horizon. "Maybe."

"If the answer is only maybe, then why can't we wait for tomorrow?" I ask.

"Because we need to keep moving. The farther we get, the harder it will be for anyone to track us," Dad explains as he organizes the climbing gear.

"Who's going to follow us?" Hank asks, settling further back from the edge than before.

"Disease Containment. Eventually, they're going to come looking for us." He swings the ax over his head. The metal makes contact with a peg, sounding a loud *ping* that reaches the world below, scattering birds into flickering black clouds.

His words conjure the image of the bored-looking workers with short, slicked-back hair and DDC stamped on their fitted black suits. The woman who gave the talk in our classroom last year had a voice so monotone that I had a hard time keeping my eyes focused as she read statistics off of her tablet. I can't imagine those people leaving their tiny little building to hunt us down. "The Department of Disease Containment is responsible for keeping records of people's travels and the spread of the disease," I correct him.

"They're responsible for a lot more than that. They run the Institute. They're the ones that will investigate our untimely deaths."

Dad drops the rope down the edge. I watch as it skitters across the uneven surface, uncoiling as it falls. In my mind, the DDC woman runs up to the edge of the ledge, brandishing her stamp at us and yelling hoarsely.

"They'll look for us because we passed the test?" Hank asks. The image evaporates.

"They will, if they know you passed."

"Then why did we bother running? Isn't it already too late?" Hank demands.

"I said *if*," Dad snaps. "I know someone on the inside who should be able to erase your results. No results, no suspicious disappearance. Come on. Let's get going."

Whoever Dad knows must be pretty powerful.

"This is just like the wall in the obstacle box!" Hank says as Dad helps him clip onto the rope. I watch him step over the edge, resting his weight between his feet and the rope.

"It's like ten walls from the obstacle box," I correct him.

"Yeah, well, I'll still beat you down," Hank chides.

"Never in a million years." Every single one of Hank's times in the obstacle box is faster than mine.

"Alright kids, pay attention. We're going to have to use the same rope." Dad is all business. None of us question his ability. One after another, we follow him down.

The descent isn't as steep as it looked from the top, but the granite is slick where the rocks have recently sloughed off the surface. Our progress is painfully slow. My mind fills with questions with every pause we take. I want to know who will erase the test. "Dad?" I ask as Hank reaches the next waypoint.

"Yes, Kara?" His voice is tentative. It's my turn to scramble across the smooth surface.

Grains of fine sand crunch underfoot as I take my first few steps. It isn't so bad if I lean forward. "Who's going to erase our test results?"

"A very old friend. Kara, please focus." He sighs.

I lean back and step again. "What kind of a person can make a whole test just disappear?"

Both of my feet slip at the same time, driving my knees toward the surface as I slide down. The rope glides through my fingers like fine silk.

"Kara!" Dad's scream is closer than it should be.

All at once, the line tightens. My skin is hot where friction burned holes through my jeans. I cling to the rope with both hands. My eyes are clamped shut and my heart is racing with the uneven pattern of panic.

"It's okay. I got you." Dad's soft voice is right next to me.

I peer through cautious slits. He's two feet away. Hank is pressed up against him and they're both holding the rope. I could reach out and touch them.

"Try to get your feet back under you," he coaches.

It takes longer than it should, but I end up back on the rock, resting my weight on my legs. I trace the strata of sparkling black and brown streaks that haven't been eroded by weather with my eyes, not daring to let go of the rope. The answers will have to wait.

After an hour, my hands ache from holding on. Hank makes my complaints audible below me, but Bruce remains stoic above. Dad keeps vigilant watch on our descent. When we run out of rope, we all cling to the cliffside while he clicks the release and prepares the next hold. We won't be able to collect the pegs above us, but at least we won't lose the rope.

"Won't somebody find those pegs?" Bruce asks.

"I can't move them now. By the time anyone starts looking for us, we should be far away from here." Dad sounds confident. I try to feel confident too.

"I thought you said they wouldn't look if our results were erased?" Hank asks.

"I'm trying to keep us ahead of all of the possibilities, Bud," Dad says. Hank hates it when Dad calls him 'Bud.' I glance down and notice that he doesn't look like he hated it this time.

The trees are closer now, but we're still very high. For the first time since the slip, I dare to let go of the rope. I put my hand out in front of me to measure the sun in the sky. I can fit four fingers between the base of the sun and the horizon. We have more than an hour before the sun sets. I wonder if we'll still be on this wall when the dark comes. My hands are raw and red from holding onto the rope for so long and my arms ache. I feel mechanical, like my gears need to be oiled. That's how Hank described his own arms. He says he wishes he could have built us a descending machine.

As the sun sinks lower in the sky, mosquitoes begin to buzz around my head. One of them is sucking the blood from Bruce's ankle just above me.

"Can you get the disease from a mosquito bite?" I ask.

"You can get lots of diseases from mosquitoes," Bruce responds.

"You know which one I mean!" I snap. He wouldn't think it was funny if he knew about his ankle.

"You can only get the disease from direct contact," Bruce says.

"Not mosquitoes?" I press.

"No, Kara, not mosquitoes," he insists.

When we reach the ground, the trees cast tall shadows, making it seem darker than it is. I look up to the sheer face where I slipped. An eerie orange glow blankets the surface, making it look otherworldly. I decide that it is another world. Up there, where we used to live at an energy management facility and Hank and I hadn't passed a test. It's hard to imagine never living in that world again.

After a long moment staring at the sun glinting off of the past, I turn away. It's time to learn about our future.

I KEEP my eyes fixed on the dancing orange and yellow of the firelight as my head spins with what Dad just told us. The government doesn't want to find a cure for the disease. The Division of Disease Containment's real job is to keep track of people who figure out the truth and make them disappear. The Institute is meant to train scientists to be agents of the government—the government that doesn't actually want to help people. The dissenters are the only people who know the truth. They hide in the Deadlands to fight back against infection… and the government wants them all dead.

Thick chunks of rotten wood crackle and glow red under their white-ash surfaces. The heat reaches me in rising currents that make my face feel dry and hot against the cold dampness.

"Do you believe they really aren't working on a cure?" I ask.

"Maybe. But it's sort of hard to believe, isn't it?" Hank answers. His feet drag through the earth as he scoots himself closer so that our conversation stays private. Dad walked off to make contact with the person who's going to get us out of this mess, or our "dissenter liaison," as he put it.

"What's harder to believe, that or that people who live on the outside are the ones who are actually working on a cure?" His voice is as quiet as the hiss of water evaporating from the logs drying out next to the flames.

"Both," I say, turning my head to watch the shadows that dance across his face.

"Invalid response."

"Dissenters are harder to believe," I decide.

"Yeah. What are they fighting against?"

"A government that doesn't want to cure the disease." I repeat Dad's explanation.

"It doesn't make sense." Hank shakes his head.

"Do you think the Institute can really change people like that? Make them hollow and obedient?" I curl my legs back from the fire, wincing at the burn of overheated fabric.

"Maybe a little—like the Milgram experiments," Hank offers.

"But every scientist?" In the narrow passageway of my mind, the disapproving faces stare down at me from the hallway portraits. *They aren't stern, they're empty.*

"I don't know. I mean, he was there, so he knows something we don't, right?" Hank shrugs.

I exhale, overwhelmed by the strangeness of it all. "At least it means there won't be any near-dead."

"Dad said 'shouldn't be' not 'won't be.' He said there were mixed reports but that where we're going should be clear," Hank corrects me.

"Yeah. Well, that's better than what we learned in school." I watch him again. He's dragging a twig through loose earth to create a rough sketch of a stick man with stink-lines and x's for eyes.

"The *propaganda*, you mean?" He swings the stick back and forth, erasing the picture.

I think about Dad's word. The thought is too big to make total sense. "He's probably sort of right. There's bad stuff mixed in with everything good they've done. Every organization has weak points."

Bruce approaches us tentatively, holding two steaming tin mugs in one hand and one in the other. Hank looks away from him, making a scornful sound with his shoes as he shuffles back to his spot.

"Are you going to stay mad at me forever?" Bruce asks. The air coming from his direction is cold. I move so that I'm closer to Hank again.

"You too, Kara?" He sounds wounded. Maybe he thought he still had my allegiance because he always takes my side when Hank's being a jerk. Maybe he deserves it.

"I brought you guys dinner. The package says it's chicken noodle." He thrusts the hand with two mugs at me.

The rich, starchy smell wafts up as I take the cups, making my mouth water. Each one has a fork sticking up from the contents. One red, one green. I hand Hank the red one. "Is this the same stuff as last night?" I ask Bruce's back.

He turns his head, one eyebrow raised as though cautious of a trap.

"It's actually good," Hank exclaims though an overstuffed mouthful. He parts his lips and steam escapes, mingling with the smoke from the fire. I take a more cautious, measured bite. Everything in the mixture tastes exactly the same, but even though carrots and chicken shouldn't taste like each other, it's delicious.

"That's because it's cooked tonight," Bruce says. His body is pointed toward the fire now. His jacket is zipped all the way to the top so that the collar is flipped up into his overgrown hair. He brings his cup up to his lips and sips. He has the blue fork.

"The marvels of modern science!" Hank says between mouthfuls.

Bruce smirks.

"You can sit down, you know," I say, taking another sip of the salty broth.

He pauses, weighing his desire to join us with the risk of our scorn. "You're not still mad at me for keeping secrets?"

"Yes," Hank says without pause.

"That's what I thought," Bruce huffs.

"It doesn't mean you can't sit," I say.

He does, but the distance between him and us is noticeable. I take in a few more mouthfuls in silence. Bruce scoots one of the drying logs into the flames. Smoke fills the air until the log catches and the heat pushes it upward.

"Did you know all of it?" I ask, too curious to keep the silence.

He sighs.

"No lying," Hank snaps, putting his empty mug on top of the dirt that used to be his art canvas.

"Pretty much," he admits.

"People on the outside?" I ask.

"The lies about the outbreaks?" Hank adds.

"Yeah. Dad told me the first year I had to take the test," Bruce says.

"And you believe all of it?" I ask, eyes wide.

"I do," he says.

"That the government doesn't want a cure? That dissenters are looking for a cure and the government wants to hunt them down and stop them?" Hanks eyes are big too.

"Why would Dad lie about it?" Bruce counters. His fork tings against the side of his mug as he sets it aside.

"But..." I start, then take another bite of noodles while I try to formulate the nebulous thing that's floating right behind the fog of too much information at once.

"But what? He knows more than we do. He went to the Institute. He's seen what they do firsthand."

"That was a long time ago. And he got bumped out of the Northern Laboratories program into Energy Management, so maybe he doesn't really know everything," I say, finding the words to match the feeling.

"He said that he and Mom went to Energy Management on purpose—to escape," Bruce corrects me.

"Right. With the help of dissenters on the inside, working against the government," Hank says. The thought of it is exciting, if not terrifying.

"What's so hard to believe?" Bruce asks.

"People on the outside. No near-dead. I mean—you've seen the videos! Everyone's seen them. They're real." I ignore the fact that I normally hate talking about the near-dead in the dark. "Besides, Bruce... what about those people?" I remind him of the transport vehicle leaving the hospital.

"I trust Dad," Bruce concludes. The conversation fades against the crackling fire. I fix my gaze on a lump of charred wood that's crumbled away from the center of the glowing mass as my soup turns cold. Thin lines of pale orange flicker and blink back at me.

"I can't believe you didn't tell us," Hank says into the fire.

"Are you going to hold it against me forever?" Bruce asks.

"Depends," Hank says. I glance over at him. His eyes are bright and mischievous.

"On what?"

"How badly do you want us to forgive you?" I ask, in on the plan.

Bruce looks back and forth between us as realization dawns. "Oh geez! You guys are too old for this," he protests.

"How badly do you want back in?" Hank repeats.

"You know those stories are a bunch of crap," Bruce says, but it's obvious he's going to give in.

His words have new meaning, but I'm not ready to give it more thought. Not tonight. There's been enough thinking.

"Do it," Hank whispers.

"Do it," I repeat.

"Dad hates them." Bruce is sitting up now. His words don't match his face.

"Dad's not here." A smile creeps across Hank's face.

"Dad's not here." We've won.

"Which one do you want? Deadlands rebellion or—"

"Henry Endgal!" We both shout. Bruce smiles. He already knew what we wanted.

"A hundred years ago—" he starts.

"One hundred and twenty-three years ago," I correct.

"Don't ruin this, Kara," Hank moans.

"Facts matter," I argue.

"One significant figure," Bruce says, shutting us both up. I settle in, leaning against Hank and watching the fire as Bruce's voice drives my mind back in time. We're home, camping in the backyard under the blinking light of the reactor.

"It started when the bees disappeared," Bruce starts again.

"That's how Dad starts the story," Hank objects.

"Do you want it or not?" Bruce thrusts his face into his hands, but he can't hide his enjoyment. "Fine. Imagine what it would be like to wake up one day and all the food is gone. There is no bread because all the wheat in the fields is dead. Crops shriveled on the vine and rotted on the ground. The war started because there was no food."

I can see Dad approaching through a split in the flames. His canvas jacket hangs on his narrow shoulders. Tucked under his arm is a data tablet. I protested the second he pulled it out, but he explained that his was altered so that no one could use it to track us. He's still too far away to see his expression.

"The livestock started to die first. That's just the way it is with famine. People killed each other over cans of food. Then came the bombs. Then came the disease," Bruce continues.

This is one of the parts where Dad always used to jump in and correct us. In Dad's version, the disease was in the bombs. *A tool of war.* But Bruce is sticking to the story. Dad looks pleased. I watch as he stops to listen to the fireside tale. He can't see me, so he doesn't know that I see him. Instead of joining us, he turns to kneel at our pile of supplies, intending to give us this night before we have to believe something else.

"Skip to the good part!" Hank begs.

"Before Henry Endgal, people used to believe that it was the dead come back to life, but those were the dark ages."

"Impossible!" Hank interjects with childlike glee.

"What would *you* think if your neighbor came banging on your door with his face half-rotted off?" Bruce moans, his arms flailing in the air. "Can I borrow some sugar and eat your entraiiiiiiilllls?"

When we were younger, we would squeal with delight at this line. Bruce would lunge forward at our kicking legs in a mock-attempt to tear us to pieces. Tonight almost feels like that.

"A lone hero in a bloody, barren world. Henry discovered the truth. With a bloody scythe in one hand and a tiny vial capped with nothing more than a thin film of melted wax in the other, he crossed the great plains in the dead of winter. His mission was singular. Against all odds, he intended to rally the last stand against the mounting numbers of near-dead and end the disease that should have destroyed mankind…"

Somewhere in the night, something small screes a shrill cry to the night, and an owl hoots. It *almost* feels like before.

"WHY ARE THEY CALLED COYOTES?" I ask.

"It's a really old term. It dates back to when people used to smuggle other people across country borders," Bruce says.

I imagine quick, angular people climbing hills of radioactive dust in the wasted land to the south. They peer out of thick cover, on high alert against invisible threats.

"They're not actually coyotes," Hank says.

"I know that. How come we didn't learn about them in school?" I ask.

The trees are getting thinner. Between clusters of pine, the anemic grass reaches up to my knees. The yellow flowers make the tall grass look sick. *It shouldn't be so pale when it's so close to water.* I glance back at the skeletal remains of an old structure. Jagged, rotting boards jut out from the front like a broken-toothed smile. The grass surrounding it is even paler than where we're walking. It makes me wonder if the old structure has something to do with the unnatural color. Like the bombs in the story…

"They aren't supposed to exist. If the government admitted that there were people on the outside moving people in and out of cities it wouldn't make them look too good, would it? I mean, nothing is supposed to be able to get in or out of the City States without the DDC knowing about it, right?" Bruce says.

"Maybe that's the reason for all of the infections," I suggest. *Maybe the barn is an infection.*

"No. Dissenters are even more careful," Bruce says.

"They wouldn't have to be if they had the cure," Hank says.

"Working on it isn't the same thing," I say.

Further ahead, Dad stops to wait for us.

"Maybe a cure is impossible. Maybe there are too many mutated strains and that's why the government is mostly focused on killing them," Hank speculates.

"Then why would they tell people they can help? What about all the people that go for help?" I ask.

Hank shakes his head, clearly still trying to make sense of it for himself. Bruce has mostly left the speculations to us, unwilling to put himself in a compromising position after being re-accepted. Hank's eyes brighten, as if he's suddenly stumbled on a suitable explanation.

"Actually..."

"Quiet!" Dad throws his arm up in the air and cuts him off. The word is low and sharp—the sort of sound we don't dare disobey.

I stand frozen in the ocean of yellow grass. A gentle breeze wafts past us, tousling the wisps against one another. Dad is staring out across the grass at a lone figure that walks with unnaturally swaying arms. Its body rocks back and forth, as though each step threatens to upend the whole venture. It stops and looks around as if it's forgotten what it meant to do. From far away, just standing there like that, it looks like a person. A sad and lonely person that doesn't know where it's going or what it's doing.

"What's it doing here?" Hank whispers.

As the locomotion process starts again, I pull my eyes away from it long enough to look at Dad. He puts his finger to his lips, forbidding even the quietest whisper. Tilting his head, he indicates that he wants us to walk forward, away from the ambling figure.

I obey, falling in line with Hank but keeping my gaze fixed on the strangest thing I've ever seen. We've watched videos, but this seems so different—it's *real*. It occurs to me that it doesn't look as rotten as they are supposed to look, or as scary. The faded blue shirt is torn from the sleeve down to the torso. The black smear around the cuffs must be old, dried blood. But otherwise, there are no visible injuries. The way the collar is buttoned all the way to the top reminds me of the woman behind the hospital. It's as though one minute it was a man dressing for work, and the next it found its way into an open field.

Dad leads us in a wide arc around the wandering creature. As we get closer, I can hear the strange noise it makes, like a breathy whine. The sound is almost mournful, as though he were in a great deal of pain. I can't see its face anymore, but I'm certain that it's a he—unless the disease made it lose most of its hair. The sun glints off the back of the slightly greyish skin that looks as if it were stretched too tight across the back of its skull.

The creature cries again, and the sound comes out as if it were leaking through multiple holes. A horrible thought occurs to me.

"Dad? What if it's not all the way gone? What if he's still a person?" I whisper as quietly as possible, but the sound of my voice carries across the tops of the grass.

The man's head snaps up, alert and discerning. The head bobs up and down, swiveling on the base of its neck until it faces us. The whine is louder now, transforming into something more urgent—something hungry. The unnatural gait is faster now as the creature lunges in our direction.

"Kara, Hank, get back. Now." Dad pulls the lashing pole from the side of his pack and holds it out in front of him, ready.

Bruce pulls his lashing pole out too, but stands back, waiting for instructions.

The man who got lost on his way to work is gone. He doesn't look human anymore. He looks angry. The breeze picks up and drags a terrible stench across the field, making me gag. The thing's mouth is open unnaturally wide, tilting the head back so that the milk-white eyes look sunken into the too-tight skin. Underneath the flapping shirt, there's a large, festering hole where his sternum should be. I imagine that's where all of the sound is leaking out.

When the thing gets close enough, Dad flings out his lashing pole and catches the creature around its open mouth. The buzz of the electromagnetic wire is nearly drowned out by the creature's wail. Dad pulls back against it, nearly toppling the unsteady thing, but it manages to keep its feet and pull back with surprising strength. Dad spreads his feet, pointing his front foot directly at the flailing body before him, and wrenches forward. The creature pitches backward. Dad twists the handle of the lashing pole, and the blade punches through the side of the creature's cheek, forcing its mouth open even wider.

"Bruce, I can't get the angle right to kill it. I need you to do it," Dad grunts, turning his pole so he can step back from the frantic thrashing. He's breathing heavily with his effort.

I nearly cry out when Dad scrambles, almost losing his footing. Hank grabs my hand and squeezes hard.

"What do I do?" Bruce asks.

"Twist your pole so the blade is exposed and stab it through the eye," Dad grunts. He twists his own pole so the thing finally loses its balance, falling to the ground with a terrible shriek.

Bruce hesitates. I can't see his face, but I imagine he's grimacing. My hand aches from how hard Hank is squeezing. I can feel my nails digging into his skin, but I can't make myself let go. Bruce thrusts his pole forward and down, right into the thing's eye. Even from behind, he looks scared. The creature stops thrashing immediately, as if Bruce had merely pressed an off switch.

Dad's shoulders sag with relief, and his body relaxes. "Good work, son," he says, releasing the current in the wires so the pole comes free of the dead thing.

Bruce doesn't respond. Dad takes the lashing pole from him and tosses it aside, then turns him away from the corpse. Bruce's face is white. I look away from it, not wanting to think about how similar his pallor is to the dead thing's. Instead I look at Hank. His eyes are fixated on the corpse. His lips are slightly parted, and he's breathing in short, quick bursts, as if he were in a trance. "Did you see how fast it changed?" he whispers.

I nod, unable to find words as I join him in staring. In some ways, it was exactly like we were taught—dangerous, animalistic, contagious… But it died so easily. *And what was it doing here?* The body is splayed out where it fell, one arm flopped out to the side. A silver link bracelet with a single dangling charm rests on the limp, oddly contorted wrist.

"It isn't right," Dad says. The words are like a thread pulled too tight.

"What do you mean?" Bruce asks.

He isn't dressed for a trip to the outdoors, I think. Maybe he isn't even a he. *An it.* Hank squirms free from my grip.

"Where did it come from?" he asks, stepping forward to get a closer look.

"Stay back!" Dad snaps, stopping him mid step.

"I don't think it was supposed to be here," I say, looking over the corpse and across the field to the broken structure. It couldn't have come from there, either.

"No. I don't think so, and that's a problem," Dad agrees.

Bruce nods, as if he'd been thinking it too. "There shouldn't be any near-dead in such an isolated area. It doesn't make sense for the disease to show up outside of populations."

"It's supposed to be controlled. No unpredictable outbreaks anymore," I add.

"We need to go." Dad walks over to pick up the lashing poles.

"Maybe he was running away too," Hank speculates.

"I don't think so. I think we're being followed," Dad says, putting his arm across Hank's shoulders. "Come on, Bud."

Hank shrugs it off. "Da-ad!"

As everyone else moves away, I turn to look at the body again, hesitant to leave it.

"Kara. We need to keep moving," Dad calls after me.

"We can't just leave it," I say, feeling sad and sick at the same time.

"We have to."

"We need to bury it," I insist.

"No. That would take too much time," Dad says, walking over to me.

"We *killed* it," I say, barely stopping the wail that threatens to bubble up from inside of me.

"It was sick. It would have died anyway." Dad drops to his knee to look at me.

"It used to be a person," I say. The tears are hot and ready to come.

Dad kisses the top of my head. "I know." His head dips as he loses some of the firmness that held him up during the encounter. "I'm sorry. We had no choice. I *need* to protect you."

"Can we bury it?" I ask, hopeful.

"If it was following us, then maybe it's better to bury it anyway. Then no one will know that we killed it," Hank offers.

Dad is quiet for a long time.

"We can bury it."

By the time the whole burying ordeal is done, it's too late to keep going. Dad marches us through the dark back into the cover of the trees. There, he decides that it's too risky to set up a full camp. No fire, and we need to set up a barrier alarm for added protection. The barrier is a series of detectors that are linked together via optical sensors that connect in a square. The alarm will sound if anything crosses them.

Bruce hasn't said much since he killed the thing. I'm leaning against him, certain that I'll never fall asleep again when Hank pulls himself up so his face is close to mine. I squint at him through blurry eyes. His eyes are bright and blue. His hair is lighter than everyone else's. It's reddish, like Mom's hair. He has a mischievous look on his face.

"I thought you were with Dad," I say, careful not to disturb Bruce.

"I made you something, Kara," he whispers.

"What is it?" I ask, leaning forward.

He flicks his hand, and the air around it begins to glow a pale blue. It illuminates his face and casts shadows on our unpacked supplies. "It's a night-light."

I hold out my hand, and he gently places the glowing ball into my palm. The air is warm, but it doesn't feel like I'm holding anything. I look at the light. Once again, he's made something out of nothing.

"How did you do that?" I ask.

"Look," he says, pointing at the top of the light at a dark spot I hadn't noticed before. "If you touch it here, the light will go off." He shows me.

Now I'm holding nothing but a black spot and a mess of fiber-optic wires so fine they're almost invisible. It's made of *almost* nothing.

"The graphite conducts your body's electricity; you just need to start the flow. If you flip the switch the glow will stop and you can put it in your pocket. Go ahead. Turn it back on."

I touch the black spot, and this time I feel the fine wires stiffen with current as they spread out. A ball of light.

I watch the soft glow of the night-light ball, thinking that it's the most beautiful thing I've ever seen. "It looks like a full moon," I whisper to Hank.

"If you put your fingers on the wires, you can change it." He does.

"Full moon. Gibbous, crescent," he says as he changes the shape. "You can make it smaller as you get braver."

He's not making fun of me. He's helping me.

"Thank you, Hank," I whisper as I fall asleep under the glow of the tiniest full moon.

CHAPTER
SIX

OUR PACKS HANG UPSIDE DOWN on the line we tied between two trees over the fire next to our jackets and pants. Supplies are strewn across the campsite in various states of drying from our unplanned trip downstream, but our lashing poles are neatly organized. Two by the sleeping bags and two on the opposite side, next to the barrier alarm. Dad says that we're miles from where the near-dead chased us to the river, but we can't be too sure after so many encounters. So far it's quiet, but that's mostly because nobody wants to talk. We're lost.

"We're not completely lost. We know we're by the main river, we just need to make our way back toward the road," Dad says into the silence.

"What good is that going to do?" Bruce snaps at him.

I bury my head in my lap, my stomach still empty after two soups. My clothes are damp even though they were stuffed into the wet bag with my sleeping bag. I pull the night-light from my pocket and switch it on so that it glows in the shadow of my legs and peer down at it. I wish there were a way to use it to turn on Dad's data tablet—then we wouldn't be lost.

"If we can make it to the road, then maybe the coyote can find us," Dad offers.

It sounds too much like a question. Bruce huffs, crossing his arms across his chest.

"I'm not giving up—we're not giving up. This is just a minor setback," Dad says. I want to embrace his words, but they sound thin, weightless.

"It's hopeless, Dad! If you can't make contact, then we can't set a new rendezvous location. Then what? Are we going to jump in the river again when the near-dead come back?" Bruce throws his hands out, lurching his body off of the ground. Dad looks up at him, his eyes revealing the falseness of his stern expression.

Met by silence, Bruce shakes his head. "We *had* to jump into the damn river! We *had* to run! Why didn't you wait?"

"We couldn't wait. Not once they passed the test." Dad's voice is full now. He stands.

"You don't even know if they can fix that!" Bruce shouts. The burst of volume is so sudden that it makes me jump.

"I'm not going to gamble with their lives, Bruce!" Dad matches his volume. His face is red.

"What do you call this, Dad?" Bruce gestures to us. Dad's eyes follow his hand around the campsite.

"I'm trying to protect my family. Everything will be fine once the tablet dries out," Dad says.

"You're unbelievable," Bruce shouts before storming out of the campsite, triggering the barrier alarm.

Dad follows him, only pausing long enough to reset the alarm. "Bruce."

I watch them disappear into the dark, helpless.

"Dad should have let Bruce have a third soup," Hank says.

"Shut up, Hank," I snap, still staring at the darkness.

"You too? And you guys call me a glutton…"

"How can you be so clueless? Now is *not* the time to be funny," I growl, switching the night-light on again.

"It's not my fault—"

"It *is* your fault!" He looks like I just slapped him. "It's both of our faults. We shouldn't have passed that test."

"How were we supposed to do the right thing if *they* didn't tell us?" He gestures toward the dark. I imagine the fire's crackle masks voices coming from the shadows.

"It wouldn't have been hard to guess it, would it? The way Dad always says, 'you have no idea, but someday you'll understand.'" I turn my lips out, forcing my voice unnaturally low in imitation.

Hank snorts. "That's not what he sounds like."

I give him a side glance. One side of his face is orange from the firelight. "Let's hear you do better."

Hank lifts his head and fixes his gaze on me with an intense stare, clenching his jaw. "There are systems a lot better than this one, but they'll never give us an upgrade. You know why? Because they don't have to. They aren't interested in making anyone's lives better!"

I stifle a laugh as Hank brings his fists to the sides of his head. It feels wrong to laugh when things are so serious. Hank catches the change and quits the game.

"We should've guessed, huh?" I ask.

"Maybe, maybe not," he says, slumping forward so his chin rests on bent knees.

"Some geniuses we are." I sigh.

Hank sighs and the campsite returns to silence. I hold the globe up against the firelight, considering the contrasting colors.

"Tonight is a gibbous, 70 percent," Hank says.

"Hmm?" I ask.

"The moon. It's not up yet, but it'll be a gibbous with 70 percent exposure when it rises," he says.

I push the wires until I'm holding 70 percent of a sphere. "I knew that. I just wasn't thinking about the moon."

"What were you thinking about?"

"Dad and Bruce."

"Yeah."

I return the moon to full, then back to gibbous again. "Too bad you can't fix the tablet."

"I can't do anything until it's dry." Hank shrugs, then adds, "Even then…"

I imagine the inside of the tablet—circuits and wires with burnt connections that can't be repaired without the right equipment. Water is an insulator, but not the sort of water we were in. The water inside of the tablet was full of leached minerals and dissolved gases. *Ionic.* Conductive until dry. There's no telling how long it'll take for the enclosed system to dry out.

Hank plucks a long strand of grass and begins twirling it between two fingers absently. The fire shifts, and a spent log crumbles, embers spilling across the dried ground. Hot ash rises on the current and wafts gently toward Hank's grass. Hank spins the blade like a fan, forcing the ash in the other direction. *That's what we need for the tablet. A fan.* I watch Hank twirl the blade again.

I lean over and pull the tablet from Dad's pack.

"What are you doing?" Hank asks.

"I'm going to dry the tablet," I tell him, pulling a blade of grass.

"How?" he asks, crawling over to investigate.

"I'm going to use the heat from the fire to make a pressure differential and blow hot air through the system vent," I say, rolling the grass into a tiny tube.

"Why didn't I think of that?" he asks.

"Because it's not always your turn to be great," I say, setting the tablet down low in the cool earth. After some tinkering, I can feel cool air moving toward the fire.

Hank pulls out his tool kit and starts fussing with the smooth edge of the back panel. "It'll work better if it's exposed," he says.

Impatient to get the process going, I roll up Dad's map and use it like a billow to really get the air moving. I blow until I'm dizzy, then stop to ask, "How's it looking?"

"It looks… good," Hank says, after a pause, squinting in the light of his headlamp.

"Should we try it now?" I ask.

"Not yet. I don't want to short anything. I didn't bring a soldering gun."

I push steady breaths of air into the fire, making the embers glow so hot that they turn white. My face burns from the heat, but I don't stop. Hank uses the thin tube of grass like a vacuum brush, gently running it over the fine gold lines that will bring the tablet back to life.

"I think that's it." He lifts it up to study our work.

My stomach flips. "What if we're wrong, and it shorts?"

Hank slides his finger across the power switch. I close my eyes, afraid to see nothing.

"Got it!" His jubilation reaches me through the darkness.

I open my eyes. His face is glowing in the white light of the tablet screen. "We have to tell them!" I squeal.

I'm on my feet, rushing toward the trees as Hank replaces the back of the tablet. Without thinking, I run through the barrier alarm. My arm glints red from the optical sensor before the thin hum of the alarm begins. I run on, assuming Hank will reset it after he crosses the line. I follow the narrow swath of light from my headlamp, swinging it slowly through the trees as I search for Dad and Bruce.

Hank's arm brushes against me as I listen over the alarm's whine for any indication of where they've gone. "Where do you think they went?" he asks, holding the tablet to his chest as he sweeps the woods.

I hear Dad's voice first, from far off. "Kara! Hank!"

Then the soft sounds of shifting through the undergrowth. Bruce calls out to Dad, "To the right, I see light." Then at us. "We're coming!"

I rush toward them, returning their cries. "Dad, Bruce! You'll never believe what we did…"

Dad crashes into me, throwing his arms around my shoulders and pulling me close. "Where are they?"

Hank stomps up behind me, and Dad pulls him in. Bruce runs up holding a lashing pole. "What happened?"

"We fixed it," I say.

"What?" Dad asks. His arms are like iron bars across my body.

"Everything is fine. Hank and I fixed the tablet," I say.

"What triggered the alarm?" His grip loosens.

"Oh, that was me. Sorry." My face flushes—it's definitely burnt.

Bruce walks back to the camp and switches the alarm off. Dad drags us after him, back to the light of the fire. Inside the barrier, he stops and kneels in front of us. He's been crying. "I thought something happened." His voice catches. He grabs my head and pulls it into his chest where my forehead brushes against Hank's. "I'm sorry. I shouldn't have left you."

"I'm sorry I ran off." Bruce puts his arm across us, and his body shakes.

Hank pushes away from the hugging mass, fighting the interwoven arms of affection in a way only he can. "Dad. Dad! Did you hear Kara?"

Dad releases us, wiping his eyes. "What's that, Bud?"

"We fixed the tablet." He pushes it out toward Dad, who looks down at it, stunned.

"You clever boy!" Dad grabs it from his hands, running his fingers across the edge so that the screen glows white.

"It was Kara's idea," Hank admits.

"How did you do it?" Bruce asks. He's looking at me.

"I used convection." I smile.

Dad leans forward and plants a kiss on my forehead. Hank ducks before he can repeat the action on him. "My brilliant children!" He beams.

CHAPTER
SEVEN

"I'M COMPLETELY EXHAUSTED. I couldn't possibly be more exhausted than I am at this moment." I began preparing this speech as Dad pressed us into motion in the pre-dawn light after too few hours of rest.

"Is that so?" Dad sounds amused. He presses aside a mass of needled branches from a fallen tree, looking back to study my unenthusiastic trudge.

"It is. I know it. I've never been so tired in my life," I explain. My argument is fortified by two days of marching toward the new rendezvous location with nothing more than quick stops. We choke down dry packets of tasteless food and lay still long enough to fall asleep, but not long enough to stay that way.

"That's probably true," Bruce suggests, letting the branch swing back to its original position.

"This is worse than tired!" I moan. My feet scrape marks in the dirt. It takes more effort to walk like this, but the feeling of my sore legs dragging underneath me is satisfying, so I continue.

The scuffing sound mingles with the water lapping at the bank of the creek that's just come into view. According to Dad's map, we'll walk around it, then continue west to the road. I stare at the sun as it sinks into the trees, wishing it meant we could stop.

"There is no truth like the truth Kara speaks," Hank chimes in. I look back to see that he's joined me in the foot-scraping march.

"Oh, how the mighty have fallen," Dad teases, reaching back to ruffle his hair.

"No more soup. What did you expect?" Hank shrugs.

I turn my head away from the sun, unable to stand the ache of squinting into the orange light. I blink twice before the surroundings become clear. The forest thins into grass and fern along the waterline at the top of a steep hill. *Who knew there could be so many hills?* Two large trees grow together near the bank next to a large rocky formation. Behind them, the forest thickens again, but here is a natural clearing. The area is open and has good visibility. It's like our surroundings are begging us to stop and rest.

"We'll rest when we get to the road," Dad says, making Hank groan.

"But Dad, look at this place," I beg.

He stops walking. I hold my breath, afraid to hope that he'll relent. His expression is thoughtful. "It's just another half day's walk to the road if everything goes well."

"If," Hank points out.

"It's been quiet since we went in the river," Bruce adds.

Dad studies us, the hard knot in his jaw wavering as he relents. "Maybe we should rest."

We cheer. It's what we all want.

"Grass. I'm going to make a bed right here in this grass." Hank puts his hands out in front of him and staggers forward until he's touching the ground. He drops his bag to the side and lets out a dramatic wail. "It's like a pillow!"

I let my body fall to the ground. The same grass ripples as I fall back into it, relieved. This place is too perfect to turn down.

"It's decided then," Dad laughs, loosening the belt to his pack as he watches our dramatic collapses.

"I'll build some lures, and we can try to fish," Hank says, sitting up suddenly. His body hums with renewed energy.

"Where do you get your energy?" I ask, propping my head up on a tired and reluctant bent elbow.

"I'm borrowing from the future," Hank says, fishing out some fiber optics from his pocket.

"We'll rest tonight. If we hurry tomorrow, we shouldn't have trouble making the rendezvous." Dad smiles, pulling the kettle out of his pack.

I settle in to tying thin strands of string to make fishing lines as Dad and Bruce set out to gather wood for a fire. The sun disappears, turning everything into a darker shade than it was before. This place is so peaceful it's almost singing. It feels alive. I think about the alive feeling as I work. Since retreating to the mountains, I've counted more than twenty species of bird. We've seen rabbits and marmots and some evidence of predators. Dad thinks that bears are still gone this far south, but that the predators might be foxes or coyotes competing with wild dogs for resources. I wonder how far south we have to travel before everything is dead. Will we cross a boundary between green and dead, or will it taper out to the scorched Deadlands we learn about at school?

I don't want to worry about it tonight. Everything is too perfect and my mind is too tired to process the possibilities. As Hank sinks the first line into the water, I lean back and close my eyes. I try to picture a community in the south. At first all I see is red, dead earth like the pictures from school—satellite images of a barren land that look like another planet. I try to put plants in those pictures and add water. Most of what I plant in my mind shrivels and dies, but I notice that a few take root and grow near the water. I decide that's where I'll add the houses for the people to live. Tomorrow. We'll meet our coyote and leave these woods. Then I can imagine the rest of it. Then we'll be there for real.

CHAPTER
EIGHT

MY FINGERS DIG into the soft bark of the tree I'm using to stay upright. I grit my teeth as I prepare to take another step. *I can use the crutch if I need to.*

I shake my head. *It's just one step.* One step should get me to the next tree. Then the next. I push hard with both hands and move as fast as I can to relieve the awful pain. The edges of my vision turn black as I fall into another tree. I wrap my arms around it, panting from the effort. Sweat pours down the back of my neck, making my hair cling to my skin in the cool evening air.

I rest my forehead against the rough surface. The road is maybe one hundred meters away, if even that. I'm almost there.

"I can't do it," I whisper to no one. When the no one doesn't respond, I move the discourse into my head. *Not another step. I can't. It's impossible.* Hyperbole, though a useful tool, is absent from this assessment, I imagine telling Hank after he accuses me of exaggerating. I carry on this fantasy of a conversation as a distraction—a denial of the truth.

I don't have a choice. I can't figure out whose voice tells me this. I urge myself forward, promising that the coyote is still waiting. I'll see him peeking out from cover, cautious, but happy to see me. I won't have to make my way alone anymore.

Just one minute, I beg. Only long enough to catch my breath. I let heavy eyelids shut out the fine green moss that covers every vertical surface. *I'll count to ten. That'll be enough.* I pretend I can shut out the cold that bites at my damp hair, sending aching shivers through my sweat-drenched body. *One... two...*

I jerk my head up, the remaining tendrils of the dream slipping away into the mist that's settled around me. The sudden motion makes my whole body swim. It's dark. I rub my hand across the deep, bark-shaped grooves stamped into my forehead as I try to make sense of my surroundings. The shadowy outline of the guardrail where the road cuts through the trees lies at the edge of visibility. I look up to see the pinpricks of light that make up the swirling arms of the Milky Way, blinking with atmospheric turbulence.

I fell asleep.

I have to move again, before I lose more time. The coyote won't wait forever. I push off of the tree. This time, a sound escapes me as my foot drags across the ground, sending waves of pain up my leg. I grasp the thin, smooth bark of a sapling as it sways under my weight.

"One down," I encourage myself.

Six trees without needing the crutch. The sweat is back. There's too much for it to just be exertion. I take another step, holding a branch as I swing my body forward. A painful twinge shoots up my calf and creeps into my hamstring where it radiates heat that's spreading. *Fever. Infection? Shock?* Bruce would know.

Thinking his name makes me suck in a sharp breath of cold air. I wasn't ready to think it. I breathe out slowly and will my body forward. As the trees thin, I'm forced to pull out the lashing pole I turned into a crutch. Step, pause, shudder, drag. Thirst burns at the back of my throat. I'm dehydrated. My backpack is nearly empty. I tried to carry more water, but even with the crutch, I couldn't support it. I have to get to the road. If I stop, I die.

Resting my back against a large spruce, I look up into the sky, searching for the waning crescent that should have risen by now. *I won't take another step until I see it.* My eyes settle on the thin slice of moonlight as it dances across the treetops on its way toward the sky. I reach into my pocket, searching for the night-light that isn't there as Hank's voice whispers inside my head. *Waning crescent, 12 percent.*

I force my eyes shut, pulling my hand out of the empty pocket.

The last three steps to the guardrail happen all at once. My fingers wrap around thin metal that digs into my palms as I hold myself upright, triumphant in my accomplishment. I lean into the thick square post that holds the triad of rails in place, relieved to have completed the journey. When I do, the whole structure sways as the loose bolts wiggle in holes made too long ago, now spongy with dry rot. Steadying myself against the motion, I look out onto the road.

It's empty.

"Hello?" The word is quieter than I mean it to be, tentative. I clear my throat and try again. "If you're hiding, it's alright to come out. I'm sorry I'm late."

The words die in the night, cut short by the thick fog that blankets everything. With numb, fumbling fingers, I fish out my headlight and switch it on. I swing the dim slice of light back and forth across the black asphalt, not certain what I'm looking for.

No one's coming. The thought breaks through my denial, sapping the little energy that remains. I'm three days late for the rendezvous. All of the effort to make it to the road— nights without sleep, days spent moving instead of looking for water— for nothing. I'm alone.

My body shakes, my eyes sting with tears, and my head starts to swim from too much air. I don't know if I'm about to cry or faint.

"It was supposed to be safe," I scream into the night. The proclamation is followed by an agonized sob, but no tears come.

There was no warning.

The thoughts vibrate through my mind as I stare at the empty road.

They learned. They aren't supposed to be able to learn.

I won't make it much farther on my own. Not without water.

They worked together, like they were communicating. That shouldn't be possible.

The road travels from north to south, cutting through the thick woods and connecting the City States to the Institute. It's the only maintained road on the outside. If I travel south long enough, I'll have to leave it in search of the remains of an old world.

They killed but didn't eat. They always eat.

I turn my head south and wonder how far I'll have to go before someone finds me. A transport vehicle headed to the Institute, maybe. I imagine climbing the steps into the vehicle and sitting next to the others. I picture the grief and fear etched on their faces and colored in with the hope that the Institute promises—treatment. A cure. I imagine myself dashing that hope away. *There is no cure. They don't want to fix you.* I imagine their faces turning angry as their humanity fades away, taking me with it.

I can't go to the Institute. Even if I survive long enough to come across a transport vehicle, I couldn't bring myself to go to the place we were running from. The place they died to keep me from…

I am alive and they are all dead.

Gradually, my breathing returns to normal and the urge to scream at the nothingness subsides. The numbness remains, fighting back against the violent shivers that provoke my body into a thousand micro-movements I don't have the strength to fight. I have to at least try to make it south, to find the people Dad promised would help us— to find the people who want to end this nightmare.

Resolved, I urge myself back into motion. I slip off the pack and toss it over the top of the guardrail. It hits the ground with a thud worthy of a much bigger load. I swing the crutch over to the other side. Moving so slowly that it might be dawn by the time I've got both feet on the road, I climb the first two rails and sit at the top. Cold metal digs into my glutes. Carefully, I swing my good leg over the top, bracing myself for the inevitable wobble of the structure. When I'm steady, I look down. My foot dangles about a foot above the road. If I can get my other leg over, I should be able to slide down.

Slowly, painfully, I drag my left leg over the edge, pointing my right foot toward the road and letting gravity pull me down. At the moment my momentum takes over, my left foot catches against the rail.

My right foot swings back, missing the asphalt and forcing my whole body to pitch forward. For one second, I'm flying, then realization strikes and instinctively I tuck my shoulder. The impact knocks my breath out as I roll toward the center of the road. I blink and everything goes dark.

CHAPTER
NINE

I'M SITTING *in my own data port in sixth year. It's our annual health lesson. The Institute scientist is dressed in a neat lab coat and wearing bright blue synthetic gloves. Her blond hair is cut short against her neck, but wisps of her unkempt mop brush against her forehead. If it weren't for these unruly strands, she would look so neat and perfect that I might question if she were real. She smiles a perfect smile as our data port screens project our health lesson.*

"Through the efforts of the DDC, our cities have become so healthy and regulated that infection is nearly a thing of the past. But with increasing activity outside the force fields, it's important that you always follow all of the rules."

The health rules. Our standard for survival. Without everyone's cooperation, we risk an outbreak. Still. Even now. Always we must stay wary of an outbreak. I watch the statistics run across my screen and rapidly click through to create my study file. I will receive a perfect score on our assessment. I've tuned out the almost-perfect scientist.

"...Transferred through fluids. Blood, saliva and contaminated water supply are the largest risk. Infection rate is 100 percent. Irresponsible behavior and open wounds are the only risk factors left. This is how you are infected..."

The smell of wet tar assaults my nostrils as things blink back on. The perfect scientist's voice fades away with the shifting fog. Gritty asphalt digs into my cheek. I try to get up, but my whole body groans in protest, acutely aware that it's beyond its limits. Still, I'm relatively unscathed. My thick canvas jacket protected most of my body from impact. Only my face was exposed. I sit up, scratchy gravel pieces rubbing against my body as I move. I brush my hands across my face, checking for scrapes—nothing major, but I feel the fresh blood as it makes its way to the surface of my forehead. I've broken all the rules.

The squeal of brakes pulls my attention away from my blood-smeared fingers as blinding headlights steal my vision. I bring my arm up to shield my eyes from the bright glare and squint to make out the shape of a vehicle. It's the same sort of vehicle that's used to run up and down the barriers and tunnels that separate the cities from the outside. *A maintenance vehicle.*

The driver blares the horn, and I scramble to find my feet, failing twice. On the third try, I am nearly to my feet when the car door slams. I look up, crouched unsteadily on trembling legs. The largest man I've ever seen stands just behind the headlight so that I can only see his silhouette. When he moves, I see the outline of the lashing pole in his hand.

"I'm human!" I yell, putting my hands up as though they could protect me.

He stops just in front of the vehicle, keeping the pole pointed in my direction. I can see the tension in his raised shoulders. "Are you hurt?" His voice is deep. There's uncertainty hidden behind its depths.

"I fell. I'm injured. I'm—" My whole body shakes with fear. I don't dare hope that he is who I hoped to find on the road.

"Are there others?" he asks, standing fast to his position, his weapon still aimed with the glinting blade exposed.

I make a snap judgment, certain of who he must be. "We were supposed to meet someone here three days ago."

I catch a flash of recognition. It's only there for a moment, causing a shift in his demeanor before it fades away. For that briefest moment, I'm bolstered, but it doesn't last. The cool confidence leaves me as quickly as it came. *He's not the coyote. That's impossible.* I sink to my knees, unable to hold myself up any longer.

"We?" The lashing pole tips back. I hear the slink of the blade retreating before he sets it against the vehicle and walks into the light. As he approaches, I make out the details of his person. His girth is not just an illusion—he's a thickly muscled man, maybe in his thirties or forties. His skin is so dark that he would disappear in the night without light. He wears simple clothes, fitted pants and a thick canvas jacket that is the over-sized twin of my own. It makes him seem famil-iar. I hold my breath, hoping that I've made the right decision.

"Four of us." I let the words out without daring to think of their meaning. I run my hands across the loose pieces of asphalt, eager to distract myself.

He stops in front of me and stoops down. His massive frame blocks the light and casts strange shadows across what might otherwise be a kind face. With arms resting on his knees, he looks me over. His eyes are wide and searching. "Where are the others?"

I shake my head, unable to speak. *There are no others. And it's my fault.*

He lets out a heavy sigh, as though resigning himself to something. I watch his expression, but it stays kind, if maybe a little pained. "I'm sorry. I'm going to help you. Your name is Kara, right?"

He knows my name. I look at him again, consumed by disbelief. "You're the coyote."

"That's right. But call me Simons. It's nice to meet you, Kara." A small smile brightens his face as he offers me his hand. I take it tenta-tively, and he shakes it vigorously, nearly shaking a smile onto my face. It doesn't come, and I wonder briefly if my face still makes that shape. Without further discourse, he lifts me up with firm but gentle hands. I wince as my leg stretches out beneath me.

"Is it an open wound?" he asks, pausing to look me over once more. He turns to take in the blood-splattered pack I left at the road's edge, concern writ across his furrowed brow.

"No," I say. *That blood isn't mine.*

He nods, then swings a massive arm around my back and scoops me up off the ground. My body tenses with the swift motion. He crosses the road in two massive strides, stoops down to retrieve my pack and the lashing pole crutch, then turns toward his vehicle.

"How are you still here?" I ask, staring down to where my jacket crumples against his. They're nearly identical. His is infinitesimally more faded than mine, but that could be a small matter of a few more hours in the summer light. They could be from the same shipment. I imagine him pulling the jacket from a brown supply box with the government goods symbol on the top and brushing at the creases.

"I ran into trouble the morning of the rendezvous. I couldn't mobilize until today."

I hear the passenger door open before he swings around so that I'm facing forward, looking at the empty road I may never have managed to get up off from without help. I grab the door frame as he eases me into the front seat. He gives me a long, searching look before closing the door and walking back to the driver's seat. *Trouble.* If he was close, then there's a good chance he means the same trouble that—

The vehicle dips from his weight as he settles into it. Time is moving funny. I know it takes longer, but I feel like there is that one second that he moves to sit, and now we're driving. I blink, fighting the most pressing urge to let my eyes rest that I've ever felt. *I have to know if he saw it too.*

"Was it near-dead?"

He glances over at me before returning his eyes to the fog-drenched road. He nods, then rummages in a sack on the seat between us and pulls out a large canister. He twists the top and hands it to me. "Drink this."

I grab the canister from him and take several fast, deep, greedy gulps. It burns down my throat before hitting my stomach like a block of cold ice, making me choke and sputter.

"Easy. Try taking smaller sips," he suggests.

I cradle the canister and begin to take a series of smaller sips. The refreshing liquid makes its way down my throat, satiating my burning thirst. I will it to wash the rusty taste from my mouth. My tongue and cheeks still feel gummy and thick. "Thank you," I say, more grateful for this than anything else.

I swallow again, then return to the topic. "A whole lot of them?" My heart flutters. A jolt like an electric current buzzes down my arms, making my fingers tingle.

"I imagine it was the same incident that left you alone." He doesn't look at me this time. His face crinkles like he's still working something out for himself.

"You don't think there could have been more than one group?" I ask, apprehensive of what I want to ask.

He shakes his head. "Groups are rare. More than one… not anymore, anyway."

"It must have been, then." It comes out a raspy whisper. I clear my throat and take another sip as the buzzing in my limbs intensifies, making me feel like I'm somehow separate from my body. "Did they… act different?"

He looks at me again. "Different how?"

"Like they could think—or at least work together…"

My heart flutters as I wait for Simons' report.

"No." The word is definitive, but his voice is soft. Still it lands a blow across my chest that makes my whole body feel like lead.

"Are you sure?"

He slows the vehicle as it enters a severe curve. The vehicle banks with the road, and the acceleration makes everything spin.

"Kara, I don't know what happened to you out there—I know it must have been terrible, but… that's just what near-dead do. They don't think or decide or work together. They eat."

I stare out the windshield, blinking back tears. *They didn't eat.* The sentence is trapped inside.

"Whatever you saw—or think you saw—" He pauses when my breath shudders, as if waiting for me to break down. I exhale. The numbness has swelled so that it fills my chest. When I don't cry, he continues. "No one could blame you."

I think he'll say more, but he lets the topic go. It hangs in the cab compartment for a moment like a heavy mist before diffusing into the night. The vehicle hums and groans the sounds of engine and exhaust, but inside there is only silence. I try to focus on the path ahead of us, lit up by the headlights, but my eyes are blurry with sleep. I think that the time might slip by me again. I shift in my seat, unable to get comfortable, but afraid that if I'm able to I won't be able to stay awake.

"Did you make it to the road all on your own?" Simons' voice is smooth and deep, like a river at the front of a spring. Fast-moving water whose fingers are as cold as death. But his voice is warm.

"Yes." I almost forget to answer. I'm slipping. His persistent gaze makes me uncomfortable. He's looking for something. I slump down in my seat, afraid of what he might find.

Finally he speaks. "The fact that you didn't give up is pretty impressive."

I don't feel impressive.

"The best I can do tonight is get us to a safe house. It won't be anything special, just a couple of beds behind a closed door," he says.

I haven't slept on a bed in… weeks? *No. It hasn't even been two weeks since we left.* The idea seems foreign.

"Thank you." It comes out as weak as I feel.

"From there, I'll see what I can do."

His statement is strange. If he's a coyote, can't he still get me to safety? Have things changed now that I'm alone? I open my mouth to inquire when a pained moan issues from the back seat. I look to Simons. The deep creases of concern wrap around his face, revealing his angst. The worry lines look as if they manage to travel around his ears and continue on to the back of his shaved head.

He calls out, softly, "We're almost there, baby."

He's traveling with someone else. I'm so tired I must've missed it. I twist around to peer into the back seat. Behind a screen, I can just make out a mound of blankets and something moving within. A whimper escapes from their warm depths.

"Hang on and I'm gonna take care of you. Just a little further," he comforts the mound in the back seat.

"Who is that?" I ask.

He responds quietly, the anguish tangible in his voice. "That's my girl, Trudy."

"Is she…" I know the answer to the question I can't quite formulate.

"It was such a cold night. I pulled us off the road to build a fire. They came before the sun rose, and one of them got her while we were running." His voice is tight and low, like it's the only type of sound he's able to make right now. He's holding the steering wheel so tightly that the edges of his palms are white.

His explanation is like a hot knife in my belly. I forget to breathe.

"I killed it, but not before it got her bad."

She's infected. One of them. Neither of us seem able to say it. "How old is she?" I ask, at a loss of anything better to say.

"She's seventeen last month," he replies, glassy eyes fixed on the road. "It hasn't gotten to her head yet," he suddenly adds. I'm not quite sure if he is reassuring me or himself.

Neither of us speak again. I fix my gaze on the road until the dark asphalt blurs in my vision and then goes dark around me. Time moves forward without needing me to account for it. I'm sinking deep into cool waters. The muffled sounds of the last weeks echo through the pool like rushing tides. Below me, the icy fingers of the rushing water. Winter melt. Cold death.

I jerk upright in response to the slowing of the vehicle, forcing the sleep from my mind. Simons pulls the vehicle off of the main road onto a gravel path. The way is scattered with broken branches and under-growth and is so narrow from the encroaching woods that I'm not certain we'll be able to pass through. The vehicle bounces and shim-mies as we traverse the unmaintained road, but it never once threatens to stall or tip—it's been built for exactly this type of terrain.

After several minutes bumping across the road, the dark outline of a small building comes into view between branches that scrape across the windshield. Simons rolls the vehicle expertly toward the front of the building, which is little more than a shack, before cutting the engine. Leaving the headlights on, he clicks his seatbelt off and looks over to see that I'm awake.

"Give me a second and I'll be back for you," he says.

I nod at his reassuring words, thinking about how I don't have much of a choice.

The vehicle sways with his motion as he exits the driver's seat and opens the back passenger door. With a gentleness that seems contradic-tory to his mass, he lifts the mound of blankets that contains his daughter. He pauses long enough to cradle her against his chest and whisper soft comfort into her ear, caressing thick black hair caked with blood. As he disappears into the shack, I reflect on the depth of his love for a daughter he will most certainly lose and decide that I don't mind being forced to rely on him.

CHAPTER
TEN

"I CAN DRIVE you to the south end of the road. They're looking for someone that can meet us there and get you the rest of the way." Simons' legs are bent at a nearly comical angle as he sits on the edge of the low cot that served as my bed for the night.

"How long will that take?" I ask, blinking up at him as bright light pours through the single-pane window on the east side of the room. The glass is cracked so that the light casts a rainbow of color across the arm of his jacket and my mud-caked pants.

"About a day down, then another day for me to turn back around and head to the Institute," he says, folding his fingers together where they rest at the peak of his knees. Though he tries to hide it, I don't miss the quiver of uncertainty.

"Why so long?" I ask. The words burst out of me, loud and petulant. He's worried that his daughter won't survive the extra trip. I look over at the mass of blankets that barely rise and fall with the fading life they contain.

"There's a transport vehicle making its way from the Capitol, then there's the regular supply run. We're going to have to wait both of them out to avoid detection," he explains.

"What if she can't make it that long?"

Simons sucks in a quick, sharp breath in response to the bite of my question. He lets the air out slowly through flared nostrils before standing. His head is only inches from the ceiling. "Trudy's strong. She'll make it."

He ducks his head as he walks through the doorless passageway that joins the sleeping area to the kitchen. A second later, there's a loud bang as Simons releases his frustrations on the shack. The entire structure shakes with the impact, and I wonder that he managed not to cry out. Then, as if nothing had happened, I hear the sound of a kettle lid and pouring water. Three steps and he sets it on a surface—*the wood stove.*

With great effort, I right myself in the bed. My entire body aches, begging me to lie back down. Gritting my teeth, I swing my legs over the edge of the cot. Chunks of mud crumble from my boots when my feet touch the split wood flooring, adding to the layer of grime that coats the ground from years of neglect.

The blankets across the room shudder a breath, drawing my attention from the dirt-crusted floor. I watch as the breath is repeated, one, two, three, four times before returning to the shallow rise and fall of before. *Maybe she wasn't breathing before.* The thought makes me cold inside. That the willowy girl with lips so cracked they're dark with dried blood might be so near death that she would stop breathing without anyone noticing…

Simons says that Trudy's strong and that she'll make it, but I'm not so certain. I don't think he's so certain either—not a two-day trip, anyway. She needs immediate medical attention or she won't survive long enough for the disease to take hold. The Institute is her only hope. Simons knows it. Last night, he explained that the dissenters have the technology to put the infected into cryogenic slumber, but Trudy needs immediate medical intervention. Without it, cryogenics won't save her.

The crutch is leaning against the north wall. I reach out and pull it toward me as footsteps tread back and forth across the kitchen, managing meal preparation and worry by virtue of the same motion. Simons isn't a coyote anymore. He's going on the inside. He'll become a volunteer for the Northern Laboratory program to report on its inner workings. He'll travel with his daughter, keeping vigil over her body until the day a cure rescues her from her cryogenic prison—if she survives long enough. Either way, his life is theirs the second he crosses the threshold into the Institute grounds.

Outside, a moss-draped Sitka sways in the breeze. I lean heavily on the knobby branches that make the brace for my crutch as I shuffle through the entryway. Simons is standing at the stove, pouring boiling water from the kettle into speckled black tin cups. I can see the tension in the knotted muscles of his back as he stirs the cups' contents. Beyond him, behind a sagging counter, the wood splinters outward in a gaping hole where he punched through the shack's thin wall. The smell of something sweet wafts over to me, reminding me of rainy Saturday mornings. Cups in hand, Simons turns. His eyebrows lift when he sees me, but he doesn't speak.

"I'm going with you," I say.

He stands, stock still and too large in the tiny kitchen as he digests my words. Only the wiggle of a tin mug as he shifts his grip against the too-hot surface reveals his inner workings. He sets the mug on the table, shaking the burn out of his hand. "It's too risky. Once you go in, I can't guarantee that we can get you back out again."

"It's too risky not to. Trudy might not be able to make the trip down and back." I tell him what he already knows.

"What if I can't get you back out?" he asks.

"I don't need to get back out. I'm going with you." I shrug, then make my way over to the wobbly table with the flimsy metal frame. Simons watches me move but doesn't intervene.

When I manage to lower myself onto the cracked canvas of the rusted chair, he sighs, then, grabbing the other mug, he joins me.

"We promised your dad I would get you south."

"He wanted to get us to the dissenters. Going south was only a product of that."

He folds his hands on the table, then stares into them as if they held the answers. He speaks slowly, choosing his words very carefully. "Your father didn't want you to go to the Institute—or the Northern Laboratories. It's why he didn't wait to run."

"Dad's not here anymore!" I spit at him with so much venom that he should think it's his fault he's gone. I take a deep breath, trying to calm my racing heart. "It's my decision," I say.

"I don't think you understand the risk. Being a volunteer is dangerous. The dissenters—"

"You're going to be a volunteer to help the dissenters. You're doing it to put an end to the disease and…" I gesture toward the bedroom. "To make sure she makes it. That's what I want to do."

He studies me, his face a mixture of desperation and apprehension. "You're too young to be sure about something like this." He doesn't look as certain as his words sound.

"I don't want anyone else to die. I want to end this."

I watch as he chews his lip, still staring deep into the pink of his thumbnails. When he looks up at me, I land the final blow, the one that will guarantee our journey north. "We can save Trudy together."

Without another word of dissent, he slides the tin cup over to me. The hot metal threatens to blister my skin, but I hold it close.

"Oatmeal with brown sugar. Trudy's favorite," he says, picking up the black handle of his spoon.

CHAPTER
ELEVEN

THE SUN IS high when we make our final preparations to leave the shack. Trudy is tucked in the back, steadfast with the rising and falling breaths that keep the blankets in motion. I'm leaning against one of the thick beams of lumber holding the metal awning of the deep-woods shack, waiting for Simons to help me into the vehicle. After loading the small dining pack he used to prepare our breakfast, he leans through the driver's door, reaching toward the middle of the vehicle to pull a small electronic box from the space just below where the equipment is built into the dashboard. Standing up straight, he looks it over as though he's considering its value.

"What's that?" I ask.

"It's a communication box—an *illegal* communication box," he says, moving toward the shack. On the porch, he turns back to consider me. "I want you to think for a minute. You don't happen to have any papers with you, do you? Things like messages, or maps?"

"I've got a map," I say.

"A paper one?" he asks.

I nod.

"It's best if we get rid of that," he says.

I open my pack and relinquish the map. He takes it and adds it to the communication box. Setting them both on the table, he exits the building, letting the door shut behind him. Reading my expression, he says, "In case we get searched on our way in."

"Will they be safe here?" I ask, fighting the ache that makes me wish I didn't have to leave Dad's map.

"Someone will come by and collect them." By the way he says it, I know he means *some dissenter*. The thought lessens the ache.

"That's it, then," I say.

"Time to go," Simons agrees, offering his hand so that I can limp up to the passenger door. He lifts me inside and sets the crutch down at my feet. I scoot back and pull the buckle across my lap as he crosses into the driver's seat. Without a further remark, he turns the key and points the vehicle back toward the road. Despite my best efforts, I feel myself fading moments after we rejoin the maintained asphalt. I fight it as long as I can, but I can't resist the comfort that greets me on the back side of my eyelids.

The next time I open my eyes, I can tell immediately that several hours have passed. The light has that uncanny richness to it that only happens when the sun is low. Ahead of us, a large structure towers in the distance. Gates stretch outside of our view on either end of the entrance, attached to walls made of thick concrete that disappears on either side into the dense growth of the woods. The walls are meant to keep the structure safe from the outside world, but as we approach it, I can't help but think it looks the other way around.

"Do you know what it will be like on the inside?" I ask, trying to calm my mounting apprehension.

"I know there's some sort of expedited screening process, then the volunteers get registered," he says.

I force myself to sit upright as the structure crawls out of the woods, growing with each passing second. *We're going to it, not the other way around,* I remind myself.

"It's so much bigger than I thought it would be," I whisper.

"There's more here than just the hospital," he says.

"You mean the DDC?" I ask.

"That too."

The thought of being so close to what we were running from makes it seem like the fractions of seconds in between each of my heartbeats are too long. I take a deep breath, trying to calm myself.

"You okay?" Simons asks. He reaches out and puts a hand on my shoulder.

"Yeah." I tear my gaze away from the structure to look at Simons. His head is tilted so that he can watch both me and the road. Behind the kindness, I can see the sorrow and fear that weigh him down. I'm suddenly overwhelmed with the realization that I should be the one reassuring him, not the other way around. "Yes." I sound more confident this time.

"Do you want to turn around?" Simons asks.

"No. We've wasted too much time," I insist, afraid that he might actually turn around.

"If you want, maybe I can try to find someone to get you out once things are settled?" he suggests.

"Going on the inside is a dissenter job, right?" I ask.

He nods.

"Then that's what I want," I say, clenching my fists inside my pockets to bolster my resolve. Dad wanted us to be a part of the solution. This is a part, just as much as anything else could be.

The vehicle rolls to a stop in front of the towering gate. In large metallic print above the entrance, a sign reads *Institute of Scientific Education and Disease Treatment*. A large screen appears at the entrance, and a voice prompts us, "Welcome to the Institute of Scientific Education and Disease Treatment, what is the nature of your visit?"

Simons responds in a loud, clear voice, "I've got a patient in need of immediate medical attention."

"I'm sorry, did you say patient?" the female voice asks. The tone assures me that the source is very human.

"That's what I said," Simons confirms.

"One moment, please." The intercom buzzes with interference. I lean forward to try and get a better look at the screen, which appears to have remained grey during the exchange. Leaning in, I can see the faint outline of a woman with impossibly short hair and a slim black suit talking into an earpiece. She shakes her head, then drops her hand back down. Simons rubs his hands backward and forward on the steering wheel as he waits, failing to hide his agitation. I note the large knot of his tightened jaw, and it makes my insides ache.

"Do you have confirmation of infection?" The voice breaks through the static.

"No, but I can promise you she's infected. Your doctors will take one look at her and agree, and I need them to take a look at her." I wonder if she can see him on her end.

"Just a moment," she says, making me as tense as Simons looks.

The vehicle's engine hums against the intercom's static as we wait. After a few seconds that pass like several minutes, the gates swing open.

"Please drive forward to the yellow line and follow all instructions. Thank you for visiting the Institute." This time when her voice disappears, there's nothing but silence. Simons puts the vehicle in drive, and the engine shifts into motion, rolling us toward the bright yellow line that seems to glow in the late evening light.

I'm busy thinking about how strange the woman's salutation was. *Thank you for visiting the Institute...* As if we've just shown up for a quick tour. When the vehicle comes to a stop, a flash of brilliant light forces my attention back to the present. Above us, a row of floodlights shine down, making it nearly impossible to see.

"Remain in your vehicle until you have received further instructions," a blaring voice demands.

Squinting, I detect half a dozen individuals approaching, garbed in biohazard suits.

"What's going on?" I ask, fighting the rising panic as the suited staff opens the vehicle doors.

"Stay calm and do what they say. You'll be okay," Simons says as the suited individual at his door directs him to place his hands on the wheel and remain still.

I take a deep breath, trying to force myself to remain calm as a suited hand grips my wrist and pulls with steady force. "Please come with me."

I comply, allowing the suited arm to remove me from the vehicle. When my right leg touches the ground, I reach back in the vehicle to grab my crutch. The suited person yanks me back, causing me to lose my balance and collapse onto the ground.

"She's got a weapon!" the person shouts. It sounds funny coming through the respirator.

Someone else joins them, grabbing my other arm and forcing me forward. "Hands on the ground now!"

I cry out as my body is forced forward. *Just do what they say*, I remind myself, reaching out in front of me as far as I can.

"It's a crutch! She's injured. It's just a crutch," Simons yells. I can see his feet pointing toward me under the vehicle.

"They're clear. Get her up," one of them says.

I'm lifted with the same roughness. Someone brings my hands behind my back and binds them with magnetic twines as if I were a prisoner. Two of the suited captors start to drag me away from the vehicle. I struggle to engage my legs in an effort to move of my own free will, but my body is no longer responding to my commands. As we move away from the vehicle, I hear a commotion. I twist my body to look back at Simons, who is struggling against his own bindings.

"That's my baby. You need to be gentle!"

"She will receive proper medical care. If you would just come with us—" one of the suits urges him.

"Let me go with her. I want to go with her!" Simons continues to fight them. His eyes are wide and scared.

"You need to come with us," the same suit tells him as a fourth man joins in the struggle to force Simons away from the vehicle.

Two suits remain at the vehicle with lashing poles, preparing to open the back doors. I crane my head to see, but we enter a building and the doors shut before I get a chance.

CHAPTER
TWELVE

WE PASS through two doors and enter a long corridor dotted with plain wooden doors. The entrance to the building and then into the corridor opened automatically, as if anticipating our approach. The two suits drag me across the slick black tile without remark. I try to look through the foggy plastic cover and into the face of one of them.

"Where are we going?"

The one on my left turns their head and looks at me. "Screening."

We stop at the door at the end of the hallway, and the person on my right flashes a badge in front of a sensor. The door swings open to reveal a waiting area. The walls are blank white and lined with old-looking brown chairs with silver metal arms and legs. Righty loosens their grip and gestures for me to enter the room.

"I can't really walk right now," I say, giving silent Righty my most incredulous side-eye.

"Someone will bring you some assistance," Lefty says, shifting their grip as if to help me into the room.

"We're not supposed to engage," Righty hisses.

"Who's going to report me for putting her in a chair? You know the cameras in this building are visual only." Lefty shrugs, then continues to help me into the room, easing me down into the nearest chair.

Righty huffs. When Lefty returns to the door, they snap it shut, leaving me to contemplate the room's starkness on my own. I reach up to brush away the sweat that has accumulated at my hairline again. My body aches from the harsh treatment. I consider the strangeness of the whole situation. *Maybe they were afraid of me.* Maybe they think I might be infected.

Simons said that everyone that goes to the Institute gets screened for the disease, so maybe it's as simple as that. I shake my head. That's the reason for the suits and the security and even the rough treatment. *They're just scared of the disease.*

"Are you sick?" A timid voice draws me out of my introspection.

I look over to see an old man sitting in the far corner. *How did I miss him?* Maybe I am sick. "I don't know," I tell him.

"You poor child," he says, bringing a weathered hand up to his trembling lips. After some more fussing and mumbles I can't quite interpret, he settles again.

"I came here with my wife from hospital," he says. The statement is clearly an invitation for me to share my story.

I look down at my feet. "I came here with a friend and his sick daughter," I say.

Before the man can follow up on his inquiry, the door opens again. Simons has to duck his head under the doorway to enter. Once inside, he pauses long enough to look around until he settles on me. The door shuts, and he takes a seat next to me. That's when I see the side of his face is covered in blood. His eye is swelling rapidly, forcing it shut.

"What happened?" I shriek.

"I'm okay. Are you?" he asks.

I nod, staring at his mangled face with wide eyes, at a loss for words. They didn't let him go with Trudy.

"Is this your friend?" the old man asks, oblivious to the terrible thing that just happened.

Simons turns his head so he can look at the old man through his good eye. There must be something about him that makes it difficult to pick him out of a room. I wonder if he disappeared back when he was home as well.

"Yes," I say.

"So we're friends now?" Simons asks me in a low voice that doesn't invite the old man into further conversation.

"I think we're going to need friends here," I say.

He smiles, then opens his hand for me. I place my hand in it, and it disappears into his embrace, making me feel immediately better.

The door on the other end of the room opens, and a woman with short hair in a white lab coat enters, holding a ratty-looking pair of crutches. She sweeps the room, settling her gaze on me.

She offers the crutches to me, and I release Simons' hand so that I can take them. As I scramble to get my feet underneath me, the old man speaks up. "I should be next. I've been waiting for hours."

"Someone will be here for you shortly," the woman says without turning. When I'm steady on all four appendages, the woman beckons. "Please follow me."

The crutches are much easier to use than the one I fashioned for myself. I stop at the door long enough to glance back at Simons. He offers a small slice of a smile. "I'll find you on the other side, friend."

The door closes, shutting us in a very small, dark vestibule. The woman places her hand on a sensor that flashes green, then scans her badge on a screen just above the hand pad. The door clicks, offering her access. She pulls a metal handle and holds it open for me. "Go on in, I'll meet you on the other side."

"This is screening? For the disease?" I ask, even though I've already been told as much.

"Don't worry, it's very quick," she says, urging me forward.

I make my way forward into the dimly lit room and see a yellow line across the center. Just before the yellow line, there's a large red X. I stop at the X. The door closes behind me, and there's a whooshing of air as the lights flicker on. I can hear a faint electric buzzing coming from somewhere in the room. Studying the surroundings carefully, I discern a subtle wave in the air in front of me—something like a mirage. I suspect a force field. My mind spins with the strangeness of everything about this place. Why is there a force field in the middle of a dimly lit room with steel double doors that closed and locked behind me? A door on the other end of the room opens. The thin slice of yellow light stretches out across the floor and sweeps out like a crescent omen. The yellow glow is blotched out in shadow as something stumbles in.

I watch in horror as one of the near-dead wanders into the room—right in the middle of the Institute! The creature is like a poster picture of the ones we see in the videos—decaying on the outside, dark grey skin peeling away to reveal putrid and twisted muscles. Its eyes are milky and sunken deep into the emaciated skull that looks as though it's been sucked dry. A violent shudder begins deep inside of me and travels outward, making my hands and legs tremble as slick sweat coats my exposed skin. I stand my ground, gripping the rungs on my crutches to cease the terrible shaking in my hands. To stay calm, I focus on the shimmer in the air—the promise of security. I think of home, and my heart rate slows.

Suddenly, the shimmer disappears, and I can smell the decay. Icy cold death. Lost futures. The instant the force field goes down, the creature notices me. In a sudden fit of rage, it thrusts itself forward, hungry for my flesh. Somewhere amidst my terror, I find myself mesmerized by what the thing can do with a decaying body. It's like watching the dead come back to life. I can see the tendon and muscle movement through the paper-thin grey skin. Where the flesh has ripped and been sheared off its body, the muscle quivers and leaks dark blood. A terrible, gasping growl emanates from its throat, rising in intensity until it's nothing more than a high-pitched scream.

Though in imminent danger, my mind processes the information as if I were creating a study file. As if time has paused for me, I consider the situation: sight, sound, scent, scenario. Then time starts again, and I know my next action. I brace myself against my left crutch and raise my only weapon—the other crutch, ready to strike and go down fighting. But just as soon as the force field disappears, it re-engages. The beast, mindless in its attack, continues its lurch for my flesh and makes direct impact with the energized barrier. There's a loud sizzle as the creature's body burns against the electric shield. It shrieks but doesn't stop. I lower my crutch and watch the carnage. Pieces of flesh melt away from the skeleton, while others sizzle and smolder like meat dropped directly into coals.

A door on the opposite side of the room from the one I entered opens, and the short-haired scientist walks in. She puts her hand on my shoulder and says, "Congratulations. You've passed screening. Welcome to the Institute."

It's like she doesn't even notice the thing behind us throwing itself into the burning force field. There's a sickening gurgle that makes me look back over my shoulder. The top of the creature's head has melted off. The arms are twitching as the open neck sizzles against the force field, and the body slumps lifelessly to the floor. My stomach rises into my throat before it sinks down low. Regretting my curiosity, I look away from the mess and meet the scientist's gaze. She hasn't even blinked.

"That's how you screen people?" I ask. My mouth feels like it's stuffed with cotton balls.

The scientist places her hand on my shoulder and guides me out of the room. I can't smell the thing anymore, but the stench is burnt into my nostrils forever. The steel doors close behind us, and as I hear the lock slide into place, I try to imagine a lock sliding into my brain, to trap the terrible memory there for good.

"The patients don't attack other infected. It's the fastest way to receive an accurate diagnosis. Volunteers can't be admitted if they're infected. It would compromise *everything*." Her voice almost sounds like a laugh.

I watch her face, perplexed by her carefree demeanor. She saw what was in that room, but it's like she isn't affected by it. I scramble to process her explanation, but I end up stuck on one word. "Patients? That was a patient?"

She laughs at this. Her head tilts back, and her bright eyes close into little slits as she shakes her head with amusement. "They're all patients. Some are just further gone than others."

"But it killed itself. How can that be the best way to screen newcomers if they kill themselves?" I demand.

She tilts her head to the side so that her short hair hangs, as though this angle might give her more clarity. "Well, aren't you a curious one?" Her pale lips curve up into a polite smile that doesn't reach her eyes.

She rights herself and gives my shoulder a firm tug. I follow her into another hallway. "There are more than enough patients. Losing a few throughout the course of a day is a small price to pay compared to our safety."

She leads me to another metal door, keeping a firm hand on my shoulder. She places her other hand on the sensor before flashing her badge. The lock clicks, and she turns the knob. *How can there be so many patients? Where do they all come from?* I'm about to ask her when another door bursts open. The blond scientist whirls around. I can feel the pinch of her nails through my jacket, as if she were afraid I might run off from her.

"Professor Amos," she breathes, still keeping a firm grip on my shoulder. Clearly, she wasn't expecting anyone else.

"Rio," the other woman responds with a harshness that matches her severe appearance. Everything about her comes across as sharp. Her eyes are piercing, and her nose comes to a small point. Even her lips are fine and small and gather to a point. She has an ageless look about her. She could be thirty or sixty.

"Can I help you with something?" Rio asks. The hesitance in her voice makes the difference in their positions clear.

"I'm taking over this case. You're dismissed to process the next volunteer," the pointy woman responds.

Rio's hand shifts, but she doesn't release me. "I'm supposed to take her to—"

"I've got her orders right here. She needs to be taken directly to surgery, as I'm certain you realize," Professor Amos snaps.

Rio opens her mouth as if she were going to protest, then snaps it shut. She looks down at me, then back at the impatient expression of the waiting woman before relenting. "Right away, Amos."

When she releases my shoulder, I nearly lose my balance. The pointy woman rushes to my side and plucks me up. She's surprisingly strong for such a small woman. I look up at her, curious, and she brings a finger to her lips, glancing at Rio's retreating frame. I follow her gaze, noting the way Rio attempts a quick backward glance. She waits until Rio turns away, then produces a small syringe. I only have a second to acknowledge it before she plunges it into the top of my shoulder. I feel the pinch of the needle right where the collar of my jacket brushes the back of my neck.

The world swirls to black as the pointy woman calls out over an intercom. "I need a medic in receiving."

CHAPTER
THIRTEEN

I'M STILL NOT USED to the lights here. I've never been anywhere with so much light. We used to make light—my mom and my dad. Energy radiating out to the nearby cities. Precious light that we never wasted. Now it's everywhere, leaking from the ceilings and pouring out into unoccupied halls. *This is what it must be like to travel to the sun.*

There is nothing remarkable about the room I'm in. There's a white door against the white wall with a metal handle. It and the mirror are the only things that aren't white. The tile on the floor is large and white. It looks smooth like porcelain.

It's difficult to tell how long I've been here. Things all blurred together starting in the hallway, and it's difficult to stay awake when the medics come to silently change bandages on my leg and administer medicine through an IV. Every one of them looks like her. Their hair is short, their coats are white, and their gloves are blue. I'm still at the Institute.

I blink at the beeping instrument at my bedside. The sound must have woken me. I shift so that I can get a better look at the thing making the sound as I struggle to put the pieces of my memory together. I remember being dragged from the car, the old man and the brown chairs, Simons' face and the monster in the room...

The sound of the door draws my attention away from the beeping machine. I turn my head, expecting to see one of the short-haired medics in the crisp white lab coats and white pants with blue gloves, but it's the pointy woman. Instead of short hair, she has braided hair that's tucked tightly into her coat. She strides over to the machine and presses a button that stops the beeping. In the resulting silence, she pulls the empty bag from the metal hangar and replaces it with another.

"What is that?" I ask.

She looks down at me, as if surprised to find me awake. "Antibiotics. Pain medication. Saline," she says in the same crisp tone she used to address the other scientist—*what was her name?*

I push against the bedding with stiff arms, trying to sit up. She puts a hand across my body to stop the motion. "You need to remain still, or you may compromise the healing process."

"Healing process?" I scrunch my nose. From somewhere in the depths of my mind, a conversation surfaces. What about my leg—is it salvageable? Is it even *worth* being salvaged?

My eyes refocus on the back of the woman's head as she finishes changing the IV and resetting the solution. "What's wrong with my leg?" I ask.

She turns, meeting my wide-eyed stare with her own sharp gaze. "You've had surgery."

"What kind of surgery?"

"The tissue couldn't be salvaged. The interior has been rebuilt," she explains.

A panic rises inside of me. "Is that why I can't feel anything? Is that permanent?"

She shushes me. "You'll heal. The synthetic tissue should communicate with your nervous system after some time, and it'll be like nothing ever happened."

It seems too good to be true. I study her face for some clue that she's only appeasing me, but her face is inscrutable.

"Where is Simons?" I ask, suddenly aware that he must be overwhelmed with concern.

"I'm sorry, who?" She raises a thin eyebrow.

"The man I arrived here with," I say.

She shakes her head. "I have no idea what you're talking about. You arrived on a city transport under presumption of infection."

I balk at her. "No. I was with a man—he's very big, I'm sure you could pick him out—"

"You must have been delirious with fever," she says, walking away from the bed toward the door.

I think she's going to leave, but she stops just under the metal hinge and reaches up to the back of a little black box with a blinking blue light. The light stops blinking. I watch her with wordless confusion as she strides confidently across the room to a data station buzzing with electronics and indicators. She looks at the screen with a puzzled expression and says, "That's strange. I can't get a display on this thing. I better do a full reset."

She presses a button, and the screen that previously displayed crisp, clear data denoting my health goes black. I hold my breath as she turns away from the blank screen to face me. She returns to my bedside and places a hand on the crisp white sheets that cover my unfeeling leg.

"Why did you come here, Kara Mason?" she asks. Her voice is quiet and urgent.

"I came with the man I told you about—Simons," I say.

She snaps her head back and forth, rejecting my explanation. "Why didn't you go south?"

My mouth falls open with the realization of what she knows. Is she also on the inside? I pause, unsure if I should trust her so quickly.

"People risked their lives to keep you safe," she says.

"Trudy wouldn't have made it." I try to explain without revealing too much.

She brings her right hand to her head, placing an index finger on one temple and her thumb on the other and letting out an exasperated sigh. The data port screen flickers blue, forcing her attention. She glances at it, then at me. Her words are hushed and urgent.

"I can't believe you could be so stupid. You aren't safe here. I have no idea if I can keep you hidden. You were supposed to go south! Why didn't you just go?"

"I wanted to help…" I whimper my weak explanation to her unforgiving face.

"What do you think you can do that we can't?" She laughs.

My face flushes at her rebuke, making me feel small. "Maybe Simons can get me out?" I suggest.

She shakes her head. "It's not that easy. You can't just walk out of here."

The data station beeps, signaling the end of its reboot. She glances at it. Her expression tells me that this conversation must come to an end.

"I will do what I can, but I can't make any promises. Just…" She glances up at the ceiling as if it might hold my redemption. "Keep your mouth shut like your life depends on it because it does."

With that, she stands, brushing a non-existent wrinkle from the lap of her white suit with a blue-gloved hand. "Your recovery looks to be right on track. Another medic will check on you, and we'll see if we can get you cleared for solids tonight."

She offers a bright, empty smile before turning to the door. Looking up, she says, "Oh, look at that—the camera is off too. There must have been a power glitch."

She reaches up and presses a button that brings the blue light back to life. Opening the door, she addresses me once more. "Try to get some rest. That must have been a traumatic trip to take. All alone on a vehicle full of infected people. You poor thing."

The door shuts behind her, leaving me alone with the buzzing machines. I look in the large mirror on the wall directly across from me. My hair is ragged and matted from lying in bed. I'm not dirty anymore. Against my white medic bed in my white patient robe with white sheets covering the white bandages on my leg, my face looks pale and narrow.

A machine whirs through a cycle, then clicks. A light blinks on the little device attached to my leg, and some medical information is sent digitally to some other location where a medic will decipher it. I will the information being transmitted to be innocuous, afraid that it might somehow reveal something about me to the wrong person.

CHAPTER
FOURTEEN

"GET UP. NOW," a voice prompts me from the darkness of slumber.

I open my eyes to see the pointy woman's face only inches from my own. I blink, thinking that maybe this is a dream, like the other strange one I've been having where I open my eyes and there's a man standing at the end of my bed. He's just standing there wearing a crisp white lab coat over a black suit, looking at me. He sees me open my eyes, but he doesn't say anything. I blink and he's gone. At the end of this blink, the pointy woman is still there.

"Did you hear me? Come on. Up!" she urges, pulling my hand and shifting my body so that I'm sitting up.

"Where are we going?" I ask, using the hand she doesn't have in a vice grip to stifle a yawn.

"A dorm just opened up next to mine. I'm moving you there," she says.

I look around, awake finally, and notice that the data screen is blank, and the buzzing I came to associate with my stay in this room is absent. With swift and practiced hands, the pointy woman removes the IV from the back of my hand, replacing it with a wad of gauze and a strip of white medical tape.

"Here, slip this on over the gown. Are you strong enough to walk?" she asks, helping me into a lab coat that's the twin of hers. The back of my hand brushes against the stiff fabric, sending a chill down my spine.

"Um. Walk? I can't walk," I stammer, searching her face to see if she is making a joke.

"Your leg is fine now. It's only partly numb to spare you from the discomfort of your nervous system rewiring to incorporate the new tissues." She brushes a dark strand of loose hair behind my ear before placing a pale and narrow hand on the shoulder of the lab coat. Everything about the gesture seems counter to her personality. It was gentle and caring.

I look away from her hand and into the seriousness of her face. "I don't know if I can."

"Alright. Let's have you try. I can get crutches if necessary, but we'll be less obvious if you don't need them. Come on. I'll help you at first." She offers me her hands, and that's when I realize she isn't wearing the blue gloves. Her skin is cool against the clammy warmth of my hands.

"What's your name again?" I ask, deciding that I can't just keep thinking of her as *pointy woman*. Maybe she'll forgive me for not remembering.

"I'm Amos," she says.

"I'm Kara—"

"Mason. Scientists, volunteers and everyone else who works within and as a product of the Institute is referred to by their last name," she corrects me.

Standing is strange. I can feel the cold tile under my bare right foot but on the left side— nothing. I bend my knees, and the left one stays put, knocking me off balance.

"Easy. Try again," she urges, keeping one hand on my elbow.

"Am I going to be a volunteer?" I ask, finding my own balance again so that her hand on my arm is more of an accessory than a necessity.

"I'm not sure yet."

This time, I take extra care to think about the motion I want to accomplish. *Lift your left leg, point your toes, then bend the knee.* I watch in amazement as my body responds, going through each motion as if it were completely natural. The whole process is painless. *Feelingless.*

"Because you're going to try to hide me?" I ask, remembering our clandestine conversation. I'm taking a gamble saying this out loud, but the data port is blank and the blue light above the door isn't blinking, so it seems like a safe bet.

She gives me a sharp stare meant to warn me against such bold statements. "Yes."

I take another step, this time with my right foot so that the entirety of my weight is being supported by a leg that feels like it's not there. Then another. *Three... four...* five steps and I've made it to the other side of the room. I turn around, teetering on legs that aren't quite ready for what I'm asking them to do. "How are you going to do that? People know I'm here. The other scientist, the people in the biohazard suits, doctors and medics..."

She watches me take the five steps required to return to her side. Her thin smile does little to soften her features, but I like it anyway. "The young woman that arrived in the transport vehicle with the rogue maintenance worker and his daughter was never processed, so there is no formal report of her arrival."

"What about the people who saw me? Won't they recognize me?"

She puts her hand on my shoulder and turns me toward the door. Her stride is quick and confident and her hand is sure as she compresses the lever and swings the door open into a wide hallway filled with noise. Bright lights bounce off of the floor, creating a distorted reflection on their white surface. Two men in lab coats walk past us, deep in conversation about something on the shorter man's data tablet. In the distance, a grey-haired man guides a group of young-looking individuals in dark blue lab coats out of a room, instructing them to follow him to patient 04582. With Amos's hand planted firmly on my shoulder to steady me, we pass through the door side by side, our lab coats billowing with the rush of air as it shuts behind us.

"Let me ask you a question, Mason," she says, keeping her head up and her face bright but neutral as we wade through the hallway. "When you're walking down a street, maybe at the end of a school day, how many individuals do you notice?"

"I don't know. Fifty? One hundred? It depends on the day," I say.

She pulls me to the right so we don't disrupt the path of two individuals wearing lab coats over their black suits. When I turn my head to get a better look at them, she gives me a little jerk, forcing my eyes forward.

"And how many do you recognize day after day?" We pass through double doors held open by a sensor, then turn left. Here, the floor changes from pristine white tile to dark, matted carpet.

"Maybe one or two people. There's a man who always wears a brown hat with a wide brim—I would recognize him."

"Exactly! You might notice one or two people who obviously stand out in a crowd, but if everyone looks like they're supposed to be there, you don't notice them," Amos says, clearly pleased with my answer. Her explanation makes me think of the first near-dead we saw standing alone in the field in dress clothes. He definitely didn't look like he belonged there.

"I'm going to hide you in plain sight, right where no one will look for you," Amos continues.

"Is someone looking for me?"

She stops in front of a door with a faded brass handle and looks me straight in the eye. "I don't know yet, but I have to assume that you're not just going to slip away. You shouldn't have been able to pass that test. Not a year early, but you and your brother did. You're the only ones who did."

Hank. My body aches like more pieces of it are missing than just the insides of my leg. I blink hard and fast to keep the tears from coming. I don't want Amos to see me cry. She opens a door and reveals a room that looks like a snapshot from my past. A dormitory with a brown cot and a desk. There's a small, neatly folded stack of clothing at the foot of the cot. The ghosts of a hundred mornings getting ready for school flood my memory until I expect to hear Bruce yell at us that we're going to be late if we don't hurry.

"You'll stay here for now. Until I can figure out something better to do with you," Amos says, urging me in and shutting the door behind us.

I don't answer. Somewhere deep in my mind, Hank is pounding on the bathroom door, demanding I come out or get ready to share.

"Mason!" she snaps, bringing me back from the ghosts.

"Yes?" I ask, fighting the sting of tears.

"I said my room is right next to this one. I'll come get you every morning. Don't answer for anyone else. Do you understand?"

I nod, well aware that there's no other acceptable response. "Yes. I understand."

"Good. I'm going to bring you along and slip you into a different group each day for now. I will take you, and I will retrieve you. Unless I have given you direct instructions, you will do absolutely nothing. You will not converse with anyone, you will not roam anywhere, and you will only answer to me. Here. With me. In training. Understand?"

I nod. She's so serious. Urgent. I don't dare argue with her.

"There's something I need to take care of. I'll be back to check on you in a little while." She turns to leave.

Before she can open the door, I blurt, "Will they be looking for Hank, too?"

She stops, stunned by my words. I don't blame her. I didn't know I was going to say them either.

"There was a report of an incident," she says, speaking very slowly.

Incident. How could such an innocuous-sounding word hold so much? My heart is thudding in places it shouldn't be. I swallow, trying to move it down out of my throat. Amos stands at the door for a long, quiet moment, waiting for the rest of a conversation that never comes.

"I have to go. I'm sorry, Mason," she says, before letting the door shut me into the room filled with memories.

PART TWO
THE INSTITUTE

CHAPTER
FIFTEEN

THERE AREN'T any white suits in my size, so Amos has me put on volunteer clothes to follow her around today. She says that no one should notice as long as I keep my lab coat buttoned. If they do notice, she said, then I'm supposed to say that's all that was left in the decontamination room. Then I made her explain that there are decontamination rooms attached to every laboratory—in the medical building and the school building—for clean-up. Usually decontamination rooms have clothes for scientists, interns and volunteers, but sometimes the laundry schedule is off, so it's not an unreasonable explanation. That's the only thing she gave me permission to say out loud today.

"Remember, not a word when we're around others," Amos says as we exit the medical building and follow a slim cement walkway that cuts through short-clipped grass before it joins a concrete circle at the center. The circle connects all of the walkways and buildings on the campus. It looks like the spokes of an ancient wheel, or maybe the face of a clock that hides the inner workings of a hundred turning gears.

"What about right now?" I ask, noting that the nearest people scurrying by are out of earshot.

"Do you always like to push boundaries?"

"Not once I know where they are."

She raises an eyebrow at this, then turns inside the circle. "We're headed to the receiving building right now. That's the first building you were taken to. Behind us is the medical building, which, as you know, houses all of our resident scientists." She gestures to our left, which would be noon on a sundial. "The low building there is the interns' quarters, and"—she points to three—"this path takes you to the transport structure where vehicles and cargo are stored."

I follow her gesture and note an even smaller building tucked back by the wall. "What's that?" I ask.

"That's another residence building. It houses volunteers in training."

My face lights up at her explanation. "Is he there?"

"Of course."

"Can I see him?" I ask in a high-pitched whine.

"Absolutely not when someone can see you."

There must be some other time that I can. I don't think Amos is sloppy with her words. I wait patiently to see if she will finish the thought. There's a long pause while I watch her face turn from stern to soft.

"I'll see what I can do."

Her words elate me. I fall into step with her as we continue toward the receiving building. "What are we going to do in the receiving building?" I ask.

"You aren't going to do anything," Amos corrects me. "I'm going to investigate a reported personnel anomaly."

"What does that mean?" I scrunch my nose.

"It means I'm going to do my job, and you're going to quit asking questions," she says as we pass through automatic steel doors that slink into a firm lock seconds after granting entry.

I remain Amos's silent shadow as she approaches a woman with a shaved head sitting behind a tall counter. "Good morning. I'm here to look into an incident from a few nights back," she says, prompting the woman behind the counter to produce a slim folder.

Amos takes the folder wordlessly, but instead of opening it, she holds it against the data tablet she carries tucked under her arm. The folder beeps, and Amos returns it to the woman behind the counter. Two taps later, her tablet screen glows with the contents of the folder.

As she reads through it, the woman behind the counter pipes up, eager to be helpful. "I talked to Rio and Jenkins—they were both on shift that night, and they both swear there was a third party."

"For their sake, I hope there's a reasonable explanation. Can you imagine what sort of consequence there would be for an undocumented person on the Institute campus?"

The young woman's olive skin turns nearly as pale as her lab coat. "That would be bad."

"Without a registration, how would we know if this supposed individual was even screened?" The sharpness in her voice has returned. I watch as it cuts the scared scientist on the other side of the counter.

"I'm sure if you talk to Rio—"

"That will certainly be part of my investigation. I plan to hold anyone and everyone accountable for a potential outbreak on Institute grounds."

She tilts her data tablet, and the screen goes black. Tucking it under her arm, she turns away from the counter and says to me, "Shall we get started then?"

I glance back at the woman behind the counter as we pass through another set of automatic doors. She looks so scared that she might start crying. Before the door closes, I see her pick up the handset to the same type of receiver the woman on the screen used the night Simons and I arrived.

I turn my focus back to our surroundings. When I confirm that we're the only two people in the hall, I whisper, "This is about me."

"I thought I said no talking?" Amos glares down at me.

"There's no one here. And the cameras in this building are visual only," I say, still keeping my voice low.

"How do you know that?" she asks, a look of genuine curiosity on her face.

"One of the scientists in the biohazard suits said so."

"Those were volunteers," Amos corrects me.

"Does that matter?" We're nearly to the door at the end of the hall. I suddenly wonder if the old man will still be waiting on the other side.

"It does. If they weren't, then I couldn't make you disappear so easily," she says.

"You can do that?"

"That's one of my primary duties here," she says.

I can't tell if she's referring to her official position at the Institute or her position with the dissenters.

"What is your position here?"

"I'm an auditor. My position includes all things from statistical analysis of job distribution to investigation of aberrant occurrences within the Institute grounds."

"That must be useful."

"It is. I'm also an adjunct Instructor for the scientific intern program, which can be just as useful at times. Enough. Mouth shut." She gives me a look that suggests there's no room for arguing.

I compress my lips together, biting my tongue to force away the questions that ache to be released, and fall behind Amos as she swings open the door to the waiting room. My eyes move directly to the back corner in search of the old man, but he isn't there. Instead, there are five new people sitting in the brown chairs, fidgeting and uneasy as they await screening.

"Good morning, prospective volunteers," Amos addresses them cheerily. A few wary eyes glance in her direction, but others keep their vigil watching the floor. "I'll be performing an evaluation of the screening and intake process today. This should not affect you in any way, but you may catch a glimpse of me as you move through the process. Thank you for your cooperation as you wait in these challenging first phases of your entry to the Institute."

Even the wary eyes look away from her as she sweeps across the room and scans her badge at the opposite door. I wonder why she addressed them like that. No one gave me any information when I arrived. The sting of my teeth sinking into the fleshy mass of my tongue keeps the inquiry at bay as I follow her into the small vestibule.

I recognize the steel double doors that contain the screening system, but Amos bypasses those and scans into yet another room. As we wait for the green light and sound of sliding locks to indicate her clearance, I consider asking her another question. Before I can even intake a breath, she gives me a sharp look, her eyes wide and angry, warning me to keep my mouth shut.

The door slides open, and we pass into a room no bigger than the entry vestibule we were just in. Inside this room, another scientist waits—a young man with short-clipped black hair wearing the blue synthetic gloves and white lab coat. He looks up from his data tablet, and I watch his expression transform from curiosity to one of barely masked panic.

"Professor Amos," he stammers, nearly dropping the stylus from his left hand.

"Just an audit, no need for formalities." She offers him a cool, thin smile that makes him swallow hard and fidget with the stylus against his tablet screen again.

He nods, opens his mouth to offer cooperation, then changes his mind and turns around, obviously not forgetting Amos's watchful eyes on the back of his stubbly head. When he turns, I realize what we're here to observe. We're staring directly into a window that looks into the screening room.

The force field barrier is invisible at this angle. It looks as if nothing is separating the thrashing creature from the man standing directly opposite. A sound that reminds me of home signals the power surge of the force field re-engaging. It's the sound of the in-rush of power to the storage cells that relay with the power grid. I don't remember hearing it on the night I stood on the opposite side of this window.

The nervous scientist glances over his shoulder at Amos, who looks busy and critical staring into her tablet. "I'll be right back."

The door clicks shut, leaving us with the hum of the transformer relaying energy to the force field. I count the seconds it takes for the scientist to walk from this room to the other door to retrieve the volunteer. The door opens on six. The volunteer jumps at the sudden entry of the scientist, who beckons him into the next hall. I watch the soundless interaction, enraptured.

"Normally, we keep the patients restrained like this. A new screening patient had to be developed the night you arrived, which is why you saw what you did." Amos speaks as if she could read my thoughts.

I take her words as a cue that it's safe to talk right now. "Why didn't they just process us in the morning?"

"If you had been processed in the morning, there's no way I could have intervened. Too many people would have seen."

"So you orchestrated the whole thing?" I ask, amazed that any one person could have so much power.

"I had help. We knew to expect you after Simons sent his last message."

"How many of you are here?" I ask with a rush of excitement.

"More than anyone would expect," she says, nudging my shoulder to draw my attention to the next patient—a man in slim, green pants with a canvas jacket and a tired look hidden by a tuft of overgrown hair. The scientist opens the door for him, and he takes a hesitant step toward the X, not seeing what's on the other side of the force field yet.

The doors shut behind him. The scientist will be returning to this room now. With the last second of privacy, Amos says, "But don't you dare think that means there isn't any danger here. There's danger around every corner. Everything is under scrutiny. Everyone is monitored, and there's no room for mistakes."

The lock on the door clicks, and she falls silent, looking busy with her tablet once more as the scientist returns to the room and checks something on a control board.

"Who's doing registration processing today?" Amos asks, managing to sound simultaneously threatening and disinterested.

"Um… Rio," he stammers.

"Exactly who I want to speak with." Her tongue clicks. She dims the screen of her tablet and tucks it under her arm just as the force field shuts off.

I hold my breath, knowing what to expect and hoping that the tired-looking man knows too.

But it doesn't happen. The three seconds pass in anguished silence as the chained patient stands docile, completely unaffected by the man on the other side of the room.

"Another one," the scientist says as he uses the stylus to mark something on his tablet.

Amos pauses long enough to ask, "How many?"

"Two so far today from the same transport," he answers, shaking his head as if he can't believe it either.

Amos gives him a curt nod, then opens the door to exit. She urges me out ahead of her, placing a firm hand on my lower back as if to steer me away. The scientist follows behind to complete his duties.

At the door on the opposite side of the vestibule, Amos fumbles with her badge before managing to place it against the scanner. The extra seconds it takes to allow us access is enough for me to overhear the scientist.

"We're going to have to transport you to patient processing."

"What? Impossible!" The tired man's voice is higher pitched than I imagined.

"There are cryogenic options—"

Amos's strong hand forces me through the door to complete another task.

CHAPTER
SIXTEEN

"HE WAS ONE OF OURS," Amos explains as she hurries me back across the path toward the medical building. Her meeting with Rio was short. It turns out there were only two people on that transport vehicle after all, but the volunteers got their orders mixed up and brought the infected girl into the receiving building by mistake. Rio forgot to purge the air vent before cycling the force field and got a false negative. It was lucky for everyone that Amos was passing through and heard the cries of the distraught volunteer in the waiting area. That's what Amos's official report says. It's impossible to tell if Rio believes it or if she's too scared to argue.

"What will happen to him?"

"After testing in the patient intake, he'll be sent to cryogenics," she says.

"Even if he doesn't want to go?" I ask.

"No one objects to the cryogenic process. The alternative is too horrible to consider," Amos promises me.

I fall silent at this, unsure if there's anything proper to say in response. The alternative is terrible. Definitely too terrible to think about, anyway.

"I've got to report my findings to the audit board now. You can't come with me."

Amos's statement pulls me away from the dark corner inside my head. "Where will I go?"

"I'm dropping you off with an intern group for a few hours," Amos says as we approach the medical building. The entryway is free of personnel, and it suddenly strikes me as odd how few people are moving around on such a large campus.

We pass through the doors, and she takes us down a busy hallway, stopping at a door marked with the word *laundry*. Casually, as if there were every reason for two scientists to enter a laundry room, she opens the door and strides in.

"Take off that lab coat," she says, flipping through a hanging rack of freshly laundered dark-blue coats.

I obey, shrugging the coat off of my shoulders. Amos takes it from me and hands me a new one. Without missing a beat, she explains, "Interns at the Institute wear dark blue lab coats so they're easy to tell apart from the resident scientists. You'll blend right into the back of the class. I know the professor I'm leaving you with. He hasn't looked at an intern in the last decade—not really. He won't notice you as long as you keep to the back and keep quiet."

"What about the interns? Won't they notice an unfamiliar face?" I ask, alarmed by what she is asking me to do.

"Professor Hugo is the most rigid, demanding instructor at the Institute. No one will have a spare moment to notice you," she insists, still rifling through the laundry.

"Seriously? You keep saying that no one will notice me, but this place has been close to empty all day. And now you're putting me with interns? I would notice if someone new suddenly just showed up— even if she didn't say anything!" My heart beats loudly in my ears. I'm pushing too much, but Amos seems delusional.

She stops what she's doing and looks up at me, lips pulled tight. "Mason," she says, her voice measured and patient. Behind the thin word, she's holding back a mountain of exasperation. "This campus houses three hundred resident scientists and the entire functioning branch of the DDC. There are several hundred interns—whom, might I add, are constantly getting shifted through our various programs—and dozens upon dozens of constantly rotating volunteers. We also regularly host government visitors and rotating workers from other areas. At any one time, there are countless people on shift, and those shifts rarely overlap or stay consistent. It would be a miracle if someone recognized you."

"If there are so many people here... where are they all?"

"The Institute runs on a tightly regimented schedule. So long as you adhere to it, you may remain invisible," she says, returning to her search. She lifts one of the large bins full of dirty coats and exclaims, "Ah, here it is," producing a data tablet that appears to be the twin of her own.

"How did you know there would be a data tablet in the laundry?" I ask, watching her turn the slim device over.

"Even I needed a little help to pull this off," she laughs, then extends her hand to offer the tablet to me.

I take it, trying not to seem too eager to flip through the comforting archives of data. When I look into the smooth black of the screen, the glassy pool instantaneously changes to grey and prompts me—*register owner*. I glance up to make sure I'm not about to err. Amos nods, assuring me that I'm allowed. I tap the screen, and it intakes my metrics, making a map of the blood vessels in my retina and the depth of the valleys time has yet to etch on my face. I imagine the heat as the infrared signal marks my fingerprints where they grip the back of the device. The screen flickers white, and the imprint is done—the tablet is mine.

I've never had a personal data tablet before. The ones we had at home were part of the school program and thus required manual entry of my personal identification code to access.

"The tablet is yours, but don't get any ideas. All tablets within the Institute grounds are traceable. Every keystroke, every note, every search and every communication," Amos says.

That sort of defeats the purpose of having a personal data tablet. I don't say it out loud.

"Alright, let's get you to your class," Amos says, turning me back toward the door and opening it with the same confidence she used to enter.

I follow her, only wishing that I could look as purposeful as she does striding across the reflective tile. I look down and notice that I don't have to try as hard to look somber as I did a few weeks ago. The thought does wonders to make me believe I'm blending in. *Hiding in plain sight.*

"Take notes. Treat everything the professor says as important and keep your face buried in the tablet unless he asks you to look at something. If he does ask, be the first to look. Don't dare get caught not following directions," Amos says. Her voice is casual but quiet as we pass through yet another busy hallway. Some of the multitude of people at the Institute are becoming apparent, but still no one notices us.

Ahead, I see a group of younger people in dark blue lab coats gathering by a pair of doors meant to partition off the expansive hallway. Amos walks right through the group of gathering interns. They part for her like dark swells of water moving away from the shore. At the far edge of the gathering, Amos gives me a nudge to indicate that this is where we will part.

I step into the mass of navy just as a clipped voice addresses the group, "Per our lesson last week, which Zoribiatus strain manifests first with abnormal pigmentation of skin tissue caused by swelling of extravascular fluid of the lymph system?"

I take a half step behind a very tall boy with short, dark hair whose fingers are flying furiously through his notes. Forcing my attention away from him, I bring my own tablet up to my face and open a fresh study file. Instead of scouring old data, I type silently and furiously to create a new one. The act appears identical to what the other interns are doing. As my finger flies through the airspace above the tablet to recreate the professor's inquiry, a student responds.

"Strains of the ZCB family."

"Incorrect."

I delete the response, daring to catch a glimpse of the professor and the unlucky intern. Professor Hugo is an unassuming man in a crisp white suit and lab coat buttoned all the way to the top. His thinning hair is clipped short and combed neatly to one side. Behind wire-framed glasses, piercing green eyes reveal a meanness. He points at the boy next to the incorrect intern, prompting him to say, "The ZCC family manifests first with abnormal pigmentation and swelling of the lymph nodes. Those same symptoms are present in the ZCB family but often follow the manifestation of lesions."

"Correct," he says, turning his head two degrees back toward the incorrect intern. "Make a note."

The professor turns. The motion is so fluid that it makes him look like he's riding a mechanical swivel. His head doesn't even bob as he makes his way down the hall. The interns seem to have anticipated his motion because they fall in step behind him all at once, making me think of the way surface tension can pull a hundred drops of water upward, defying gravity. I scramble to follow, making sure to stay near the back.

"We're going to observe three instances of the ZCC strain today and make a direct comparison to manifestation with the ZCD family. I will expect by the end of this lesson that you should manage to differentiate by sight alone the three main strains of Zoribiatus that are still circulating amongst the population."

The professor continues his lecture as he guides us through locked doors that offer entry with the scanning of his badge and remain open until the last intern passes through. Our pace is hurried as we make our way down a very different hall than the one we left. It's not that the architecture is different; in fact, it's exactly the same as it was on the other side of the locked doors—drab, white and reflective. But these halls are empty save for our group and two women in thick, yellow protective wear and blue gloves that pass over their elbows.

This is where they keep the infected.

"Case number one came to us only just this morning. As you will observe, the patient is in the very early stages," Professor Hugo says, scooping the patient file out of its bin at the end of the bed.

"Excuse me—are you a doctor?" the pale woman in the hospital bed asks. Her eyes are puffy, red, and completely reveal her terror.

"If you are asking if I'm a medical professional, then the answer is yes," Hugo responds, flipping the chart page and turning away from her.

Her mouth drops with unspoken words as he addresses the class.

"This is patient 58624. She tested positive for ZCC strain two and is scheduled for cryogenics by the middle of next week."

"Mary," she says to Hugo's back. "My name is Mary."

He ignores her, and so do the interns, though the task is more difficult for some of them.

"Here is the most common stage of disease you will see in newly infected. With study, tell me, what do you note?" The professor's eyes travel across the sea of furiously typing blue.

"Swelling in the neck."

"Discoloration of the lips and tongue."

"Thinning of the hair."

"Greying of the sclera."

Answers punctuate the sterile room, each one soliciting a quick nod from the professor. At the last one, his lips tick upward.

"Ah. Very good…"

"Miller."

"Miller," he agrees, not really caring. Donning a pair of the elbow-length blue gloves, he turns back toward Mary and clicks on a little light I hadn't noticed him holding. "Often, discoloration of the sclera and other ocular tissue is masked by the increased blood flow in a distressed patient."

"Is this really necessary?" Mary asks as Hugo tilts the light to illuminate her eyes, causing her to blink.

"You are admitted to the Institute for treatment, aren't you? The Institute, by nature of necessity, is an academic hospital. How can we provide you with what you require if we cannot study the thing that will otherwise kill you and so many others?" His questions aren't intended to solicit an answer.

With a gloved hand, he pulls aside her medical gown, revealing her naked form. I try to keep my eyes away from the look of horror that marks Mary's face as Hugo continues the lesson. "Note similar early manifestation markers that show changes in the pituitary system."

It's a command that the interns obey eagerly.

"Lack of body hair."

"Discoloration of the areola and vulva."

"Loss of epidermal elasticity."

"Correct. A final note before we move on to the next patient—this strain can often be detected by discoloration of the nail beds, but that shouldn't be relied upon for definitive diagnosis without at least one other indicator."

He releases the gown, which wafts down to cover Mary's thoroughly scrutinized body. She reaches out to hold the flimsy material as sobs distort her withering body. I ache for her and the way that no one else seems to acknowledge her presence.

"Our next patient is an anomaly," Hugo says, ignoring Mary's wailing. He places his gloved hands through two holes in a metal container and removes them again, without the gloves. He turns to the door, leading the way out of the room.

I force myself not to look back at her as the door shuts, muting her terrible sounds. I'm certain that doing so makes me less human than I was before I walked into the room.

Hugo continues with the lesson as if this were perfectly ordinary. "A third-year intern, infected on Institute grounds during a routine patient processing. Perhaps that's something for all of you to note, hmm? A reminder that our safety systems are in place for a reason."

I catch several students exchanging wide-eyed glances with one another as Hugo brings the cohort into the next room, which is much smaller than the previous one. The door clicks shut behind me, forcing me to step in close to the other bodies. I hold my tablet close to my chest, unable to see through the shoulders and arms of the other interns as Hugo speaks.

"What makes this case interesting is the difference of the sequence of manifestation of the ZCC strain of Zoribiatus by virtue of the contamination. Here we see extensive tearing of the abdominal region, which we shall call entry point one."

"That's sick," someone whispers.

"How is she even alive still?" another voice responds.

Hugo's voice cuts the exchange short. "Entry point two, as you can see, is the gash running from the base of the skull down through the clavicle."

The interns hum with unspoken questions. From how it sounds, the patient in the bed was nearly torn apart. Though I can't help but be a little curious, I'm thankful I don't have a front row view of the carnage.

"Professor Hugo?" A hand appears above the interns.

"Yes…"

"Miller again. Was all of this damage done by one patient?"

The other interns look up from their tablets at her question, clearly interested, though I can't tell if they're interested in the answer or the boldness of the intern who asked the question. I hold my breath, afraid for her, and eager for the answer.

"Miller." This time, her name matters. "One patient can do much more than this. That's why you're here."

A sea of heads snap back down to their tablets.

"Who can tell me the primary differences in manifestation?" Hugo inquires.

"Major pigment change at the site of the wounds."

"Necrosis of the flesh at each injury site."

"Very good," Hugo manages to say without a hint of encouragement. "Who can tell me how order of injury was determined?"

The room falls silent, each student relying on another to pluck an answer from the data. The medical port beeps with the steady rhythm of the patient's heartbeat.

"The difference can be determined by fluid output from each injury. Entry point one has a darker discharge, though not by much."

Miller again. I wonder if she's the only one with the correct answer or the only one brave enough to test her mettle.

"Correct. The last patient we will observe today is in the final stages of disease progression. He is from the donation program, and you should expect to see him on the dissection table within the week." Hugo presses through the bodies toward the door, finished with this room.

I sink away from the door, fitting through the small gaps between busy bodies waiting for their next assignment. I wait for the interns to clear the room, eager to keep my inconspicuous position in the back for fear of being asked for an answer I don't have. When the room is nearly empty, I dare to glance at the occupant. My heart stops when I see Trudy's mangled body.

CHAPTER
SEVENTEEN

LYING on my side on the thin mattress, I stare into the white glow of my tablet and wait for the clock to turn today into tomorrow. Without losing track of the digital time display, I distract myself by cruising through the notes from today's lesson.

Why did the professor lie about Trudy? Amos wouldn't address it with me, likely because she didn't feel safe discussing the subject of her falsified audit in the building. It would be simple to assume the explanation is straightforward—that in order to make me disappear, Trudy's story had to be likewise changed. Yet it doesn't seem right. It's not possible that the other scientists on the Institute grounds would overlook such a blatant lie about something that never happened. There are too many people that would know it wasn't true.

Nothing at the Institute makes the right kind of sense. There's an air of mystery to the way things run that goes much deeper than Amos's work for the dissenters. The Institute is enormous. Even with my limited tour, it's clear that the medical facility is packed. We walked past dozens of closed doors adorned with patient numbers. Every time one of the yellow-garbed hospital volunteers opened a door, they would release the sounds of distress—the moans, shrieks and sobs of patients forced to face the hopelessness of their situation while someone takes samples of their blood and puts their bodies on display.

I close my eyes as if shutting them might shut out the sounds that echo in the tiled halls of my mind. Their cries blend until they sound just like *them.* The sounds of hundreds of rasping screams combined with the rustle and smack of cloth, skin and wet, meaty flesh moving together. I shake my head, attempting to shut out the chorus of death, knowing that I can't stand what comes next—when they all go quiet.

I open my eyes to a screen that's gone black. I lick dry lips and taste the metallic tang of blood. I bit my lip. I wipe the blood away with a shaky hand and check the time. *One minute.* I rise from the bed, each movement made with extreme care so as not to make any noise that might rouse Amos on the other side of the wall. Slipping the volunteer clothing back on, I make a final check of the time before heading to the door.

Amos was waiting for me in the hall juncture when the interns were dismissed. She took me around the back of the building, on a different route back to the dormitory halls. Just before the floor turned from tile to carpet, we passed an emergency exit. There was no scanner mounted on the wall next to the door, and the little device that hangs above the hinges was absent of the blinking blue light. I figure it's the best chance I have of getting out of the building undetected. Thanks to the predictable regimen of the Institute, all I have to do is get by the cameras.

The hall is so dark that it's easy to detect the blinking blue lights in the distance. I duck down and crawl toward the back wall, hugging the surface and scooting past until I've made my way to the dark niche that holds the exit point. I approach the door, running my fingers across the edges and feeling around the hinges and the handle for any indication of wires or a sensor that might trigger an alarm. Nothing obvious. It would be easier to tell if I had a light. The thought makes me ache for the little night-light. I didn't dare bring the tablet for fear that the *everything* Amos warned me would be traceable might include location. I don't know who besides Amos might check on me, but I don't want to find out, and I don't want Amos to know what I'm doing either.

Outside, the cool night air beckons with an aching familiarity. I slip into it, holding the door open long enough to wedge the little brown cloth I took from my bathroom into the hinge. I turn away from the door and look across the campus grounds. A fog swirls ghostly shapes above the clipped grass, seeming to skip over the walkway before coalescing again on the next patch of greenery. It makes the walkways look even more like spokes on a wheel. I imagine someone at the helm of a ship steering the Institute through the ocean of forest that surrounds it.

Moving quickly, I head directly to the low building next to the concrete wall that acts as a divide between this world and the one outside. The night is quiet, absent of the sounds that kept me awake long after Dad, Bruce and Hank drifted off. The sensation of silence is strange. It shouldn't be possible to keep the wild completely out. There should be some evidence of the life that grows on the other side—an insect's drone or a night bird's song. The only proof of our location is the smell of damp earth and the sweet sharpness of forest growth.

The volunteers' quarters are completely absent of windows on all but one side. I make my way toward the glow of soft light that seeps out from the window on the far side that looks out onto the concrete wall. The window looks into a common area crammed full of couches and chairs, most of which surround a large viewing screen. The screen is blank, and the couches and chairs are empty, as is the thick slab of a wooden table with benches askew on either side. In the back corner of the room, a single low-watt bulb illuminates a chipped wooden coffee table and the red-orange fabric of a squat chair. Across from the empty chair sits the shadow of a very large man, slumped forward with long legs stretched out toward the empty room.

My heart leaps, making me jumpy but thrilled to have been right about finding him. I move away from the window and try the door. The handle turns without obstruction, granting me access.

Simons looks up at the open door, curious about the interruption. "Kara? Is that you?" he asks, as if he doesn't dare believe his own eyes.

"It's me," I say, letting the door click shut behind me.

He's up before I can take another step, crossing the large room in a matter of seconds. He puts one massive hand on each of my shoulders and looks down at me, confirming my existence. "I wasn't sure I'd ever see you again," he says in a soft, low voice.

The warmth of his hands on my shoulders engulfs me, causing everything to rush in at once. All of the loss, terror and uncertainty of the last week wash over me. Without thinking, I throw my arms around his waist and hold tight as the sobs overwhelm me. Simons flinches from the suddenness of the act, then wraps his own arms around me, enveloping me in what comfort he has to give. We stand like this for a long time, neither of us saying a word to each other, until I've spent all of the anguish that's built up inside of me.

As the blubbering turns to hiccups that catch in the back of my throat, I'm suddenly aware of the thing I've just done. I release the big man, wiping my eyes with the rough fabric of my sleeve in an attempt to quell the flow of tears.

Simons reaches out to pat the top of my head. "Are you okay?"

I nod, still working to regain some composure. "I'm alright," I say, too embarrassed to look at him through the tears that don't seem to want to stop.

"Come sit down with me," he offers, steering me back toward the little sitting area.

I follow him to the low chairs and take a seat opposite him, my knee brushing against the chipped edge of the coffee table. I run another sleeve across my face, still not ready to meet his gaze. I bring the damp sleeve down to my lap and mumble at my feet, "I'm sorry for that."

"It's alright, Kara. You've gotta let it out sometime. There's nothing to be embarrassed about," he encourages.

I sniff, keeping my leaking eyes on my feet and my attention on the strange buzzing in my arms, wondering what happened. "I was fine before I came here," I say.

"Kara, you lost your family. You're not fine. There's nothing wrong with not being fine." Simons leans forward so that his face is level with mine.

I think about how much I miss Hank and Bruce. About how I wish more than anything that Hank were here to make fun of my tears. I wish Bruce were here to describe how the process of tear production is linked to the emotional center of the brain. I want Dad to bring me a hot cup of tea and tell me I won't even care about any of it tomorrow morning. But they aren't here, and I will care. The tears return, but I dare to look up at Simons anyway. His eyes are rimmed red with grief and exhaustion. It looks like he hasn't slept since we arrived, making me think that maybe he isn't fine either.

"I miss them," I say.

"Do you want to talk about it?"

I consider his question. What could I say? Would I tell him that Hank is better than me at almost everything? That Bruce wants to be a medic? That before all of this happened, I believed everything the schools taught? Or maybe he wants me to describe how they died…

I shake my head as the last of the tears mark wet trails on my cheeks. "No. That's not why I came."

"Okay," he says, his torso wobbling on unsettled legs. "That's okay. We don't have to if you aren't ready."

"Thanks," I say, somehow feeling marginally better knowing I don't have to say anything.

"So what brought you here?"

"I saw Trudy today—well, yesterday, but I saw her."

Simons' eyes brighten, but his jaw tenses as he grits his teeth. "Is she okay?"

"She's alive. The infection is pretty bad though. I read her chart—she'll go to cryogenics at the end of the week." I don't tell him how she was used as an example in a lesson.

He puts his fingers together and sinks his face into his hands so his chin is resting on his thumbs, closes his eyes and exhales. The tremor in his hand is so subtle that I almost miss it.

"That's a good thing, right? It means she'll be stable enough—that she won't die from the attack?" I don't know if I'm helping or hurting.

Simons wipes the corner of his eye, composing himself. I wonder if I should tell him that it's alright to let it out. I don't. It's too strange to offer an adult that sort of advice.

"It's good," he says once he's got himself under control. "It's as good as I could have hoped for, at least."

Watching him suffer makes me question my intent in coming here.

Is it cruel to put the burden on him? I chew my lip until fresh blood seeps out.

"Whatever it is, just tell me," he says, reading my hesitation.

I decide that I would want to know if the situation were reversed. If it were Hank, or Bruce or Dad.

"The professor told the interns that she was a third-year student at the Institute. He said that she was injured by not following safety procedure during an experiment." The words come out all at once, stumbling over one another to be gotten over with.

Simons lets out a shocking burst of laughter. There is nothing merry about the sound. It's cold and bitter, filling the empty room with its uneasy, angry vibrations.

"Why would he say that?" I ask.

Simons runs the fingers of his left hand across his bottom lip in a slow, contemplative motion. The laugh has dispersed from the area, but it left its coldness in his piercing gaze. "It's a cover-up. They don't want anybody to know about the attack."

"Why would they hide the attack? Don't they want people to be scared of near-dead outside of the cities?"

"Oh, they do. But if there's even a hint of their involvement, then they'll want to cover it up. They can't have anyone who isn't high enough up to know better suspecting that they're the ones controlling the near-dead populations."

His explanation sends an electric shock down my arms. "How could they control them? How could anyone control them?"

"They don't exactly control them. Nobody could do that. But they sure seem to know how to move them around when it suits them," Simons says.

"No. That's not possible." I shake my head. If someone can control the outbreaks, then why wouldn't they put a stop to them?

"Do you think that such a large group would go unnoticed so near the Institute? Do you think the DDC wouldn't know about something like that?"

Simons' questions are too similar to what Dad said about the near-dead. *This is why he thought we were being followed. He thought that the*

DDC was sending near-dead after us. If it's true, then the DDC must also know about how they behave together.

"Why?" I ask, still wavering between certainty and disbelief.

"What do you think would happen if people knew it was safe out in the world?"

"It isn't," I say, crossing my arms across my middle and holding them close against the chill.

"It isn't," he agrees. "But it's not dangerous like they say it is. It's dangerous because they *make* it that way. To keep people scared. To control them."

"That's sick," I whisper, afraid to say it any louder.

Simons' fingers are pressed together and splayed out wide. He nods, keeping his thumb balanced on his chin as he does. "It's why we exist," he agrees.

If everything Simons is suggesting is true, then things are so much worse than even Dad believed.

"It's about more than a cure," I say, looking around the room again, afraid to spy a blinking light.

"It is," he agrees.

"Is it… safe in here?" I ask, glancing at the blank screen.

"The cameras in here are motion detectors—all visual," he assures me. "But we don't want to be overheard if we can help it."

My whole body hums with nervous energy. I resist the urge to jump up and burn it off, pressing my clammy palms into my knees instead. "Do you have help here too?"

"I do. I'm assuming that means you do?"

"A scientist—Amos—she took me from the receiving building. She's hiding me," I say.

He blinks at me, bringing his hands together over his bouncing knees. "Amos," he repeats her name.

"I think she's—"

"Don't say it," he cuts me off, eyes wide with warning. "Don't ever say it out loud, no matter where you are. Even if you think it's safe."

I bite my lip and taste the old blood.

"Does she know you're here?" he asks.

"No."

He lets out a heavy sigh. "I'm sorry, Kara. I shouldn't have brought you here. I don't know what I was thinking."

"You had to. You had to save Trudy," I remind him.

He leans forward and places his forehead in his hands. "No. It wasn't right. I was selfish. Bringing Trudy here doesn't guarantee her safety, and I've gone and compromised you."

"Don't talk like that," I snap, surprising myself. He looks up at me with raised eyebrows.

I take a deep breath. "Trudy is your daughter—she's your family, and you had to do it or you would have lost her. It's like you said—it's alright to not be fine about it all. I'm not. But since we're here together, we can be not fine together."

Saying it makes me feel grown up, which makes me less scared. Simons straightens out in his chair and offers me his hand. I take it, and I'm even less scared than before.

CHAPTER
EIGHTEEN

THE FOG IS EVEN THICKER NOW that dawn is approaching, but the campus is still quiet—too quiet for the last moments before sunlight creeps over the horizon. I cross the giant wheel quickly, blending into the fog as I move toward the hazy lights that line the outside of the medical facility. I creep around to the back of the building toward the door I left propped for my return, slipping into the shadowy entryway. I run my fingers along the door, searching for the exposed lip of the door that the rag should produce, but find nothing. The door is level with the jam, creating a nearly seamless surface. The rag is gone.

Uneasy panic drips down the back of my neck, making my heart beat faster. I try to keep my breath steady to fight off the mounting alarm. *I have to get inside before someone finds me.* Leaning against the rough concrete wall, I close my eyes and try to think. There has to be another way to sneak into the building.

I can't just walk through the main entrance. It doesn't matter how much confidence I have; no one will believe an extra short volunteer without a yellow suit is scheduled to cruise through the entrance at 4 a.m.

The thought gives me an idea. At no point in time throughout the day did I see a single one of the medical facility volunteers coming or going from the facility. They must have their own entrances. I make my way along the building, keeping out of view. Three-quarters of the way around the building, I find what I'm looking for. The door opens automatically at my approach, so I walk through it as if I'm meant to be here.

The artificial light reflects off of the floor, making everything too bright. A sterile, chemical smell assaults my nostrils as I move too quickly down the hall. The metal screech of a distant door makes me jump. I taste the metallic tang of adrenaline as I duck down a side hall in the opposite direction from the wailing. The sound of the door closing echoes in the distance, replacing the terrible cries. A lone individual travels down the hall, covered feet squeaking against pristine floors. I count each footfall until, on twelve, another lock clicks, and a new cry fills the halls.

I move toward the double door entryway, eager to avoid the volunteers making their early morning rounds. Another door opens behind me, making me quicken my step. When the wailing ceases, I hear two sets of footsteps. I don't stop to see if they're looking in my direction; instead, I hurl myself around the corner into the main hall. The double doors are locked fast. The only way through is the flash of a badge that I don't possess.

I curse silently as I decide on my next move. It would be folly to wait for someone to pass through the doors. I could be stuck for hours, and Amos would discover me missing long before I made it back. In the meantime, some volunteer would surely note my presence and report me. My best chance is to retrace my steps and hope that no one is guarding the front entrance.

The volunteers' rounds have a rhythm to them. I count the beats between each door passage, jumping from hall to hall on my way back to the exit. I stop in a vestibule as another, yet-to-be-detected volunteer exits a room two doors ahead of me. I wait to see what the volunteer will do. She looks up the hall, then turns her head south, her braid coming loose from her suit when she does. She re-tucks it, then approaches a mounted receiver on the opposite wall.

"I need a gurney in the main hall. Patient 5826 is deceased."

She hangs up the com with a heavy sigh, then turns. I press my body against the wall, too afraid to breathe and reveal myself. She rubs a bare arm against the seam where her face mask presses into her forehead before re-gloving and opening the door to return to the silent room. The second the lock clicks, I sprint toward the exit. If I'm caught now, someone will certainly think I'm a loosed patient.

I make it to the exit just as another door opens, followed by the racket of a rolling cart. The door doesn't open automatically. I reach out to press against the handle, but it doesn't budge. That's when I see the scanner mounted against the wall and realize that of course the door only allows one-way free entry. They aren't trying to keep people out of this area—they're keeping them in.

I'm trapped. The thought makes me dizzy with panic. I throw myself against the wall as the gurney turns into the main hall, ushered by two more yellow-clad volunteers. They stop in front of the silent room, and one of them knocks. The door opens, and the volunteer woman grants them entry.

"Transport for the dead!" The knocker announces in a cheery voice.

"You're sadistic," she says.

The three volunteers roll the cart into the room, and the door snicks shut behind them. I reel in the silence. The medical building is secured to keep the patients in. Only volunteers and scientists can move between the areas. My only chance of getting out is with one of them. Long seconds pass without any ideas. Adrenaline seeps out of me in waves of stinking sweat and noisy breaths. Somewhere outside the locked doors, volunteers vacate the low building and make their way toward hasty training. I wonder if it would be too much to hope that some of them have training here.

The door opens again, and two volunteers exit, pushing the loaded gurney into the hall. The body is covered in a long, white sheet so that I can only make out an outline.

"I really thought this guy would make it to the end of the week," the door knocker says.

"Nah, man. You didn't see the panel of tests the doc ordered on him. A program like that was sure to make it quick," his partner answers.

They point the gurney toward the doors on the opposite end of the hall and begin rolling it.

The door opens again, and the woman calls after them. "Hey! You forgot to finish the report. I can't release the room for cleaning without it."

Knocker groans. "C'mon. Can't you do it? Those dang things take forever. We gotta get your buddy here to the morgue."

"No way," she says. "He's not going anywhere, and I'm not getting bumped to cryo crew for breaking the rules."

"Come on, let's just do it. I'll co-sign for you," Knocker's partner offers.

Knocker sighs, kicking on the brakes to the gurney. "Everyone around here is such a stickler for the rules," he moans as they both return to the room where the volunteer woman stands scowling.

I stare at the shrouded body. A door in the north hall opens, releasing a pained cry. Thirteen steps later, another door closes. I know what I have to do, but the idea makes me sick. The dead don't run.

I duck below the door where the three volunteers stare into a data port. Standing next to the body, I'm certain I'm about to make a terrible decision. I tremble as I contemplate how much the sheet reveals. A man, emaciated but tall, who died with his mouth wide open. The sheet reaches over the gurney's suspension system, promising me cover for my terrible idea.

At the very last second, I decide to at least opt for a little bit of protection and shove my arms into the holes next to the door. My hands return to me clad in the thick blue gloves. I pinch the sheet awkwardly through the thick layer and lift it up just enough to duck under and swing my leg over the center-v in the suspension system. I ease myself down until I'm straddling the thin metal bar, then tuck my legs into the crook on each side. I grip either side of the hollow metal slab that holds the body, my hands already sweaty inside of the thick nitrile.

The door to the silent room opens again, and the transportation volunteers return to the gurney. My stomach flips, and all my muscles tense as one of them kicks off the brake and the whole thing rocks into motion.

"What a waste of time," Knocker laments.

"Rules is rules," his partner says.

The gurney shimmies across the floor, its racket almost deafening. I'm thankful for it, certain my breaths are too loud.

"I'll get the door," the partner offers, releasing his side.

The gurney swings wildly to the left, causing me to lose my footing. My shoulders ache with tension as I think with all my might, *leg up!* My foot brushes against the ground before I manage to snap my leg back up and hook it around the suspension.

"Warn me next time, dude. You know these carts are worthless," Knocker snaps, slowing the cart to a stop.

The lock clicks, and the double doors swing open. Knocker lets out a grunt as he pushes the gurney back into motion.

"You ever notice how it always feels like these suckers are heavier dead than alive?"

The partner joins him on the other side of the doors, and the jerky motion of the cart steadies.

"I don't spend much time lifting live patients, myself," the partner responds.

Knocker snorts at this, and the cart turns to the right. "You must've gotten on somebody's good side around here."

"People 'round here don't have a good side."

The conversation dies. Five seconds down the hall, they stop. I watch another set of doors open to darkness. When the volunteers push the cart forward, the room floods with sickly yellow light. The gurney comes to a stop against a tiled wall, and a yellow-clad foot kicks out the brake again. I resist the urge to loosen my grip, letting my fingers ache with the tension.

"You scan him in?" Knocker asks.

"Yep. According to this, someone's on their way to process your good buddy here right now," his partner answers.

My stomach clenches.

"That's quick," Knocker says.

"Maybe you were right about his untimely demise."

"Yeah. Frederick here seemed like a fighter."

"That his name?"

They both move away from the gurney, back toward the door. I let a foot slip silently to the ground, unable to hold my position any longer.

"Yeah. He said it every day for a week and a half. After a while, it just sort of stuck with me," Knocker says.

The door opens, and both volunteers step back to let someone enter. I can see the bottom of a white lab coat as the newcomer sweeps past them. I sneak my leg back up, wincing at the soft groan of the suspension system.

"He's all yours," Knocker says as he and his partner exit the room. The scientist doesn't respond. I watch the bottom six inches of the scientist approach the gurney.

The automatic door shuts, leaving me alone with the scientist who's about to expose me and the dead that brought us together. Before I have a chance to even think, the sheet flies away from the gurney. The scientist puts one blue-gloved hand on the surface and ducks down so that I'm staring straight into Amos's very angry face.

"Mason."

CHAPTER
NINETEEN

"WHAT ON EARTH WERE YOU THINKING?" Amos hisses at me the second her dormitory door closes, shutting us into relative safety.

I open my mouth, too aware of how dry my throat is. "I—"

"Never mind. I don't want to know—I don't care to know," she corrects herself.

"I'm sorry," I say, stepping back and sitting on the edge of her cot, avoiding the crisp crease of her tightly tucked cover.

"No, you're not." She stops pacing and faces me directly. "You're sorry you got caught. You're sorry I found the cloth you stuck in the door, but you certainly aren't sorry about your idiotic plan."

She continues, her voice shockingly piercing for how low she keeps it. "You have absolutely no idea how dangerous what you did was. No idea what I'll have to do to keep it quiet. No idea what we're going through to try and keep you safe. You don't understand."

"Then help me understand," I snap, throwing my arms out so they smack either side of the brown bed cover.

Thin eyebrows rise over the glowing anger that radiates outward from her glare. "What do you think I've been trying to do? If you would look outside of yourself for one second, you could see that's exactly what I've been doing since the day you tagged along with Simons to the Institute."

"Well, you're not doing a very good job of it," I mumble, crossing my arms and looking away from her accusatory expression.

Amos lets out a frustrated sound that prompts me to glance up at her. She puts thin fingers up against her forehead as if she were pushing back against a nagging pain. "I don't know what I expected. You're just like your father. Immature, impatient and completely selfish."

"He wasn't any of those things," I say, anger rising inside of me, making my ears hot.

Amos drops her hand to study me. An involuntary smirk contorts her face. "Do you want me to lie to you? Should I tell you he was a great man, invaluable to our cause? Is that what you want to hear?"

I stare at her, unable to formulate a response.

The smirk disappears, replaced by a cold look of contempt. "No. I won't lie to you just because he's dead. Your father was a fool. In the end, he helped no one. If you don't learn your place, you're going to end up just like him."

Her words hit me like a punch to the nose—the kind that turns a sibling spat into an all-out brawl. White-hot starbursts explode behind my closed eyes, turning my vision into colorful spots. Standing from her bed, I give her the most hate-filled glare I can manage. My fingers bite into the flesh of my palms, and my whole body vibrates with an electric disdain. "I'd rather be dead like him than hollow like you."

I force my way past her, reaching for the door. I can't stay here a second longer. Amos blocks the door as I compress the handle, preventing me from making the dramatic exit my heart craves.

"Let me go," I say, keeping my eyes fixed on the grey of the door so that her form is a blurred white mass in the periphery of my vision.

"I can't do that," she says, placing a cool hand on top of mine.

"It's not your decision." I resist the urge to pull my hand away.

"It is. You wanted to be here, remember?"

"I wanted to be a volunteer—with Simons," I correct her.

"That's not an option," she says.

I let my hand fall from the door, finally looking at her. "Why not?"

I watch her face change. The deep lines that accentuate her sharpness soften; in their absence, she looks sad and tired. "Because I can't just let you die if there's a chance I don't have to."

She steps away from the door and sinks into the chair at her workstation, resting the palms of her hands on her narrow legs. I move toward her, too curious to let anger rule me. She lets out a heavy sigh before saying, "There is no higher mortality rate on earth than for a volunteer. They're laborers. Whether it's at the Institute or in the Northern Laboratories, their fate is the same, but at least here, the end result is almost always infection. Up north, where they deal with the developed disease, it's often much, much worse."

"How long?" I ask, taking a cautious step in her direction.

"Six months."

"How is that possible?" I ask.

"There are always more volunteers. Many more than scientists. They're disposable bodies—integral to the way things run. Without them, we would lose too many scientists," she says.

"How can there be so many of them? The disease is supposed to be nearly gone in the cities, and… people on the outside—they wouldn't come here. If they're on the outside, then they don't believe in what the Institute and the Northern Laboratories are doing." The illogic of what she's saying makes my head spin. There can't be so many volunteers.

"The problem is much more complicated than even your father understood. I can't explain it to you—not even here, but I promise I'm being truthful about this. About the volunteers and about the danger," she says, some of her usual steeliness returning.

My whole body feels numb save for my left leg, in which a dull ache has taken up residence.

"What about Simons?" I ask.

"He knew what he was signing up for," she says.

"Six months?"

"If he goes to the Northern Laboratories," she confirms.

"And if he stays here?" I ask, a glimmer of hope returning.

"He won't. His daughter is scheduled to go north. He'll go with her," she says, stomping it out before the flame can catch.

"And there's nothing you can do about that?"

She lets out another heavy sigh. "Six months is an average. There are volunteers who make it longer, of course."

"So there *is* something you can do."

"I didn't say that," she corrects. "But there are people who help."

My whole body slumps with relief. She notices it. "Don't get too attached. There's a good chance he'll be gone by the time you make it up north."

I look up at her, perplexed. "What do you mean?"

Amos smiles, clearly pleased with herself. "I've got a plan for you —*we* have a plan for you. We're going to send you to the Northern Laboratories."

The shock of her statement puts a chalky taste in my mouth. "I'm going to go to the Northern Laboratories?"

"That's right. It's the perfect solution, we all agree. And it was easy. When the DDC officials realized that you'd been located—on Institute grounds, no less—they were eager to absorb you into the program. I mean, can you imagine what they went through, knowing that they lost the only individual to receive a perfect score on the placement test? And that was after the addition of the—"

"Perfect score?" I ask, losing the thread of her explanation.

She stops and studies me, blinking. "Yes. Didn't you know?"

I shake my head.

"No one has ever gotten a perfect score. No one has ever passed the test on their first try—not until you and your brother, that is. And taking it a year early was notable, so they're very interested in you."

"His name is Hank," I say, cutting her off again, unable to stand the cold way she refers to my family.

"I'm sorry, Mason. You and Hank did something remarkable, but you—it's the reason we're able to do this," Amos says, as if it's the most exciting thing that's ever happened.

"What if I don't want to? What if I don't want anything to do with any of this? With the patients and the lies and the volunteers nobody cares about?" I ask, gesturing to her room as if it housed the entirety of the Institute's foulness.

"If you can do this, Mason, then we might be able to use you for something significant—something that could put an end to the DDC's activities inside and outside the City States." Her last words are spoken in such a hush that I almost don't believe she said them.

"What are they really doing?" I ask, nearly mouthing the words.

Amos's eyes glisten with fevered excitement. "You can stop them. What happened to you never has to happen to anyone else, ever again."

Her dorm spins, and the floor is no longer stable. I step backward until I trip onto her bed. When the back of my leg makes contact, a sharp pain shoots outward, causing me to suck in a fast breath. I close my eyes in a desperate attempt to stop the room from pitching. Amos joins me at the bed, putting a cold hand on the side of my face.

"Mason. Breathe," she commands from far away.

She turns away to rifle in her desk drawer. When she returns, she kneels down and puts something in my mouth, forcing me to swallow the bitterness. "That's it," she encourages, "nice slow breaths. Keep breathing."

Slowly, the room stops moving, but everything is still far away. Amos resumes her position next to me on the bed, pulling strands of hair away from my face and twisting them into a tight braid that she tucks into the back of my suit. When she's done, she turns my head so that I'm looking at her through dull eyes. "Better?" she asks.

"I don't know," I answer honestly.

Her eyes are sympathetic. "It's okay. I know I'm asking a lot from you."

I shake my head. "It's not that."

"What is it then?" she asks, straightening the collar of my volunteer suit—the one that belongs to the people who aren't expected to survive.

"What happened…" I start. A knot in my stomach creates a sharp pain that makes it hard to breathe again so that I can't finish the statement.

"I know," she says, pulling me so that I'm leaning against her. She places a hand on the side of my head. The gesture is awkward, as though she hasn't shown affection to someone before. Still, it's comforting. "That's why it has to be you."

I pull my head away from her shoulder so that I can look at her. "What has to be me?"

"You're going to bring us the cure," Amos says, a thin smile warming her peculiar face. "That's what the Institute and Northern Laboratories are all about, after all."

I know her statement is a lie, but there's a purpose to it. She's hiding what she can't say within it.

"Why does it have to be me?" I ask.

"Because you know what's at stake. You've seen the hive."

The hive.

This has everything to do with the strange behavior I witnessed. I open my mouth to question her, and she puts her hand over it before I can make a sound. We cannot speak about this. Not even here.

"Can you do this? For us?" she asks, reaching out and squeezing my hand.

I look at the woman sitting next to me, overwhelmed by her duality. She is both Institute and dissenter. I don't know which part of her is more real. In one breath, she condemns my father and dismisses the volunteers, yet in the next she seems to stand for everything I want to believe in. I've never been more conflicted about one person in my life.

"I'll do it."

CHAPTER
TWENTY

TWO NIGHTS after Amos shuffles me into the mix of new interns, I'm following the foggy pathway to the volunteer commons again. Though I don't think that Amos approves of my visiting Simons, I'm certain she knows I have no intention of stopping. Before dismissing me, she pulled up a map of the campus grounds to show me the portions dedicated to the intern program. At the same time, she mentioned a pathway tucked out of view of the other living commons and the majority of the surveillance cameras. It's a longer route that takes me along the concrete wall straight toward the window into the commons.

Tonight, I'm not wearing a volunteer suit. Instead, I'm wearing the white-and-blue jumpsuit issued to all interns. Amos gave it to me before bringing me into the mix of new arrivals in the intake building. The roster of new interns is altered to include my real name and real scores, but it has a falsified date of birth and school year. This, she told me, was done with full support of the DDC supervisors, who are just as eager as she is to alter the records, albeit for different reasons.

I don't quite understand the DDC's reasons for admitting me into the intern program. Amos assures me that it has everything to do with my performance on the test. Part of me wants to believe her. It matches up with what we're taught in the city school system, but that's also why the explanation feels false. If the Northern Laboratories don't need the best and the brightest to find a cure, then what do they need them for?

And then there's the training within the intern program—so much like Dad described it that night by the campfire. It's presented as a meritocracy. The better we perform across all disciplines, the higher we'll rank within our cohort and the more likely we'll make it to the top, granting us acceptance into the Northern Laboratories program. Unqualified interns will be shuffled into other programs—energy management, Institute positions, DDC personnel...

But there's more to it than our performance. Amos already told me that I'll need to stay at the top of my class in order to succeed. They'll expect nothing less from the girl with the perfect score. She also told me that it'll be a lot harder than I think. It was easy to get top grades in the school system. Less than one percent of the city students qualify for the Institute. But here, everyone qualifies, plus they've all got four additional years of formal education.

Amos agreed to tutor me, but it might not be enough. And there's the other portion of the intern program—the part that wasn't formally announced. I think of what Amos said as I creep away from the shadow of the concrete wall... *You need to become callous to the infected, regardless of disease stage...*

I think of Trudy. She's a patient, but she's still a person. I could never be callous toward her. Yet Amos insists I must. Thinking these thoughts makes me feel guilty, as if I intend to betray Simons. I'm not supposed to care about him either...

The commons are busier tonight. A few volunteers are gathered in front of the data screen watching an old movie. Simons is sitting in the back by the light. There's a game of checkers set up on the chipped coffee table. The board is set up so that the red checkers face the empty seat, as though he's expecting my company. Kids always want to play the red ones.

I smile at the thought of him waiting for me to play a game, but the smile vanishes when I remember that today is also the day Trudy was scheduled to be processed into cryo. He's waiting for me because I'm the only one left he has to wait for. I suddenly don't want to play the red checkers. Tonight, I want to be an adult. I want to be there for him the way he was there for me.

Sitting down in the chair across from him, I feel very adult, like I'm digesting the weight of the world. Simons smiles a sad smile as I flip the board and move a small black plastic circle. I lean back and wait for him to start the conversation. I know it's the right move in the way that someone who has done something again and again knows. As if someone has imparted the wisdom of a hundred years upon me. Or maybe it's just the knowing of our shared anguish.

"I made rank today," Simons tells me.

"What does that mean?" I ask.

"All the volunteers headed to the Northern Laboratories are scored during training. I'm at the top now," he says, moving a piece.

"Does that mean you'll be safer?" I ask.

"They'll see my scores. I should get a better assignment based on that," Simons says. He offers a weak smile.

He takes my first piece so that it's my move again. I wonder if I should ask him about Trudy, or if he didn't mention it because he can't stand to talk about it.

"When are you going?" I ask instead.

"There's a transport scheduled to go north next week. Trudy and I will be on it," he says, breaking the seal by saying her name.

"Are you alright?"

Simons nods his head as he moves another piece, but everything about him suggests that he's not. "They let me see her before she went in. She looked strong, like her color was better than before."

He can't mean the color of her wounds, which were already festering and grey days ago. I don't dare ask about it, though. "So you got the report about the successful procedure?"

"That's right. They even gave me a printout of her statistics—her chances of complete recovery with a cure," he says, a trembling hand moving toward a pocket in his volunteer's suit. My heart aches with the unspoken truth. No one intends to cure Trudy. Simons' printout is one of hundreds handed out to volunteers to string them along and convince them their sacrifice is worthwhile.

"I guess somebody better get busy working on that cure then," I suggest. These are the only words either of us can speak in mixed company. Though I know Simons knows the same truths about this place as me, I can't tell what he believes anymore. Maybe seeing Trudy was too much.

"That's why we're here. We've both got jobs to do, and if we do them well, maybe things will work out," he says, promising me he's not as broken as he seems.

"That's right. And I know what my job is now," I say, hoping this piece of news will give him some comfort.

"Oh yeah? What's that?" Simons asks with a half-smile as he moves a red piece across the center divide in the board.

"I'm going to the Northern Laboratories, too. Amos told me. I joined an intern cohort two days ago." I move my black piece against the edge of the board.

I look up to gauge Simons' expression. He looks straight back at me. My revelation removed some of his sadness, but not in the way I thought it might.

"No," he says.

"I already agreed," I say. I smile, but not because I'm happy. It's a sort of nervous, involuntary facial tic whose wild inappropriateness I can't seem to stop.

"Tell her you changed your mind," he says, putting his hands on his knees in a way that makes him very large.

"I can't. I'm registered. The DDC approved it."

He leans into a hand, pressing thumb and forefinger into his temples. "Kara, I wish you had talked to me about it first," he says, his voice softening.

"You didn't talk to me about your job. You didn't tell me about the six months," I shoot back at him, letting anger cover my fear.

He looks over at me, his brow scrunched to contort his face. "Did Amos tell you that?"

I nod.

"Did she tell you the average rate for a scientist in the Northern Laboratories?"

"No," I say, unable to control whatever emotion is running my mouth.

"Last year, it was one in five," he says.

"One of the five didn't survive?" I ask, all pretense of what I do or don't know gone.

"Only one out of every five survived the first year," he corrects.

I swallow, a large mass forming in my stomach. It must be ice because the room is suddenly too cold. "That can't be right."

"We just went over the Northern Laboratories statistics in training today. It's supposed to help us understand how critical our position is, I suppose."

"How is that possible? What could they be doing that causes so many deaths?" I want to reject his statistics. It has to be an error. Some sort of lie to manipulate the volunteers.

"I don't know, but I'm sure I'll figure it out soon enough," he sighs, reaching out to move another piece across the board.

My stomach does a nervous flip. "I don't want you to go," I say.

"I don't want *you* to go."

It's too late now. I doubt anything could be done to change the course of either of our lives. We resume the game, unable to manage the conversation. After a few uneventful moves, I take a red piece. This seems to bring Simons back to life. He lets out a silent huff of a laugh.

"Guess we're still in this together," he says.

"Both of us going north."

"It's where the answers are, I suspect."

"What do you mean?"

"Since I got here, there have been three transport vehicles from the cities. The folks I've talked to have all come here with someone sick— that's at least one infected person for each volunteer, sometimes two or three. That's more than fifty infected just since we got here. Those numbers are way too high," he says, moving another piece so that the game is a stalemate.

"Amos says there are always a lot of volunteers. She said *it's compli-cated*, whatever that means."

"Other people here from the outside are saying it's not natural the way the disease is spreading," he offers, drawing my attention away from the board.

"Do they think that…" I look around, trying to indicate our surroundings, "they're *responsible* for it? Not just aware of it?"

He hushes me with his eyes. "They do. I do too. King me."

"I'll see what I can figure out," I offer, relinquishing one of the captured reds.

"No." He looks at me sternly, like a father looks at their child, meaning for me to listen. "You stay safe. I'll do what I can up there. We have to work together."

"Alright. We'll work together. I'll do my part here, and you do your part up there—by surviving."

Two new volunteers wander into the commons and take a seat at the large wooden table. Simons looks over at them and says, "Enough now."

I nod my assent. They're near enough to overhear our conversation.

"So, what's going on with that leg? It seems like it was pretty bad when we got here," he says, switching to an innocuous topic.

"It's not my leg anymore. The insides are synthetic."

"It's still your leg. Just because they fixed it doesn't make it theirs."

I watch as his king takes two of my pieces and find my winning move.

"True," I agree, standing from the game. I need to make my way back before someone misses me.

Simons stands to walk me to the door. When I turn to leave, he stops me.

"They'll try to change you, Kara, more than you can imagine," he says, one hand holding the door and the other on my shoulder.

"I know." I want to tell him that my dad already told me as much, that Amos is already preparing me for it, but we're out of time. Instead, I just put my hand on his.

"Don't let them."

"I won't," I promise.

CHAPTER
TWENTY-ONE

PEOPLE ARE DISAPPEARING.

In the last three years, the combined functions of the Institute and the dissenters working in its midst can't explain the magnitude of disappearances. Interns have vanished from my year, and the rumor is that they have from other cohorts, too. Volunteers who are ready to head up north work in the laboratories with the interns, which makes them the best source for head counts. My cohort is down to twelve, and the ones that are gone haven't just joined other programs. Though we've lost a fair amount to energy management and non-research clinical positions, I can't say for certain what happens to the others. We aren't meant to know.

I hover in the shadows outside the volunteers' quarters. Since Simons left, whenever I find a quiet moment alone, I take a walk by this back fence and linger as long as possible near the window. Lately, I've ended up slipping back into the intern quarters without making any contact, but when I first started, someone would almost always meet me. At first, it was someone Simons trained with, then it was someone who knew him, and so on.

It went on like that until the woman I met with disappeared. No one would speak with me for a long time after that. One night while I waited, a volunteer poked his head out the door and hissed at me, "You keep that up and you're gone too, little intern!"

Today is the coldest day this year, and this year has been the coldest year at the Institute yet. It seems fitting since it's my final year. My breath makes frosty clouds that only I can see, and my hands protest the air's bite. I can't wait much longer. One after another, volunteers retire until the room is nearly empty. Finally, there is just one volunteer sitting on the orange couch and watching the large screen. I watch as he notices he's the last in the room. He turns the screen off and walks over to the light switch. The room goes dark, and I almost miss the creak of the door in the darkness.

"You the one the other volunteers talk about?" His voice is low and quiet. I squint to make out his approaching shadow. He's tall.

"Unless there's more than one of us," I reply.

"I'm surprised you're still around. You must have someone protecting you. Any chance that could extend to the people you talk to?" He leans against the wall, facing me, and rubs his hands together to fight the cold.

"I just keep quiet when it counts."

He looks over my shoulder, then turns to look over his before focusing on me again. "You call this being quiet?"

"I know where the cameras are and when eyes close."

"The volunteers talk about you. You come here looking for information?" He crosses his arms against his body.

"I believe there's something happening here, in the cities, up north… I'm sure of it. Too many people are disappearing."

"Right, right. And lemme guess, you're the answer to the problem, little intern?"

"I didn't say that. All I want is information."

There's a pause while he decides. I shiver against the cold.

"Okay. How can I help?"

"I've been trying to keep track of the disappearances. I want to know about the labs." I can't keep the excitement contained. It's been so long since I've had an informant.

"Slow down!" He puts his hands out as though he were keeping me from pouncing on him.

"I'll take anything you've got," I say, taking a deep, biting breath.

"I overheard a conversation tonight between a couple of guys that are getting ready to go. They said there were more volunteers than interns in the halls today. Said the interns are dropping like flies."

"How many volunteers per group in the labs?" I ask.

"Five per group."

I bite my lower lip and shiver. "Have there been accidents?"

"There's always accidents, but we don't know anything about that." There's something strange about his choice of words.

I study him in the dark, trying to read the words he isn't saying. "Anything else?"

"Not tonight. You'll know it when you see it," he says before disappearing.

His absence brings the cold back. The wind wraps its arms around me, and I turn to sneak back into the intern housing. There's only one cohort ahead of mine, and there aren't even five interns left. The last I heard, there were ten in that group. They're disappearing faster at the end of the program.

It's dark in the intern quarters. The doors slink shut, and I wince at the sound, hoping no one is awake to hear it. I untuck my braided hair and let it loose for the night. I'm the only intern who wears her hair braided like Amos's. I couldn't stand to cut it short. I hoist myself up into my bunk and ease my tired body down onto the stiff bedding. I should sleep the moment my head hits the pillow, but my mind is racing. I pull the small bundle of wires out from its hiding spot inside my pillowcase. It lacks the elegance of Hank's design, but the basic principle is the same. Eventually it'll be a ball of light. I squint in the dark so that I can proceed to insert each fiber-optic wire into the conductor.

"Where do you go?" The question startles me from my work. It came from the bed below me.

"Tucker, has anyone ever told you that you ask too many questions?" It comes out a hissed whisper as I shove the wire cluster back into its hiding spot. I'm terrified he'll wake someone else.

"You were with Amos?"

I wonder if anything could get him to stop. Amos has been trying. "Yeah. Shut up and go to sleep."

It might be safe to pass information with the volunteers, but not with the other interns—not even Tucker, who would be all too eager to join me. He sighs heavily, and his bed creaks as he turns within it. My own bed shudders from his motion. I guess he can take a hint sometimes.

I abandon my project and settle in for a few hours of rest, wondering who will disappear next. I wish it could be Smith. Of all the interns, he is by far my least favorite. Since the first day, he's left a bad taste in my mouth. He moves around surrounded by a posse of followers who act like he runs the Institute. He exudes confidence as if he's happy to be here. But I suspect he's the kind of person who isn't meant to disappear.

If I maintain my positions, then I will be first to choose my research specialty. I've known what I'll pick for years—since Amos first mentioned it. I want to study the hive behavior of multiple patient groups. I'm certain it's the explanation for what I saw—the way they moved so quietly and seemed to learn from one another. And the scientists have named it. They study it in the Northern Laboratories just the same as every other possible discipline, but down here, the information is classified.

The only things we've learned about hive behavior have everything to do with what *isn't* the cause. There isn't any communication because patients don't possess those neurological capabilities. There are no higher brain functions once the disease sets in, which makes the hive behavior phenomenon even more nefarious. If the patients aren't capable of hive-coordination, then what causes it? And why did the group that Simons was caught up in not behave the same way?

Everything about hive behavior suggests that it's present anytime there is more than one patient present, but Simons swore he saw no such thing. They're never together at the Institute, so I can't confirm any of it. My only hope of solving the mystery is to become a hive studies expert up north.

Someone starts in their sleep—a nightmare from today's training, surely. We spend all of our time ignoring the horrors we face every day.

We pretend we aren't fazed by the rotting flesh and animal snarls of the patients. We act so frequently that we've actually changed—we've become callous. Day after day in the labs, handling severed pieces and prodding shrieking flesh. Those of us that couldn't adapt are gone now.

There are twelve of us in here. Me, Tucker, Smith, Lau, Janson, Nguyen, Roy, Lewis, Evans, Ward, Cox and Trevino. I wonder how many names will be left once we head up to the Laboratories.

CHAPTER
TWENTY-TWO

"WHAT DO you think the fitness test will be like?" Tucker asks as he slips a lightweight white helmet with blue grid lines over his short, sandy-blond hair.

"I don't know," I say, clipping my own helmet to the straps at the collar of the form-fitting white suit with blue lines that stretch across it like circuits.

We follow the instructions given to us by the video in a small prep room, zipping the suits all the way up so that we're covered from head to toe for the assessment. The training suits fit against our bodies like a second skin. So much so that it was difficult to get them on without worming around and bumping into each other. It's the sort of close quarters and lack of privacy we've grown accustomed to, but I still can't stand it.

"Hey peewee, your scar is showing!"

I turn to catch Smith snickering at his wisecrack with the usual group of lackeys. He holds his helmet tucked under one arm as he uses the other to rub the top of his dark, close-cropped hair.

"You come up with that one all on your own?" I shoot back before rolling my eyes and turning away. My fingertips brush against the thick, nubby scar that runs from the back of my knee up my hamstring and around my hip. It bulges out almost two centimeters thick, visible in the mirror.

"You never told me where you got that monstrosity, Mason. You saving the good stories for your last moments before cryo?" he calls at my back.

"Witty as ever, Smith. It's no wonder you seem to struggle so much to barely chase my scores."

I shake my head, intent on saying something to Tucker when I'm struck by something bulky. The blow knocks me to my knees and steals my breath.

"Gee, Mason, I'm sorry. I sure didn't mean to hit you like that. I was just practicing that kick move from fitness class. You should really do a better job of watching your back." Smith oozes false empathy as his mates fail to stifle their guffaws.

Lau offers me his hand, and I take it, pulling myself to my feet.

"You should know better than to turn your back on Smith," Tucker whispers as I brush the nonexistent dust from my white suit.

A door opens, and a tall man in a black suit and white lab coat enters. He doesn't have to do anything to get our attention. He's a DDC official, as denoted by the black suit and slim golden badge adorning his crisp, ornamental lab coat. Officials like him are behind every single decision regarding our futures. Though the rest of the interns don't know the truth behind the DDC's function, they still comport themselves with cautious reverence. The entire group snaps to attention.

"Good morning, interns," the man greets us in a falsely cheerful voice. Behind the syrupy ruse is a man with too much power.

The interns return his greeting with curt nods. Satisfied, he continues.

"As you complete the last portion of your training here at the Institute, officials from the Department of Disease Containment will be assessing your performance and reassessing your ranking."

I swallow hard against his words. There has never been a mention of the DDC's involvement with our rankings. I can't help but worry that it might threaten my position. I give my cohort a quick side glance and catch the stunned looks on their faces.

"The next phase of the assessments will be extremely difficult. Unfortunately, not everyone will qualify for a position at the Northern Laboratories. Much of that will be based on your performance and our analysis. The first of these is, of course, this test. We'll be measuring both your physical and mental aptitude for the demanding and dangerous work that is required of those of you who will be traveling north."

There's a shuffling of feet followed by snickers. I look back in time to see Smith shove his elbow into Janson's side, shutting him up.

"Excuse me?" The DDC official raises his voice in the direction of the commotion.

"Nothing, sir," Janson wheezes under his breath.

"Very well." The official nods before tilting his data tablet and peering down at the roster. "I'll be calling you back one at a time for your assessment. You will be given further instructions by the administrator."

His eyes travel across his screen until he makes a match. A smile brightens his eyes as he says, "Janson, you're up."

Janson pales before stepping forward. Soft hisses follow in his wake as he makes his way to the front. The official opens the door, and they disappear into the assessment area.

When the door shuts, Smith lets out a burst of dark laughter. I catch his ruthless grin in the mirror. "That's the last we'll see of poor ol' Janson, I guarantee you that."

A flicker of rage bubbles up within me, but before I can turn to confront him, Tucker grabs my wrist. Instead, I follow Tucker and Lau to the opposite wall and sit against the mirror to wait as far out of Smith's sight line as possible.

One by one we're called back. Smith goes third, and Tucker goes sixth. When it's my turn, I leave Lau wringing his hands and tapping his feet in a nearly empty room and follow the official into a space small enough to be mistaken for an antechamber. The official looks me over curiously before exiting the room.

Following instructions, I slip the helmet's visor plate over my eyes and compress the small blue button at the connection point between the suit and helmet. The darkness is absolute. There isn't any sound either, making me wonder how such complete sensory deprivation is possible.

In the darkness, waiting for something to happen, I'm left with my thoughts. There are too many of them. After so many years managing not to, I think of my family. I think about Amos and her half-truths. There's still so much that I don't understand.

Things are bleeding together and making my heart pound. I think of Simons. I think about the night he left.

He's standing in our corner, the lamp glowing low on our red-orange chairs. No checkers tonight. I throw my arms as far around him as they'll reach and bury my face in his jacket. He moves immediately to comfort me.

"Please be careful," I whimper against the thick canvas of his jacket.

"I will. I promise." His words are soft and quiet and just as warm as always.

"Don't die?" It comes out like a question. I want it to be a demand. I try again. "You can't die. You aren't allowed to die."

"I'll stay alive," he says.

I want to believe him.

"You still need to be careful. You need to be more careful. You need to be strong." He presses his hands down on my shoulders.

"I will. I'll make it to the Laboratories. All you have to do is stay alive, and we'll figure out the rest." I know I can keep these promises because they're all I have.

"I better get to the truck," he says.

I nod, wiping the tears from my face, unable to say anything for fear of revealing how much it hurts. He opens the door, and I think that he isn't going to look back. I think that I'll never see him again, and the thought is almost too painful to think.

Before the door closes, he turns back and looks at me again. "I'm going to wait for you, Mason."

I believe him because I can't stand to lose anyone else.

"Control your heart rate." The voice comes across crystal clear in the helmet. It must be transmitted.

"How?" I know I say it, but I can't hear my voice. I try again.

"How?"

Silence. In the nothing, my panic amplifies.

There's a crackling and then I can hear my own breath, raspy and quick.

"Take a breath," the crystal-clear instructions ring through again.

I obey, afraid to speak and not hear again. I hear the sound, a slow breath drawn in deep, ending the quick ragged breaths that used to mark my existence. A mechanical beeping sound joins the chorus of my slow, deep breaths. My heartbeat. As I breathe, it settles into a steady rhythm.

"Better. This is the control you must maintain."

I don't know if he can see me, so I speak, and this time I can hear myself. "I understand."

"We're going to do a series of exercises to establish your physical aptitude. Just nod when you are ready."

I do, beginning to relax. I'm not trapped in nothing anymore. Even though it's still completely dark, I can hear and speak. The benefit of the helmet is the absence of the sterile smell. There's nothing. It's not warm or cold. I could almost imagine I'm floating in space. It's completely surreal, unlike anything I've ever experienced.

"I'm going to initiate the first simulation. You're going to see an exercise area in front of you. Wait for instructions."

I nod, then, as if I burst out from the ground, light surrounds me. I have to blink against the change. My mind grabs onto the light—I'm in the medical center—I blink again, and I can see something else. I'm outside.

I don't just see the outdoors. I can *feel* it. A gentle breeze dances across my face and tickles the hairs on my arms, making them stand up. I can *smell* it. Sun-baked dirt and fresh-cut grass. Slightly rusted metal and rubber. Hot tar. I'm in a school play yard, standing in the center of the blacktop. Ahead of me, the wooden ledge of the obstacle box is flaking. There are two rows of tires buried halfway in the fine-grain sand. Metal bars zigzag across and lead to a wall with a mix of rubber grips and steel bolts. On the opposite side, a net made of intertwined ropes reaches back down to the sand, then two poles shoot back up into the air. The poles are slick and painted purple.

"Does this location look familiar?"

I nod.

"I like to start with something you're familiar with. This is your school training yard."

"It's so real. I can smell it!" The breeze picks up, and loose sand dances across the blacktop, rubbing against my bare shins. I know I'm wearing a full body suit, but when I look down, I see grey training shorts instead—the kind we change into at school. My legs are bare and pale.

"Go ahead and walk to the tires."

I take my first step tentatively. My feet move easily across the blacktop until I reach the wooden ledge of the obstacle box. I kneel down and touch the frame. Flakes of stained wood crunch against my fingers. I stand again and stick my foot out to determine if the hard wood stop is actually there. My shoe connects with it. Before the simulation, the room was completely empty. Flat. As many steps as I've taken, I should be touching the wall. I stick my hand out and don't feel a wall. I step up and place my foot on the wooden ledge. My tread rubs against the wood. I put weight on it, and it gives a little. I step over the ledge and into the sand.

Two steps in the sand and the illusion is complete. I'm *actually* walking in sand. *Real sand!* This is so much more than a simulation. I kick at the ground, and the sand catches in the breeze. I close my eyes to keep it out. I wonder how long my eyes would sting if I kept them open. Would they still sting when the simulation was over?

"Your first exercise is going to be the tires. Step from one to the next and keep your balance."

This is a simple exercise. I used to do it at top speed. We would stand in line and run circuits. I would skip every other tire and stretch my legs as I bounded from one to the other, perfectly balanced.

I move deliberately, aware that I'm being assessed and afraid that my synthetic leg might let me down. My legs recoil and retract, responding perfectly to every command. All the clumsiness of my early days at the Institute seems to have vanished. I step from one tire to the next. I'm using the tire set that is closely spaced. I used to call this one fast feet. I could move in a blur from one to the next. Now I can see each step, broken into their series of movements controlled by the muscles and joints hidden beneath my flesh. The Institute has changed me.

"Good. Move to the other set," I'm prompted.

My body is warm and humming now, my heart steady and active. A fine slick of sweat beads on my forehead.

When instructed, I move to the zig-zag bars, weaving through the metallic maze using only my arms, swinging my torso and legs like a pendulum to propel myself forward. The obstacle box is so much like the one back at home that I might actually be there.

I'm fourteen again, and I haven't taken the aptitude tests yet. Bruce and Hank have to wait until my class is done before they do their training. I've already beaten Bruce's time, but not Hank's. He's still faster than me, but not by much. I can almost hear the squeals and cries of the other students on the course. From their midst comes Hank's taunt of *"not a chance, smaller half!"* In the afternoon, we'll return to our lessons, but right now I'm free.

My feet crunch in the sand with a satisfying sound every time I release the bar.

"Let's have you try the wall."

The administrator's words destroy the illusion, forcing me to remember where I am. I'm not at school. This is not a free play warm up, and there will be no maze trial. I won't beat Hank's time. Hank is dead. For the briefest moment, I'd forgotten. But now everything comes crashing back. The mechanical beep that blended into the background jumps into my consciousness. My heart is racing again. *This is a simulation.*

"Remember to control yourself!"

I take a few deep breaths and shake my head, amazed that it was so easy to forget. My skin is clammy, partially because of the sweat, partially because of the panic. The breeze, so welcome before, chills me now.

"Mason, the wall."

I shift my focus back to the obstacles. The wall is tall—maybe five meters. My mouth is dry. I'm not certain if I'm nervous or if I'm still recovering from the shock in the simulation. I walk toward it. My movement is confident, and soon I'm confident as well.

The rubber grips bolted to the wall are warm from baking in the sunlight. It's midday in the simulation, and the sun is almost directly overhead. With one hand at eye level and the other at my shoulder, I pull myself up and toward the wall. My right foot finds a grip immediately, and I bend the left until my foot brushes against one of the steel pins. I climb, one hand, one foot, then the other hand and foot. The motion has a rhythm that lulls me.

I reach out again, lost inside my own head as I search without really looking for another handhold. My hand brushes against a flat, rough surface. I look more closely and realize that the wall has completely changed. It's no longer painted wood with bolted-in pins and hand grips. It's now the sheer face of a stratified cliff.

CHAPTER
TWENTY-THREE

I REACH out to hook my fingers against the jagged edge of a crack that runs parallel to my body all the way up the structure, which has grown significantly. What used to be a five-meter tall wall in a school-yard obstacle box has turned into a towering cliff with at least twenty more meters yet to climb. Bracing myself, I look down to see that the sand below has turned into craggy rocks that reach up like broken fingers out of the surf of a turbulent shoreline.

The toes of my shoes are wedged onto a slim ledge created by past erosion. The swelling of waves so far below makes my head spin and my heart quicken. Gripping the sheer face with all my might, I turn my head upward, leaning in until my cheek is pressed against the cold surface of the cliff. A gust of wind whips violently across the sea, forcing my body to the left and further into the sheer face, making my position even more precarious. The air carries the taste of salt and the sulfuric smell of the life hidden by the choppy and foamed surface of the water. Though I've never actually been to the ocean, I imagine that the simulation has captured the experience completely. It's a fight to remember that I'm not really here—if here actually exists outside of this tiny room.

"What is this?" I whisper into the cliff. My fingers begin to tremble from the cold and the strain of holding on.

"It's your decision what happens next, so you better make it fast," the administrator says. His voice rings clear and loud over the roar of the wind and the crashing waves, as if separate from them.

I study the cliff as it presents itself around me, then lift my head to find the way to the top. As far as I can tell, there isn't a clear path—not even a whisper of grips or footholds that might take me where I suspect I'm meant to go. The slim crack my right fingers are buried in only takes me another body length upward, and that's only if I can keep my grip with my feet dangling over a whole lot of nothing. In addition to the lack of hand and footholds, if I do decide to climb, I'll have to be careful to mind the gusts or risk falling. There isn't a good way down either, not that I want to even attempt a descent. The memory of sliding down the granite slope as Dad rushed to tighten the line makes my stomach do flips until I can't stand to study the sheer surface below.

I remain motionless, unable to decide on a course of action. Behind closed eyes, the dark gets darker, prompting me to look up. Dark clouds race across the sky, blotting out the sun and carrying ominous thunder that competes with the sound of the crashing waves. Fat drops of water fall from the sky, splattering against my bare face and arms.

"You're running out of time, Mason," the voice prompts.

"It's impossible. There's no way up or down," I reply, trying to keep my voice level. A bright flash of light pierces the sky. At the same time, the air fills with the roar of expanded air collapsing around a torrential downpour.

"That's correct. What are you going to do?"

The fingers on my right hand slip away from the little sill that's become too wet to hold. Before I can lose my balance, I swing my arm over and hook it into the crack just above my left hand. Carefully, I slide my feet so that my body isn't bent, all the while unable to forget the sensation of falling. There's no rope this time.

Another flash of lightning brightens the stormy sky, this one even closer than the last. With it comes the realization of what the real danger in this situation is. A seaside cliff is bombarded day in and day out with ocean mist. In addition to that, the wet rock leaches minerals, making it a giant conductor. If the lightning strikes, the whole thing will surge with electricity.

Logic tells me I'm supposed to climb—to use the crack to make it to the next impossible hold. But I can't bring myself to do it. I keep thinking about the last descent, when we were running from the invisible DDC threat that hunted us down. I'm supposed to climb up and find safety at the top, but my body won't respond. Even with both hands on the only possible way up, I can't progress.

Thunder roars as the sky lights up behind me, promising that the final blow is on its way. I'm certain that if that happens, I'll automatically fail whatever this is. I'll fall onto the jagged rocks below. If I'm lucky, the simulation will disappear, and I'll just hit the hard ground which used to only be about four meters below me.

The ground! I blink away the water pouring down my face and dripping from my eyelashes. This is a simulation. The room didn't grow to accommodate this cliff. Even if the laws of physics don't apply in a simulation, they still do in the real world. If I jump, I should hit the ground. Sure, it might hurt, but it's better than letting lightning strike me and discovering what that feels like. I study the ocean below. The uneven rocks only stretch out a couple of meters from the cliff. Beyond that, the ocean darkens, revealing its depth. *Maybe if I hit the water it won't even hurt.*

My mind made up, I wiggle my fingers until they're at the bottom of the crack, allowing me to reposition myself like a spring against the wall. With one solid burst of motion, I push against the surface, forcing myself not to think about how far down it looks. My body flies outward, away from the cliff. My heart thunders in my ears. I shut my eyes to force away the panic of what it looks like I'm doing.

It stops raining. I point my legs downward, preparing to crumple upon impact. As my feet touch water, my whole body folds over itself, absorbing the impact. The water disappears, replaced by a hard surface. The pain is unreal. My vision turns grey and then black.

I'm released from the medic center after several hours of testing and a few dozen images of the synthetic tissue in my leg. It's dark outside by the time I make my way back to the intern housing. I'm released with the good news that there's no serious damage. The synthetic tissues are strained, but less so than my own tissue. My right leg will be sorer than my left leg for a day or two.

Amos came into the room before I was released to exchange words with Garth—the voice of instruction from the simulation. It turns out that Garth isn't just the medic responsible for measuring our performance in the fitness simulation; he's also the man who rebuilt my leg. I should be grateful to him. My leg is as good as new and has been since the day he built it, but he's so intolerably unpleasant that I refuse to allow myself to feel anything pleasant toward him.

I was awakened from my crumpled mess on the training room floor by his angry screams of indignation about how I threatened the integrity of his cutting-edge work. He huffed and paced, throwing an exasperated hand against his grey eyebrows and running it back across his bald and wrinkled head before re-situating his thick glasses atop his bulbous nose. He wouldn't even look at me. All he wanted to talk about was the waste of resources on a child. Amos said I needed to forgive him for his surliness.

"What he lacks in affability, he makes up for in brilliance. He's been invaluable to our work here."

Her words aren't lost on me. Garth the angry medic is on our side. Still, I'm certain I'll be content to never have to interact with him again.

The intern quarters are emptier than usual but filled with a nervous energy that I notice the moment I walk through the automatic doors.

"Mason! We thought for sure you weren't coming back," Tucker greets me, swinging his gangly legs over the edge of his bunk to stand.

"Where is everyone?" I ask, looking across the sea of bunk beds to count heads. There are only four heads looking over in my direction—Tucker, Nguyen, Lewis and Smith.

"They didn't come back from the simulation. I—I don't think they're coming back..." he stammers, running his too-big hand along the back of his neck.

"Lau?" I ask, staring at the empty bed across from my own.

Tucker shakes his head, then looks away as if he could hide the disappointment writ on his face. "I waited, but he never came back out."

"What's the big deal?" Smith calls across the room from the perch atop his bed. His intern suit is rolled up to expose the dark flesh of his hairy legs. One foot sticks out over the edge of the bed, bobbing up and down in a carefree dance.

"Are you telling me you're not upset that Cox isn't coming back?" Tucker asks.

Smith shrugs. "Cox was weaker than I thought. I'm no more disappointed that he didn't make it than that Mason did." He looks over at me, his dark eyes glowing with hatred. "You got my hopes up for a second, but I knew better. You're like a virus—hard to kick."

"Happy to disappoint," I say before turning to my own bed. I hoist myself up, eager to shut out the day. In the dim light, the dark cluster of wires barely stand out against the brown fabric of my bedspread. *My moon!* I lift them up, my heart stuck somewhere in the back of my throat. I know I left them tucked in the back of my pillowcase. I never forget to hide them. My hands shake as I roll gentle fingers across the would-be night-light. The wires come apart, split at their connection points. The core of each one of the fiber-optic cables has been shattered. They're completely useless now.

My ears are hot with anger. I fold my hand over the mess and close my eyes, careful not to register an outward reaction. Only one person is capable of such a malicious act, and I refuse to give Smith the satisfaction of knowing what he's done.

TWENTY-FOUR

THE REMAINING interns line the halls, prepared to complete the observation evaluation. Instead of our normal navy lab coats, we wear white over our blue-and-white intern suits. The lab coats are fastened up to our chins, and our hands are covered by blue synthetic gloves. Only our faces are exposed. Vulnerable flesh that I can't help but think of now, as we prepare to witness the full manifestation of every known strain of the disease. We're in an empty hallway, sterile and white—things I've come to associate with death. We are sterile and white. White suits, blue gloves, short or tucked hair. We're here to observe and record.

The hall is lined with windows that begin halfway up the wall and stretch toward the ceiling. The glass, we have been informed, is double plated. They are vacuum sealed, impact resistant, shatterproof safety from what lurks in the rooms they reveal. The windows are double sided—the other side looks like a regular wall. It makes me think of the screening room.

Through every window is a different Zoribiatus patient. Each one displays a different stage or manifestation of the disease. We have access on our tablets to subsets of data. We're meant to match each patient to their profile. Date infected. Stage and strain of disease. Point of infection. Projected life span and date of development.

Likely, the most difficult feature of this evaluation will be to accurately determine the development timeline. During development, patients are resurrected from cryogenic slumber and prepared for the laboratory setting. Some patients have been stored for decades, others for months. None that we observe today are naturally developed. These specimens were defrosted and brought to their current state in an acceleration chamber. Once patients are animated, the disease progresses from wherever it left off. We must determine what stage each patient had reached pre-development.

It is illegal to develop a pre-stage patient unless they have given their explicit consent—*a donation*, the Institute calls it. A patient who still has their mind cannot be developed so that the disease takes over. It's a measure meant to protect patients and appease any living family. It was won in the same vote that established *volunteer* as an allowed career choice, before the voting system was abolished.

Amos stands at the end of the hallway in her pure white lab coat, her voice echoing as it reaches us at our various stations. We mark our observations on our tablets as we listen to her instruction. "You have one hour to complete your diagnoses—"

The door at the back of the hall opens, the hollow metal clank echoing in the open space and cutting off Amos's instruction. I tilt my head so I can catch the activity. Three DDC officials make their way through the door, tablets in hand. A fourth enters, ushering in two very pale-looking interns in white lab coats.

"Excuse the interruption, but due to diminishing numbers, we've decided to collapse the F2 intern group into this one. I would have given notice, but the decision has only just been made, and we thought that this would be the most efficient way to converge before the final cull," the fourth DDC official announces.

Amos's face remains impassive, but I catch a nearly imperceptible rise in her right eyebrow. "Very well. Have they not completed their evaluations? The F2 cohort should be advanced?"

"There were… delays. F2 interns were participants in the darkling trials. There are measures in place to have them caught up by the end of the week," the official says, waving the two interns forward into the mix before joining the other officials along the back wall.

I recognize the second official as the same man who handled and observed the fitness assessment. He stands a head taller than the woman to his right. They each stare over the slim black of their tablets, ready to take notes on our performance. I glance away from them and down to my own tablet, where the lists and statistics stare back at me, ready to be matched to the correct patient. I imagine the officials staring at their own lists of statistics and data and making matches. Only their tablets contain information on us.

"Very well." Amos offers a curt nod. She draws her lips into a fine pale line as she resumes her instructions. "As I was saying, you have one hour to make your diagnoses. Advancement requires 95 percent accuracy in your clinical diagnostics and 85 percent accuracy in developmental diagnostics."

The margin for error continues to shrink. The Northern Laboratories require nothing less than perfection—perfection in our laboratory practices and in our compliance. I catch the smirk that flickers across Smith's smug face before he turns to study a patient at my back. His shoulder turns ten degrees past the window, and I realize that he's not watching the patient—he's studying the new interns. I follow his line of sight to the two new bodies engrossed in diagnostics. Smith is studying them for weakness. The tall boy taps nervously through a list, organizing strains and symptoms. A single bead of sweat drips down the back of his neck, visible just below the reddish-blond curl of his barely overgrown hair.

Where the boy seems edgy, his female counterpart moves with confidence. Her fingers dance across her tablet as she looks up periodically at the patients behind each window. There's something familiar about her, but I can't quite place it. Instead, I abandon the thought and busy myself with the assignment.

Though the information on our tablets is extensive, the assignment is fairly straightforward. In each room, a patient stands, or sits, or ambles placidly. They look harmless and grotesque. One example has no arms. There is a jagged humerus protruding from the left shoulder, dripping wet with blood and platelets. An infection seeps down all the open and exposed areas—he's certainly an example of strain BC. I assign the patient a projected life span of twenty to thirty-four hours.

This is part of the marvel of the disease. A Zoribiatus patient can survive mortal wounds, terrible infections and massive trauma much better than an uninfected individual. Their system doesn't shock, and their organs don't shut down. The heart has to stop due to lack of blood or the brain has to shut down from loss of glucose or blood or pressure. They survive what we cannot.

A female patient stands in the room directly across from the armless patient. She appears to be in good physical condition. Her skin is pale and intact, showing almost no sign of infection. She's dangerous. I fly through the notes on my data tablet to give her diagnosis. Strain AG—rare. Infected intravenously during an early outbreak before proper testing was in place. The virus penetrated her blood-brain barrier immediately. Her infection takes deliberate study to identify. Her eyes are pale and milky, and there is greying of the flesh around her areola and nailbeds. When she lets her mouth fall open, I note that her tongue and gums are grey.

All of the patients are naked. We are supposed to observe the entire form. It makes me think of the patient in the treatment room. *Mary! My name is Mary.* At least these creatures are unaffected by what's happening. I make a note about the absence of a male patient's genitals. One stringy gland protrudes from a weeping wound where entrails bulge and have begun to spill out. I give him a prognosis between seventy-two and one hundred twelve hours. His head and cardiovascular system are in good working order.

After a silent hour of work, Amos addresses the group. "We are entering the behavior portion of the evaluation. Please ensure that you've completed all that is required of the basic diagnostics, as you will not be able to access this portion of the evaluation once the behavioral phase has begun."

I run over my work, checking for any errors or missed categories, completely immersed in the evaluation.

Tucker shoots his hand up, catching Amos off guard. She gives him a quick scowl before looking over at the row of officials.

"What is it?" she asks.

"Will we get to see the hive mind?"

My eyes nearly bulge out of my skull. I look up, unable to believe he would be bold enough to ask such a question. Behind us, the officials reference their rosters. At the start of the program, Amos told me that the instructors keep notes on the interns that anyone at the Institute can see. I wonder what the officials are reading about Tucker right now.

"No. Only the Northern Laboratories is capable of handling that area of study." Amos turns her back to Tucker, signaling the end of her receptiveness to questions.

We've been over this before, but Tucker never quits. He never accepts the glossy half-answers the Institute instructors provide. It's part of what I love about him, but it also makes me afraid for him.

Smith raises his hand, a malicious smile crossing his crooked lips.

"Put it away, Smith," Amos says without a hint of amusement in her voice. This makes me smile an invisible expression of satisfaction.

The smirk vanishes from his face, replaced by a shadow of anger. Smith isn't often deterred.

A buzzing sound echoes through the hallway. On the other side of the windows, we can see the telltale shimmer of force fields in all the rooms. On the opposite side of the laser barrier, the floor opens up while somewhere underneath, gears turn. The familiar female intern joins me at the nearest window.

"Professor Amos?" she asks, not bothering to raise her hand.

Amos lifts her head toward her to acknowledge the inquiry. Accepting the gesture, the intern continues, "Where do you source the cadavers for feeding?"

"From recent deaths. Most of the cadavers are donated to the government from city hospitals. Natural deaths. Other diseases. Injuries," Amos explains.

We forget about other causes of death. The entire system is exclusively focused on Zoribiatus. It's the one that always kills. Every other disease plays fair. Cancer doesn't jump out and infect you if you hold someone's hand while they take their last breath.

The intern nods, and a section of her dark, glossy hair falls forward. She quickly tucks it behind her ear with a decisive gesture that brings the recognition to light. *Miller.* She is the intern who had all the answers on my first tour of the medical facility.

I force my attention away from Miller as the cadavers appear. It's time to get back to work. The gears slow as the slab they lay upon fills the holes in the ground. Row after row of death. Some of the cadavers are old. There's a very small cadaver across the hall that makes me glad to be standing so far from it. I know what I'm about to see, but I'm still not ready for it. All of the cadavers are clean—meticulously scrubbed and dressed so that we can truly see and evaluate what the patients can do when they feed.

I can hear it because I know what I'm listening for—silence. The buzzing stops, and I count to three. It happens all around me. Docile patients change into ravenous beasts. A faint buzz returns as some of the force fields re-initiate. We'll get to evaluate and categorize both today. A feeding frenzy and suicides. I mark on my tablet which rooms the force fields were re-initiated in and let a sigh of relief escape when I see that the room with the very small cadaver has been secured.

Amos's voice rings out over the gruesome sounds of carnage. "You have twenty minutes."

We get to work. A good deal of the information that we'll need is only available in the first moments after a kill has been made. Though the hunger-lust is only momentarily sated, it becomes increasingly difficult to perform diagnostics amidst the carnage. My fingers fly across the tablet as fingers, teeth and bones rip into flesh around us. Shrieks and wails and sizzles add to the terrible chorus until I feel my heart pound in my fingers.

I close my eyes, and the wet, sloppy munching sound amplifies. I swallow, and my stomach churns. I have to open my eyes to take my notes. I don't have a choice. I'll feel better when I make myself work again. Focus on my mission. Pass this exam and get to the Northern Laboratories. I look ahead. The armless patient's humerus bone is jammed between the ribs of its cadaver. It pulls against it, causing blood and meat to slush and spurt while it dives its face deep into the intestines, only periodically turning its head to take deep, wet, gasping breaths.

I note that the other patients are eating the intestines first, making me think of a lesson I learned at home. When wolves hunted, they would eat the intestines of their prey first. The digestive tracts of the prey would provide quick nutrients to the wolves that would replenish the energy they spent on the hunt. The patients exhibit a similar strategy. Hardwired evolution. I note this.

The patients who are prevented from their meals are quieting now. They push their faces as hard as possible into the laser barrier, and it melts away their flesh until it damages their brains enough to kill. They fall to the ground, sizzling. I don't mourn for them. As I finish the assignment, I check the interns. Their faces are pale.

A patient has hollowed out its cadaver and is using its hands like crude scoops. There's no sign that the carnage will come to an end. Patients are known to gorge to the point of bursting their stomachs. In the laboratories, a patient has been measured to eat upwards of fifty pounds of flesh and bone in one instant only to turn around to attack again. And they starve more slowly than uninfected individuals do. On record, a patient has gone nearly three months without eating before succumbing to disease. It isn't the starvation that kills the patients; the disease finally just decays the brain. As I watch the patient without genitals whose torso is open, I decide that these details are worth noting in my report.

Liquid has begun to drip from the torso-tear. He's bulging below his ribs in an unnatural way. There's a little pop as the thin skin that hold his intestines bursts and they spill to the ground below him. Still he continues to eat. I can see his stretched stomach in the hole now. I wonder if the stomach will pop like an over-filled balloon.

It doesn't. I make note of it and sent my report off as the timer ticks down its last seconds. The hall is quiet. Our screens turn white to announce the completion of the assessment, and I'm glad to be done with it. I don't know how much more I can stand.

The windows fade, turning to reflective mirrors so that we can all see our somber faces. *I look more and more like them with each passing day,* I think. I wonder if there is a symbol in those mirrors. Before I can think on it for too long, the building shudders. The lights flicker slightly as the rumble moves through the hallway, announcing that the patients have been incinerated.

"Thank you for your participation. Results will be posted by morning. You're dismissed." No one speaks as we file out.

CHAPTER
TWENTY-FIVE

"DENIED?" I try to keep from shrieking as I confront Amos about my research proposal.

She puts her hands on her temples, frustrated, then pushes away from her desk and looks at me. "Yes, Mason. I have denied your specialty request. You won't be doing hive studies."

I step toward her, holding the tablet out between us as though it were the embodiment of her betrayal. "I've done everything you've asked me to. I've passed every test and followed every instruction. You can't do this!"

"Of course I can do this!" she snaps, standing from her desk to shut the door behind me. In my boiling anger, I've forgotten to be careful. The door clicks, and she whirls around to grab my shoulders. "I did do it, and you are going to accept it and move on as though it were what you preferred!" Her words are a restrained hiss. She's yelling without letting her voice carry.

"Tell me why," I demand, refusing to lower my voice to match hers.

She slaps me. The sound of her slender hand smacking against my cheek rings out in the silence it brings. I'm suddenly ashamed of my outburst. I look into her wide, anxious eyes and know that I've crossed a line. "I'm sorry, Professor Amos," I mumble as quietly as if we're speaking in the open halls.

"Insubordination is not tolerated at the Institute." Her words are a show for anyone who might overhear our conversation.

I shrivel under her expression of severe warning and let the tablet fall onto the brown blanket that covers her bed. I've been counting on my top rank to give me access to the research that will give me the answers I cannot find hidden at the Institute. I won't be able to discover the truth of what happened to my family if I can't study the thing that took them from me. "I want to study the hive," I whisper.

"If I let you do that, then I may as well sign your death warrant. I haven't invested in you for nothing," she whispers back to me.

I'm so tired of everything she doesn't say, of guessing at what she knows and what I think she tells me. Does she mean that it's deadly for me to study the hive because the area of research is fraught with danger, or does she merely mean to keep me hidden and safe in the Northern Laboratories as she's done at the Institute? "I can handle the demands," I say.

"That area of research isn't for you," she says.

I chew on my tongue, forcing myself not to scowl as the quiet settles over us. Amos lowers herself down onto the bed so that we're sitting side by side. In the glow of my tablet screen, I can see the mark of her refusal stand out red over my specialty petition as it calls attention to the empty space between us.

"Is there anything I can do to change your mind?" I ask.

"No," she insists, still looking forward. Her hands are folded between her knees. She doesn't look like a professor reprimanding a student.

"If I don't, you know Smith will," I say, looking down at my feet.

"That's fine. I'm certain he'll excel." Her words make me grimace.

"What do you want me to choose?" I ask, letting some of the resentment welling up from inside me creep into the question.

"Would you even bother to take my counsel, Mason?" She meets my resentment with frustration.

I sigh. Amos wants to help me. She has since the day I joined the Institute, and all I give her in return is resistance. We fight each other from opposite ends of the same side, and neither of us has made any progress.

"I want to know what you think," I tell her. It's the closest I can come to a peace offering.

She looks at me. The look carries the weight of everything she could say to me but doesn't. "Infection science," she says.

Infection science. Such an analytical field of study. I imagine months of coding programs to run complicated algorithms for speculative calculations. Every experimental design I create will depend upon data from other scientists—cell reproduction rates, Zoribiatus strain types, cryogenic statistics. I crinkle my nose as I ponder the finer points of such a monotonous future. Out of the corner of my eye, I catch Amos smirk at my distaste.

"That ought to keep me nice and safe." I punctuate my statement with an extended eye roll.

Amos shakes her head. "No, Mason. You can't think like that. There's no such thing as a field of study that will keep you safe. The Northern Laboratories are a treacherous place. The wrong experiment —even the wrong idea—can result in the worst possible end." It's the first time she hasn't left the warning in the subtext.

Infection science. In theory, it's a predictable area of study. The disease is well controlled, and outbreaks are less and less common all the time—if we're meant to believe the government's reports. In fact, as far as the government's statistics are concerned, if things continue on their current course, infection science will become obsolete before I reach my tenure up north. My research would highlight the government's resounding success in controlling the disease. I stick the tip of my tongue out and bite down, mulling the idea over.

On the other hand, I would spend my time analyzing the statistics of every patient who makes their way to the Northern Laboratories. This might give me a chance to understand where they're all coming from. Our lessons indicate that every infection results from excursions outside the safety of our cities, but there doesn't seem to be a reason for so many people to venture outside. Something strange is happening, and Amos is steering me in a direction that promises an explanation.

"I'll do it," I tell her, more curious about the potential of the topic than resigned to it.

"It's a wise choice. You've got great potential in the area of program coding."

I laugh. Though I've improved a great deal since my first lessons, she and I both know that program coding has been one of my biggest struggles. "Are you sure you haven't confused me with another intern? Have we mixed up our meeting times?" I smile despite my previous frustration.

Amos turns toward me, erasing the empty space between us. She looks so serious that the smile drops off of my face, and I'm nearly worried that she'll slap me again. "Mason." Her voice is so low I have to strain to hear it. "You are absolutely and completely brilliant. We both know it, so there's no need to pretend between us. You have the power to bring studies from the Northern Laboratories to an entirely new stage. No one has ever been in your position before. You must not waste your abilities in foolish pursuits. Do you understand me?"

I swallow away the dryness that coats my mouth. I've changed so much under Amos's instruction, but deep down, I never gave up my own heart. She knows it, and she's asking me to set it aside. I don't know if I can. The very thing she helped me preserve through the intern program keeps me from being able to pledge myself entirely to her designs. I need more time to make my decision.

"I understand. There will be no foolish pursuits," I say.

Her head dips, and all of the tension leaves her arms. I feel a small amount of shame for lying to her. Her hands drop, and she gathers herself to stand. When she makes it onto her feet, she's transformed into the picture of the phlegmatic professor. Her voice is level and clear as she says, "I think you've made the best choice, and I appreciate you consulting me on your decision."

Our conversation is over. Her tutelage is over. I'm a scientific intern, only months from graduation and departure. I won't return to her room again without invitation. "I appreciate your guidance," I respond in kind as she opens her door to dismiss me.

"Now don't be late for your experimental assignment."

The door closes without my acknowledgment. I move quickly so I am not late to the laboratory.

CHAPTER
TWENTY-SIX

I'M NOT the last intern into the laboratory. With significant relief, I notice Tucker slip in right as the professor begins the summary of our prescribed work for the day. I flip over the protocols that appear on my tablet as the details of my visit with Amos intrude upon my focus. I wonder if Smith has noticed that hive studies is available yet. Without being obvious, I glance across the lab benches to where he sits. His tablet is unattended on the lab bench, and he looks bored with the assignment. I understand not looking forward to pulling flesh samples from a live patient, but I don't understand his boredom. The work we do is too dangerous to be boring.

The shrill sound of a metal stool scraping against the tile floor draws my attention to Tucker, who is breathless as he takes a seat right next to me. I suppress the urge to say something to him as he settles in and opens his tablet. Professor Hugo is also watching him, waiting for the hand that will inevitably burst into the air with the usual barrage of questions.

"Incubation studies done up north indicate that there is much still to gain in the field of variant strains; however, once the disease manifests, the timeline of disease progression is very predictable," Hugo continues his lecture.

I glance at the notes for our assignment. This is not an experiment, but rather an educational exploration. We're the thirty-second class to perform these particular tissue tests. We're learning the proper protocols and procedures for the work that we'll do without instruction. The life span and disease progression studies are so well documented that they're easy to ignore. This thought stirs up another as I continue to rifle through the standard procedures—this is the sort of data that my studies will draw from up north. I purse my lips together but keep my expression neutral as I sit within my ever-shrinking cohort.

"Why don't we have access to any variant strain statistics? Can we see the broad strokes of the pattern? Maybe we could overlay them with the smaller variations in manifestation life cycle and discover some correlations?" Tucker doesn't even wait for his hand to be acknowledged.

"Your assignment is limited to the exploration of well-documented data. *If* you're selected, you can bring your inquiries to your northern studies." Hugo doesn't even look up to respond to Tucker's questions. His voice carries his disinterest in Tucker's inquiry, but there's a sharpness in the way he moves his hand across the roster that suggests he's not so unaffected.

"But we're almost ready to go to the Northern Laboratories. I only think, with that in mind, that we could—"

"You're not in the Northern Laboratories yet," Hugo snaps, cutting off the rest of his question. Tucker's hand hits the lab bench with an unenthusiastic thud.

"I'm just saying, it would be nice to learn something useful," Tucker grumbles to himself. His words are loud enough for the rest of us to hear, and I want to smack him for it.

"The most useful thing you can learn at the Institute is to focus." Hugo is looking right at him, his long, slender fingers pressing into his tablet so intensely that his knuckles are turning white. The way Hugo stares at him makes me think of what Amos said so many years ago. *Professor Hugo hasn't looked at an intern in the last decade—not really.*

He's looking now.

Tucker sighs but doesn't look up from his own tablet. A green light flips on above the doorway behind the professor, accompanied by a strident buzzing that announces the approach of volunteers with our experiment subject. The professor glances up at the notification alarm and addresses the class. "It's time to garb up."

The room fills with the sounds of synthetic materials brushing against metals and fabrics as we pull our suits over our lab coats. The screech and moan of seats mark our preparations for the contamination that's about to walk into our midst. Someone coughs into the crinkly sleeve of their suit as the room falls silent, and Professor Hugo moves from his lecture podium to the metal trough built into the ground. Long metal poles reach up from the corners of the trough so that the patient can be secured for our sampling purposes. We've watched variations of this procedure before, but working with live patients has been reserved for our final moments at the Institute. The trough will fill with the gore of the thing as we remove pieces. The setup works to both teach us how to handle ourselves around live patients and to reinforce our indifference to the daily horrors we'll experience.

The door opens, and a small group of volunteers shuffles in, dragging a thrashing, restrained patient. The tallest of the volunteers glances up from his task and catches my eye. Recognition sweeps over me as I identify him as the young man who met me in the dark. His eyes dart back down to the task the moment after they find mine, and I struggle to identify the thing that I saw in the brief and silent communication. Worry? Warning.

We move toward the staging area, our yellow protective suits crinkling and rustling together to create a quiet racket. Over the din, I hear Miller whisper something to the other intern from her year, Horne.

"There should be five volunteers in a transport group, not three."

She's right. None of the other interns seem to take notice. I try to catch the volunteer's eye again, but he doesn't look up. His lashing pole is wrapped around the patient's wrists, keeping them bound behind the creature's stinking body.

"Protocol states that the first task in any experimental procedure is to what?" Professor Hugo asks, splitting his attention between the volunteers and us.

"To confirm restraint at every step." Tucker rolls his eyes.

"That's correct. Perhaps you find this lesson to be beyond your skill level, Tucker?" His voice raises at the end of the question in false curiosity.

"I only think that we might be able to learn proper procedure and experimental norms while simultaneously investigating new topics. I mean, maybe then the Northern Laboratories wouldn't be the only location actively working toward a cure," he spouts, oblivious to Hugo's impatience as discontent fills the lab.

Professor Hugo looks down at his tablet while the volunteers move into position. The tall volunteer stands rigid behind the patient, keeping his pole tilted while he holds the wrists so that it looks like he's wrenching the creature up into a standing position. I consider his stance, which seems strange compared to the maneuvers Simons used to describe.

"Tucker, you're up first. Secure the trough lashing and pull your first sample." Hugo casts a quick glance at the patient, then at Tucker, who collects his sampling kit.

My eyes are drawn away from Tucker again, back to the volunteer configuration. The hood comes off of the patient's head, and I notice that there isn't any lashing security. The two volunteers trade their lashing poles for the lashing apparatus on the trough, placing the attachment on the patient's elbows.

The stringy muscles and bulging veins that hold the patient together reveal that the patient isn't secure. One strong pull at the restraints and the arms will pull apart, bursting blood vessels and stringing muscles and tendons through electromagnetic lashings like the frayed edges of a torn garment.

Tucker makes his approach. I don't have time to think. I grab Tucker's protective suit and yell, "Stop! Tucker, don't move, it's going to get loose."

The action startles him so much that he loses his footing and stumbles backward, the pieces of his sample kit flying into the air before scattering across the white tile floors. He knocks into Smith, who shrieks at him, equally surprised by the suddenness of his fall.

"Watch it, you worthless slab of patient food!" Smith in turn knocks into Horne, who steps into Lewis.

No one has time to react. The patient breaks free from its own arms.

The violence of its forward motion startles the two volunteers, forcing them off of their feet before they can finish their tasks. The tall volunteer's lashing pole drops as the creature leaves the rest of itself behind. Its high-pitched, open-mawed cry is punctuated by small, startled cries from the onlookers.

The patient lurches forward and falls right where Tucker would have been if I hadn't managed to pull him down. Blood streaks the tile and runs back toward the metallic trough as the creature scrambles to find its feet and lunch at the same time. The two fallen volunteers back out of the trough as quickly as their bodies will carry them, forgetting about their jobs and their lashing poles.

I watch from my position amongst the interns for what feels like an eternity, my hand still grasped tightly to Tucker's suit. The creature continues its wild thrashing, blood splattering across the room and onto the pale yellow of our protective covers, making its way an inch at a time toward Tucker's feet.

"Back! Everyone stay back!" Professor Hugo commands, taking a large step backward and out of the periphery of the patient. The class responds, shrinking away from the squirming, gory mess as it struggles to find its feet.

Tucker tries to back up and rams into Smith's shin. Smith curses, then kicks him square in the head so that Tucker flops to the ground, stunned.

The patient accelerates, crawling on exposed bone toward Tucker.

"Grab it!" I shout, looking over the patient toward the volunteers. Two lashing poles lay in the trough, unreachable next to the patient's snapping jaws. The third still sits limply in the grip of the tall volunteer.

There isn't time to order anyone into action. I launch myself, using all of the force I can muster to spring past the shrieking, creeping thing and wrench the lashing pole free from the tall volunteer's hands.

The pole is lighter than I remember. I fling it toward the patient's head and let out a terrible wail, channeling every last fiber of my focus so that the electromagnetic wire engages with exacting precision. The moment I feel the pull of the tool engaging around the skull, I bring one hand over the other, twisting the pole to release the deadly blade.

The spear enters the patient at the base of its skull, plunging upward through the brain stem and into the pulsing mass of diseased matter, cutting off the creature's snarl at its midpoint so that the only sound in the room is my scream. It totters on its fleshless arm stumps before slumping to the ground. Tucker pulls his feet clear of the sinking mass, his eyes wide with shock.

I twist the blade back into the lashing pole and then out again, pulling up so the blade slices through and crunches out of the skull. It makes a sickening squelching sound as I disengage and reengage it again and the skull opens into a bloody, pulpy mess in front of me. The room is silent when I drop the lashing pole.

"Whoa, Mason," Tucker breathes, finally finding his feet.

I want to say something to him, smile and reassure him that he's still alive, or scream at him for being so infuriatingly dense, but my face is stuck and unable to respond to my brain's commands.

"I told you to stay back." Professor Hugo's voice pulls me from my shock.

"It was going to get Tucker."

Professor Hugo studies me, his expression vacillating between curious wonder and haughty scorn. I resist the urge to shiver under his silent scrutiny. Finally, he looks away, saying, "This will go on your record."

He turns to the group and snaps, "To decontamination, then screening, everyone!"

There's a pause before the flurry of motion of interns eager to escape the nightmare scene of the laboratory. Professor Hugo looks back at me and muses, "Top rank, wasn't it, Mason?"

I nod, finally finding the ability to move again.

"Follow orders if you want to stay there," he warns.

I take one last look back into the lab before entering the hot spray of decontamination solution in the antechamber connecting the lab to the screening hall. Professor Hugo is standing over the cowering volunteers and speaking into a communication device. The tall volunteer is looking past the corpse into nothing. He looks up right as I turn away, and I catch a glimpse of sorrow.

I'm certain I'll never see any of them again.

CHAPTER
TWENTY-SEVEN

FOR THE FIRST time since the meeting about my specialty, I walk down the familiar corridor that leads me to Amos's dormitory. Today is graduation day. There will be a small ceremony, then, without any further pretenses, I'll be a scientist. As usual, the halls are empty. The years have taught me that it's not hard to pick the right time to move around unseen in such a structured place. I knock brusquely on Amos's door, hoping that she hasn't left for the ceremony hall yet.

The door swings outward, and Amos faces me. We're the same height now, both of us small in stature but reaching our potential. Our hair is fixed in the same braid, tucked into our suits—hers grey and mine brown. She smiles when she sees me, and it covers the tension that I glimpsed the second the door swung open.

"Mason, what brings you here?" Her voice is artificially cheery.

I shrug. Now that I'm facing her, I'm at a loss. All purpose has left me as the unknown approaches. "I just wanted to say goodbye."

Amos nods, taking in the billowy white robe I wear for the ceremony. "Come in, but we don't have much time." She gestures me forward.

As the door shuts behind us, I think about how small Amos's dormitory is. The familiar desk seems stunted under my gaze, and standing here now, the room feels cramped. We've outgrown this meeting space. Amos is overdressed for the ceremony, wearing the formal white suit that denotes her status. She'll be handing out ceremonial certificates to the graduates before we take photographs that will be sent to the scientists' families. They'll be mounted on the walls as payment for their sacrifices. Visitors will acknowledge the accomplishment, and the houses will temporarily be less empty.

I take in a deep breath and grasp at the words that lay just below the surface. "Will you be notified when our transport reaches the Northern Laboratories?"

Amos nods. "We'll receive a general update." Her response is formal. She's standing stiffly, like she's holding something back. "I'll be keeping tabs on you through my own contacts as best as I can."

It's my turn to nod. "You'll be able to read up on my research through the general government updates."

This statement breaks the tension. Amos grasps my forearms and squeezes hard. "Mason, you need to be so careful. All of the caution and control you've learned here may not be enough once you're in the Laboratories."

"I understand."

"What you did—the way you saved Tucker—I don't think you even begin to understand how dangerous that was."

Everyone knows about the incident. It nearly cost me my top rank. People started paying more attention to me afterward.

"What was I supposed to do?"

She shakes her head. "You can't save everyone. Especially not up there. Stick to your specialty. Stay far away from hive studies and focus on the cure."

She's telling me I should have let Tucker die. Professor Hugo suggested it, the incident review suggested it, but I never would have guessed that Amos would agree. I open my mouth to argue, but her stern expression keeps my words from coming out. I bite my tongue.

"You've already done everything you can for Tucker. It's his responsibility to stay alive up north. Remember that," she says.

"Just keep my head down and work on the cure," I grumble. I have nothing left to lose, so I ask her the questions that always float just under the surface when we're alone. "What is it that you aren't telling me? Why don't you just say it so you don't have to worry about what I might do wrong?"

Her eyes are sharp and piercing as they search me. Tension is writ across her face. She holds her breath, making the room uncomfortably silent.

She lets the air out slowly in a measured and controlled exhale. It seems to deflate her until she appears smaller than me. "The hive is the absolute most dangerous research topic. No one who isn't meant to studies the behavior. If they do, they don't live long enough to find the answers they're looking for."

I spit out an exasperated breath. She isn't telling me anything she hasn't before. I bite down harder on my lip and begin the reframe of what I want her to tell me.

She doesn't give me a chance to ask. She squeezes my arms and says, "Mason. Won't you just work on the cure?"

Her eyes nearly glisten. For a moment, I want to give her what she's asking for. I shake my head, more to clear it than to deny her.

"Of course I'll work on the cure, but I can't spend the rest of my life wondering."

She looks away from me for a moment and moves her hands so that they grasp mine. Her skin is cool, coarse and wrinkled. She tries again. "There are some things that you aren't meant to know."

I squeeze her hands and force her to look at me. "There isn't anything else?"

She shakes her head. "No." It's a lie.

I drop my eyes to hide my frustration. "But if you can find the cure, then it doesn't matter."

This is all that she'll give me. A plea to give up. I'm not sure what I expected.

"I'll be careful," I promise.

I make my way to the ceremony hall without looking back.

PART THREE
THE LABORATORIES

CHAPTER
TWENTY-EIGHT

AMOS HANDS me my diploma and grants me my scientist emblem, a small golden pin that fastens to the collar of my uniform. My picture is taken with the president and the chief DDC officials to be displayed throughout the City States. I shake hands with so many people and congratulate my colleagues. There's a small feast provided for the attendees with tiny yellow cakes that have sticky, sweet tops. Before being released to meander amongst our peers, we toast our accomplishments.

"To the new scientists—our future," the tall DDC officer says, holding up his skinny glass filled with a bland, fizzy beverage poured from ancient-looking bottles.

I turn away from the groups of quietly celebrating scientists, government and DDC officials. Hank should be here. I should be standing here with him, only a few years from now. Bruce should be well into his career as a medic. He could visit Dad on travel permit. *If we hadn't run.* Amos hasn't brought up my dad's folly since that night. The strain it put on our relationship has mostly been ignored, but not forgotten. In my darkest moments, I'm afraid that I agree with her—that the Institute really has changed me.

No. She's wrong. If we hadn't run, there's no guarantee that Hank would be here with me. That's what they want me to believe. Resisting the urge to fling the delicate glass against the floor, I rush toward the corner of the room, where Tucker and Miller have congregated away from the fanfare.

"It's almost like we accomplished something important," Miller says as I join them.

"We did. We're going to the Northern Laboratories," Tucker responds, eyes wide with excitement.

Miller offers him a skeptical side glance but doesn't say anything. I shrug and take a small sip from the glass, acting my part. The fine bubbles tickle my upper lip.

"It's important to someone," I say.

Miller's eyes flash bright at my statement, but I don't meet her gaze. Instead, I survey the room filled with lies. Across the long, decorated table, Smith stands in a crowd of DDC officials. Without their lab coats, they're dark and angular, or maybe it's only my imagination making them so sinister. He shakes the hand of the tall man as another man whose back is to me pats him on the shoulder. He looks positively gleeful surrounded by such admiration. But what did I expect? I might be top of the class, but Smith won. He's going to be doing hive studies. He's the right man for the job.

I could've been the right person.

"What are you doing cowering in a corner?" Amos hisses at us.

Her presence startles me. I didn't see her cross the room.

"A quiet moment before we depart," I offer.

"You'll have nothing but quiet moments from now on. If you know what's good for you, you'll get out there and shake hands with the people who made you!" Amos allows her gaze to travel across the three of us before lingering on me.

"Yes, Professor Amos," we all reply, as though the conventions of the Institute are now a part of our makeup.

I amble toward Horne, who's mid-conversation with a white-suited government official I don't recognize.

All of the fanfare and pomp end promptly as an announcement on the main Institute intercom notifies us that the transport vehicle is ready for departure. The new interns and their instructors head toward their dormitories while the new scientists pack their meager supplies for the journey north. Instructors plan lessons for the next group of interns, and government officials board their hovercrafts and return to the Central Capital City.

I gather what few things I possess and toss them into a slim sack, lingering on the shattered mess of wires that I never turned into a night-light before tossing it in with my data tablet. Just as I'm about to head for the door, Tucker pops his head back in.

"There's a delay. The driver says it's a poorly functioning fuel cell." He shrugs.

"What're we supposed to do?"

"We can wait here or out there. Scientists are allowed delayed boarding, but the volunteers have to remain on board to monitor the cryogenic cylinders while the vehicle is on standby," he explains, then pauses, waiting for me to make the call.

I look back over the empty intern housing. Even though no one has come to clean it for the next group, it's cold and sterile. "There's nothing here for us. Let's go wait by the vehicle."

Tucker nods and follows me out the door.

"I wonder if they've already received files with our profiles on them," Miller says, kicking at the ground so that her bag sways back and forth from where it dangles on her arm.

"What do you think? That they sit in their rooms at the end of the day and read through the information on the newest recruits?" Smith scoffs, tightening the strings on his own pack so that it sits flush against his back.

"I know I would." Horne shrugs, the divots of his pock-marked face exaggerated in the shadowy lights.

I imagine myself years from now, eagerly reading through the data of new recruits.

"Isn't it strange that we don't get any information on who's already up there?" Tucker asks.

"Who cares? All that matters is that we fit into our required roles and serve the bigger purpose of the laboratories," Smith says. I don't suspect that these are his words, or that he meant to blurt them. He shifts uncomfortably and looks toward the vehicle, grumbling. "What's taking so long?"

We finally board our transport in the grey light of early dawn and leave before the sun makes its way above the horizon. I don't get a chance to catch more than a glimpse of any of the eight volunteers we'll be traveling north with. Forty patients are secured in cryogenic deep freeze, nestled in metallic tubes kept cold with the truck's massive engines.

What will the scientists think of this delivery? Do they receive a transmission of the graduation ceremony? The five of us represent a paltry eight percent of the interns that arrived at the Institute. Twelve scientists were assigned to Energy Management—I'm certain about this count because their work was recognized at the ceremony, but the others weren't even mentioned, as though they never existed. Even the interns seem to forget that our quarters were once full, and it's not like we can talk about it—not with so many dark suits listening for dissent.

This is what Dad saw. He knew that the deaths started before we make it north. I was foolish not to believe him. Now that I'm here, it's so clear. There are always whispers—a few minor accidents during training, so insignificant that they aren't reported and don't show up on the manifest. But the next day, an intern doesn't show up, and never does again.

The accident where Tucker was almost killed is the only one that ever made it into an official report, and that was filled with as many lies as Trudy's health record. Amos doesn't want me to try and save him if it happens again. I look at Tucker now. His chin rests on his fists, and his elbows dig into his lap. His short, sandy hair is unkempt, as though he's been running his fingers through it. His long, skinny legs stick out in front of him, bouncing over his feet, as disquieted as his mind.

We're all silent now as the reality of our journey sinks in. Someone coughs. It echoes throughout the silent vehicle, disrupting the quiet against the hum of the engines. "'Scuze me," the cougher apologizes. No one answers.

Several hours pass with nothing but the droning engine and crunching gravel of the road to distract us. A couple of tablets glow in the vehicle, but otherwise it's dark. I wonder where the sun sits in the sky now and think about what it will be like so far north. This time of year, there isn't much light.

"It stinks in here!" Smith blurts. His words ring in the metal box as a blight against the silence.

"It doesn't stink; it's just stuffy," a volunteer replies.

"Stuffy? Is that the scientific term?" There's contempt in Smith's voice.

"Who cares if it's the scientific term? That's what it is." The volunteer doesn't back down.

"I don't think it's stuffy. I think you reek." Smith laughs at his own joke. I can see Miller's lips twitch. Smith notices as well.

"I mean, you would think they'd shower you before putting you on here with us!"

Tucker looks away, and I catch his eye. He doesn't intend to do anything. The other volunteers are likewise silent as Smith establishes the pecking order, eager to erase his earlier spurted statement.

"We'll see how good you smell after a day or two without a shower." The volunteer is defensive, but not mean. Maybe he wishes he hadn't responded.

"I'm not worried about my smell. I'm worried about what happens if we get delayed. Hasn't anyone wondered what happens if we run out of coolant? What happens when the patients thaw and then try to tear us up?" He isn't really worried. He's picking a fight. He knows that at least some of the patients on this transport are related to the volunteers.

"They're still people," the volunteer objects.

"They're *patients*. Sure, maybe you might have a few moments with them. Enough time to say goodbye before their eyes cloud and they tear you to shreds. Maybe you'd have enough time to blow a hole through their middle so you could watch your own guts pour out as Mommy eats you!" Smith goes in for the kill.

The volunteer stands, and I see him for the first time. He's broad and has thick, dark hair. Every muscle is tensed under his jacket, ready to strike, but I can feel his restraint. The other volunteers must feel it too because they don't move to stop him. He's much larger than Smith. He takes a sweeping step across the aisle to stand in front of Smith, who's also standing with a smug, satisfied look on his face.

"Are you going to strike me?" he taunts.

"No." The volunteer's voice is flat.

"Then why'd you come over here? Wanted to know what greatness looked like, huh?" Smith has balls. He's an idiot.

"I wanted to see your face, so I could smile when I watch you get torn to pieces from your own arrogance. I want to be able to recognize you." The volunteer isn't dumb.

Smith holds his smug smile, but the life has gone from it. Not even he is arrogant enough to ignore his own mortality. He holds the gaze of the volunteer as a quiet tension settles over the two of them. No one else speaks. No one moves.

Smith turns first. The volunteer takes his hand away from the roof railing and creates more space. Smith sits, making a dismissive sound. "Go on, then. I don't need to waste my time on an idiot who failed aptitude tests."

It's what separates us from the volunteers. They're here by choice, while we're forced to be here. Smith says it like it makes him better. We're told it makes us better, but I think it makes us cowards. Every single volunteer reminds me of Simons.

I can't stay quiet any longer. "Maybe you're the idiot. After all, you *passed* the aptitude tests."

Smith scoffs. "That makes me a genius."

I don't miss a beat. "That's right. Geniuses willingly sign their lives away just to prove to the world that they're good enough." I'm keenly aware I'm talking about myself.

"That's right. They do," Smith says with pride.

I continue. "You know what I think? I think everyone who *doesn't* pass the aptitude test is a real genius. They get to keep their lives and make their own choices."

"Some good choices these geniuses made." He waves his hand at the volunteers. "They went ahead and choose to throw their lives away anyway."

I'm about to let it drop when he says one more thing. He looks directly across the way at the volunteer, who has returned to his seat. "It's probably your fault they're in those freeze-tanks."

The volunteer didn't hit him before, but I'm not so sure now. I don't want to find out. I use the seniority granted to me by my placement. Arrogant prick or not, Smith won't defy me. "That's enough. Switch places with me, Smith. Maybe you'll get along better with the other scientists."

He can't keep up the good boy image if I file a report against him. He grumbles and stands. I step out into the aisle and walk to his seat, letting him pass me. He mutters something under his breath, and I'm certain it's derogatory, but I couldn't care less. He repeats it to Tucker, who doesn't make eye contact. The glow of his tablet brightens the transport as I take his seat. Directly in front of me is a coded cooling tank. Next to the tank, I have a full view of the volunteer Smith was harassing.

The volunteer looks over at me, and I smile apologetically. I can't take away what Smith said, but I can let him know I don't agree with it. He smiles weakly in return, then closes his eyes. We return to the silence. The whole vehicle shudders and rocks. There's a loud grind of gravel under the massive, knobbed tires. I turn on my tablet to pass the time and ease the tension.

Hours after the day's last ration, everyone's asleep. The vehicle rocks back and forth; the sound of earth passing under us has become white noise. Smith is snoring. A volunteer in the back matches his cadence. I don't dare turn on my tablet for fear that I'll disrupt someone. I try to keep my eyes closed in case sleep decides to come but keep opening them and glancing around.

"You can't sleep either?"

The voice is so quiet that I have to look to confirm that I actually heard it. The volunteer's eyes are open, and he's watching me. I shake my head. "It's always hard for me."

"Me too." His voice is kind. He sounds younger than I first thought. His size made me think of Simons, so maybe I overestimated his age. It's dark in here and difficult to see details.

"What's your name?" I ask.

"Jorey." It could be his first name or his last.

"Mason. It's nice to meet you, Jorey." I smile. I don't know if he can see it.

"It's nice to meet you too, Mason."

We're quiet again. It's quiet for so long that I think he's fallen asleep. Someone near the back shuffles and adjusts their position. They're still asleep. I can hear the steady breathing of rest. I take a deep breath and think about my heart rate, hoping it'll help me relax.

"Thank you for moving him." Jorey's still awake.

"You're welcome."

"Why did you do it?"

"I didn't want to spend the whole ride listening to him be a jerk."

Jorey lets out a quiet snort. "I'm sure we still have a little bit of jerk left to endure."

"I'm sure. Try to stay out of his way."

"I didn't mean to instigate."

"I'm sure you didn't."

"I wanted to hit him."

I wanted to hit him. "Why didn't you?"

He's quiet, thinking about his answer. There's something about him that I can't quite describe. I want to trust him.

"I can hate him all I want, but if I hit him, he has the power. He can punish me and he'll know he got to me—"

"He knows he got to you even though you didn't hit him," I interrupt.

"Sure. But if I maintain control, then he doesn't know how far he can push me. He doesn't really know me."

It's quiet again, and I realize I miss whispering. It makes me think of Simons. It makes me feel less lonely. I don't want the conversation to stop. "Do you know your rank?"

"I used to be third."

"What rank are you now?"

"Technically, if you ask me, I'd say I'm still third, but I'm ranked first."

"Explain." I like how deliberately he seems to think things through.

"We lost two volunteers right before the trip. They were number one and number two."

"What happened?"

"I don't know. They were just gone."

"That's what happens with interns."

"They disappear?"

"There are whispers. They have accidents; they get infected."

"Those are the rumors that move around the volunteers," Jorey says.

"What do you think?" I ask, eager for a co-conspirator.

"I don't know what to think yet."

"Yet?"

"Just because I'm not sure now doesn't mean we won't know more later."

We're quiet again. Someone snorts and flails. After a few minutes, everything is settled and quiet again. I'm starting to get sleepy, more relaxed. I'm smiling.

CHAPTER
TWENTY-NINE

TIME PASSES SLOWLY. During what I presume are the daylight
hours, I work on my first experiment design like the other scientists,
sleeping an hour or two at a time without heeding a schedule. Our
meals are bland and small. Even Smith is quiet. We take turns pacing
the aisle up and down the transport vehicle to stretch our legs and
keep tedium at bay. The volunteers play a pattern game. Sometimes
they use prime numbers; sometimes they use multiples. I suggest they
try the game with roots, and Jorey wins.

At night, while everyone else sleeps, we talk. I tell him about
Simons. Part of me wants to tell him everything—about the night on
the road—but I don't. I'm twenty, not seventeen. I arrived with the rest
of the interns, so when Jorey asks how I met Simons, I tell him the
truth—from before. I leave out the other details.

Jorey asks me if Simons is still at the Northern Laboratories. I tell
him I think so. Amos never answered me explicitly, but she always
nodded when she dismissed me for the night. I think she was telling
me then, but I can't talk to Jorey about that either. We have to be careful. We have to keep conversation safe.

Neither of us talks about before. I don't tell him about my family
or the energy facility. He doesn't tell me about his family. I don't
know where he's from or what he did before because it doesn't

matter. When we run out of safe things to talk about, we play the game. Sometimes we make our own patterns and wait for the other to identify them. Jorey's good with numbers too. I wonder which part of the assessment he didn't pass, or if he's like Bruce and failed on purpose.

We stop once for two days. The vehicle shudders and sways precariously in the high winds while sleet pounds the sides, making it so loud that we have to shout to be heard. Visibility outside has to be zero. We can't see because there are no windows. More than anything, I miss being outside. When it's quiet again, I tell Jorey this. He agrees. We each make predictions about the phase of the moon. His is whimsy; mine is calculated. He guessed first, but I agree.

We arrive midday on the fourth day. We wait, giddy to see the outside, but when the back of the vehicle rolls open, we're not outside. We're in a massive receiving building made of steel and concrete. Artificial lighting spans the ceiling and dots the walls in a hexagonal pattern, providing more light than we've seen since the Institute.

We file out of the transport vehicle and into the building, our bodies stiff and sore from the long journey, and stand in a row, ready to be received. An elderly woman in scientist's garb and several volunteers are there to accomplish the task.

"My name is Shelby. I'm the senior scientist here at the Northern Laboratories. I'm here to receive you, assign your living quarters and give you your first laboratory assignment." She holds the transportation manifest.

The volunteers move around her to transport the cryo-tanks that hold new patients. They move into the vehicle and use devices they wear on their wrists to scan the labels on the tanks. There's a quick beep as each one is scanned and the data is sent to the manifest, where the flash of information reflects on Shelby's glasses. Shelby isn't interested in this information. She observes us.

"Volunteers, please follow Cortez to intake. The team leads will organize you," Shelby instructs them.

I look at Jorey. He nods. I lift my fingers—a small wave until next time. Maybe he'll get to see Simons before me. The volunteers follow Cortez through a door that he has to scan an ID badge to open. They're gone now. A familiar panic creeps into my fingertips. I flex my hands and breathe out slowly.

"Scientists," Shelby addresses us. "We'll be issuing you your ID cards on site. From this moment forward, you will have to re-activate them every twenty-four hours. You'll all be reporting to your senior scientist. Your first experiments are due to be submitted by the end of this week."

We follow Shelby to the opposite end of the receiving bay. The volunteers unload the tanks and follow a lit path to a third door out of the hexagonal receiving bay. There's one large door for each of the walls, and each path lights up as it is followed. Shelby uses her ID card to open our door. The room is white and clean—just like the Institute. *I feel at home already.*

Shelby refers to the manifest on her data screen. "Miller."

She steps forward, and Shelby indicates the screen and port on the wall. "Place your face here, eyes open for retinal scan. Hands here and here for prints. A blood sample will be drawn, and all of the information is recorded on your ID card. Never take off your ID card unless you're in your own room."

Miller follows instructions, quiet and quick. When she pulls her head back, a small card appears from a receiving slot. Shelby hands it to her. "You're assigned to Dunn. Cure experiment 1086. The data will be available anytime you log into a station. Your room is marked electronically with your name. Only you may enter it unless you change the parameters, which you can do from any station. You are dismissed."

There is no conversation, only instruction. Miller nods, and the pathway in front of her lights up.

"Horne," Shelby calls next. He repeats what Miller did, flinching when the blood is drawn. His face is covered in a nearly translucent fuzz of unshaved facial hair. He picks up his ID card and swallows. I watch the bob of his over-sized Adam's apple and decide he's nervous.

"You're assigned to Fischer. Kill experiment 8226. Dismissed." He walks away. I didn't see his reaction, but I don't imagine Horne would enjoy working on kill experiments. His footsteps echo down the white tiled hall as he recedes.

"Smith. You're assigned to Sima, cure experiment 4771." He flinches. He wanted to kill. Of course he wanted to kill. Before hive study became available, his research specialty preference was micro explosives.

"Tucker, you'll work under Ko. Kill experiment 6255."

Tucker exits the white hall, and I wait in the silence for Shelby to say my name. I know I'm next, but I wait for her to instruct me. She's also waiting for something, watching me. I watch her back. Her grey hair is braided like Amos's, but she looks older. Her mouth is closed so that her lips purse together, as though she is thinking something over… thinking me over.

"Mason."

It's not a command. I nod and wait. She wants to watch me, so I let her.

"Top of your class. Twenty years old. Chose infection science."

I nod again.

"It says here that you interrupted patient protocol during instructive experimentation in defiance of a direct command from a senior instructor." She reads off of her tablet before returning her studying gaze to me and asking, "Do you have a death wish, Mason?"

"No more than anyone else here." They're the first words I've spoken today.

Shelby nods. "Go ahead."

I step toward the wall and place my head against the first slot. There is a blue light against a dark screen. I detect the small motions as the light takes micro laser readings to map my retina. My hands, one in each slot, rest on similar screens, and the same lasers read my fingerprints. There's a fast, sharp sensation on my right index finger. My blood is now cataloged and imprinted on my file. The data is recorded on my ID card. As I remove myself from the scanner, I think about what Shelby read from my report. There is nothing about what would have happened if I hadn't acted. Nothing about the lapse in volunteer procedure or Hugo's failure to identify safety breaches. I grab my ID card the moment I hear the *tink* of it against the white slot. My face looks back at me, unsmiling. I look small with my hair braided and tucked, dark against the white background. The ID card has a timer counting down the hours and minutes from its generation. The timer began at 24:00:00, and the numbers blink rapidly down.

I wait to be dismissed, but Shelby remains quiet. The silence stretches out until something loud clangs on the other side of the building.

"Follow me," Shelby says, turning abruptly. There's no lit pathway to guide us.

CHAPTER
THIRTY

I FOLLOW Shelby through a series of doors that she accesses with a quick swipe of her card. We pass a small group of volunteers who acknowledge her with quick nods and bowed heads. She addresses each of them by name without turning her head in their direction. A freight elevator opens at the end of the hallway, and Shelby calls out to the exiting volunteer, "Hold, please."

The volunteer gives her a curious look but stops long enough to hold the door so that we can enter.

"Thank you, Diaz," she says, waving her hand to dismiss him before pressing a large red button inside the lift.

I don't dare ask her where we're going. At the Institute, it was easy to find the creases between the clockwork that drove the system forward. Things aren't as straightforward here. My stomach flutters as the elevator accelerates and stalls. The doors open without the flourish of a *ding* to announce our arrival. Shelby extends her hand to invite me to exit.

I step out into a frozen hall. My breath catches in my throat as my body responds to the shock of such a dramatic temperature change. All around us, pathways extend along row after row of cylinders. Between each, there is only enough space for passage. I walk out to the metal railing that guards the suspended metal gangway and look down. The earth drops out from under me as I stare down what looks like an endless hole lined with more of the same.

"Do you know where we are?" Shelby asks, joining me at the railing.

"Cryogenic storage," I answer, still looking for the bottom. *Trudy's in here somewhere…*

"This is one of only six locations in the Northern Laboratories that are free from audio recording," she says, folding her tablet under the crook of her arm.

Ah, so this is why she's brought me here. "I see," I say, tearing my gaze away from the rows of contained bodies long enough to study her again. "What are the others?"

"The energy receivers on the outskirts, of course. The bathrooms, the training rooms, the dining hall and the receiving docks. The official list of audio-free locations is much longer, of course," she answers, walking to the end of the gangway and absently glancing at the frosted glass of a storage cylinder. Behind the icy film, the obscured outline of a patient stares back.

I approach but try very hard not to look at the sad shadow of humanity. "We just came from the receiving docks," I say.

"Where every person up north focused their attention on the new arrivals," Shelby admonishes, leaving me feeling naive and foolish.

It makes me think of our speculations before loading the transport vehicle, only now I don't wish for the curious eyes that peer at me from invisible corridors. Now that I'm here, the Northern Laboratories seem far more malevolent than Amos ever could have described, though she did try. Perhaps this is why Shelby chose cryogenic storage, as opposed to the bathroom, to have this conversation.

"Do you know how many patients we house at the Northern Laboratories?" she asks, following my gaze as my eyes travel across the sea of cylinders.

I perform a couple of quick calculations before offering my best guess. "I'd say, maybe half a million? Probably more."

She nods. "You're wondering where they all come from."

"It's listed on their manifests. I could go through each one in the coming years and have an answer," I say.

My response draws her attention from the rows of frozen bodies. Her eyes bore into me with the same chill that seeps in through the openings of my suit. "Is that what you plan to spend your time up here doing? And what about the cure?"

My breath catches in my throat. I'm completely unprepared to answer her question. *What if she isn't who I think she is?*

She speaks before I can answer. "You seem reasonably intelligent, Mason—and I don't mean because you're at the top of your class. At least, I hope there's more to you than that. You'll be told that a cure is impossible—that there are too many strains and mutations. Zoribiatus is compared to a cancer, but I promise you that it's no such thing."

"You believe in a cure, then?" I whisper, amazed that we're actually talking about it.

"There is a cure. But you must never speak of the search for it. Your position up here is contingent upon your ability to stay hidden until it's time," she whispers.

My head spins. Amos never dared to speak so plainly. "What are we really doing up here?"

"Whatever you're told to do," she answers, her voice returned to a normal volume. All conspiracy has left us. When I look at her again, there's nothing of the urgent intensity that drove her to confess so much. We stare into the frozen abyss for another minute before Shelby returns to the elevator. I follow her, looking back at the stacked cylinders containing bodies—some viable, some not.

When we reach the top, Shelby indicates a lit pathway, saying, "You're assigned to me. We'll begin with cure experiment 5042. Log in right away and grant me access to your room. Do not grant anyone else permission for unauthorized entry besides me without my permission, do you understand?"

I don't understand. "Yes."

"I'll be watching you closely, Mason. There will be no further quixotic antics up here. You are dismissed. Please review our schedule after you rest." She steps aside and allows me to walk past her down the lit hall. I walk in the same direction as the others, and Shelby falls in behind me.

The hall leads us outside. I'm overcome by an excited thrill as the bright sunlight touches my skin. The air is frigid, somehow colder than the cryogenic area. A gust of wind bites my lungs and stings my nose and eyes. I blink back against it, so exhilarated that I forget to walk. I'm taking in everything I can see—the low concrete structures that dip down into the ground, the distinct divide—a large building with the only visible window. It's the exact image we were shown the day of our first lesson, but the cold makes it real.

Shelby clears her throat. "Go on and get inside, there's a storm on its way," she rebukes me gently.

I cross my arms across my chest against the cold and move toward the facility. My ID card opens the door instantly. There's a puff of air and a sucking sound before the door slinks closed behind me. The lighted pathway glows ahead of me, and I follow it. To my left, I see a large room filled with long tables and benches—a cafeteria. There's a waiting room with a few visiting volunteers dressed in fitted suits alternating brown and black in blocks.

Several more turns down the lighted halls, and I reach the scientists' living quarters. I scan the doors until I find my name. Mason. My ID card offers me entry to the tiny space. The room is nearly identical to the living quarters at the Institute. I hope the blankets are warmer than they look. The cold hasn't left me since I came inside. The indoor temperature is survivable, but cold. There's a workstation with a chair and a large screen. Next to it is a port for my personal tablet. The room is tiled with brown rugs.

The bathroom is likewise small and built for efficiency. A mirror, a sink, two drawers with standard-issue toiletries. The shower has a wired pump for cleansing solutions and two spigots for directional water usage. A brown towel hangs at arm's reach from the shower door. There is a toilet that hides perfectly behind the open door. Within it is a measurement sensor for remote health monitoring.

After an intensely satisfying shower, I brush my hair until all of the knots and tangles are removed, then find a new suit in a drawer. I use my ID card to turn on my data station. Everything I could ever want is right at my fingertips. I want to dive in and start putting pieces together, but I stop myself. I have to be patient. I have to blend in. I must refrain until I understand what's safe.

The first thing I do is follow instructions. I authorize Shelby for entry into my personal quarters and look up my assignment. Cure experiment 5042. I read Shelby's profile, the details of the experiment and my data quotas. There are report times and experiment lengths. I'm about to select the details and go through them when I notice the blinking word at the top of the screen. *Welcome.*

I touch the word, and the screen transforms. An internal aerial view of the laboratories is highlighted by small blue, red, white and yellow dots. I can select each area and an information drop down appears next to it. Outside is the receiving dock, with the hexagonal concrete and steel building. There are concrete and asphalt pathways covered in snow and ice. Like the cryogenic storage, most of the facility is below ground. There are two divided areas with the larger building in the center. White lights line the path to the cure labs, which are divided by the scientists who run the experiments. Red light highlights the kill labs. Each area shows overhead walkways, glass barriers and data rooms. I can't see all of the details unless I select one and zoom in. The kill labs are all reserved by scientists—leads.

There's another area that's dark. It's behind the red-lit kill lab areas. I try to take a closer look at it, and a message appears on the screen. *Under Construction. Restricted.* I won't be able to learn more about it here. I highlight the yellow-lit living quarters instead. The volunteer halls are adjacent to the scientist halls, and the common area is located at the junction between them.

The volunteer rooms are endless, hall after hall, and most are filled. The scientists' resident quarters are small by comparison but likewise full. I pull the statistics to confirm that there are dozens of scientists but hundreds upon hundreds of volunteers. This is all it takes to keep the whole facility running—less than a thousand warm bodies. Has it always been this way? I'll need time to understand.

There's another area—green. I touch the large reinforced room, and the whole thing lights up. *Training facilities.* There are changing rooms with lockers. It's divided into three different training sections, and there's a schedule next to it. I bring up my ID card, and the schedule dissolves into a message. *Mason. Training TBD. Requires neural mapping —20:00 in the neural labs.* We'll train here. *But for what?*

The blue-lit area comes up as *cafeteria*. Dining hours are set and fixed. If we don't report frequently enough, we'll be automatically put on medical restriction for observation and monitoring. Dining is open so that scientists and volunteers can report at the same time. I'll be able to visit with them. *Simons.* It's been so long. I'm not even certain that he's still here.

No. He promised.

I select the search option and type in his full name. I hold my breath as the information loads. I see his face.

> *Moe Simons — Volunteer, 3-year resident. Senior.*
> *Assigned as lead to team 136 of 214*
> *Team 136 Current Assignment: Screening maintenance*
> *Assignment Duration: Reassignment week-end*
> *Current Location: Volunteer selection — replacement.*

Simons is selecting a new team member for his crew. I know it's unreasonable to hope that he would pick Jorey. But… Jorey was ranked first. Maybe that'll be enough of a reason for Simons to pick him. *Technically third.* I smile. I like the way Jorey views the world.

I notice something else. Amidst Simons' profile, there is an option —*send message.* My finger trembles as I reach out to communicate directly with my old friend.

CHAPTER
THIRTY-ONE

I'M SITTING on the stiff, brown couch in the meeting area between the two residence halls. Then I'm standing. I can't decide. I can't be still. Simons responded to my message almost immediately. He'll meet me here before the dining hour.

I'm not even sure he'll recognize me. I've changed, but I feel like a kid again as I wait. I nod at volunteers as they move through the area to return to their quarters to get ready for the dining hour. Some seem upbeat, others barely able to stand on their own two feet. The haunted eyes all file in from one hall—the one with red lights.

I'm craning my neck to look down those red-lit halls when I hear a familiar voice.

"I'll be damned, Mason; you did grow up!"

My head whips around and then up. He stands so tall behind the brown synthetic chairs. Though I have grown, Simons is still as large as ever. It's like he's back from the dead. *But he never was dead.* The volunteers moving in and out of the area seem far away now. *This is real.* I force the tears stinging at the edges of my eyes to stay where they are.

"It's good to see you again, Simons." My voice is foreign to me. Adult.

Simons steps over the chair and takes a seat. I want to hug him. I want to cry. I want him to tell me everything that's happened, but I can't do any of those things. Not right now. I'm a scientist, and he's a volunteer. There are rules. Our reactions and behavior have been trained. Someone might be watching. Instead, I do the only thing I can do. I sit across from him and say, "I've missed you."

He smiles. "That goodbye was a hard thing."

The anxiety I've been carrying for so many years melts away. We made it. Both of us.

"How have you been?" I load everything I can into that question. He soaks it up.

"I am still standing. I've seen a bit of everything, and I'm still standing."

I can't help but let the big, stupid smile spread across my face. "I can't believe it."

Simons smiles, too. "A happy reunion."

There's a lot I can't ask him right at this moment, but we can still talk. We just have to find the right topics. "You chose a new volunteer for your team?"

"You've been checking up on me?" His voice is loaded with false incredulity.

"Somebody's got to keep an eye on you." I can't get rid of the grin.

His disappears. "Yeah. I lost a team member last month. I try so hard to keep them safe, but sometimes it's impossible."

My whole face slumps into concern. Maybe this is the wrong topic.

"A small selection this month, but their stats were good," he says with a lighter voice.

"I rode up with them, you know. Who did you pick?"

"Top-ranked kid. Jorey." My heart sings. He can see it. "He knows you."

"Yeah. We talked on the way up," I confide.

"That's what he said. You talked about me." The life is back in Simons' voice. He's leaning forward into our conversation with his hands folded over his knees.

"Don't be vain, we talked about lots of things!" I reach forward and push one of his massive hands.

The room is quieter now. Most of the volunteers have made their way to their rooms. Some of what Simons and I had is still intact, but some of the pieces are missing and will take time to rebuild.

"I'm glad you picked Jorey," I say.

"Well then I am, too."

"You can protect him."

His eyes darken, and his hands come up to his face in an old familiar gesture. "I can't protect him from everything. But I always do what I can."

The gravity of his statement grounds me. We're in the Northern Laboratories now. People don't mysteriously disappear up here. Up here, people die.

A stout, thickly muscled woman walks from the living quarters toward us. "Simons! You can't tell me you're not hungry. Let's go, Richards is waiting!"

Simons leans back, and the woman notices me. I suspect from her expression that Simons doesn't spend much time talking to scientists. Simons' face crinkles into a smile, and he says, "Carmen, I'd like to introduce you to my old friend, Mason."

I stand and smile at Carmen. "It's nice to meet you."

Carmen nods at me, then speaks to Simons, "You're friends with a scientist?"

Simons nods in my direction. "This one's alright, I promise." She seems content with this.

"Let's go eat," Simons says. I follow him to the cafeteria.

As we walk toward the cafeteria in an increasing mass of people, Simons falls back so that he's parallel to me. He places his hand on my shoulder, and we slow, but don't stop. I'm amazed at the number of people walking in this hall. I glance up at Simons, and he looks down at me. His voice is low and quiet.

"You need to be careful, Kara. The scientists watch each other. Something is happening here. Things always seem to be going wrong."

There are so many questions I want to ask, but now isn't the time. Instead, I respond with my own information. "People at the Institute disappear. More than sixty interns should have graduated. I think one of the scientists was supposed to die, but I saved him. The rest just disappear. Jorey says the volunteers do, too."

Simons nods and asks, "Do you trust Jorey?"

"I think he has promise."

"What sort of promise?" he asks. I have to listen hard to hear him above the increasing volume of chatter.

"He's smart and deliberate. Everything about him suggests he's telling the truth."

"Alright, that's good enough for me just now," Simons concedes.

EVERYTHING HAPPENS FAST in the Northern Laboratories. We wake up, shower, report to morning dining hour. We attend our experiment designations, report to evening dinner hour and train. We build our experiments and submit them, then review each other's work. We sleep, and we train again.

On the first day of training, the five new scientists, along with the new volunteers, had to report to the neurological laboratory to be *scanned in*. The process consisted of a thorough mapping of our neurological pathways so that we could be input into a massive database that controls the training simulations.

Every night, our training covers one of the crucial strategies for survival in the event of a patient outbreak—or that's the official explanation for the need for such intensive training. It seems a lot more like the sort of training we'd receive if we were expecting to go into combat. It's only one of the great mysteries of the Northern Laboratories. Another is the emphasis on the kill labs.

The cure labs are sparsely furnished and meticulously sterile. The floors are covered in a dark tile that prevents the reflection of the overhead lights and reduces the glare. The lab benches likewise are matte and dark, providing a blank and non-offending surface for hours on end of tedious experimentation. They are where I spend the bulk of my waking hours, pouring over a screen and trying to apply the complex code and algorithms Amos had me study to make programs that will give me predictive answers.

My experimentation focuses on disease classifications, disease developmental life cycles and infection control. Though I have particular interest in the evolution of the disease since the first outbreak, my first two designs on the topic have been shot down by the review board. They have requested that I focus my designs on the measurements of prevalent strains of Zoribiatus's response to current clinical treatment. The rationale, of course, being that in the last two decades, several treatments showed enough progress to move into clinical trials. But the more I look into these studies, the easier it is to see that none of the treatments ever had a shot. I think I'm meant to be the first line of defense against prospective cures.

The earliest strains of Zoribiatus were cured by treatments created in the Northern Laboratories. The cure created a wave of hopefulness that fueled the reconstruction of the cities and spawned social development. Rather than the close of a terrible chapter, however, the era of the vaccine turned out to be the eye of the storm. The second outbreak occurred just as rapidly as the first, only less predictable. The new strain of vaccine-resistant Zoribiatus was more destructive than the original. The mass panic and hysteria of the second outbreak was anticlimactic by comparison to the original outbreak.

The Northern Laboratories were already established and prepared to receive patients, and due to the volatile and dangerous nature of the new strain, the kill labs were born. While the cure labs stretch out with corridors, subsections and networks of rooms to house the plethora of experiments that are perpetually ongoing, the kill labs host only one experiment at a time. This is due, predominantly, to the dangerous nature of the kill experiments.

Already, people have died. I don't have to guess about it either. There's no time for whispers up here. On the third day of my first stint in the kill labs, I watched a fresh volunteer get torn limb from limb. It was his first experiment task. He screamed until the patient ripped his trachea out of his throat. After the room was incinerated and sterilized, nobody ever mentioned it again. When I tried to ask, Shelby silenced me before the words could escape.

This is one of the most troublesome things about being up here. It doesn't *feel* like a medical research facility. It seems a lot more like a military organization with an emphasis on research and development —particularly the development of weaponry. The medical research comes across nearly as an afterthought. Something to keep up appearances while something else more complex and far more sinister is happening.

None of us can speak about our suspicions directly, but it seems that at least Miller and Tucker share some of my suspicions. I sit with Horne, Miller and Tucker at one of the long cafeteria benches and lose myself to the din of hundreds of voices. Smith never sits with us. It's like there was already a seat slotted for him among a group of the more senior scientists. He's taken a particular liking to a scientist named Fischer, and the feeling seems to be mutual. Sometimes I notice him looking our way derisively and laughing with his new cohort.

There isn't much safe to talk about. Horne is as persistently silent as he is unhappy. I think it has something to do with his assignment. It happened in the first week. I found him sitting alone at the end of dining hour and staring into nothing. He told me his specialty was changed and he was on a new project. He hasn't been the same since. Now, when he isn't lost in some deep, terrible thought, he nods along to conversations and offers a weak smile to accompany his strange, watery eyes. The rest of the time, he can't be reached without earnest effort.

Miller is as sharp and decisive as the first day I caught a glimpse of her. She's as unmoved by the odd explanations for things up here as I am, but she's becoming more vocal, like Tucker, who has taken to idolizing her. They're together in nearly all of our quiet hours, which makes me feel like the odd one out. It's hard to get a word in edgewise when they get going, and I don't know if they've taken my warning about safe locations to heart.

When I can get away with it, I sit with Simons. His large body blocks mine from being viewed by the other scientists so no one will question why I'm hanging around the volunteers. They're a group of five: Simons, Carmen, Diaz, Richards and now Jorey. I don't talk much when I'm with them. I just listen.

"Did you hear about the transport vehicle that came through today?" Carmen directs her question toward Simons, ignoring my presence. I get the impression that she doesn't like me very much.

"Yeah, I did. Pretty strange to have a transport from the Institute only a few months after the new scientists." Simons nods, only taking enough time away from his meal for this response.

"Dunn says it's a government guy, not a scientist," Carmen says.

"He was dressed like a scientist," Diaz says, pointing his fork at Carmen in disagreement.

"You'd look like a scientist too in that fancy suit, Diaz, but just because he's wearing it doesn't make him one," Carmen replies, lifting a thick, dark eyebrow as if to challenge him to argue with her.

"He's a scientist," Simons ends the quarrel. There's a pause while he takes a long drink to wash down a large bite. "His name is Rick Orman, and he left on some sort of assignment back when I first got here. He's a weapons guy."

"That's right!" Richards chimes in with new recognition.

"So you know him?" Carmen's heavy chest presses into the table as she casually pushes her dinner tray aside. There's a commanding presence to her that nearly rivals Simons', but only just nearly. Overwhelmingly, there's only respect between the volunteers, and especially toward Simons.

Again we wait while Simons clears the food he's taken in. Jorey glances at me from across the table and smiles. He's timid in the group still, but he fits in. I found him one night in the cafeteria when I couldn't sleep shortly after our arrival. He was sitting at the window watching a storm. I sat with him, and it felt like it did back in the transport vehicle. Since then, we've found each other at the window several times. It's nice to have someone to talk to. Not everything with Jorey is about the scientists, or the laboratory, or death. Mostly we just speculate about the world outside.

"He's an unpleasant person, and you don't want to cross him," Simons says of Orman. "He's more senior than he looks, but he gets pulled off-site often, to deal with outbreaks or something like that."

I glance across the dining hall to the table where the most senior scientists—and Smith—are dining. Orman sits amongst them, neatly trimmed beard and salty hair slicked back. He stands out from the others. It's as if he thinks he's too good to be grouped among them, sort of like Smith when he stands in rank with our group of new scientists. I study him from across the room, trying to place the strange feeling of familiarity that crawls under my skin.

Suddenly he looks up, straight into my eyes, and realization strikes. I convinced myself years ago that the strange man staring down at me in the medical facility was just a hallucination, but now I'm less certain. *It can't be. It doesn't make any sense.*

I tear my eyes down and away from him, hoping to make it seem as if it had just been a casual glance. Shaking my head, I tell myself that it's just something about his mannerisms. He comes across more like a DDC official, and that's got to be it more than anything. High-ranking officials always put me on edge. I reflect on the two seconds of eye contact. *I'm acting paranoid. All I saw was a man catching someone looking at him. There was no recognition.*

"You okay, Mason?" Jorey asks, pulling me back to our cafeteria table.

"Yeah, I was just thinking that the new guy looks like a creep." I force myself to smile.

"Sure does," Jorey agrees.

"Did you see on the schedule that he's running a training program?" Richards asks, pushing his empty tray away and straightening his wire-frame glasses. Simons is the only one of us still eating.

"Just don't stand out," Simons warns, finally pushing his empty tray away. It's the group's cue that dinner is over. They all stand to ready themselves for training. I walk in Simons' shadow until I'm parallel to the table with the new scientists, thinking hard about not standing out.

As I drop down to sit next to Horne, Simons turns his head to me. "See you at the simulations, Mason."

I nod at him as the group leaves the dining hall.

"Why do you eat with them?" Miller asks me, pulling my attention away from the departing volunteers.

"I know Simons, from before," I say.

"But they're *volunteers*." Miller squishes her face as she says it, making her eyes small.

I shrug, in no mood to explain myself to her or anyone else.

Tucker twists his body toward Miller, his foot knocking against mine. I watch him, his long arms bent and his whole body now pointing at his person of interest. "I can get why Mason does it. The volunteers do all our dirty work. If you want them to do a good job, spending time with them could encourage them to work harder for you."

Miller nods. Her short black hair brushes against her cheeks before she tucks it behind her ear on one side. She flashes a quick, brilliant smile toward Tucker. "I guess that makes sense."

Their bodies are facing each other completely now, and I roll my eyes while no one is looking. I glance at Horne, who as usual is silently pushing his food across his tray, not looking at anybody and not talking.

"What were you saying then, about the contradictory results in your experiment?" Miller is back to pretending that I'm not there. I listen, like I do when I sit with the volunteers, hoping to hear something useful.

Tucker's eyes light up conspiratorially; he tucks his head in over the table, and all four of us lean in as if we're in on it. "It's strange, is all I'm saying, like the body is almost pre-programmed to prolong death in a way that couldn't be a natural expression of disease." His voice is low, and he's mostly talking to Miller.

"Do you think it *isn't* natural?" Miller's voice is louder than she meant it to be. She winces.

Their conversation is too obvious. I glance at Horne, who is back to pushing his food around and nudge him. "Let's go get ready for training."

He nods and follows me out of the cafeteria. I glance back at Miller and Tucker to see a group of senior scientists chatting with them now, Rick Orman among them.

"Did you get your experiment peer review back?" Horne interrupts my gaze.

"Yeah, mine got torn apart, and I have a meeting with my experiment authority about it. What about you?"

"Mine was cleared through. I have to meet with the assigned scientist group for training." His voice wavers, as though he's in shock over the whole thing.

"What's the experiment about?" I ask.

"I'm not really supposed to say." Horne shrugs. His shoulders slump as though it's become too much of a burden to hold himself up any longer.

"Is that part of what bothers you?" I ask.

He shakes his head, his forehead crinkling. "I suppose. Part of it."

"Are you going to be alright?" I ask him, concern mounting as the depths of his turmoil sink in.

"I don't know. I suppose so." Ahead, our paths split.

I put my hand on his shoulder in the only gesture of reassurance I can think of. I give it a little squeeze and feel nothing but bone beneath his suit. "See you out there," I tell him before heading to my room.

THIRTY-THREE

I'M late to the kill floor. My morning experimental design conference with the investigative authority ran long. He went through my design submission line by line, scrutinizing every detail. By the time we finished, I had to run to make it to screening before my ID card expired. Now I'm worried I'll be chewed out by the lead scientist for being late on the first day of a new experiment.

I rush up to the entry door and scan my ID card. It swings wide, and I enter without thought. It's quiet. My eyes sweep around the room for the other scientists and land on the floor where Miller is splayed out as though she fell reaching for something. Crouched over her body is a patient dressed in torn clothes, blood dripping from its face and hands. The patient is mid-feast, hands wrenching up one of Miller's broken ribs.

I'm stuck in place, unable to process the scene. *How could this happen?* Where are the other scientists? The volunteers? I'm supposed to be a fourth on this project. There's no one else in the room. Miller was alone with this patient.

How could things go so terribly wrong?

The squelching sound stops as the patient looks up from Miller's corpse.

It breathes a raspy, wet sound that echoes in my mind from miles away, then moves clumsily, slipping in the pool of blood it created, trying to stand. All of its focus is on me now. I turn to run, but the door has already shut behind me and won't open again. A room won't open from the inside when a patient is present.

I fight to remain calm as the patient finds its footing, pressing against Miller's middle and the control console to right itself. On its feet, the patient is much quicker. It lurches toward me with outstretched arms, gurgling low in its throat. I fling a chair between us and jump across the room, still looking for any sort of weapon.

"Help!" I scream at the top of my lungs, throwing the other chair between myself and the patient, who screams in mindless frustration.

No one responds. A quick glance at the hall cameras confirms that there are no volunteers on the floor. I'm alone with Miller's corpse and the patient that tore through her. I'm not sure what to do. There isn't enough time for a rescue from another location. I won't be able to survive long enough. I have to kill the patient somehow.

This patient is incredibly fit—early stage manifestation with no obvious external injuries. The only blood present seems to be Miller's, but I can't get a good look at it while I scramble to keep away. *I guess this is why we're trained to make such fast diagnoses.* The patient's foot catches on the leg of the chair, and it falls forward. I take a quick side step and slip in Miller's blood, landing hard on my elbow and making eye contact with her lifeless face. Then I see it.

Just behind her, where her arm is bent at an unnatural angle, is the cannon gun she never got a chance to use. As the patient finds its feet again, I reach across Miller's still-warm body and yank the weapon clear. I compress the trigger, causing the barrel to kick back against my body as it launches a huge, hot burst of energy at the approaching creature.

It shrieks in agony as the blast bursts and spreads overheated flames across its entire body. It only takes a couple of seconds for the patient to fall, a mess of hot ash and smoldering bones on the clean, white floor. My breath comes out as a sob of relief.

As the panic drains from me, I realize there's sound outside the room—others. The door opens, and two volunteers in bio-suits enter together. I drop the gun and reach for the control station to pull myself up. One of the volunteers grabs my arm and hoists me up.

"Mason! What happened?" It's Jorey.

I shake my head and look at him through the film of his mask. "I don't know. I was late. Miller was alone with the patient…"

"Are you hurt? Where are the other scientists?" He supports me and guides me around Miller's body.

"I'm fine. I don't know where the other scientists are. There are supposed to be two others—Sima and Orman?" I'm so grateful that Jorey is one of the responding volunteers.

"We're supposed to take her to quarantine," Carmen interrupts our conversation.

"Quarantine?" Images of the inter-city quarantine facilities flash through my mind. "Shouldn't I just go through screening?"

Carmen squares her body to mine. "Yes, quarantine, Mason."

"Shouldn't I just go to screening?" I repeat my question.

"I guess the scientists don't know everything around here!" Carmen's statement comes out as a bark.

It stings, making me want to yell at her. I'm the scientist and she's the volunteer, and regardless of her being on Simons' team, I have the overarching desire to put her in her place. "Explain, volunteer Carmen!"

Jorey jumps at my words. I might be Carmen's superior, but she's Jorey's. Pulling rank as a scientist makes me feel as low as Smith, but I can't make myself care enough to stem my anger. I wait for her response.

"There have been instances with some strains of the disease in the Northern Laboratories where an infected person doesn't show in screening immediately," she responds. Her voice is flat, and I picture her hating me and wishing for me to be infected. I mask the creeping guilt with my own anger, my insides folding over themselves all the while.

"So I'll go into quarantine?" My voice is soft again. I want to apologize. Seeing Jorey and Carmen in bio-suits reminds me that I've been exposed. I'm covered from neck to toe. My hands are gloved, and only my face is exposed, but maybe that's all it takes. Miller's blood is certainly contaminated, and I was wedged against her body.

"A scientist will report to quarantine and give you the details of your situation." Carmen's voice hasn't changed.

As we leave, she depresses a button on her wrist. "Kill floor three is cleared for incineration."

"HEY, MASON! WAIT UP!" Tucker calls out as I head toward training.

I shake my head, not wanting to take part in another conspiratorial discourse. We both know that Miller's death couldn't have been an accident, but it's not safe to talk about it. I've already said too much, but still he hasn't relented. He isn't taking it well, and I'm tired of not being able to help him.

At first, I was willing to talk him through what I knew. I told him about my time in quarantine, and how I tried to look up the recording of the incident on kill floor three only to find that all the visual feeds for that date and time were missing. There's no formal incident report, no review of the procedures—nothing. The only thing I could find was Miller's scientist file, which noted the date of her death and listed the cause as "patient accident."

Not even Simons was able to gather information on what happened. He couldn't determine what volunteers did the patient development and delivery for the experiment, and he suggested that the volunteer files might have been tampered with.

"What's the hurry?" Tucker demands, pushing though slower-moving volunteers and scientists as he fights to catch me.

"I'm not in the mood tonight, Tucker," I say without looking over.

"It's not like that! I have news." He grabs my shoulder so that I have to stop walking and face him. His hair is slicked back and away from his furrowed brow as he pleads with me to hear him out.

My heart aches every time I look at him now. His eyes are dull and sunken in. All of his excitement left with Miller. I know how he feels. Sometimes I notice the same shadow darkening my own face. But he doesn't have Amos to help him through it. All he has is me.

"Okay. What's the news?" I ask under my breath as volunteers move past us.

"It's Horne. He's gone." Tucker's voice is a mixture of wonder and angst.

"What happened?" I ask, feeling a pang of sadness for another loss. *Not Horne too...*

"I don't know. I was hoping you could find out—you know, like you did before?"

"I'm not sure what you think I can do that you can't," I lie.

"I don't know what it is you do, exactly. Miller figured it had something to do with your coding specialty. She said that you learned the master code used at the Northern Laboratories, so I figure it has to be related to that," Tucker ventures.

I keep the shock from my face. *He thinks I have access to the main system.* At least that's better than him suspecting I have anything to do with dissenters. "That's definitely not true," I say, forcing a bemused smile.

"It was just a theory," he shrugs.

I turn away from him, eager for space to process what happened to Horne.

"Mason, please?"

The desperation in his voice makes me turn back to him. He looks so distraught. "I don't think I can stand for him to just be gone like Lau," he begs.

"Fine," I sigh. He's managed to completely disintegrate my resolve. "I'll see what I can find," I say, turning to make my way into the training room. Tucker moves quickly to follow me.

The training room is designed to run complex simulations. To the observer, or the simulation instructor, we look like a group running on a stationary track with large, non-descript objects moving toward us. The track functions as a running platform that responds to obstacles based on the pre-programmed algorithms for each workout—in this respect, the simulations share a crossover with my research. I've found that I'm quite adept at working on program simulations when I work with a team that needs to do simulated practice for their experimentation. I suppose that's one aspect of my research that I don't hate.

Under normal circumstances, there are three separate training experiences run in the room. Endurance and agility are run on a track that moves underfoot as we are presented with a variety of obstacles and tasks that require us to both think and act quickly. Weapons are almost always run by Orman, which is the primary reason I avoid it. I can't shake the feeling that he had something to do with Miller's death. He was the lead scientist for the experiment, and there's no explanation for his absence.

The majority of us have been in some variation of weapons training since we were old enough to hold a gun, which makes the training seem redundant. The exercises we perform go so much further beyond the scope of what's required for safety in the Northern Laboratories that it adds to the sense that there must be another reason for the training. We aren't military, but we train like we are.

Redlining is my least favorite training category, and it's about as grueling as it sounds. Individuals infected with the Zoribiatus disease lose the portion of their brain function responsible for communication of fatigue. Though it may seem inconsequential, this is part of what makes them so incredibly dangerous. Human beings are capable of incredible things physically, and often the main inhibitor of our true abilities is our mind. Our precious minds cost us a level of physical efficiency and ability that the Zoribiatus disease cures in a reasonably healthy patient—when an uninfected human sprints at top speed for an extended period of time, the mind stops the body before the muscles reach exhaustion. When a Zoribiatus patient sprints at top speed, the only thing that stops them is muscle failure. The physical exhaustion occurs significantly past the point that the mind determines is the critical point, which can, in dire situations, result in an individual being overcome by a Zoribiatus patient.

There are only two hopes for someone to outrun a Zoribiatus patient—the first is to hope the patient's physical condition has deteriorated enough that they lack the coordination and muscular support to sprint. The second option is to increase your own ability to run at top speed as long as possible in hopes that you can find safety. The only way to increase the time to physical exhaustion is to train your mind, which only occurs by forcing your body to this point over and over again until your mind increases the duration to exhaustion. Nothing is more painful.

Tonight, instead of regular training, we're doing an annual cataclysmic disaster response scenario—my first. We'll work together to safely evacuate and destroy the Northern Laboratories just like we would if an irreversible outbreak were to occur. The entire simulation is based upon the structure of our facility, and we'll perform pre-designated tasks within the ever-changing landscape of the simulation.

I wander into a crowd of volunteers, hoping to shake Tucker so I can speak freely. I glance back and confirm that Tucker has been grabbed up by Smith and a few other scientists. I shake my head, both amused and concerned. I don't know how much longer Tucker can keep this up before he ends up with the other missing persons.

"Oh, good evening, Mason." Richards' soft voice pulls me from my thoughts.

"Oh, hi." I look over at him as others situate the helmets on their heads in preparation for the simulation. I notice he's alone. "Where is everyone else?"

"Shelby gave Simons some sort of special assignment. He took Carmen. I haven't seen Jorey or Diaz yet tonight," Richards says as he pulls the straps out from his helmet.

Before he can place it on his head, I put my hand out to stop him. He raises an eyebrow over the wire rim of his glasses as a wordless question. In a full room we're alone, so I ask in a low voice, "Do you know what happened to Horne?"

His head drops, and he nods. "I heard he infected himself while running cultures in the cure labs. It's really too bad. He was taken into cryo just before dinner."

The confirmation of the news leaves me feeling hollow. Horne's actually gone then. He isn't dead, exactly, and I suppose if I really wanted to, I could go out to the containment area and visit him, but I know that I won't. The Northern Laboratories keeps close tabs on who enters cryogenics without an assignment.

I shove the helmet onto my head and attach the straps, knowing that I'll be late to the session. I leave behind thoughts of Horne as I jump into the impending simulation.

CHAPTER
THIRTY-FIVE

SWEAT STINGS in my eyes as I break through the barrier that separates the mainframe computers from the rest of the facility. I've been running for over an hour, killing patients and making little progress toward my simulation assignment.

A horrible snarl pulls my attention away from my stinging eyes and burning legs. I whirl around to send a burst of energy straight into a patient's skull. It drops with an unenthusiastic thud at the doorway. I grab the chrome-lined chair and use it to shove the body outside the sensor area so that the door will lock shut when I get the system online again. The sound of screams, accompanied by the buzz of more pulsar gun discharges, travels from somewhere below. It never feels like a simulation when things are out of control like this.

I hurry to my task before more patients can make their way up. From this room, I'll have visual access to the entire structure once I bypass the corrupted power distributor and recalibrate the satellite signal for energy redistribution. The ground vibrates as the simulation manifests another explosion somewhere within the building. There's enough energy from the backup generators to read the signals from the power grid and find the corrupted unit. My fingers fly across the screen as I re-work the circuitry. With my other hand, I pull up the network for satellite communication. I have the whole system running a reboot in a matter of seconds.

The screens flash to life. As I watch the hordes of patients make their way through hallways littered with debris from the explosions, I wonder why the simulations never seem to be able to re-create the hive behavior. There are enough grouped patients to create a hive response at every convergence point, yet their behavior remains consistent with the typical manifestation of the disease. Maybe Smith has an answer for this. I've never been assigned to one of his hive experiments, but I suppose I could ask him directly. I get the impression he wouldn't tell me. Even if he weren't a completely self-absorbed jerk, I'm not certain he *could* tell me. Projects like his and Horne's seem to operate on a different level of security.

More screams. The simulation won't end until I can restart the automated destruction sequence for the facility. I open up the main access panel and get to work, wondering how possible this particular disaster is. There are so many backups in place to keep the destruction sequence active. If only one thing goes right in a catastrophe, it would be the destruction sequence. *We might all die, but the Northern Laboratories will burn.*

As I work, I notice something strange in the way the program displays on the screen. There's a discrepancy between the simulation-based program and the actual program I learned for this task. Do the simulation programmers realize their mistake? It occurs to me that I might be able to verify the error if I can access the original simulation program. It shouldn't be difficult to do, considering how similar the interface is to the one I use in my own research.

My curiosity gets the better of me, and without any further thought, I connect my personal interface with the one in the simulation. With a couple of quick changes, I'm in. Instead of line after line of simulated code, I'm looking at the actual simulation program as it runs in real time. My observation screens transform so that I'm no longer looking at scientists and volunteers running and killing patients. I see the simulation as it is—masked participants in a virtual experience. There are no patients, only shapeless masses rising up from the track to interact with the users.

Adjustable magnetic fields are built into the entire physical system and work to pull the billions of metallic points in the fiber-optic track into any number of complicated shapes and structures, making one room infinitely capable of creating any experience. This design, along with the virtual masks that generate the events dictated by the instructor, make simulations the most powerful tool in the Northern Laboratories. The suits generate an electromagnetic signal that communicates each individual's perception to the other participants for a completely shared experience, and I have a bird's eye view of the entire thing.

I marvel at the system, looking from room to room as the simulation puts us through our paces, and completely forget about my virtual task. I look down at my hands, which are gloved, and up my arms, which are covered by my scientist's clothing. Unlike the participants on the screen, I still appear to be wearing simulated clothing. On the screens, I can see things as they are, but if I look around in the room, I'm still fully immersed in the simulation.

How is this even possible? I marvel at the duality of the situation and wonder if Miller was more correct than even I knew. *Is this why Amos wanted me to learn the code?* My head spins with the implication as I watch line after line of program run across the screen. I notice that a section of the program appears to be actively changing. I flip through and expand the section to see that it's referencing section 005 of the training room. I find the corresponding area on the display screens and note that there are two participants in that section—Tucker and Smith. Something strange is happening.

Section 005 converts to standby mode outside of the simulation, and the safety stops disengage. I read it in the program and note the corresponding red light that flips on in the room to indicate that the electromagnetic failsafe has been disengaged. Tucker continues on as though nothing has happened, moving toward the rail that leads to the overhead escape hatch. He must not be getting the warning that the section failsafe has disengaged.

I pull up the section on my own screen and try to re-load the activation sequence to bring it out of standby mode, but all I get is an error message. I don't have access to the safety mechanisms within the simulation. I look back to the screen to see that Smith is backing away from the area. He's moving, one step at a time, out of the affected section as if he were aware of the program error. I toggle the screen display so that I can view the simulated experience and confirm that there is no indication of the error within the experience. Smith knows something.

I flip the screen back into the real view and confirm that the red light is still blinking warning outside of the simulation to inform the program director that there's an issue with the safety and wait for the situation to be corrected. A minute passes, and nothing changes. The red light continues to flash, and Smith proceeds with his stealthy retreat.

The section code changes again. This time, the structural components are altering. *That shouldn't happen.* The simulation is meant to recreate the structural layout of the Northern Laboratories facility. If the structure of the room changes suddenly, it would defeat the purpose of the program. I suspect that this is what Smith knows. He's two steps away from moving into section 006.

It takes a few beats to figure out the intention of the program changes, but when I do, I know, in no uncertain terms, that they'll kill Tucker. *Program stop change for greater than one section occupant. Program structure interface floor change -20.* The second that Smith steps out of the quadrant, the floor will disappear out from under Tucker, and he'll fall twenty meters to the track base. Without the safety stops, the fall will kill him. Smith is almost out of the room.

I dive into the program, begging the interface to allow me access to the structure component of the simulation. I call up the change first —*floor +20.* Then the parameters—*Program stop change for greater than one section occupant.* The last command area requires section entry. The screen fades into a sectional map of the training room as Smith takes the last step to exit the section.

Tucker will fall into nothing. The moment I select the section and enter the sequence, I'll stop that from happening. As I drag my finger across the screen to choose the section, I smile to myself. *Hank isn't the only one who can make something out of nothing.*

It happens so fast that I nearly miss it on the display screen. The floor fades away, then reappears so quickly that Tucker barely staggers with the loss of his footing. At the same time as the change glimmers across the screen, there's a loud clank of metal grinding against something hard and unmoving. The impact is so severe that it shakes the entire training room and knocks me off of my feet. Before I can see what happened, everything turns black. The simulation has been terminated.

I reach up to the straps at the sides of my helmet and yank it off to escape the nothingness as the track sinks below me. All around me, scientists and volunteers are pulling their helmets off and looking for the source of the disruption.

The program directors must have located the safety error and shut down the simulation to bring the section out of standby. They must not have access to the safety mechanisms when the simulation is running either, but then I see it.

Next to where Tucker stands, confused and uncertain, the millions of fiber-optic strings that make up section 006 stretch into the ceiling as a solid mass. A steady trickle of blood drips down and collects at Tucker's feet—Smith's blood.

The panic of my mistake slams into my chest, making it hard to breathe. When I selected section 005, I must have dragged my finger across section 006 too. The same change that saved Tucker's life forced the floor base of section 006 into the ceiling, crushing Smith.

I move with the other stunned participants, numb and sick. I didn't mean to do it—I only wanted to save Tucker.

The track groans as the fiber optics release their hold on the ceiling and sink back into their standby positions. Smith's body returns with the track floor, a crushed and bloody mess. I look away from it, unable to stand seeing what I've done.

Low whispers travel like a ripple through the group of onlookers as the victim is identified.

"Smith."

I peer into the crowd, looking for anything to distract me from the horrible thing that's happened—that I did. I spot Jorey saying something to Richards, who nods. Jorey looks at the remains, then away, head low. He didn't really want to see Smith dead.

"What happened?" Orman's demanding voice forces my attention back to the scene. He's peering down at what's left of Smith, a look of disgust altering his typically sharp but detached expression.

"I'm—I'm not sure." The program director scurries over to where Smith lies on the track, holding his tablet in one hand and a helmet in the other.

"What do you mean, you aren't sure? This is your program! Tell me what happened!" Though his words are harsh, his tone is cold.

"It wasn't! Someone altered the program—I watched it happen while I was running the standby reset for sector 005. It—it happened so fast," the program scientist stammers, terrified.

"How could someone alter the program?" Orman continues his inquisition.

"I don't know. But—it looks like maybe there were two competing interferences."

I swallow against the lump that is my heart pounding in my throat and wonder if they'll be able to trace the changes back to me. Maybe I should just admit to it now and explain what was about to happen to Tucker.

"I want a full investigation, and I expect answers!" Orman snaps. The director nods his head, clearly intimidated, before scurrying away.

He's nearly running in a straight line away from Orman toward me. I step to the side as he passes and hear him murmuring to himself. "… Impossible to determine the source…"

I'm safe. The knowledge doesn't sit well. I look away from the fleeing man and back to the horrible scene I've created to find that Orman is staring at me. Adrenaline surges through my body and makes my muscles want to twitch, but I force myself to be nonreactive. I tell myself he isn't looking at me.

CHAPTER
THIRTY-SIX

THE TRAINING ROOM is cleared out so that Smith's remains can be dealt with. I rush into the locker room and jump straight into the showers. I can't wait to wash the guilt away. I wash again and again, willing the experience to fade away, but every time I close my eyes, I see the drip of blood as it runs down the section 006 divide.

The memory mingles with the others until the blood isn't dripping and pooling on the training room floor—it's smeared across the trampled grass in the clearing. My heart rate spikes as the room begins to fade. I'm about to lose control.

I reach out with my eyes closed and shut off the water so that I'm standing alone and naked in the shower stall. I have to regain control. In the still of the moment, I conjure up the details of the training room floor, just as Amos taught me to do years ago. I force myself to picture Smith's body lying on the track, distorted and crushed. I follow the trail of blood to Tucker's stunned face and Orman's look of cool fury, picturing everything in sharp, terrible detail, and then let it fade.

Orman's voice turns into a dull murmur. The red of the blood turns grey, and Smith's body becomes a smear on a map somewhere far away...

I'm always surprised how well this technique works. If I allowed myself to, I could forget everything. I grab a second towel and wrap my hair, heading toward my locker to dress.

I step out of the bathroom and into the open area, expecting it to be empty. Instead, Shelby is sitting on a bench, wearing her crisp, white lab coat, waiting.

"You surprised me," I say, unable to hide my reaction.

"I meant to," she says, keeping her hands on her knees.

"Is there something you need? I didn't think that we had any advisory meetings, and according to the schedule, I'm not working on one of your experiments for another few months," I gush, feeling exposed as I walk toward my locker.

"You're correct," she says simply, still not moving from her position.

I crawl into my suit and pull it over my bare flesh as quickly as possible. I can feel her watch me as I braid my wet hair with shaky fingers.

"It was quite a strange sequence of events this evening, don't you think?" she asks.

My fingers pause. Water drips from the tips of my hair, making me think of the blood dripping down the wall. I turn the blood grey and make my fingers continue their task. "It was terrible," I agree as I stare into the locker space before me.

"I don't think that it was supposed to happen like that," she continues, as though she were making a casual observation about poorly collected data.

"No. Do you think there was a program error?" I ask, making certain that my voice remains measured and even. I think of my heart rate ticking its accelerated beat in the simulation suit and the way Garth scolded me for letting it run away. I feel like that right now.

I take in a slow, even breath and turn around to face her, telling myself that I'm in control. She is small and old, but I'm still terrified of her in this moment, and she knows it. She straightens her glasses and stands. Her white lab coat billows with her motion. "It must have been. Sometimes it's just a terrible accident."

I nod, pretending I'm naive enough to believe her. She walks to the exit, her stride strong and confident. It doesn't even begin to reveal her true age. She stops and looks back over her shoulder. The motion causes her silver braid to pull out from her collar.

"Remember, Mason. You can't save everyone." She turns back to the door, tucking her braid as she leaves. In the silence, the thud of my heart inside my chest is a piercing scream.

CHAPTER
THIRTY-SEVEN

IN THE GLIMMER of my workstation, my hands appear white and ghostly. Tucker's dead. It was a very straightforward accident during a kill experiment. It wasn't even the patients that got him, it was a weapon malfunction. The thing irradiated the entire team, killing everyone in the room within hours. It was just an accident.

The message on my screen blinks again, and I pull my eyes back up to the task.

Do you wish to confirm the experimental specialty switch?

They're all dead now. Miller, Horne, Smith… and now Tucker. Tucker didn't deserve to go. He asked the questions I always wanted to ask but wouldn't dare to. I wasn't good to him. If I hadn't been too scared to try it, there might've been a chance to save him—to pull him into the shadows and teach him to wait the way Amos taught me. It's too late now.

I'm the only one left. I'm an actual statistic—the one in five, but I don't feel safe just because I beat the odds. If anything, I'm even more terrified. I close my eyes and see Smith's blood dripping down the track. I see Miller's open chest filled with ragged bones. I open my eyes, and the message prompts me again. *What are you going to do, Mason? Amos isn't here to stop you now…*

I think about what Shelby said after Smith's accident—*you can't save everyone.* I couldn't save Tucker. I killed Smith. Now, at the close of my own research, his specialty is obtrusively available. All I have to do is reach out and grab it before it shows up on the roster of available topics at the Institute. I can claim it for myself and begin finding answers to all the deaths.

There are far too many accidents for a research facility like this and never any consequences. It's like someone wants it to happen. Not to mention the amount of time and resources spent on training. It doesn't fit.

I think back on Garth's bemoaning of wasted resources at the Institute. By all accounts, the government seems to keep close watch over the flow of work. There has to be a greater purpose to the training. It's something I've suspected since arriving, and I'd bet that it's somehow connected to the deaths—the *accidents*, and the slew of infections since Horne.

Simons lost Diaz to an infection just two weeks ago. There isn't an explanation for how it happened, either. The infection didn't register right away, and he cleared screening. No one realized it had happened. It took weeks before any symptoms showed up. That sort of thing shouldn't be possible up here, but he wasn't even the only one.

Simons picked a new volunteer for his team last week—a woman who arrived with her entire family in cryogenic storage. The night after he selected her, we sat together and listened to her story. Her husband had been infected on an exploration outside the city and had unknowingly infected their daughters.

With many tears, she delivered them to the Scientific Institute for treatment. After watching them disappear behind the curtains, she walked directly to the building next door to register as a volunteer. We listened, respectful of her suffering but calloused by our own—except Richards, whose kind heart and soft demeanor seem to be impenetrable against the horrors of our existence. He moved to comfort her immediately.

Richards has been here the longest, since he was almost as young as I am now. He traveled up north with his pregnant wife and no explanation for how something so horrible could happen in the city. Every time I feel like I can't keep it up, I think of the volunteers. Simons has been here for four years, and Richards for nearly twenty. If they can keep going, so can I. I think of how much worse they have it. A near miss for a scientist is almost always a fatality for a volunteer team.

I reach up onto the screen and press my finger on the flashing word.

Confirm.

I will take over hive studies. Amos isn't here to keep me from it. I've made it to the Northern Laboratories, and yet I've learned nothing. It's time to do something about all the deaths. I need to search for the answers that no one wants me to find. Soon, I will have access to every facet of the research up here in the Northern Laboratories. I'll leave infection studies behind—leave Amos behind.

Let someone else find the cure. I'll gladly participate in their studies, but I can't promise another second of my time to someone else's plan. *Let Shelby pine for a cure.* Whatever is happening in the laboratories has to be related to the hive mind. And it's not just up here—it's outside the cities too.

It's time to dedicate my research to understanding how the patients are able to work together as I've seen them do before. I've never seen it up here because I've never worked with the hive, but that all changes now. The screen flickers as my current research slips away into the archive database and Smith's work—my work—uploads into my workstation.

A message appears at the bottom of my screen, making my breath catch in the back of my throat. I almost expect it to be from Amos, as if she were sitting at her own workstation at the Institute, watching me and waiting for this very moment. I shake my head and tell myself that such thoughts are just paranoid nonsense. Amos won't know before my peers, and it's too late to receive communication from another scientist. In the wake of my initial panic, I know that the message is from Jorey. He's the only one who reaches out in the dark.

Phase of the moon tonight?

I smile, eager to tell him about my decision, and reply.

New moon. See you in a few.

"TIMED KILL EXPERIMENT 8020: subcategory gasses. Trail 24," Shelby speaks into the microphone as we set up the recorder.

The kill lab floor is clear of all but the two of us. The switch in my schedule occurred almost immediately following the change to my specialty. First thing the following morning, the schedule read that I would be working on the kill floors with Orman and Hersch. After breakfast, the schedule changed again, and I was assigned to a cure project directed by Shelby. Finally, at the close of laboratory hours, things landed the way they've played out these last weeks— Shelby leading the experiment with me as her secondary recorder and Orman as our third. Working near Orman makes me uncomfortable. He's always watching me with the same strange expression, and it's been worse since the accident. There's a knowing quality to his looks that's difficult to ignore.

To make matters worse, for some reason my natural response to this restless nervousness manifests as contrarian outbursts. If it weren't for Shelby's stern countenance and watchful eye, I'm not certain what the outcome of this week might be. Likely another horrible accident. I can hear Orman's haughty, uncaring voice as he tells of the tragic events to everyone else who was working in the cure area across the facility, in another corridor, evaluating the disease under a microscope, growing cultures and testing pharmaceuticals at the time of the incident.

I picture the faces of the other scientists as they take in the story, knowing full well that it was unavoidable. Something is far more likely to go wrong in the kill labs than in the cure labs, after all. Or maybe they'll watch it happen on the lab's closed-circuit cameras as the whole gruesome scene plays out for them in high definition. I wonder if anyone watched what happened to Miller before the recordings disappeared. The live stream can't be interrupted. I'm lucky for this. If it weren't for the live feed, Jorey and Carmen wouldn't have been so quick to pull me from the lab the day Miller died.

Shaking my head, I pull myself away from the gruesome thoughts of my own demise and return to my checks. I spot Orman walking down the corridors on the cameras. His imperious swagger and cocksure demeanor are nearly as unmistakable as his well-groomed silver-laced hair. Depressing the speaker button, I address him as he walks up to the gate. "Orman, have you been screened in the last twenty-four hours?"

Shelby gives me a sharp look of warning, and I wince. I'm overstepping my position again. Orman's likely to take this attack on his authority personally. Once again, I've over-corrected myself right into a confrontation.

Orman holds up his digital clearance card to show the time stamp since his last visit to the screening room ticking down at 23:53:46. "Mason, you're such a stickler for the rules. Let me in and let's get down to business."

"Cut the attitude, Orman, or I'll put you with the volunteers," Shelby cuts in, replacing my finger on the depressed speaker button with her own. She's taking the spotlight off of me by taking ownership of my actions. Being the most senior scientist in the labs, not even Orman will push very far with Shelby despite his rumored appointment within the DDC.

There's a quick rush of hot air as the gate slides open and the door locks release. Orman turns the knob and walks in. "Sorry I'm late, I let my screen card get a little too close to expiration. I just couldn't pull myself away from this week's experimental records."

His eyes settle on me in that way that unnerves me, and I tell myself it's just the guilt over what happened to Smith.

"I don't want to hear your excuses. We've got six patients to end today, and I'd rather just get it done." Shelby snaps his statement from where it hangs in the air.

"I'm thrilled you're in such high spirits today, Shelby. This must mean you designed the experiment," Orman comments as he deftly punches commands into the database. He looks over at me and winks. It's the first time he's specifically acknowledged me, and it's strange.

I almost want to smirk back at him because he's right. Shelby's always in a particularly foul mood when we're about to execute one of her kill experiment designs. Instead of acknowledging the strange wink, I keep my eyes forward and focus on my task, listening to the thing inside of me that seems to know better than to engage with Rick Orman.

"We're online, and the pathway is lit. Should I signal for the patient?" I glance toward Shelby for her cue, and she offers me a curt nod.

"Orman, we're waiting for your signal, so if you could stop picking your teeth long enough to man the pulsar gun, we can get this thing moving." Shelby shoots Orman a disdainful look as he removes his finger from his mouth and mounts the behemoth weapon.

"It's not like sitting atop the world's most precise nuclear laser gun with my sights set on the near-dead is a difficult job," Orman says lazily. No matter how serious the endeavor, he never seems worried for his own safety. I can't decide if it's neurotic audacity or something more sadistic, but I know that I'm not the only one disquieted by his cavalier attitude. I've heard the same comments from volunteers. Where the rest of us are weary, Orman is callous. He's the best shot of us all, and I'm certain he enjoys it. "Locked in and ready to destroy."

"That's more like it," Shelby says. "And I prefer that you don't refer to the patients by the colloquial term 'near-dead.'" She makes another entry in her database and addresses me, "Signal for the patient."

The speakers crackle as my voice rings through to the holding room. "We're online, and the transportation pathway is hot. Proceed with the patient."

A series of buzzes and clicks resonates down the corridor opposite the one where scientists enter. We observe the procession on the cameras.

In about two minutes, we can see the group in front of us just as clearly as on camera. Five volunteers surround one patient. It's Simons' team. I recognize them easily, including the woman Simons only just chose. Her hands shake as she tightens her grip on the lashing pole, holding the patient's right arm firmly behind its back. The rest of the volunteers glance at her uneasily as the patient squirms and twitches under the restraints.

The group leads the patient into position. Their motion is like a fine dance they've rehearsed so many times. They extend their arms so that they are separated by the full five-foot length of their lashing poles in a starfish configuration. A sixth volunteer approaches from the hall with a ladder and places it behind Simons, at the head of the starfish and directly behind the patient, then steps across the threshold.

Simons climbs the ladder so that he's standing on the top rung. Just a foot above the ladder is a floating walkway. He latches his lashing pole onto the locks built for this purpose. Once the lashing pole is secured in place, he pulls himself up onto the walkway and depresses the speaker button. "Lashing secured—verification requested."

I zoom in and confirm that both locks are engaged. "Lashing confirmed, signal volunteers to retreat."

Simons gives the signal.

Richards grabs the ladder and backs away. In unison, the four volunteers unravel their lashing poles from the bundled patient, and the thrashing the volunteers were controlling becomes evident. They back carefully away and stand on the opposite side of the glowing blue line on the floor. After Shelby and I verify their positions in the room, the laser cage is engaged. With a near-silent hum of light, the visible blue barrier fills the space where the room is divided by the line.

"Simons, you're clear to release the patient." I signal over the speakers.

Simons carefully unlatches his lashing pole with a strong and calm circular movement. With his fingers depressed on the magnetic release, the wires repel one another, and the patient comes out of its package like a nightmarish gift.

Free now, the patient only stands still for a moment before crouching down on its withered haunches and looking overhead with dead, white eyes. Without seeing, it zeros in on Simons and leaps straight into the air. It misses the floating walkway, which was constructed to be out of reach from even the strongest patients. When it lands on the ground, it notices movement on the other side of the cage and lunches forward. Richards jerks back, startled by the lunge, and trips against the ladder. The action causes him to fall against the back wall where the top of the ladder hits the control panel.

Inside the laser enclosure, the floating walkway that suspends Simons over the patient shudders before one end dips down, released from the ceiling.

"Here we go!" Orman says under his breath. Maybe I only imagine the hint of a smile crossing his face.

"Hold your fire," Shelby hisses at him. Perhaps she saw it too.

Simons is halfway across the walkway, heading toward the upper exit. Before the patient manages to hoist itself up, Simons launches himself off the walkway, and Shelby engages the top laser barrier. When the patient reaches upward again, it contacts the laser barrier and shrieks as flesh melts away from bone.

It collapses on the ground and thrashes about before regaining its feet. The entire left side of its face is melted and dripping like a bad paint job. It shrieks again from instinctive frustration before poising for another strike, tearing the rag of former clothing from its chest.

"That was close," Orman breathes.

"Alright, let's get this over with," Shelby says, "before something else goes wrong."

While the patient shrieks and thrashes around in the laser cage, the sandblasters begin their work, shooting a fine stream of silica particles into the molten-light pathway. In moments, the lasers dim out, and a thick, transparent glass box remains, encasing the patient. The pressure test comes back positive, confirming the seal.

"We're ready to go," I signal Shelby.

"Begin the nitrogen purge," Shelby says. "Recording time to death in five… four… three… two… one…"

I depress the purge button and flip the nitrogen lever. The hiss of the gas is muffled through the thick layer of glass as it swirls into the cage and flushes out the oxygen. The patient continues its blind rampage without registering the change in the air. Its breathing pattern remains steady at first.

"100 percent purge reached in 2:32," Shelby records into the log. Reading the oxygen sensor, she adds, "Respiration steady, oxygen output is 10 percent below human output."

We watch silently as the patient continues thrashing. The exposed sunken chest heaves in and out with a quickening urgency, stretching tight grey flesh, but there is no cognitive response. It thrashes again toward the walkway and pounds its melted flesh against the glass in a fixated frustration, smearing a thick, greyish blood on the walls.

"Does anyone else get tired of this cruel and unusual treatment of patients?" Orman inquires sarcastically. "Wouldn't it be kinder to just put them out of their misery with a quick laser blast?"

"Orman, you know the patients don't realize they're suffering. Their central nervous system is the first to detach completely from the brain upon neurological development. But if you want to go give him a reassuring hug, be my guest." I sigh deeply, forgetting not to engage.

"The DDC requested respiratory data, and we are obliged to provide it. Now quiet, you two, we have full response." Shelby draws our attention back to the patient.

The patient is now the perfect picture of someone suffocating to death without realizing. Its respiration rate has doubled from the initial purge and its breath is shallowing. The oxygen respiration censor reads *not detected,* and the room falls silent again. Several minutes pass like several hours before the patient slumps against the glass and slides to rest on the floor. Shelby stops the death count.

"Death at 24 minutes and 41 seconds. Patient remained fully unaware throughout the experiment. End experiment trial 24." She stops the recorder and turns toward me. "Take Simons to quarantine."

CHAPTER
THIRTY-NINE

THE DINNER HALL echoes with the noise of hundreds of overlapping voices. The kitchen faces the exterior wall, where the only window in the building lets in light in the summer. The floor is concrete, and the ceiling is tile, causing the multitude of conversations to blend together into a cacophony of life. From the entrance of the hall, it's impossible to distinguish who is saying what.

As I walk down the mess line, grabbing a hunk of cornbread and some over-seasoned chili beans, I catch a few familiar voices—Orman's droning on about his next experiment to Fisher, Hersch and a few of the weapon-hungry volunteers sitting nearby. "What it really comes down to is the efficiency of a laser's ability to transfer heat and gamma radiation into the target. How do we improve that? Conductivity, of course!"

I act like I don't see the group and shuffle discretely to the other end of the hall, nearer the window. It's mid spring, so we've missed the precious hours of sunlight that may have shown through the window earlier in the day. Instead, we're treated to another spring ice storm. The ice falls just as often as the snow up here, only with more fury, as though nature is hoping to penetrate our souls and extinguish our wills for good.

I've lost myself staring into the storm, both forlorn and sympathetic, when a familiar voice brings me back to the symphony of life. "Am I going to be able to show my face in the presence of Simons any time soon?"

"Richards." I look over at the slight man with thinning brown hair and smile.

"I can't believe I did that. I'm usually so much more levelheaded, and Simons knows it. Is he all right?" Richards is only picking at his food, thoroughly distraught.

"I'm sure he'll be fine. He cut his leg when he jumped, but his risk of contamination is low. The patient had regular strain ZCC, no record of dormant contamination. We'll have him tested and cleared from quarantine by the end of the week," I reassure Richards as I take my seat next to him.

"Does it happen often?" the new volunteer woman speaks up.

"Does what happen often?" The woman's eyes are wide with a fear that almost masks the deep shadows that settled before she made the journey. Losing your whole family is hard; traveling along with their frozen bodies to volunteer in a facility that kills patients with the same disease infecting them is harder—even if there are supposedly other departments working on a cure.

"Mistakes… quarantine… do people—volunteers—get infected often?" She finds her voice and finally meets my eyes. Hers are bright green underneath her fiery red curls. Everything about her is small except the look of steely determination. A mother separated from her children.

"It happens." I keep my gaze on her face. I'm cold now, but I never became heartless. I live in the scientist quarters, but my heart belongs amongst the volunteers. "You're less safe here than you were back in the cities, but I'm certain you knew that."

She glances away to blink back emotion, then meets my gaze again. "I know, it's just different—being here, seeing them every day and having to get so close… and *catching* them…" Her face scrunches with disdain.

"You're a natural," Jorey chimes in. "I've never seen someone work so efficiently with a lashing pole. It's like she was born with one in her hands."

"She's very good," Richards confirms, testing his standing with the team to see if all is forgiven.

"Better than you ever were," Carmen laughs. Her large body vibrates with the sound. A shadow crosses her face and makes her stop laughing. Simons is in quarantine. Richards might be—at least in part—to blame. She glances at him, and it looks like a glare. He shrinks in his seat, playing conspicuously with his chili.

"So you have a reputation after only a week in action?" I inquire, hoping to change the subject from Richards' error.

She blushes, but I catch the subtle upturn at the corner of her mouth before she can conceal it. Jorey smiles, interpreting her modesty as acceptance of his observation. Carmen grunts as she returns to her chili, and Richards keeps his head low.

"I'm Frances," the woman says, volunteering her hand.

"Mason." I nod at her gesture but don't accept her hand. Frances returns her hand to her side shyly and focuses on her plate.

Just as a new silence overcomes our group and we're lulled into the general hum of the dining room, an implacable voice interrupts from behind me, sending icy fingers of adrenaline down my spine. "Mason, I hope to see you on the firing range during simulation training hours tonight?" Orman's fishing inquisition is unmistakable.

"I'm scheduled for endurance and agility tonight," I retort without looking up.

"Shame," Orman condescends, "It's been far too long since you were in one of my training groups, and I'm giving a great lesson on targeting tonight."

"I'm certain I'll survive without your instruction, Rick. I'm one of the best shots up here." I match Orman's belittling tone by referring to him by his first name in front of the volunteers.

"There's no harm in improving." I sense his eyes burning into the back of my head. "I'll have to check the records and see why it's been so long since you exercised on the firing range."

I keep my eyes forward and my mouth shut as I listen for Orman's steps to be drowned out by the hum of the dining hall. Somewhere inside my head, I hear Shelby scolding me for my brazenness. I've been bribing the schedule master to get out of weapons exercise, content that no one noticed. Of course Orman would notice. He always seems to be watching me a little too closely.

"You got endurance and agility? I do too." Jorey smiles. His whole frame seems to lighten up—which is saying something with Jorey. "I bet anything I'll whip your butt!"

I smile back at him. "You're on."

CHAPTER
FORTY

I WALK with the group toward training, lost once again in their conversations.

"Really, the trick in weapons training is to mind your own business and avoid Orman. When he notices you, just act like his subordinate and let him best the target. He's good at what he does, and he'll often give good advice... he's just an arrogant prick," Carmen advises Frances as they join the group. "Anyone else have weapons?"

"I've got redlines tonight," Richards says, making a sour face. "Going to be tough without Simons."

"What's the purpose of all this training?" Frances asks, raising an eyebrow at Richards' statement.

Carmen shrugs. "Everyone has their own theory about it. I think it's research. We're some sort of test subjects for a program they're not telling anyone about."

"I think it's military training. We're a secret army preparing for an unknown threat," Jorey says, then looking over at me, he adds, "Mason thinks so, too."

"It's best not to get too speculative out in the open," I say as we turn toward the training room. Carmen looks away from me, and Jorey winces.

At the entrance to the simulation room, we part ways and join our training groups. Along with Jorey, I notice Walker, Dupont, and a few other scientists reporting to endurance training, but the majority of our group is volunteers. Glancing at their feet, I also notice that many in the group are newer arrivals. Every scientist is given highly efficient synthetic foot protection, but volunteers are only given sets as they become available—often recycled from former volunteers.

Today's group instructor is Twining, a tall, thin scientist in his second decade in the Laboratories. Twining's specialty is cell function and neuro-communication. In the cure labs, he designs experiments to investigate the differences between cell function, communication and reproduction in patients versus uninfected individuals. His specific knowledge makes him exceptionally skilled in designing endurance training. He's taken over for the last program director, who was unable to come up with an explanation for Smith's death.

"Tonight, we're going to be simulating urban escape," Twining explains.

A few of the volunteers cackle amongst themselves as Twining describes the course activity. He clears his throat nervously, failing to pull the group into focus. I suspect there are always eyes on his performance. He calls out for attention, silencing the extraneous chatter. In the crowd of jovial participants, I observe a new face. This guy is younger and seems more at ease than new volunteers usually are. He's tall and lean, and his hair is atypically long. There's something easy about him that makes me wonder what he's doing here. None of the typical sadness and despair are apparent, and his easy smile and hearty laugh seem to attract the other volunteers.

Before I've taken in the new volunteer completely, we're instructed to put on our helmets for the countdown. Out of the dark nothingness, there's a flurry of sound and then sight. I glance at the other participants and note that we're wearing city clothes. Jorey takes his mark next to me on the far edge of the track. Two people over from us, I spot the new guy stretching lazily. When the buzzer sounds, we all take off with a jolt, pressing forward with a relaxed determination.

We're on a deserted street in a large city where the twilight sky and crisp air are suddenly so real that it sends a chill through me. I hear Jorey breathing steadily beside me and the measured footsteps of others nearby. For a big city, it's eerily calm. Though a breeze wafts through the buildings, the air is stale and dead—this is an infected city. I take new stock in the silence, listening carefully for warning signs of near-dead—*patients*—wandering the streets.

"How's this for a fresh new scene?" Jorey breathes as he trots along next to me.

"I fail to see the point of urban training," I reply. "It's not like any of us will ever see a city again!"

"That we know." Jorey laughs, then immediately falls silent. "You hear that?"

I jerk my head to the left and search the alleys as we pass them. There's a subtle rustle beneath the silence that makes certain the presence of infected within the simulated city.

"Time to shut up," I whisper. Since Miller's death, even in a simulation, the sensation of being near an outbreak without protection rattles me. Measuring my pace against the other participants, I relax my gait and slow until I'm near the back of the pack without being dead last. It's difficult to judge when they'll strike in a simulation, as it is impossible with today's technology to program the simulation to actually *smell* us. Though there is always a group of engineers working steadily at the world's biggest problems…

"It's show time!" the new volunteer shouts out a few paces in front of me.

Before dismissing his remark as horseplay, I glance over my shoulder. He's not joking—from two of the alleyways the group just passed, they begin to emerge. I refrain from slowing long enough to look back again. I shake out my hands and relax my shoulders. It's time to think. We're approaching an intersection, and I need to decide if I want to stay with the main group or branch off on my own.

Jorey nudges me. "Let's break away from the group here and make a run for the city limits!"

I nod and run the tangent, preparing to turn away from the group, running shoulder to shoulder with Jorey. As we come up on the intersection, our plan is halted by the new guy. "What are you doing? You don't stand a chance if you break away from the group. This is a *city!*"

I shake my head, ignoring this man's obvious inexperience. I follow

Jorey, banking left and heading down a side street as the sun sets deeper. It's quiet again. I look back at the group as they press forward on their original pathway, pursued by a massive group of infected. Turning my head back to Jorey, I smile with smug satisfaction. We move forward easily on this side street, feeling relieved and a little clever.

The streetlights flicker on in the fading light—only half are still working. As we move forward toward the eastern edge of the city, my heart sinks. Just a few hundred meters ahead of us, the street comes to a dead end. An eight-meter-high brick wall blocks the path forward between two skyscrapers. The only way out is to return back the way we came or try one of the alleyways, which could easily be programmed to manifest trouble. We stop, facing the brick obstruction.

"Let's scale it," I say breathlessly.

"No time." Jorey gestures to one of the side alleyways. The unmistakable sound of progressing near-dead is getting louder. Their uneven footsteps bring urgency to every second we fail to act.

"Hurry, up here," I scream at Jorey. There's no point to discretion anymore. The street's now filled with infected, some with symptoms so advanced they're without all of their limbs and large portions of their flesh, others nearly intact and moving far too quickly.

Without further communication, we both scale the fire escape of the nearest building. Jorey and I match each other's climb nearly step by step as the entire structure rattles unsteadily. The metal groans as we climb past the first rise. I look below to see our pursuers gather at the bottom of the fire escape, some of them already grasping at the base of the ladder.

"It's not going to hold," Jorey gasps as we continue our desperate climb.

"No kidding," I reply, passing the third flight and frantically looking for another plan.

The structure shudders from the added weight of the climbing creatures.

As my heart pounds in my chest and the ringing in my ears starts, I notice an open window on the fourth flight, curtains fluttering in the night breeze. "There!"

He nods. We make it to the fourth-floor landing as the metal moans under the strain of too much weight. Shrieks fill the air with as much terror as the sensation of the failing fire escape. I rush up to the window at the same time as Jorey. "Go, go!" he yells. I don't hesitate to thrust myself through the window.

As I jump, the structure gives way behind me. I hit the carpeted floor with a hard thud. The impact resonates in my head and makes my joints ache. Standing up as abruptly as I fell, I turn back to the window. The dread of failing to see Jorey consumes me. Any memory of this being a simulation is gone now.

"Mason, help me!" Jorey's voice is right outside the window, and I see his fingers grasping the windowsill.

"Jorey!" I grab his wrists and brace myself so that he can pull himself through the window, which he does with ease once he has my support.

"That's why I let you through first," Jorey gasps. "You've always had faster recoveries. I would've been flat on my face." He chuckles out a heavy breath.

"We're not in the clear," I say. There's a rustling in a nearby room. The building is rancid with the stench of rotting flesh. As quietly as possible, we make our way to the door on the opposite end of the room. I breathe out slowly as I turn the doorknob. The door presses back on me as if it's weighted down. I step to the side, and the door swings open. A bloodied torso flops into the room as if it had been propped against the door. The shirt is torn and still wet with blood and fluids, but the stench makes it clear it's been here for some time.

Entrails stretch across the hall to the right. I gesture opposite the bloody trail. We take off down the hallway in an easy gait. "We need to find a stairway," I whisper.

"Over here." Jorey points to an emergency exit at the far corner.

I press against the door latch, and nothing happens. "It's jammed!"

Jorey tests my hypothesis, confirming it vehemently. "Together. One... two... three!" We press against the door with all our might, and it bursts open with a loud clank. The sound alerts the rustling creatures down the hall. Without hesitation, we jump into the stairwell and force the door closed again behind us.

"Up or down?" I ask.

"Down, we'll be trapped on the roof," Jorey replies.

We begin to jog down, our footsteps echoing through the abandoned stairwell. Just as we turn the last corner before the bottom floor, we hear a low, gurgling groan. I stop to look over the ledge. A dozen bodies make their way up from the bottom of the stairwell.

"Up!" I yell, spinning in my tracks and retracing my steps. We climb until we're back on the fourth floor. There's a loud pounding on the jammed door. The only place to go now is the rooftop. *From there…*

"We're screwed," Jorey whispers as we round the bend in the stairs on the eighteenth floor.

"Just keep going," I encourage, suppressing the growing terror. My legs are burning from exertion. I've never climbed stairs so quickly in my life. Just when I think I can't stand the burn any longer, we make it to the rooftop. We burst through the door, relieved.

"We've got to block the door," I say the moment I can speak again.

Jorey nods, and we scan the rooftop for something useful. He finds a board as thick as his hand and as tall as him and makes quick work of securing the door. With no time to spare, we succeed. The door groans under the force of the beasts on the other side. We're trapped on the roof.

"We don't have much time," Jorey says.

I look around. The building to the east of us is set just against the city wall. The town tapers off into a forested area on the other side. We're only one building away from escape. I stand near the edge of the roof, staring at our exit.

"We've got to jump," I say.

"No way. We'll never make it," Jorey protests. The door groans under the pressure of the near-dead's eager pursuit. "On the other hand…" Jorey smiles innocently.

We align ourselves at the opposite end of the rooftop. The splintering of the board makes jumping seem slightly less crazy than staying on the roof. To my knowledge, no one has ever actually been attacked in a simulation. I don't want to know what that would be like. Jorey gives me one last uncertain look before we set off. In my mind, I count off like we used to when we were kids. *Mark, set, go!* We run with all of our might toward the next building. With deft certainty, our feet hit the ledge, and we launch ourselves into the air, flailing in free fall and trying to will ourselves to the next rooftop.

I can see in an instant that we're not going to make it. I remind myself that the safety device should catch us. *Should.* Maybe someone has decided it's time for me to have an accident and Jorey will be an inconsequential casualty. He's just a volunteer, after all.

In one last desperate attempt, I throw my arms over my head and reach for the ledge. My fingers barely brush the top before sliding down the side of the wall. I don't even feel the impact of my body against the concrete. Jorey is hanging onto the edge of the roof, his legs dangling freely as he kicks the wall for a grip. I realize I'm not falling. I look up to see a pair of hands wrapped tightly around my wrist. I regain my senses and throw my other arm high into the air, where another set of hands grabs hold and pulls me to safety.

"You've got to be crazy! Why on earth did you separate? And who the hell thinks they can jump from rooftop to rooftop?" It's the new guy, and he's smiling as he looks me over.

I swallow my pride. "Thanks, I thought I would make it." I look back and see the previous rooftop swarming with infected.

The new guy shakes his head, his stupid long hair swishing back and forth. "You are some kind of crazy. I'd never do something that stupid, and I'm about as stupid as you get." He's still smiling.

I'm back on my feet, shaking out the shock of my near miss. "Let's get out of here." The whole group is watching me now. Jorey is making his way back onto his feet, slow to recover as usual.

We make our way down the fire escape and toward the woods on the other side of the brick wall. Back on the ground, I'm running easily again, only slightly achy from my impact. I'm not running beside Jorey any longer; a group of volunteers has him flanked and is pulling up the rear. The new guy jogs easily alongside me.

"That took crazy guts. I'm impressed." He smiles at me, breathing easily.

"I didn't do it to impress you," I say, noting the sting of my bruised ego. A low beeping tone alerts us to the simulation's end. The screen flickers green, then black, as the ground shifts below us and the track comes to a stop.

The new guy stops running right beside me. He pulls off his virtual mask to reveal that he's still smiling. "I can tell I like you already. My name's Eli Cain." He thrusts his hand at me.

"Mason." I take his hand. Propriety or not, this man saved my life —virtually, at least, which means he'd likely do it in real life, too. As much as the guy's long hair and relentless smile annoy me, I kind of like him, too.

CHAPTER
FORTY-ONE

ANOTHER SLEEPLESS NIGHT. This time, instead of persistent thoughts about the hive, my mind is stuck on Simons. My workstation display clicks over to 2:23 am, promising me that additional time laying prone and waiting for sleep would be futile. Sometimes I suspect that I have more sleepless nights than not, and that this somehow fuels my drive rather than breaking me down.

I consider my options. I could get up and work on my new experiment design for my first hive investigation, which would be the most responsible thing for me to do. I could see what information we have in our archives about the new guy, Eli Cain... Something about him seems off. I could take a trip down to quarantine and see if Simons is likewise plagued with sleeplessness... or I could sit here and contemplate the weather. The last thought gives me my answer.

As I have so many times before, I let myself wander through darkened corridors toward the dining hall. At this hour, it's completely empty, so my footsteps echo across the hard floors. I position myself directly in front of the window and listen to the groan of the building joints as the wind pounds and thunders against the structure. Staring through the window is a lot like staring at a black screen. Every now and then, the shudder of a fresh icy blast blurs the blackness, but otherwise it's as dark outside as it is inside. I let myself be comforted by the angry sounds of the spring storm and lose myself in thought.

"What sort of moon tonight?" Jorey's voice doesn't surprise me. He frequents the window nearly as often as I do.

"Third quarter, waning."

The bench shifts and creaks lightly as he takes his seat next to me. "I don't see it."

His voice is lighthearted, and I note that he's half staring out the blank window and half staring at me, waiting for my reaction.

"Me neither." I suppress a smile.

"What's got you up?"

"Simons," I sigh, still gazing at the nothing outside.

Jorey nods, and for a moment, we sit in silence, comforted by each other's presence. I don't want to talk about Simons. I have some confidence that Jorey knows this.

"Frances caught Orman's attention in weapons training tonight," Jorey offers.

I raise my eyebrow and glance over at his shadowed figure. He's also looking outside, but his body is angled toward me. "In a good way, or is she a target now?"

"She got top score and managed to bat her eyelashes the whole time." It comes out a half laugh. Jorey imitates a cannon gun pulled up to sight and swishes his nonexistent hair over his shoulder. He pulls the imaginary trigger and flutters his eyes, flashing a dashing smile at me that's supposed to be flirtatious.

I can't keep myself from giggling. I put my hand up to stifle it, but it echoes in the empty room, making Jorey's smile broader. "Good for her. She's got some talent. And the ability to follow instruction."

"She's a fast learner for sure. I've never seen someone pick up the job quite as fast," Jorey agrees.

"It's no wonder Simons picked her from the crowd," I observe, before immediately feeling a twinge of regret at mentioning his name.

"He's no fool..." Jorey trails off.

"What do you think of that new guy?"

"Hmmm." The sound echoes deep in his throat, and I can almost feel the vibration of his contemplation through the bench. "He's a bit... different..."

"For sure."

"He's got quite a smile," Jorey offers in a mixture of admiration and derision.

"I didn't think volunteers had anything to smile about in their first week here. It just seems strange."

I lose myself in thought again, this time reflecting on the simulation. The easy way that Cain pulled me up onto the rooftop and the casual manner with which he addressed me. Pretty brazen for a new guy. I think that I *do* like him, or at least I'm fascinated by him.

"Do you think he's attractive?" Jorey asks.

"What?" His question shocks me. Reactively, I smack his arm, then immediately wonder why he generated that particular response.

"Sorry. I was just making conversation," Jorey says innocently, rubbing his arm as if I've seriously hurt him.

I try to shrug it off and smile into the darkness. "Yeah, I know. He's just..." I search for words to describe my fixation.

"He's tall, strong, and confident," Jorey tries, then his voice turns whimsical. "Flowing locks of golden hair..." He wiggles his fingers on either side of his head for effect.

"Jorey! I didn't know you felt that way," I tease. My face squishes up in a ridiculous grin in the way it always seems to when it's just me and Jorey.

"Nobody said I did. I was trying to see if you felt that way."

My face returns to its regular shape and immediately feels hot.

"About a volunteer?"

"Yeah... I guess that's ridiculous." His voice softens, and he brushes the back of his neck absently.

"No time for that kind of thing."

"Still busy with hive experiment design?"

We change conversation topics as seamlessly as the wind changes direction.

"I'm almost done, then I'll be on review boards for the rest of the year. I could use the break for sure. It's been difficult to put together an entire experiment in just a few weeks."

"Will our team be on it?"

"I haven't decided yet." I don't want them to work on my experiment. It's too dangerous to risk the only people I have left to care about, but they're the best team in the Northern Laboratories, so it wouldn't make sense to select anyone else.

"Is that a good thing or a bad thing?" Jorey knows there's no such thing as a good thing in the kill labs.

"Every day without a death is about as good as it gets up here. You know that by now, right?"

"Today... didn't feel like a good day."

"It could've been so much worse," I offer.

"We have such a good system."

"You *do* have good systems. To other groups, this would have felt like a success."

"If it weren't for Simons, I wouldn't be alive."

"I know what you mean..." My voice trails off.

We're quiet for a long time. The window shudders in the storm. I wonder what that extent of cold feels like. I don't think that even our specialized materials and equipment would protect us from it. Still, for whatever reason, I want to *feel* it.

"It's late." Jorey interrupts the long silence.

"If we were far enough south, I might suggest watching the sun rise."

"Man, I miss that."

"The sun rising in the morning or being able to watch it happen?"

"Both."

"Yeah," I agree.

"Sun or moon?"

"Too difficult to choose." I know I'm not much for conversation tonight. Jorey keeps looking at me expectantly. I smile, then shrug. A yawn creeps up from deep inside.

"You plan to sleep at all tonight?" He looks tired. I wonder how many nights he spends at this window.

"I might just head in and finish my design." I stand from the bench and stretch, rotating my tender shoulders in and out as the night's blunder sets into my joints.

"I don't know how you do it," Jorey wonders.

"Me neither."

He squeezes my wrist. I grab his hand in return. There's comfort in the contact. We walk back toward our rooms together.

FORTY-TWO

I STUDY my reflection in the mirror, noting the deep-set bags under my eyes that make me look older and more tired than I actually am. There's a large and darkening bruise on my shoulder where I made direct impact with the wall during training. I roll my shoulder gently forward and then reverse—no real damage, just inflamed tissue and residual soreness. Tossing the towel at the mirror, I leave the bathroom to finish getting ready. If I hurry, I can stop to visit Simons on my way to the kill labs.

Our lab uniforms are tightly fitted, chemical- and tear-resistant, single-piece black suits. I stretch the uniform over each leg and pull it up high enough to slide my arms in, wincing as I contort myself to fit, thinking that things always feel more swollen than they really are in tight clothing.

Fastening the zipper at the neck, I turn the lip inward and tuck it into the uniform so that everything is secured. I check for loose pieces before strapping on my gloves and the wrist communicator. Our gloves are highly sensitive to touch, functioning on the electrochemical energy generated from direct contact with our skin. The receiver and communicator isn't so much a unit as a biological wiring system that functions symbiotically with the body's natural movement. Our bodies provide the energy to run the devices, and an intricate distribution of satellite and electromagnetic waves transfers and communicates the information. Using the gloves, we can run the entire laboratories—provided we have a screen in order to see what we're doing.

In most rooms in the Northern Laboratories, thin screens are built into the walls. The screens are built to be responsive to the touch of any gloved hand. Only the screens in our personal quarters work from the touch of our bare hands. The communicator from a single glove provides the power to a screen, but in the Laboratories, due to the number of scientists gloved at any instant, all of the screens can be simultaneously and continuously run.

Once my gloves are fastened, I do a quick touch test on my control screen at my private workstation and then open my experiment—my first investigation into the hive. Hive-mind experiments are complicated and dangerous. I knew this even before Amos swiped the specialty away from me at the Institute. Something could go wrong, and the whole team of scientists and volunteers would end up dead. But it's more than that. If I'm not careful, no one will walk away from the kill floor.

Keeping this in mind, I've tried to keep things low risk. My first design is a continuation of where Smith left off. I've only just built in the beginnings of my suspicions. Smith was investigating hive communication. Before his untimely demise, he'd already searched the entire gamut of possibilities for how the hive works. He investigated the possibility of pheromone-based communication, such as one would find in ant and bee colonies. He spent the first part of the year developing and executing fruitless experiments before claiming this hypothesis invalid. He then went through the psychology and sociology of evolutionary behavior, searching for clues for the group-think only to find no connection to the hive communication.

It's strange to read about how long he spent on each dead end before opening up another, seemingly fruitless avenue of investigation. Smith was smart, but his experimental designs read as simple and poorly thought out. From my perspective, the only option for hive-communication is one that could be created or manipulated by humans. It's a bold hypothesis, but one that's been carefully measured and constructed to exist within the logical pathway of research and aligned with government goals. It's a direct and natural conclusion based upon his documentation.

I scan through my proposal. I'm about to submit an experiment that measures electromagnetic wave frequencies for variability. I've chosen twelve key frequencies to measure based on a derivative algorithm I designed for my old research. Communication through measurable frequencies is, after all, one of the primary things that separates humans from other species.

I hope to reduce the noise and possibly, by measuring specific frequencies, increase the signal of any communication so that I can generate some hard data to supports my hypothesis. Then the real work can begin. I finish skimming the experiment. Almost everything is in order. The experiment will be ready for submission after another round of checks, then I'll be heading the project some six months from now.

I check the clock and see that I've got just enough time to refresh screening and pop in to check on Simons before I'm due in the kill labs for Orman's experiment. Not wanting to waste more time, I shut down my workstation, tuck my hair in my collar and head out. I want some answers, and I know that Simons is the only person that can get them for me.

I hurry down the halls and note that they're relatively quiet this morning. A few volunteers emerge from screening and travel in the opposite direction, toward the cure labs. The excess of noise down the hall confirms that the cafeteria is still full for breakfast. I do a quick mental check to make certain that I'm not skipping too many dining hours and decide I'm fine. My heart thuds its telltale beat as I consider all the ways I'm forgetting to blend in.

I scan my badge at intake and wait for the rush of the doors. Several cameras follow my movement toward the database. I key in the room code for Simons and document my reason for visiting. The hall door opens, and I follow the complicated maze of low-risk quarantine until I reach the window of Simons' unit. A flashing light in his room indicates my approach, but instead of greeting me at the window, I catch him running on the treadmill as if he didn't have a care.

I watch him pounding rhythmically on the stationary platform, his muscles moving easily for such a quick clip. He goes on like this for another couple of minutes, and I figure he's made it perfectly clear that he doesn't want to see me.

Real mature, Simons.

We argued about my switch to hive studies on the way to quarantine. He told me I should've listened to Amos and let it rest. I told him it wasn't his place to make those sorts of decisions, then slammed the door on him, once again the child I can't seem to leave behind.

I turn to leave, and Simons calls out, "Where are you off to? Are you too busy to wait for me to finish my workout?"

I smile, relieved that he's talking to me. "You can't say hi?"

"I've got a record to beat. What did you say yours was? 5:02?" The treadmill slows, and Simons steps off, wiping his face with a towel.

"You beat it?" I raise my eyebrow at him through the glass.

"5:43," he says, running the towel over his bald head and across the back of his neck.

"Ouch. Not even close." I can't help myself.

He shrugs. "Next time."

"How are you holding up?" I ask.

"Two more days," he replies. "How are things on the outside?"

"I wouldn't know," I quip.

We both laugh. The humor cuts the tension so that I'm comfortable enough to say, "I'm sorry about running out on you."

"No mind, Mason," he assures me. "We're all working under a lot of pressure here, and sometimes I push too hard. I forget that you're not one of my group."

"I'm more a part of your group than anyone else's group. I don't fit in with anyone here."

"You always were a bit of a lone duck," Simons agrees.

"Don't you mean wolf?"

"Nah, I meant duck. You aren't fierce enough to be a wolf. Sometimes I still think I'm talking to that little girl from the side of the road..."

"About that, Simons..."

He puts his forearm on the glass, facing me so that we're almost connected. It looks as though we're having a moment, but in reality, his large frame blocks the cameras so that our conversation can't be recorded. "You don't have to tell me what you don't want to. You don't owe me anything," he says.

"Audio here?" He asks so quietly that he might have just mouthed it.

I glance over at the cameras and nod. "Not monitored though."

He nods, then with a low voice, he adds, "You sure about that?"

"They're supposed to just be for the records. They only get checked if there's an incident."

"So they say."

"Alright, alright, enough. I need you to look into something for me."

Simons stops smiling and meets my gaze. "Everything okay?"

"Everything's fine. There's a new guy—I met him the other night in training. I can't quite figure him out."

"Name?" Simons asks.

"He goes by Eli Cain. There's something different about him for sure." I think on how to explain the series of events from training. "We did urban training in an ancient city. It was like he was familiar with the environment—like he'd been there before. He was really confident. Jorey and I broke away and nearly failed the simulation, and he led a group to the end in that same amount of time. I made a bad judgment call and almost had a fall—the sort of fall that could get someone killed, if you know what I mean. He caught me and brought us all out. His first simulation."

"Doesn't seem too strange," Simons says. "Anything else?"

"Yeah. He seems…*happy*," I say, finishing with the main thing that's aggravating me.

"Alright, I'll look into it. Don't worry too much about it, though. Strange people walk in here all the time. I'll have the information for you by the time I'm out."

"Thanks. I better get going. I'm on support for Orman's experiment today." I slip as much disdain for Orman as I can into my statement.

"Who's subbing in for me?"

"I don't know... I forgot to check the roster. Did you make a request?"

"I requested Berg," Simons says. "He's alright, and I figure he can get them through the assignment."

"I like Berg. Good choice. I better get going," I say.

"Get to it. And send my best to the team."

FORTY-THREE

I'M the last to enter the kill lab staging room. Shelby scans me in with a skeptical but knowing look and tips her head in the direction of Orman, who's fussing with his latest weapon—the focus of today's experiment. The gun is approximately the length of a rifle, but much bulkier. The charging compartment is aligned directly behind the crystal and cross-sectional with the source. Recalling the experiment, I derive the purpose of the system as a charged laser pulsar test designed for efficiency of kill by spreading the laser shot throughout the body using electrical conductivity. An over-designed blow torch, if you ask me.

"Orman, why did you choose such a large kill floor for this experiment?" I ask, referring to the extensive corridor designed for large experiments.

"I would have expected you to read the experiment more thoroughly, Mason," Orman says in his typical condescending tone. He continues as though he's stating the obvious, "We're testing three main functions of weapon design today. First, I want to test the efficiency of kill time, which we will do via direct shot, which—you are correct—can be done on a regular-sized kill floor. However, I'm also studying the range of function and scope accuracy, which, if you were in regular attendance to weapons training, you would realize are just as important as the magnitude of the kill shot."

Another militaristic experimental design. If people in the City States knew about the level of combat training and weapons design that went on up here, they probably wouldn't believe in a cure either. I roll my eyes, hoping he doesn't notice. "Of course, I'm sorry. I was distracted by the weapon design and had forgotten the other attributes of the experiment. It won't happen again."

"Spare me the sarcasm. Hasn't anyone told you to respect your elders?"

I busy myself with the recording software, checking to ensure that everything is operative. Once all of my checks clear, I bring the communication program online and queue the surveillance cameras to see the line of volunteers, armed with lashing poles and patients, waiting for their signals to proceed.

"We're live," I announce to the team.

Shelby begins documenting and starts the equipment to measure the intensity of Orman's shots and evaluate his aim and timing to correct for human error. She works without words. Orman breathes out and smiles as he relaxes his body and eases his head down so that his eye aligns perfectly in his scope. *Delighting in the kill.*

The first volunteer group proceeds down the corridor with their patient fully lashed. I notice that this specimen is nearly overdeveloped—its flesh hangs off the appendages like rags, and the oozing pieces underneath sag on the bones as if the skin, muscle and sinew are no longer intact.

The volunteer group places the patient in the target, unlashing it and stepping outside of the yellow lines. The patient stands, seemingly stunned, on the target. The face is a horrid sight—both eyes have sunken into the sockets, and the lower jaw is completely missing, giving it an expression of constant shock.

I only have a few moments to take in the patient's appearance before Orman announces in a cold voice, "Kill in three… two… one!"

A buzzing emanates from the power source, and the air around us ionizes, causing the hairs on my arm to stand and brush against my uniform. The blow strikes so suddenly and with such force that the patient could have been mid-sniff, seeking us out. The laser burns a large hole through the torso before turning bright with electric charge. The beam disperses, no longer burning along a straight path. It spreads across the patient's body, turning it into molten ashes. Just as soon as the shot fires, the whole ordeal is over, and there's only a whisper of the patient as the ashes settle on the painted target below.

"Damn," Orman curses. "I can't get the electric current to engage at the same time as the laser. I thought I fixed that!"

"Kill time was under three seconds, what are you complaining about?" Shelby asks incredulously.

"Yeah, well, I could get it to a fraction of a second if the electric charge didn't need power time," Orman replies, exasperated.

"All clear for part two," I announce, eager to get the rest of the experiment over with.

"Fine, bring in the next patient. I want to get an idea of the range on this baby," Orman says.

"Group two, you may proceed," I announce, then watch Simons' group, led by Berg, advance with the next patient.

Frances has her lashing pole wrapped around both of the patient's wrists to control its arm movement. She follows behind, bracing herself against the patient's aggressive resistance to restraint. Jorey and Richards walk along either side of the patient, lashing poles secured tightly around the torso, helping force the forward motion required for their delivery. Carmen's lashing pole is wrapped around the patient's neck, securing the hood meant to inhibit the patient's perception of the volunteers. Berg leads the way, his lashing pole also wrapped around the patient's neck, only higher. His muscles clench as though he is pulling with all of his strength to guide the patient forward.

"We've got an aggressive patient in line," I indicate to the team. "You order that, Orman?"

"A little target practice goes a long way," Orman replies, his smile clearly indicating he's looking forward to this kill.

The volunteers bring the patient to the far end of the kill floor where the second target is mapped. In order to release this patient, the suspended walkway is required. The team waits as Berg climbs the ladder and secures his lashing pole. Once the pole is secure, Richards releases his lashing pole, grabs the ladder and removes himself to the indicated safe zone on the other side of the yellow line. In unison, Frances, Jorey and Carmen release their lashing poles and begin to step away. As soon as the patient is free from the magnetic pressure of the lashing cords, it throws its arms in blind attempts to grab at the volunteers.

As it thrusts violently against its remaining restraint, the hood slips, causing the lashing pole to release. Berg notices immediately and grabs for his pole, slipping in the process and tipping directly over the handrail of the suspended walkway. He falls head first, still reaching in a desperate attempt to secure the patient, who seizes the opportunity—leaping for Berg's body. The rest of the group works quickly to regain control of the patient before it's too late. Frances is the first to get a direct hit. She flicks her pole around the patient's neck and engages the magnetic hold. The patient bucks at the restraint, reaching for Berg's splayed body.

I watch helplessly, willing the group to gain control. My eyes are torn from the scene when Shelby yells, "Orman, don't!"

I look over in time to see Shelby reach for Orman as he pulls the trigger. Her hand on his shoulder causes him to jerk to the left. There's a dull buzz as the laser shoots across the kill floor. He releases the trigger before the electric current initiates, but the hot stream of destructive light flies across the room and directly through Carmen before bursting into a smoldering welt on the wall behind.

Carmen stands motionless for a moment before slumping down onto her knees. In the commotion, Frances loses her grasp on the lashing pole, and the patient pulls free, pouncing onto Berg and tearing in with hands and mouth, pulling flesh from his neck. Berg doesn't scream as the patient tears open his body and greedily begins consuming the spoils of its kill. The blood is streaming from Berg's throat and the patient is covered in the gore up to its elbows when the buzz of the laser sounds again and the air ionizes with the electric charge.

Orman's second shot is direct, incinerating both the patient and Berg in a show of meticulous efficiency. All that remains of the gory scene is the smeared puddle of blood where they were strewn on the floor. The ashes of the kill waft slowly to the ground as if suspended by a breeze, soaking into the blood at impact. No one moves or makes a sound until Carmen groans weakly.

I grab a medic bag and rush out. The air on the kill floor is still charged from Orman's weapon, resulting in a dull metallic sensation. By the time I make it across the floor, Jorey and Richards have Carmen propped against the wall, and Frances is cradling her head. There's a large, charred hole though Carmen's stomach. Where the flesh isn't burnt, she's bleeding profusely. I fall to my knees in front of her and tear open the medic bag.

"Carmen, can you hear me?" I ask, digging frantically through the contents.

She nods in response and grabs Richards' hand. I'm still digging when Shelby takes a knee besides me and hands me a syringe. I look at it and know that she's right—it's all we can do. The syringe contains the maximum dose of the most powerful opiate we have at the Northern Laboratories. It'll kill her without pain so that she doesn't have to bleed out.

"Carmen, look at me, please," I urge. She meets my eyes with her own. "I'm going to give you something for the pain."

She nods. She knows she's going to die—we all know.

I deliver the dose and watch as she responds immediately. We remain there, huddled around Carmen, providing her with the only thing we have—ourselves. I feel a sudden stab of anguish when I realize that Simons should be here. Not just because this wouldn't have happened if he'd been here, but because he would know what to say. He could make it less terrible.

"Carmen," I begin, searching, "if Simons could be here—"

She cuts me off, her voice weak but urgent. "No... you."

I search her face, looking for an explanation. Carmen has been on Simons' team since before I arrived. She's never liked me, never made eye contact. I was sure she hated me. "I don't understand..."

"You have to find her," Carmen continues, her voice clearer. Her glassy eyes are looking out into nothing, and I think she must be delirious. The medication is working quickly. She looks at me with focus and clarity.

I hold her gaze, keeping my eyes clear and calm. I put my hand on her wrist. She's still grasping the lashing pole. The muscles of her forearm strain against my grip. Her wrist is upturned, and she releases the pole. She's trying to press something into my hand. Unable to tear my eyes from hers, I take her hand without looking and feel a thick, slick piece of paper. I accept it from her and take her hand in mine. It won't be long now.

"Find her…" Carmen whispers again, so softly that no one else can hear. It's smothered by the blood that is slowly filling her lungs and making its appearance at the corner of her mouth. Her eyes don't see me anymore.

I don't understand, but I know that I won't be able to ask. Her breath shallows as she closes her eyes. With one final exhalation, she's gone. We're all motionless, unable to tear ourselves away from her body. I look down at the card in my hand. It's curled as though it's spent years wrapped around a lashing pole—a faded picture of a young woman with short blond hair dressed in scientist's clothing. Underneath the photo, a gold script indicates the scientist is Madison Carmen. I'm transfixed by the image and nearly lost by the strangeness of Carmen's request. I never thought of Carmen as anything but part of Simons' team. I never thought about who she lost.

Shelby grabs my shoulder roughly, pulling me from my stunned reverie. She looks down at the photo with an icy, warning gaze, then glances back at Orman. I quickly shove it out of sight.

"Evacuation called for Kill Floor Six," a voice calls out over the communicator. We make our way to the explosion wall with time to spare. A flash of light and a deep rumble indicate that the kill floor has been extinguished, Carmen's body along with it. Nobody says a word.

Orman brushes his uniform as if to rid it of dust before saying, mostly to himself, "What a waste. That was my best prototype."

His callous voice fills me with rage, and I speak before I have the mind to catch myself. "Your best prototype just killed someone in there, Orman!"

Orman looks at me with a mixture of surprise and derision. "Mason, what's gotten into you? We had a patient out of control, and I *dealt* with it."

Senior or not, Orman killed someone. "Before you *took control* with your trigger-happy approach to problem-solving, Frances had the patient lashed again. We could have recovered both Carmen and Berg!"

Orman laughs his cold laugh and shakes his head at me like I'm a child. "You are out of control, Mason. Whining about lost volunteers, calling them by name—get hold of yourself or I'll pull you from assignment for being unfit."

Shelby pulls herself away from the group and faces us, arms crossed. "Enough already."

Orman's mouth hangs open as if he's about to speak. I bite my lower lip to stop myself from saying anything more.

Shelby makes eye contact—first with Orman and then me, before addressing the group. "That was a ZCA strain patient. Report to screening at once, then get cleaned up and report back for your training and tasks as usual. Don't linger, it will only make it worse."

CHAPTER
FORTY-FOUR

I MAKE my way alone to my room, barely containing my anger. Yet again, I've let my hot head get the better of me, and this time I've managed to make a fool of myself in the process. Orman may be callous, but he still has the authority to make my life miserable—or worse.

Standing in the dim light between my bed and workstation, I study the picture Carmen left with me. The young woman's face is bright and innocent. It's a graduation picture like the ones they send to the families of scientists that make it up to the Northern Laboratories. The edges are frayed and jagged; the picture is faded and scuffed from years of handling while it was wrapped around Carmen's lashing pole. She must have held it for every assignment, every delivery. As far as I know, there's no Madison Carmen in the Northern Laboratories... I wonder how she met her end—or if she waits, frozen in the cryo-rooms with the rest of the patients for a cure that will never come.

Curious, I settle into my workstation and call up the records for scientists both past and present. I enter in the name and am met with a negative result. *Match not found. Enter alternative name?* She should be listed here. The graduation picture confirms that she made it out of the Institute. To be thorough, I decide to search inventory for the cryo-room storage and scroll to the index. At the bottom of the screen, I select *search by name,* and the blinking cursor waits for my next command. The program scrolls through the multitudes of archived names to find its match, then comes back without one.

Find her. She isn't in any of the records—something that Carmen must have known. How long has she been searching?

I close the program and look at the picture again before flipping it over so that the edges curve toward me. In eloquent script, a message stares back at me—*I promise I'll be back with the cure!* A broken promise to a mother who wanted nothing more than to be with her daughter. Before I can stop them, the tears make their way down my cheeks. I notice the first one as it falls on my thumb and drips onto the message. I dab the photo gently with my sleeve to soak up the moisture before it can tarnish the message. I tuck the photo into a pocket on my glove so the curvature of the picture hugs my forearm like it hugged the pole for so long.

I should stop myself, but I just keep crying. I let the sadness overtake me as I curl up on my bed. I close my eyes and try to take myself from the laboratories, from the death and hopelessness that surrounds us every day. I breathe out, tears still oozing, and think of another time —a lifetime ago—when the sun shone and green grass was more than a memory. I picture my brothers running in the open field, laughing while I fight to keep up. Keeping my eyes clenched, I focus as hard as I can until I think I can hear their voices and smell the wildflowers. The memory is near solidifying into reality when the picture greys and the sounds stop.

In a rush, the scene disappears, and I jerk my eyes open until I'm aware that I'm lying on my bed. There's no meadow, no laughter and no family. I sit up and wipe the tears from my face. I breathe out deeply and recall the kill lab. I picture Carmen slumping to her knees, the rest of the group surrounding her and her last words. I let the image sink deep into my brain until it's bright and vivid. Once I'm certain I've drawn out the entirety of the memory, I allow it to fade until it's nothing more than a faint memory—a vague story someone told me.

I open my eyes and see my reflection on the workstation screen. My face is cold and blank, and my eyes are dry of emotion. I smile a heartless and empty smile, in control again. The feeling is gone, but the knowledge is not. *Find her.* Another disappearance that no one can explain. A picture that Shelby demands I keep hidden from Orman's watchful eyes. It can't have been an accident.

My mind swims in the wake of another tragedy—another bad day up north that no one else seems to care about. *Are they just accidents?* I can't think of a way for today's disaster to have been orchestrated. It might have been a real tragedy—like what happened to Smith.

What if that's all any of it is? Accidents. Maybe the hive was never meant to kill anyone. Maybe it was just a horrible mishap. An experiment gone wrong. Maybe I'm searching for answers to a conspiracy that doesn't exist. Maybe that's what Shelby was really trying to say my first day here. Maybe the end game really is the cure…

I shake my head.

No. Today might have been a real accident, but that's not how things are done up here. Smith died because I had to save Tucker. If Tucker hadn't been put into danger, then none of it would have happened. That was no accident. Carmen's daughter is missing from the archives, just like Miller's death. Those aren't errors in record keeping. I'm not wrong about what's happening up here.

I open my experiment with a grim certainty and read the design for the last time. *Forget the algorithm.* No one will bother to check my program anyway. I delete the selected frequencies and choose from my own personal list. No more waiting and following instructions. No more blending in.

I submit my experimental design in a flurry of determination. Once it's done, I can hear my heart thudding in my ears. I'm hit with a rush of exhilaration and terror as I stare at my blank screen. I can't take it back now.

"ELI CAIN IS a bit of a vagabond, traveling around the cities as a mercenary—when he's on record, that is," Simons explains as we make our way down the dining line. He casually loads his plate with pasta, rolls, and various meats. His plate is so full the rolls topple onto the tray.

"Where did he come from?" I ask, taking less than half of the portions Simons does.

"Don't know… there's not much of a record of him anywhere. My sources tell me he turns up in general society every few months along the coasts and up the delivery channels. He offers his services as a guide, protection, and infiltration."

"Infiltration?" I give Simons a sideways glance. Cain's mysterious character is filled with curious entries.

"There are more people on the outside on our side than you'd realize. There are people that think this whole 'near-dead outbreak' is nothing more than a conspiracy started during the war. Some side let it out on the other side, and it got out of control. Of course, a lot of people think that the 'near-dead' don't really exist anymore, they're just a ploy the government uses to keep people scared," Simons explains.

"I used to know someone who believed the same thing," I say, then offer up a bright smile to mask the pain at mentioning my father so nonchalantly.

"It's not that hard to believe, is it? I mean, even if you subscribe to the old Henry Endgal folktale, it wasn't long after fighting stopped that the first cure came to be."

I have to look away. These are things I haven't thought about in far too long. I'm afraid of what other memories they'll bring. "It would be wonderful if the whole thing were just a ploy, but we both know that's not true." I shake my head, and a wobbly laugh bursts out before I can stop it.

"Yeah, well, there are all sorts of conspiracy theorists out there that believe all sorts of things—and if they don't believe it, they suspect it. The government has a mounting army of enemies," Simons says, sliding his overfilled tray to the end of the serving line so that his food shakes precariously.

"That probably explains the increased focus on weapons and defense. There's an army in here, too." We drop the conversation as we approach the group table where Eli Cain sits amongst the ranks as Carmen's replacement.

I stop Simons before we sit, lowering my voice so the words are shared only with him. "Are you sure he's a good pick?"

"Mason, you know I don't just pick anybody. My sources say he's alright, and he handled his first simulation like a natural—as witnessed by you. *Trust me.*"

Simons sits dramatically, with Richards to his left and Frances on his right. His pasta slops over the edge of his plate, and a roll topples from the pile, bumping into Cain's tray across from him.

Cain picks up the roll and studies it in earnest. Simons holds out his hand to reclaim it, but Cain bites into it, holding it between his teeth to free his hand. He puts his hand back down and takes Simons' unsuspecting palm in a warm embrace. With his free hand, he tears the roll from his mouth, and before he's finished chewing, he says, "Thanks again for having me on your team. I hope I can live up to your expectations." All the while, he keeps smiling.

Simons smiles back, amused by Cain's boldness. I offer an inquisitive look, and Simons says, "Cain, you've met Mason, I hear?"

Cain twists around, still chewing and smiling, so that he can see me standing behind him. "Well hey there, Mason! I was wondering when we'd run into each other again. I haven't seen you since training last week!"

With his back turned toward him, Cain can't see Simons wink at me—still amusing himself with this new volunteer and my lack of enthusiasm. I scowl at Simons until I realize that it must seem like I'm scowling at Cain. I switch my expression to neutral, my ears hotter than I'd like them to be. "Cain, welcome to Simons' group. You should know you've been selected for the best team."

He takes my hand enthusiastically, smearing sauce on my glove. Once he releases me, I discreetly wipe my hand on my pants. The only place left at the table is right next to this smiling fool. I sit quietly and settle in to eavesdrop on the volunteers' conversation. It's only a matter of minutes before Cain forgets I'm sitting next to him and he's busy engaging the rest of a group in a story about taking a group to the Deadlands for soil samples.

"If you can imagine what it's like getting a permit like that cleared at a city DDC office—and trust me, you don't want to—then you know the pains I've suffered in the name of an honest job!"

It's been five days since we lost Carmen. Though everything seems normal on the surface, if I study the team, I can see the subtle signs of their grief. Frances looks pale, and the dark circles under her eyes tell the story of her sleepless nights. Richards is smiling and engaging in conversation as if nothing is wrong, but he hasn't touched his food in days. Jorey is perhaps the most obvious. He just sits with the group, no smiling, no talking—his massive shoulders slump forward as if he doesn't have the strength to hold them back. I haven't seen him at the window since the incident.

Cain slaps his hand on the table, drawing the ire of some nearby volunteers. "The damn fools wanted to send out government security. I mean, picture it—those tight black suits and the slim city pistols. They couldn't outrun a puddle of mud!"

Simons takes a long drink, then guffaws slapping Richards on the back. Richards returns the gesture with a quiet chuckle before re-situating his glasses higher up his nose. Cain's upbeat tone and easy demeanor act as an unguent on the dour mood of the team. It's easy to drown out the present in his lavish storytelling. I can't study him too intently sitting so close. He's tall. Even sitting, he's a head taller than me, his shaggy blond hair reaching down to his shoulders. His arms are lanky and muscled. He's got a deep scar that travels from somewhere up his arm all the way down the back of his hand and across his middle fingers. Watching him gesticulate, I notice that he's missing some dexterity in his hand. *I bet he's got a story for that.*

Cain continues animatedly, oblivious to my observations. "You see, that's the problem with these researchers. Some of them are actually *bitter* that they didn't become scientists. Sure, if they could get a soil balance just right, they could bring crops back into the City States, but they're just researchers! Since I haven't had a day of formal education, they treat me worse than the dirt they're digging up."

Cain mimics the researchers hemming and hawing over their soil samples, drawing laughter from the team. "But when we came across a loose pack of near-dead, you better believe they fell to pieces. I've never had such a hard time corralling an expedition back to safety. No fitness, no endurance and no common sense."

I assume he's using as much hyperbole as truth as he leads the team on in his tale. I roll my eyes and push my dinner away, half eaten. Jorey catches my exasperated look and smiles. Simons nudges Jorey and folds his arms, smiling and content with the new guy. I can't tell if Eli Cain is a pain in my side or a welcome change. For now, I count him as both.

After dinner, I make my way to training alone. Though I was able to put it off for weeks, I can no longer escape weapons. After my blowup at Orman, he's been following my movements even more closely. I quit bribing the schedule master to switch me out of weapons and have, for the most part, kept my head down and my temper in check, well aware that the rumors about Orman's position in the DDC may be true.

Tonight's training is focused on the use of powered weapons. It basically consists of shooting blanks into an energy-absorbent barrier. I'm thankful the activity is stationary since I did a seriously intense redline session last night. The virtual experience is from a high vantage point, well camouflaged and downwind from our targets.

The targets are easy to hit. They wander aimlessly from side to side with little obstruction. I work through them, counting each hit to keep my mind occupied. Without thinking, I open my mouth wide in a yawn as I annihilate yet another meandering target. Before I close my mouth entirely, I notice Orman watching me. In the simulation, he's perched in a control room with thick glass casing and an extremely large pulsar gun. I figure the over-sized gun is not only simulation.

Keeping one eye on my targets, I watch as Orman fiddles with some controls, his eyes still locked onto me. Suddenly my targets become aggressive. I quicken my shooting pace, glancing at Orman again. He's watching for my reaction.

My frustration mounts as more targets appear than I'm able to take down. I adjust the level on the pulsar, trying to hit multiple targets with each shot. Just as I think I'm getting things back under control, the targets turn—all at once, like a hive. Instead of thrashing around aimlessly, they're facing me directly. I don't have any time to digest the fact that this is the first ever simulated hive I've experienced. There are too many.

I flip the pulsar to the highest level and continue shooting—six, eight targets per shot, but they still make their way over. Knowing I don't have much time before the hive is upon me, I look for something on the field I can use to deter them. A steep mountainside to my left offers a welcome solution. I fire diagonally along what I hope is the fault line and watch as the mountainside crumbles and falls onto the hoard. After the dust settles, there are only four patients left. Adding a few extra for the ones I forgot to count, I wipe out the last targets. I breathe out a sigh of relief and raise my head from the gun.

A hot rush of air brushes past me, and I turn my head just in time to see a patient fall to the ground next to me, head smoking from the laser discharge. I look back to see Orman's gun pointed right at me. Three beeps signal the end of the simulation. I take off the helmet to see Orman standing just a few feet from me, holding his over-sized weapon. His control room was part of the simulation, but as I predicted, the gun was real.

"Cutting it a little close?" I ask, keeping my voice calm and controlled.

"A thank you would suffice," Orman replies. "One of these days, you'll be grateful for my assistance."

His statement makes me think about his position—getting pulled away from the Northern Laboratories. I wonder how many outbreaks he's handled, or what else he's been sent to do. I bite my lower lip and force myself not to make any snide remarks. "Great shot," I say.

"You're welcome," Orman says, feigning graciousness with a slight bow. His salted hair, messy from the helmet, falls forward, and he brushes it back tidily as he lifts his head again.

I rack my weapon and turn to leave the track when Orman calls out to me. "Mason!"

I turn back and make eye contact, making sure to stand up straight. "Yes?"

"I'd like to talk with you about the experiment you submitted. We should set something up," Orman says before turning to use the exit on the opposite side of the track, taking his weapon with him.

I had no idea that Orman was on my review team. *This is bad.*

SNOW CRUNCHES underfoot as I make my way over the frozen ground. Just a few hundred meters behind me, the laboratories appear small, as if the snow has buried them. There's been a break in the storm, and it just happened to coincide with the sunlight, providing a false sense of warmth in the frozen midday. I use the charged wand, gripping the rubber end, to defrost the ice-encrusted hinges of the thick metal door in front of me. The stream of charged particles heats the air around the tip of the wand, spanning out until it hits the door and causes water to run down the rust-proof surface.

I disengage the infrared stream and use the blunt end to beat down a few chunks of remaining ice. I punch in the security code and scan my badge at the entrance. With a low moan, the door shudders open, granting me entry. I step into the dark corridor at the third entrance to the hexagonal receiving structure. The last thing I see before the door closes behind me is the white puff of my breath in the still-frozen air.

I wait for my eyes to adjust before moving to the back end of the corridor. The door opens automatically, revealing a large storeroom. I grab the delivery manifest and scan through the list. My heart sinks. There are no scientist supplies. That confirms it then—there won't be any new scientists this year. I'll be a rookie for another year.

I'm about to set the manifest down when something else catches my eye—energy supplies are normal shipment items, but these are odd. Frequency converters. Six of them, hand-held. They must be a part of someone's experiment design and I'm oblivious because I've been off the review board while preparing my own experiment.

I search the package description to see if I can determine which frequencies the devices cover, interested if any of them overlap with the frequencies I chose for the hive study. If they do, then I'm definitely on the right track and might be able to accelerate myself into further answers before my experiment even begins. Unfortunately, the packages have no additional information on them.

Curiosity gets the better of me, and I pull out the silken screen from my glove slip. I lay the cloth across one of the boxes from this month's delivery and gently touch the screen to cue it on. The screen lights up with the cursor blinking on the bottom. I punch in the item code for the converters and search.

After a quick several seconds, the result pops up—*Item not found.*

I search again, this time under experiment design, and leave out the item numbers in case they're inconsequential. This time, a link comes up. I touch the screen to open the link, but instead of opening it, I'm redirected to another screen.

Access Denied—Security clearance not valid. Message 046228.

I read the message again, puzzled. After my year anniversary, I should have been granted the next level of clearance, leaving only governmental security issues beyond my grasp. Perhaps my clearances haven't gone through the system yet. My anniversary was just a week ago, after all.

I look for clues about the nature of the link, but there are no descriptors in the actual code, just a scramble of numbers and letters. There isn't a category in the search results either. Undaunted, I try another option, pulling the first section of the code to search for related information.

I get two hits. The first is a document too heavily encrypted to read. The second is a video of a communication. Holding my breath, I select the video for replay. An access key pops up, prompting me to enter my security code. *Foiled again.*

I lean back against the wall, chewing my lower lip and thinking about what my next step will be. If only Miller were right and I really did have access to the master code. I think back to the training floor. It was so easy to open the program for edits. That night, I was convinced that she must have been right about Amos having gifted me the key to the Northern Laboratories.

I haven't thought about it since then, though. It's too closely associated with Smith's death, and I've been terrified ever since that Orman suspects me.

Now I wonder. Maybe it isn't the master code for the Laboratory. Maybe it's more of a workaround. I glance at the clock before I pull up the encrypted file and get to work. Pulling what I suspect to be the most likely repeated pattern key, I enter it into the video prompt and wait.

The screen scrambles for a moment, then clears into a split picture. The first is of a pristine room with a thick, perfectly polished wooden table. Around it are what I recognize as the government officials responsible for management of the Northern Laboratories, including the president and the four DDC officials who supervised our last days at the Institute. The second half of the screen is fixed on a tidy desk filled with neat stacks of labeled and bound papers. Orman's hands are neatly folded in front of him, and his hair is perfectly groomed, accentuating the peak of what I suspect is his receding hairline.

"I don't understand why you need these models. We were assured that you had resolved the problem," one of the government officials grumbles.

"I've run into a few minor roadblocks, but I assure you—they're minor," Orman defends himself with crisp assurance.

"Orman, you know we have every confidence in you, but this project has a lot of us on edge. We've put our necks on the line for this. Requesting new devices doesn't help your cause," the security administrator admonishes. His voice is tinged with anxiety.

"I've never let you down, and I won't this time either. You're right to put your faith in me," Orman insists.

"That reminds me..." the president interjects, drawing eyes from the tall DDC official. "We need to set up a meeting on that other matter..."

Orman rolls his eyes. Apparently, his haughtiness isn't even curbed by the president's committee. "I'm working on it. It's not a matter that you need concern yourselves over. The situation will be under control."

"It better be. We have a schedule," the president warns.

"The shift to manufacturing will proceed without further delay. And I will expect my project transfer promptly," Orman snaps.

"We'll hold up our end of the bargain so long as you see yours through," the DDC woman promises to the nods of the others.

"If that's all, gentlemen..." Orman addresses the crowd. The DDC woman raises her eyebrow at his choice of words.

"I believe we're reasonably satisfied," the security administrator concedes.

"You can expect your shipment within the next month," the materials coordinator adds offhandedly, scanning through what I assume is his schedule and supplies list.

"I'd appreciate it expedited," Orman quips. "It's been a productive meeting. If you will excuse me now, I've got a few things to attend to here."

Orman's screen blanks out first. The last thing captured before the screen goes blank is the security officer shaking his head. He begins to say something to the president, but the communication goes dark.

I remain kneeling in the semi-darkness, processing. The frequency converters were specially requested by Orman. He must be developing a new weapon or using them to modify some current one. Knowing him, it likely has something to do with converting low-frequency wavelengths to high-frequency ones to up the kill factor—or something along those lines. But that's not what bothers me.

Manufacturing?

Carefully, I roll up the screen and tuck it back into my glove. I finish taking the inventory and record all the supplies in the database, scanning all the laboratory goods into their proper categories. By the time I've finished, the sun is setting below the frozen horizon. The icy particles in the air scatter the light into a stunning array of low-frequency color. The fading light reflects off the snow and ice, creating shimmering illusions as far as I can see. It's what I imagine the sea would look like at sunset. Light dancing across a broken surface as the moon pulls the water from rest.

As I pull the vehicle back into the complex, I recall what Simons mentioned earlier. Deep in the heart of the cities, outbreaks are nearly a thing of the past. It would be easy, in that environment, to think that everything is back to pre-war conditions. People who live on the outskirts of the cities know the truth. I know the truth. Those whose families are involved in commerce, trade, investigation, exploration, transportation… they know the truth. They've seen the outbreaks.

Down there, they suspect the danger is a fantasy. Up here, it's real. There are so many patients at the Northern Laboratories. They don't just appear out of thin air. I need to figure out the truth. The disease isn't a ploy, but it's definitely not the real issue. It's being used as a game piece in whatever is actually happening.

My mind wanders back to the recorded communication between Orman and the cabinet. The government officials were skittish. Does Orman just have that effect on everyone, or is there more to it? The whole exchange was vague, as if they were trying to keep something under wraps. The hairs on the back of my neck rise and brush against my suit, prompting me to rub my neck.

Orman's definitely involved in something for the DDC that's meant to be a secret. That supports my own hypothesis of subterfuge. Is it coincidence that whatever he's involved in is also related to frequency communication? And what of the manufacturing comments? Thinking about it puts me ill at ease. There are some circumstances in which I'd rather be wrong, and I wonder if this should be one of them.

Over the years, everything has been stacking up. My arrival to the Institute… The disappearances… And now there are no new scientists at all?

I'm dancing along the edge of something big and likely very dangerous.

CHAPTER
FORTY-SEVEN

I ALWAYS END up on Shelby's cure team by special request. For the past year, we've been dissecting and interpreting the genetic code of the dominant strains of Zoribiatus while monitoring their life cycles. Shelby runs her experiment with fastidious precision. We're the first team to report to the cure labs and the last to leave. Every evening, she requires that we submit our write-ups for experimentation, and the following morning, she directs our next tasks based on the results of the previous day. Thus, our work is never certain, and we frequently find ourselves working toward unrelated tangents rather than the main experimental objectives dictated by the government.

I pause at the sterilization station so that a burst of ultraviolet light can decontaminate me before moving to the hand wash station. While I'm scrubbing my hands with too much soap, another scientist approaches and leans in to whisper.

"She's off on another tangent again. We are measuring the STOP signals in DNA replication today." Sima speaks in a voice meant only for my ears. She follows her exasperated statement with an eye roll.

I sigh and turn off the water. My hands drip in the basin as I scan the prep area to see who else is joining us. A genetic specialist, Sima is a regular on Shelby's cure lab team. Hersh is gowning up to enter the labs. As a close friend of Orman's, he's definitely not my favorite scientist. I suspect that Shelby didn't request him, but rather Hersh requested Shelby's experiment. Two other scientists pass through the sterilization station.

One calls out, "Hey Mason, I think I'm on your experiment next cycle."

I turn to the guy and stammer, "Oh? I didn't know they were putting out the next cycle of assignments yet... I haven't even gotten peer review or approval. Um..."

"Dunn." He offers his hand, and I bring my soggy hand up but stop and search for a towel. "For crying out loud, Mason, you've been here a whole year. Don't you think you could take some time to know your peers?"

"Sorry," I say, not really meaning it. "I like to focus on work."

Shelby enters from her office and ends the conversation. "As you should, Mason—and everyone else." She addresses Dunn's sheepish grin with a sharp glare. "I've requested culture plates and fresh cells. I want full reports of STOP frequency and replication rate by the end of the day. Volunteers are setting up the equipment as we speak, so let's not waste any time."

We finish prepping for the experiment and file through the containment barrier into the lab. I settle in at a station near Shelby and begin. The other scientists engage in trivial conversation as they work. Their conversations act as a white noise template for my thoughts. Within hours of the experiment initiation, I notice that I haven't detected or recorded a single STOP signal in the replication. I check the rate of replication to see if my cultures have died, but the rate is steady. I pull up the software for measurement and check the parameters for detection.

"Shelby, I think I've got a software bug at my station," Dunn says. "I haven't recorded a single STOP..."

"It's not a bug," Sima interjects. "There is no STOP." She looks over the culture details, and her breath catches. "This is the ZCZ strain from the recent family. Replication never stops. Shelby, how did you get clearance to test this strain?"

Ignoring her question, Shelby walks from station to station to check our data. Every single experiment confirms the same—replication from any single template doesn't stop. "Keep recording. I want a full day of data." She stops at my station and studies my records over my shoulder. I glance back, uneasy.

"Mason, why are you recording protein transport post-replication?" She points at my additional data point and punctuates her question with a raised eyebrow.

"I wanted to record the destination of each protein body to see if any were used for cell signaling," I say, feeling my head shrink into my shoulders. It was foolish of me to add a whimsical data point to Shelby's calculated experiment.

"Interesting," Shelby says, almost to herself, but then to me. "Not exactly useful for my purpose, but surely you have an objective?"

"I've just started searching for the mechanism of the hive mind, and I thought it might be an interesting side experiment," I offer. I wonder if she'll call my bluff. Smith already eliminated cellular communication.

"Very astute, Mason," Shelby returns. "About your experiment… leave your station recording and come speak with me."

I set up the auto record and check the incubator for temperature control before following Shelby to her office. We remove our lab coats before entering the containment barrier for decontamination. As I turn from side to side under the ultraviolet beam, I look back at the lab and catch Hersh watching us. I suspect he'll run off to Orman to report my chat with Shelby. Orman must have people watching me—he always seems to know what I'm up to lately.

The door to Shelby's office closes, and she says, "You're right. Orman is keeping tabs on you."

"How did you know what I was thinking?"

I follow her as she moves across the office to stand behind her cluttered desk.

"I saw you catch Hersh," Shelby replies.

"Why?" I blurt. I don't know what to do with myself, so I just stand there.

"Mason, you're no idiot. I've known that about you since before your first day in the Northern Laboratories. I know you went to the Institute early." She takes a seat and almost disappears behind a stack of papers—write-ups about her hundreds of experiments, I presume.

"That's not in my profile," I object, rubbing my foot against my ankle to scratch an itch that isn't really there.

"Of course. I know that too."

I don't reply. I just stand there, processing and fidgeting. I suddenly realize that I don't know what to do with my hands.

"What is the purpose of the Northern Laboratories?" Shelby asks, shifting papers to either side so that we have a clear view of one another. She knows what to do with her hands.

"To combat and cure Zoribiatus by means of technical force and pharmaceutical advancement," I reply automatically, quoting the mission statement plastered above every entryway I've crossed under since my first day at the Institute.

"Very good. You're nearly as good at regurgitating propaganda as you are at insubordination," Shelby muses, leaning back in her chair. She uses that word—*propaganda*. "But I know you don't buy it. You're looking for answers, and you've gotten sloppy."

"What do you mean?" Shelby has my full attention, and I forget about my useless, misplaced hands.

"Mason, why would anyone choose to join the Institute? You had your way out, and you didn't take it."

"I wanted to do something. I wanted to stop it—"

"And how many times have you been told it's impossible? How many times did Amos try to teach you? How many times have I had to shut your mouth before..." She stops talking, temporarily overcome with exasperation. She waves one hand in front of her face with a sort of absentminded *go on* gesture.

My eyes drop to the floor. "Haven't you ever wondered? In all the years that you've worked here... haven't you *suspected* there's more to the problem than a government that doesn't want a cure?"

Shelby's head rests in her hands as she slumps over her desk. Her voice is soft when she speaks again. "I don't wonder, I know. We all know, eventually."

My mouth drops, and I see Shelby in a new light—no longer the stoic heroine of the Northern Laboratories, she's a cog in the machine.

My mind races with wild thoughts. *Has my usefulness to the dissenters run out? Have I become a liability? Will she report me?* I try to speak but have nothing to say.

"It takes time up here to really understand the disease," Shelby explains. "After years studying the nature of each strain and the evolution of the viral form compared to natural evolution, you learn there's not really an explanation… a natural explanation, that is."

"We can trace the origin of the first strain," I argue, still trying to read Shelby's reaction to my existence. "It evolved from the human variation of viral Toxoplasmosis. The vaccination caused a mass extinction event, and the Zorbitoxo parasite reemerged in a new strain of Zoribiatus that was resistant to treatment."

"And why is the Zorbitoxo virus so resistant?" Shelby prods.

I think back to the foundations of genetics and pry an answer from my brain. "Only the resistant strains reproduced…"

"How could resistant strains be resistant to all forms of treatment when they were only subjected to one during the extinction event?" Shelby asks, deftly guiding me to the only conclusion—the one I've suspected yet never been able to manifest.

"It replicates without next generation fitness… It's resistant to mutation, so there is no cell death…" I say, fitting today's experiment into the puzzle. If replication from any individual cell never stops, the next generation never needs to replicate and thus mutation can never cause cell death.

It comes together, slapping me in the face. "It's manufactured," I whisper. The answer was there all along. The government isn't using the disease—it *created* the disease.

Shelby nods. "Today's experiment was for you."

"What do you mean?" My whole body feels numb and inconsequential.

"You have to stop stabbing around in the dark for answers to questions no one wants you to ask. If you know the truth, you can stop fishing for it and stay safe." She's trying to protect me.

My mind flashes back to the recorded communication.

Am I the "situation" they were referring to? Worse yet, if the disease has been perfected, then is this new strain what's meant to be manufactured? Is that Orman's real purpose in the Northern Laboratories? To keep the government's secret?

Shelby sighs heavily and grabs my hive experiment draft off the desk. She glances at it with frustration, then thrusts it at me. The pages rustle as I catch it. I look at Shelby's comment sheet cover where she has written in red ink: "No grounds for experiment." And marked "recommended re-design."

"If you don't stop your search for the truth and start working on something useful around here—control—there's not much of a chance you'll make it another year."

"What do you mean... control?" My head is spinning with new information. *Control.*

"You listed electromagnetic frequencies for measurement that are reserved exclusively for government usage. Do you think that will be lost on your reviewing scientists? Do you think Orman will overlook something like that?" She sounds more angry than inquisitive.

"Four of twelve specified frequencies... could be coincidence," I defend, realizing how foolish that argument sounds. Orman ordered frequency converters—what if I chose his frequencies? If I did, it wasn't an accident. I suspect he might know exactly how the hive communicates.

"Don't treat us like imbeciles! Every senior-level scientist can clearly see that you're searching for hive communication on government-controlled frequencies. Do you want to get yourself killed?" Shelby is once again overcome by her own incredulity.

"I didn't think it would matter," I say weakly. Of course it matters. "Nothing seems to matter around here. Nobody ever seems to care what experiments other scientists are designing. I didn't figure anyone would care." I wonder if feigning stupidity will take me anywhere. Maybe out of harm's way.

Shelby's demeanor softens, but her voice is still stern. "The other scientists don't care. You don't have to worry about them—you need to worry about the government overseers. Orman, myself, Walker... we report directly back to the government."

"Shelby, is Orman watching me because I've gotten too close to the truth?"

"Yes."

I suck in a breath. I thought I was being so careful. "Is he alone, or is he watching me for someone else?"

"You better hope he's curious for his own sake," she says. "Even still, he's dangerous."

"What about you? You report directly back to the government. Are you going to report me?"

"Of course not," Shelby says, sounding less like a senior authority figure than ever before. "I want you to blend in. I want you to survive."

"Is that all you do up here? Just survive?" I want to spit the words at her, but it comes out just above a whisper.

Shelby's eyes drop. "Yes and no. People here generally leave me alone as long as I report and review. I slip below the radar. I've been working on something."

I meet Shelby's eyes, begging her to be someone better than she seems to be. She pulls out an ancient notepad covered in scrawls. "This," she says, "is the cure."

I take the notepad without asking and flip through it furiously, taking in the formulas and indications carefully scribed across endless pages. "You know the cure?" I gasp.

"It's hypothetical—I've never tested it, and as long as I'm here, I'll never have the opportunity," Shelby explains.

I stare at the notepad, running my fingers along the edges, trying to convince myself that it's real. "This is what you were trying to tell me," I whisper. I quote her, *"There is a cure."*

She nods.

"Do they know?" I ask.

"The government doesn't care about the cure; they only want control," Shelby replies.

"That's not what I meant," I say, sighing with exasperation. I'm still too afraid to say it out loud. *Dissenters!*

"Ah," Shelby says, taking the notebook back from me and tucking it into its hiding spot. Once secured, she returns her attention to me. "Of course they know. It's all part of the plan to take away the government's control."

Control. Amos was trying to tell me so much. I missed it.

"How can they control this disease? It eats people up from the inside out. How can they use that?" I ask.

"It's a weapon. An army of mindless violence that spreads and reproduces on its own," Shelby points out the obvious.

"And when they're done with it?"

"It dies on its own. Every infected individual has an expiration date," Shelby concludes for me. The manifestation of the truth is more terrible than I could imagine.

The cure exists. It sits on the desk directly in front of me, at the hands of the most senior scientist in the Northern Laboratories, but no one wants it. I shake my head, overwhelmed. "I don't understand. If they aren't interested in the cure, and they already have their hive control… why are we even here? What's the purpose of sending new scientists to the Northern Laboratories?"

"Do you think I'm the first person to come up with the cure? I can't say definitively, but I know others have come close. You can't stop human progress, so the government seeks to control it—to contain it so that there aren't any competing forces out there. That's why we collect the most brilliant minds—the most likely to come up with the cure on their own. They end up here, where we can get rid of any problems— or direct their talents to government causes."

"Then why are there fewer and fewer scientists? Where is everyone going?" I ask, thinking she must know the truth.

"That I can't say for certain. Unfortunately, I'm just a relic of a place whose time is ending."

The reality of the situation sinks in. We're stuck up here exactly *because* we have the cure. We have it, but that's where it ends. "Why bother making a cure if we can't get it out of the Northern Laboratories? What's the point?"

A pained look crosses Shelby's face. When she speaks, her words come out very slowly. "At first, I did it just in case I ever left. So that maybe I could undo some of the damage I've helped create up here."

"And then?"

She looks up, misty eyed, as though she'd forgotten I'm in the office with her. "And then there was you."

"What does that mean?" I ask, confused and frustrated.

"You were always meant to bring the cure out of the Northern Laboratories."

"How?"

"Now you want to know?" Shelby laughs.

I sink into a large cushioned chair opposite Shelby's desk and sigh, trying to expel the weight of everything. "I don't believe this."

"Of course you do," Shelby presses. "You've always believed this, since the day you first saw the hive."

Something clicks. I jerk my head up and study Shelby carefully. "How do you know?"

Shelby looks ashamed. "I helped create the hive mind. I've played a role in every hive interaction."

The realization of what this means hits in a wave of panic. I can feel my heart pounding in my throat as my breath catches. My whole body tenses up, and when I look at Shelby, I only see the blur of her outline. I feel numb. When I stand to leave, I'm thrown off-balance by my racing mind. Shelby moves to catch me, but I fall to the ground before she reaches my side. I feel her hand on the side of my head, and it sounds as if she's calling to me from far away. Before things go completely blank, I whisper, "Why did you have to kill them?"

PART FOUR

THE HIVE

"WE'LL REST when we get to the road," Dad says, making Hank groan.

"But Dad, look at this place," I beg.

He stops walking. I hold my breath, afraid to hope that he'll relent. His expression is thoughtful. "It's just another half day's walk to the road if everything goes well."

"If," Hank points out.

"It's been quiet since we went in the river," Bruce adds.

Dad studies us, the hard knot in his jaw wavering as he relents. "Maybe we should rest a little."

We cheer at his words. It's what we all want.

I wake up warm. It takes me a minute to realize I've slept in long enough for the sun to creep above the horizon and warm my sleep sack. I don't open my eyes. I'm not ready to end this wonderful feeling. I feel rested. It's so good to be lying in the warm sack with the sun shining. This is so much better than walking. I'm smiling with my face buried in the warmth, still refusing to open my eyes.

The barrier alarm isn't particularly loud—just a persistent whining pitch. It's quieter this morning since we set it further out. It takes a second for me to realize that I'm even hearing it. Just as my sleepy brain concludes that the sound *is* the alarm, there's a secondary tone. Two areas have been breached.

I'm up, suddenly all too awake and alert. The first thing I see is Dad, standing near the ashes of last night's campfire. His sleep sack is still in his pack. Bruce is standing next to him. They look so similar. Dad's just a little bit taller. Their hair is long and greasy from days without washing. Dad's dark stubble has grown into a shaggy beard. Bruce's adolescent face is unkempt, but definitely not a beard. They wear the same expression of horror.

Hank sits up next to me and yawns. He's about to ask what's going on when Dad implores him with a stern and urgent look to stay silent. While we all slept in the brilliant morning light, our little clearing was surrounded. They're moving in by twos and fours on three sides. Opposite, at the lake, they're starting to splash into the water, making a noisy approach. There are so many I don't understand why we didn't hear them coming.

I'm on my feet as fast as Hank. Dad urges us over wordlessly. There are too many to kill. I take his clammy hand in mine and look into his ashen face. I've never been as terrified as this very moment. I'm not scared of the near-dead—yet. I'm afraid of how pale and uncertain Dad looks.

Suddenly he moves. He grabs mine and Hank's arms and stoops down. His voice is so quiet and fast that he almost sounds calm. "I need you guys to climb those rocks, and as soon as you reach the top, you're going to stay there. No matter what!"

The granite rocks are tall and narrow at the top. It'll be difficult for the infected to reach us. Dad boosts Hank up first. He jams his foot into the crevasse and uses it to pull himself up the rest of the way. He turns around, and Dad boosts me up so I can grab his hand. I scramble against the sandy surface and perch at the top. There's barely enough room for both me and Hank to keep our footing.

"Dad, it's too small up here! You and Bruce aren't going to fit." It's a whisper, but I know I'm too loud.

"I know, sweetie. Just stay up there no matter what." It's not calm I hear in his voice—It's resolve.

Bruce hands Dad one of the lashing poles. He's going to stand and fight with Dad. But there are too many of them, and they're getting close. The smell is seeping in through my pores, and it occurs to me how incredibly quiet they are. They aren't groaning or gurgling. There's no shrieking or growling. The only sounds they make are like wet, labored breathing. The ones in the lake are splashing and bobbing. Some of them are getting trampled and drown as more of them approach from the bank.

There are hundreds.

I don't want Dad and Bruce to fight. I want them to run, but it's not possible. From my high vantage point, I can see the circle of death. They're coming from every angle, shoulder to shoulder. There are only a few meters separating them from Dad and Bruce.

"Dad?" Hank's voice is high. He sounds like a kid. He sees the same thing I do.

"Promise me you'll stay up there," Dad calls back.

"No, Dad!" It's a sob. I'm crying.

"Stay up there!" he commands. We're not whispering. There's no need for it anymore.

Bruce holds two of the lashing poles at the ready. The bodies will converge from every side at the same time. He's moving to the left— away from the rocks and away from Dad. His motion is so subtle and deliberate that I'd miss it if I weren't watching him so intently. I don't want to look at the near-dead faces. I want to see my family—Dad and Bruce.

Bruce is luring the bodies away from the rocks and away from Dad. His face is so serious that he looks older than Dad. There's a trickle of sweat that runs down the side of his cheek from stern concentration. Dad isn't watching him; he's watching the onslaught.

Bruce makes his move right when Dad lashes out for a kill. When the first one drops to the ground, it's like someone turns off the mute button. Grunts and gurgles and growls and groans fill the air with an unspeakable noise. Bruce kills one by the tree. He's managed to lure a large part of the attacking pack away from us. Dad notices the break as another drops dead at his feet.

I want to scream, but I can't draw any attention to the rock. Hank is squeezing my hand so hard it hurts. Bruce kills another—*three, four, five*. I keep count for him because it's the only thing I can do. Dad takes down two at once. He's up against our rock and using it to try to make his way to the trees to help Bruce. It seems like they have a good strategy. The attackers are tripping over the dead bodies in their way, and it gives them both a little more time.

Bruce manages to grab onto an overhead branch and pull himself up so that he's killing from above. The progress of attack slows with every kill. Dad creates a wall of bodies as he makes his way to Bruce and the tree. It might be a long, hard battle, but maybe they can keep the attack slow enough to kill every single one of them.

Wet, dead hands slap against the base of the rock where Hank and I stand. There's no way up without help. We should be safe. I hate how safe we are. We should be with Dad and Bruce, killing. We shouldn't be up here doing nothing.

"I wish he'd given us our lashing poles," I say.

"We might fall off the rock and into the herd," he says.

"You're right. I wish we were down there with them, actually helping," I amend my statement.

"Me too," Hank agrees. "But we're helping. Look how many are trying to reach us instead of them."

Maybe two dozen of the attackers are piled against each other, moaning at our rock. I understand what Hank means. Two dozen trying to reach us means two dozen that aren't trying to kill Dad and Bruce. Maybe this is what Dad wanted us to do the whole time.

"I can see a break in their approach," Bruce yells down to Dad. There's a steady zap, thunk, smeck sound from their repeated kills.

"When that break comes, Bruce, I want you to run." Dad's breath is heavy. He grunts as he thrusts the end of the pole and pierces through the skull of another diseased body.

"No. We run together or not at all. I'm not leaving you," Bruce says.

Maybe Dad can understand him. Maybe he's too tired to come up with an argument. Instead of saying anything, he keeps killing. This is the only way they'll survive. I'm watching Dad and Bruce, so I don't notice the trickle of near-dead leaving our rock to join the attack at the tree.

"Hey, they're leaving!" Hank says with urgent worry.

"We have to stop them… Bring them back!" I insist. I wave my hands down at the retreating monsters.

"Hey! Hey! Come back here, you assholes!" Hank chimes in and screams with me. All the angst and fear we've held in leaves us in a wave of angry slurs.

"Fuck-faces! Get back here!"

"Come here, you pieces of shit!"

"You smell worse than shit!"

"Don't you leave! Don't you dare leave!"

It's not working. Every single one of them has gone, following the others to the tree. Soggy bodies emerge from the lake, half-drowned but still approaching. They've killed so many, but there are so many more.

"Dad! They're coming," I sob at the top of my lungs.

Hank doesn't relent. His angry screams are a desperate cry. His face is wet and stained with the salt of his tears. "You bastards! Don't you dare walk away from me!"

The herd of attacking near-dead is quiet again. I don't know when it happened—maybe at the same time they left the rock and we started screaming at them. They stumble over the bodies but don't relent. Dad can't keep up with them on the ground. Bruce pulls him up onto the branch. They're safer for a moment. But still the near-dead come.

Bruce stabs one in the face. While his pole is stuck in the dead thing's face, another one grabs it and yanks. Bruce almost loses his footing, then wrenches the pole free, killing the grabbing attacker. This time, three of them grab onto the pole, and Bruce can't hold it. Could they be learning? *No. It couldn't be. They're not supposed to be able to do that.*

Bruce's foot slips from the branch, and he almost goes over, but Dad grabs him. They only have one lashing pole now.

Dad boosts Bruce up to the next branch. I can see it bend from here. Every time Dad uses the lashing pole to kill, hands grab and pull at it. He won't be able to hold onto it much longer, and the branch above won't hold both of them.

"We have to help them," I say.

"How?" he asks.

"Can you make something?" I ask him.

"Out of what?! What do you want me to do? Should I throw rocks at them?" Hank is screaming at me, and spit is flying from his lips. Some of it lands on my cheek and mingles with my tears.

"I don't know! You can make something out of nothing. You always make something out of nothing! Do it now! Please, do it now," I beg him, losing all reason.

"I can't make something out of nothing. You know that, Kara. I use tools, I make toys!" His words come out as a desperate wail.

His anguish penetrates me, and I sob again, not caring about the spittle that leaks from my mouth. "We can't just watch them die!"

I hear a snap in the branch and squeal as Bruce clambers for higher ground. Dad yells at him, but I don't hear what he says. Bruce is hanging from a thin branch with his legs dangling. He tries to wrap his legs around the trunk and misses. He stops trying when he almost kicks Dad in the face. They have no weapons, and they're surrounded.

"They're distracted. We can climb down," I urge Hank.

"We can't climb, we'll have to jump. It's too far," Hank points out. The ropes are in our pack on the ground.

The attackers are still eerily quiet. Their strategy changes. They aren't supposed to understand strategy.

They start to push the tree. There isn't any communication; they just start pushing, all of them together. The tree shudders. Bruce swings again and uses his momentum to improve his grip. I can hear the roots snapping.

The tree dips, and Bruce swings again, but this time, he doesn't keep his grip. I hear his last word. It's a question. His eyes are wide and afraid as he reaches out and grasps for nothing. "Dad?"

They grab his leg, and he disappears in the swarm. He's screaming, and they remain silent as they kill him. His scream stops. The only sounds are those of the rocking and groaning tree behind Dad's call for his dead son. "No! Bruce! Noooo!"

Hank and I are silent from the shock. There's a ringing in my ears, and I know it's the echo of Bruce's scream.

Bruce is gone.

Hank says his name, and it sounds like a foreign word. "Bruce."

They aren't eating him. The disease should make them eat him, but they aren't. They're pushing the tree down. It's leaning so badly that Dad has to stand on the trunk to stay out of their reach. He uses the branches to keep himself from falling while the tree rocks and vibrates with every heave.

Bruce is gone. The tree will fall, and Dad will die too. I can't let it happen. I push my body to the edge of the rock and put my left foot in the crevasse so that I can push off and clear the larger base of granite structure.

Hank grabs my arm and tries to stop me. "Don't do it, Kara!"

"They're going to kill Dad!" I scream.

"They'll kill you too!"

"I don't care! Let them kill me! Let them kill me like they killed Bruce! I won't just sit here and let them kill Dad!" I yell. Dad hears me. He looks right at me as the tree goes down. He shakes his head at me. *Don't jump. Don't try to save me. Let me go.*

A loud snap announces the tree's defeat. The last thing I see is a bright spurt of blood as Dad disappears into the gooey hands that downed the massive tree. I launch myself outward, unable to stop. Unable to care. I'm going to kill as many of them as I can before they tear me apart.

I feel two things before the world goes black. The first is a jolt on my arm, like pulling something. The pressure is there. It moves from behind me, then down. The second is a massive, painful snap. I think it's my hip, but it radiates down my hamstring. The pain is so big that I can't tell where it's coming from. My ankle twists, and my body lurches to a stop above the ground. Bile pours from my mouth as I disappear in the pain and darkness.

Hank's whisper reaches me just before I pass out. "I promised I'd keep you safe."

FORTY-NINE

THERE'S TOO much pressure in my head. I feel like it's going to pop. That's the first thing I notice. Then I notice the pain. It's all I can feel… my leg. I open my eyes, but I can't see anything. My jacket is draped over my face. I'm upside down, hanging from my foot, which is stuck in the crevasse.

I try to wiggle my toes and can't feel anything else. I try to move, and all I feel is the pain. It's so bad it threatens to take me with it. I can't tell the difference between the pain of being still and the pain of moving, so I decide to move. I flex my whole body and push against the rock. The world spins. I'm still stuck upside down.

I try again, and this time, I manage to take the weight off of my foot. It slips from the crevasse, and I fall. I hit the ground, and the pain takes me with it. I choke on my bile and turn my body before everything is gone again.

The next time I'm awake, the pressure is gone but it hurts to breathe. I'm nauseous again. I hold myself up and retch, but there's nothing inside to come out. I open my eyes, and my vision is spotty. My hands are in the scattered ashes of our campfire, sticky with my own vomit.

I pull my legs under me to stand. It takes several tries before I'm on my feet. I'm afraid to look around. I know the near-dead are gone because they could have pulled me from the rocks and eaten me alive.

I lift my head. The tree is on its side. Its roots stick out like fingers grasping for the ground it was torn from. Dad's body lies next to it, torn open at the throat. His eyes are open and spattered with blood. His clothes are soaked crimson, and his arms are spread. He's reaching out, even in death, for Bruce, whose body lies just out of reach.

There isn't as much of Bruce left. His body is bent and torn. His arms lie across the grass, as if they were ripped from him and cast aside. His torso is split, smearing a foul-smelling liquid that makes footprints in the bloody, stomped grass.

I retch again, and my vision turns grey. I didn't expect to see them. I thought they would've been eaten and smeared like ground meat across the meadow. I didn't think I'd recognize them—that they'd be so… whole. That's not what the near-dead do.

I wait until I stop shuddering and the grey spots clear up. I try not to stare at their bodies and instead look around. I don't see Hank. *Maybe he got away!* I have to find him.

I take a step, and my left leg gives out underneath me. I brace myself and put pressure on it, forcing the appendage to straighten. Everything feels hot. I'm sweating just from the effort of standing. I wait until the sick feeling is gone before trying again.

Another step. It's not so bad this time—or maybe it's worse. Another step. Four steps. Five steps. I can walk. It won't be fast, but I can walk. I'll pack a bag with only the things I need and find Hank.

I'll need a lashing pole. I'll need the cooking kit. I'll need my sleeping mat—Hank's too. I wonder if I can manage both of our packs. I turn back to gather supplies, and that's when I see him at the base of the rock. His face is smashed in like something stepped on it. He's torn open, and there's nothing there below his shirt… Just sloppy, gory meat and guts. If I'd looked down while I was hanging, I would have seen him.

I sink to my knees as the memory returns. He tried to stop me from jumping. He said he was trying to protect me.

"Hank." His name comes out a choked sob.

I'm too numb to cry. My swollen heel digs into the back of my leg, and I am vaguely aware that it's touching bone, not muscle. There's a strange groove there, like the muscle is gone, maybe even ripped out.

Hank's dead, and it's my fault. Hank is dead. Hank is dead! I'm looking into his dead eyes. I could reach out and touch the bloody dirt where pieces of him soak into the ground.

They're all gone now. Dad. Bruce. And Hank.

All because I asked to stop.

"Why didn't you just tell us?" I whisper into the stale, dead air.

There's no one to answer.

If we hadn't passed the aptitude test, there wouldn't have been any reason to leave. We wouldn't have climbed these mountains. We wouldn't have gotten trapped, and nobody would be dead.

The sun is low in the sky. I've lost most of the day.

My body is heavy. The longer I sit, the heavier it gets. The pain is returning, little bits at a time. I vomit again, and this time there's bile. I turn my head so that it won't drip down and mingle with Hank's blood in the dirt.

I let the sun disappear behind the trees and below the horizon. I wait until the moon rises in the sky. It's waning. The night is nearly over by the time it's high in the sky.

My body is welded to the dirt, still facing Hank. I can't move, but if I could, I would see Dad and Bruce. I'm surrounded by death.

The moon smiles a sadistic grin down at me. I pull the night-light from my pocket—it didn't fall out when I was hanging upside down, a small miracle. I hold it up and press the black spot so that it glows blue. I push the fragile wires so that they match the smiling white slice in the night sky.

"Look, Hank, less than half now," I say. "I'm not afraid of the dark anymore."

I let the tears come again. In the dark, my mind wanders. At the first sign of daylight, I collect and organize the thoughts. I analyze the information as the scattered pieces return like fragments of a dream. In the light, the data brings questions that I can't answer.

Without thought, I start to pack my things. I take the sweater out of my pack—it's too bulky. I stuff the only clean sleep sack—the one from Dad's pack—into my bag. I take my canteen to the stream above the lake and fill it, putting the last few drops of iodine into the mixture. It'll have to be enough.

By the time I've gathered what I need and made my way slowly back down from the little stream, the sun is high in the sky. I open my bag and lay everything out to check one more time. Sleep sack, multi-tools, canteen… I don't need much to make it the last little bit to the road.

Then it hits me that I have no idea where the road actually is. *I need the map.*

I make my way on shaky legs toward Dad's pack. I can't count how many times I watched Dad carefully fold the map and tuck it into the side pocket with the sticky zipper. The same zipper growls with resistance now as I tug it into compliance. I place two gentle fingertips on either side of the thick paper colored in greens, blacks and reds. Once loose, I proceed to unfold it.

I trace the marks he made with shaky fingers until I reach the last mark—here. The path he meant for us to take is likewise marked, leading toward a red circle on the road, which carves a dark black line that meanders through the same woods we've been traversing. If I follow it southeast, my fingers land right back where we started —*home*. Only home doesn't exist anymore. To the north lies the Institute.

We've been running away from the Institute by heading almost directly toward it. The realization is strange, but I know Dad had a plan. I'm the only one left who can see it through now. I hold the map up to the sky and adjust my course.

Dad was so worried that someone from the DDC would follow us —he was certain of it. Perhaps he was right—we were being hunted. Is it really possible that the DDC has been following us this whole time? Did they use the near-dead?

Impossible! No one could *use* the near-dead. No one could control something like that!

Then why am I still alive when Hank is dead? The nagging thought creeps under my skin and makes my whole body erupt in an unsettling chill. We should have both died at the same time.

But something stopped the near-dead from killing me.

I shake my head, unable to make sense of it. Near-dead don't push down trees and kill without eating. Near-dead aren't quiet.

I pull the pack over my shoulder. When I decide what direction I'm going to head, I fold the map and put it in my jacket pocket. My finger bumps the black spot, and the night-light springs to life. I pull it out gently.

I hold the delicate glowing orb, and my hand starts to tremble. I turn toward Hank. He made it so I wouldn't be afraid. I'm not afraid anymore. I hobble over to him and place his hand over what's left of his chest. As gingerly as possible, I place the glowing night-light in his hand. I adjust it until I know it will stay and then stop. I look at him holding it and pretend he's just sleeping. I pretend his face isn't smashed and his body is whole.

I turn around before the image can be ruined by reality and walk away. As I leave the clearing, I whisper to him. I whisper to all of them.

"Thank you, Hank. I love you."

"Thank you for trying to save me, Bruce. I love you."

"Thank you for trying to teach me, Dad. I love you."

I know what I need to do. I'll find the coyote and join the dissenters.

I'll never forget them.

IT'S dark when I first open my eyes. It takes me a moment to realize that I'm in my own room, tucked beneath a layer of synthetic brown blankets, far from the bloody clearing in the mountains. My head is pounding, and I have no recollection of returning to my dorm. There's a vague sensation in the back of my mind that something has happened, but everything is fuzzy. I look at my workstation to see what time it is, but it's blocked by a dark figure.

I sit up, startled.

"It's alright, Mason. Shelby asked me to wait for you to wake up." Simons' voice pulls me from the dark like a long-lost friend.

"Simons! What time is it?" I ask, brushing my hands across my face in an attempt to wipe away the cobwebs separating me from my thoughts. The memory is so vivid. *I was dreaming about it*, I realize.

"It's around 2 a.m. They sent you from the clinic last evening just after dinner hour. Shelby said you got sick in the cure labs yesterday morning with a fever. The clinic says your immune system was down —you've been malnourished or something like that, but I suspect that's not the whole story?" Simons summarizes before waiting for me to explain what really happened.

"No," I reply, still trying to remember everything. The past keeps swimming in the foreground, making the present seem like a distant memory. I push it away and grasp for yesterday. It returns, slowly. "I was in Shelby's office. We were discussing my experiment design and…"

Everything comes rushing back, and panic sets in. The reason for the dream. Simons recognizes the change and moves to sit next to me on the bed. He puts his massive hand on my shoulder and says in a calm voice, "Whatever happened, Mason, you can tell me later. I just need to know for now that you're alright."

I breathe out deeply and resist the onset of panic. "I'm alright, Simons." I nod at him, reassuring. I force the memory down, making it grey.

Simons studies me with parental eyes before returning my nod with his own. "Alright, then, I'll let you sleep. We'll talk later." He pulls a sealed envelope from his pocket and hands it to me. "This is from Shelby. She insisted you read it immediately, then destroy it."

I take the envelope from him and hold it. "Thanks."

Simons stands and studies me again before turning to leave.

"Simons," I call out softly, afraid for him to walk out and leave me alone with my memories.

"Mason?" Simons returns my call and steps back into the soft glow of my workstation.

I avert my eyes, embarrassed. Simons shifts impatiently, and I recognize his fatigue. "You need something else?"

"No," I reply. "But what would you say—if I told you that something was about to happen up here? Worse than a mystery or a conspiracy."

Simons shifts again and lets out a long, slow breath. "Well, Mason, I suppose I'd be inclined to believe you."

"Really?" I ask, feeling like a kid all over again.

"It sounds like you've gotten some answers, so I'm just going to wait to know what the next step is," he says, affirming a level of confidence in me that I'm not sure I warrant.

"Thank you, Simons."

"I just have to ask one question," he says, rubbing his hands along the unshaven line of his jaw.

"Nothing has changed. They're still safe—for now at least," I reassure him without needing to hear his question.

"I'm not the only one who'll be happy to hear that. I'll make sure the others know," he says, relief flooding his voice.

"If it comes to it, we'll figure something out." I don't know what could possibly be done, but I owe him this much. For all the experiments, every death and each moment I forget about the families—I owe him and every other volunteer.

"I'd risk my team on your word," he says, dropping the weight of mounting anxiety. Before he turns again, he says, "Get some sleep."

Simons leaves me alone with the chill in my room. I grab a thick jacket and move to my workstation. The lights flicker on and flood my room with the impression of warmth. I flip over the blank envelope that Simons gave me. Shelby's signature adorns the seal, ensuring that hers were the last hands on the contents. I break the seal and reveal her message.

Mason,

I'm sorry to have to reveal everything to you in such a sudden manner; unfortunately, I see no better way to protect you from yourself. I can't emphasize to you enough how much danger you're in as a result of your decision to select hive studies and the development of your latest experiment. As the primary reviewer, I've rejected the experimental design based on poor backing science. While I know that this isn't true, I can only hope that Orman agrees under the guise that you'll buy my premise.

You must never speak to anyone regarding our communications. The cure and your knowledge of the situation in the Northern Laboratories must never become apparent.

Unless the government believes they have your full compliance, they'll move to eliminate you as a threat, just as they have every other threat. Orman has requested a meeting with you. The success of our plan relies on your ability to convince him that you don't suspect anything. Orman could be your greatest enemy—he's the chief administrator for government communication with the Northern Laboratories, and I suspect much more. If you can convince him that you don't challenge his authority, you may remain protected.

> *After you collapsed in my office, I administered a high dose of white blood cells and temporarily elevated your body temperature. You will check out of the clinic as only temporarily ill and malnourished. This shouldn't surprise anyone—we're all aware of how often you skip dining hours. Take care of yourself... I'd hate to have to replace you. I've grown fond of working with you.*
> *—Shelby*

She didn't apologize. What does that mean? Maybe she isn't sorry that my family's dead. Maybe she doesn't know the hive killed them? *What if she doesn't know that it happened?* I have to ask her. I can't believe that Shelby would willingly participate in an attack like that.

A blinking at my workstation alerts me to a message. I queue it up, expecting an inquiry from Jorey.

It's from Orman:

> *My earnest condolences. It pains me to hear that you've fallen ill. In light of this, I have postponed our meeting until tomorrow evening. We'll meet in my office during dinner hour. Not to worry—I've requested our meeting be catered so that you don't worsen your condition. I believe we have much to discuss.*
> *Best,*
> *Rick*

The gravity of the situation sinks in. How many have died? How many have disappeared? My mind flashes to an image of Shelby's finger on the button.

How much does she know?

I don't sleep for fear that the dream will come again. When day arrives, I prepare myself for the performance of my lifetime. I told myself that I'd know what the next step was once I knew the truth, but so far, it's not true. I do have something now that I have the answers—the cure. The cure means there can be an end. It means we can bring them all back. I just have to figure out how to get there...

I make certain to show for the morning dining hour, but the persisting knot in my stomach prevents me from getting any food down. I can taste bile in the back of my mouth. No matter how hard I try, I can't completely grey out the memories. I sit with Shelby and the other scientists—the picture of compliance and policy—but stare long-ingly across the hall toward Simons' group where the team laughs at Cain's antics.

It's hard to look at Shelby and wonder. I walk with her and Sima to the cure labs and suffer through the day's measurements in studious silence. More than once, I feel the burn of Hersh's judgmental gaze as I record data with practiced hands. If Shelby is affected at all by the circumstances of the last twenty-four hours, the change is unde-tectable. She continues to drive her experiments forward with full force, rarely blinking as the other scientists furrow their brows and scramble to keep up.

Every pre-determined data point I record has become the subject of my own scrutiny. For what purpose does the government wish to receive this data? Did Shelby really design this experiment? Why does the government need an army? Who do they intend to use it on?

Shelby's tangent aside, we've returned to recording life cycles of individual strains of Zoribiatus. Just yesterday, I would've guessed the purpose of these experiments was to find what triggers cell death or perfect incubation... Now I know that we're breeding the perfect strain of Zoribiatus to be used as a government weapon.

What exactly defines the perfect strain of weaponized Zoribiatus?

My thoughts are interrupted by Hersh, who invites himself into my workstation. "Mason, I swear you look paler today than you did yesterday." His voice is cloyingly sweet and unnatural.

"I'm actually feeling much better, thank you, Hersh," I reply, biting my lower lip and keeping my voice under professional control.

"I'm very happy to hear that," the red-bearded scientist coos. I smell the sulfuric boiled-egg smell on his breath from morning dining hour. "Shelby has a good eye to have spotted your illness and pulled you out of the labs before something terrible could happen."

I seize the opportunity to use Orman's spy against him. "Actually, I am not certain that's why she pulled me."

"Oh? Why then?" Hersh's eyes widen almost imperceptibly, the hungry hunt for information an obvious undertone to his false concern.

"Shelby wanted to let me know that she's unhappy with my experiment," I say, adding a note of dejection to my voice.

"Oh no! Why is that?" The sympathy in Hersh's voice is grossly over-exaggerated. His face is the illustration of concern. I want to laugh.

"Well," I start, adding a sigh for dramatic delivery, "she says that it lacks scientific integrity. I'm disappointed, but she's right."

Hersh's eyes dart to Shelby before returning to me. "She's right?"

"I can see her point. I didn't spend nearly enough time on my experimental design. I've been distracted—probably because I haven't been feeling well—and it's obviously reflected in my work."

Hersh nods, scrunching his eyebrows. "So you haven't been feeling well for some time?"

"I suppose not. I never stopped to assess my own health. All I've been worried about are the experiments and the screening."

The pieces fit. Yesterday, Dunn complained that I didn't know his name. Simons, whom everyone knows I'm fond of, was in quarantine. I was present for an incident in the kill labs. Diaz had a missed contamination. Even without so many sleepless nights, I'm a good candidate for a breakdown. It's so believable I have to keep myself from smiling.

I shrug to indicate that my interest in the matter has passed. Reluctantly, Hersh shuffles away from my station. Keeping my head down, I search my peripherals to spot Shelby giving me the slightest nod of approval. My hand shakes as I continue to record data. In just a few hours, I have to face Orman.

I decide that I'll start by being an exceptional suck up.

CHAPTER
FIFTY-ONE

"COME IN!" Orman opens the door to his office, welcoming me. His demeanor is almost giddy. It immediately puts me on edge. Orman is never giddy unless he's going to shoot something.

"Thank you," I say, keeping my tone in check and attempting to sound as respectful as possible. I glance around to see that we're alone in his office, which is at the junction between the kill lab and the main area that connects all the passageways. It's set up similarly to Shelby's, but where hers looks unkempt and stuffed full of years of research, Orman's office is tidy and has a lived-in look to it. Instead of piles of research and old documents, his shelves are lined with personal memorabilia.

"Are you feeling better today, Mason?" Orman asks, continuing with pleasantness in his voice, ushering me through the door. Everything I tend to identify as typical Orman behavior is absent. I never thought I'd miss it, but right now, I recognize it as dangerously missing.

"Yes, I feel a lot better," I reply. "I'm taking extra measures to rest and recover. I've really been out of sorts for a while now—maybe weeks. I think it's the stress."

He lets the door close behind him and moves to put his hands on my shoulders. I let this happen as if it were the most normal thing he could do. He squeezes my shoulders while looking down at me and smiling. "There has been so much stress lately. I only feel bad that I didn't recognize your symptoms earlier. I should have been paying better attention!"

I wonder if Hersh managed to scurry over to make his report before our meeting.

Orman releases one shoulder and allows his other hand to slide around so that I'm wedged against him, directing me over to a small table with two covered trays. He releases me from the strange side-embrace and moves to stand behind one of the two chairs. I move to sit across from where he stands, but he makes a little noise as if he's correcting me and pulls the chair from the table, offering it to me.

If this is some sort of game, I have no choice but to play along.

"Thank you," I say, accepting the seat awkwardly. His behavior is so distracting that I almost forget my plan. *I have to stay focused.*

"Of course. Thank *you* for agreeing to meet with me. I've been meaning to have this meeting with you for quite some time." Orman takes his seat across from me. I briefly consider if I would feel more comfortable sitting across from the version of Orman I'm more accustomed to—terse, haughty and controlling. This is just a different sort of controlling.

My hand shakes as I remove the lid to my dinner tray. Orman catches this and places his hand over mine. I hold my breath to keep myself from flinching.

"Let me get that lid for you. You're still recovering."

His hand is cold, but his tone is warm. I count the time his hand is on mine. Each second is like an eternity. *One... two... three... four...*

I breathe out between my teeth, making a subtle hissing noise, and remind myself to keep my cool. He's likely testing me, pushing my buttons and trying to get me to snap at him in order to find a reason to have me put on restriction. If he's trying to throw me off, it's working.

"It took some digging," Orman says as he stacks the lid on a nearby cart, "but I finally found someone you eat with who was able to tell me what you like. I guess I shouldn't be surprised... Kids are all the same: pasta!" He says it with a bit of grandiosity. He calls me a kid. *What other kids is he referring to?*

I smile to show my appreciation as I speculate on his efforts. Orman went out of his way to talk to *volunteers* and find out what my favorite food is. He's being nice.

"Orman," I say, bemused, "I never knew you had the capacity to care for others. I'm impressed."

I wince. My biting remarks could be exactly what he's searching for. *Then again, if I don't act like myself at least a little bit tonight, it might make him even more suspicious.* I search my place setting for a fork and can't find one. I look up to see Orman has left his seat and is rummaging in a cabinet behind his desk.

"Of course I care, Mason. I care about all of the scientists at the Northern Laboratories." I study him while his back is turned.

"You sure have a way of hiding it," I jab. *Don't push it!* Shelby's voice screams inside my head.

"That, Mason, is exactly what a scientist should be able to do—Ah!" He emerges from his cabinet holding a dusty bottle, brushing it with his sleeve and looking triumphant. "Do you know what this is, Mason?"

He holds the bottle out to me and searches my face for indication that I recognize it. I shake my head.

"Of course you don't; I forget you never spent much time in the cities. How foolish of me. This—" he turns the bottle so that the label faces me "—is a twenty-year-old bottle of malt whiskey I had imported from the Capitol a few years back. It took quite a few bribes—trust me —to get this here. Do you have any idea how expensive indulgences like this are? Of course you don't," he corrects himself, speaking more for his own benefit than mine. "This is a real privilege, and I believe I'll share it with you."

"What's the occasion?" I ask, growing increasingly wary.

"I have a proposition. Join my research team."

"Join your research team?" The words are thick and sour in my mouth.

"Yes," he affirms, rummaging again in his cabinet of treasures. "Since you've been attending weapons training regularly again, I've been able to measure your improvements, and I'm *very* pleased."

I smirk. The real reason for my improvements in weapons is my focus on imagining his face as the face of every target I hit.

"You're pleased." He beams, mistaking my expression.

He sees what he wants.

He pours the whiskey into two tumblers and hands one to me. "Remember to just sip this slowly—especially in your condition."

I take the glass. He toasts to his proposition before I accept, and we sip the malted beverage. I set the glass down while the elixir burns my throat. A warmth spreads through my chest. "Thank you for the offer; however, I'm not certain that it's the right position for me..."

I don't want to work on his weapons team. That's a measure too far.

"What on earth are you talking about, Mason? You're a natural with weapons, and you think fast under pressure."

I pick up the glass again so that I have something to keep my hands busy. Orman swirls the amber liquid casually and takes another long drink.

"Besides," he continues, "I suspect you'll be searching for a new area of study in light of recent circumstances..."

Finally, we arrive at the matter of my new specialty.

"Yes... I'm sad to say that my research has hit a dead end." I don't even have to try to put the right amount of bewilderment, disappointment and heartbreak into the statement. Every one of the emotions has set up shop at the front of my consciousness.

"Truly, you have my condolences," Orman says in a low voice, nursing his drink and meeting my eyes. His gaze burns a hole straight through me. "I read your experiment design, and I thought it might soften the blow of failure. We all stumble into roadblocks; it just so happens that yours are insurmountable."

I wince under his criticism. I take another sip. "Yes, it's been a rough twenty-four hours."

"Indeed." Orman leans in and places his hand on my arm from across the table. "So you'll say yes, then, to my offer? You'd be the ideal partner out in the field."

Part of me is curious. I want to see what the government is doing outside of the laboratories. I want to see where the outbreaks are and understand the plot. But I don't think I could keep the ruse up indefinitely. Not working so closely with the enemy.

I search for an escape—anything to prevent me from having to accept a position on Orman's research team—and land on the only lie I think I have a chance at pulling off. "I would love to, Orman, but I've already accepted a position on another research team."

Orman removes his hand from my arm and sits up, taking another drink. "Oh? I hadn't heard. Who has the honor of accepting you onto their team?"

His eyes are sharp and angry. I'm afraid he knows I'm lying already, but I can't back down now.

"Shelby offered me a position when she rejected my experiment," I say, the words rushing out of my mouth before I have a chance to weigh and measure each one. It's a dangerous move. I don't know if Shelby has already spoken to Orman.

"This is a new development," Orman says, a look of genuine surprise on his face. "Shelby hasn't had a team in twenty years. You were under her advisement when you arrived, and even that didn't last." He sounds bitter.

"I told her how much I learned under her advisement and asked for her guidance while I discover my new specialty. I've been flailing for some time now."

"Under Shelby's advisory. Off-limits until further notice." He speaks slowly, his voice dripping with disdain. "Why is she so interested in you?"

"I had a bad attitude at the Institute. She tried to straighten me out." Orman nods slowly, continuing to drink and study my face. His leg, crossed over his other leg, shakes as he muses silently. Still holding my drink, but not tending to it, I attempt to change the subject matter. "We don't have any silverware. Is there any on the tray? Dinner is getting cold."

Orman drains his tumbler and sets it on the table before standing and walking to his desk. "I apologize for the oversight," he says, not looking at me. "I must have forgotten to request it. We can eat with these."

He walks back to the table and presents two pearled knives with razor-sharp blades. "They're a matched set. They, like the whiskey, are also very rare and costly." His voice has regained some of its characteristic slow and sarcastic undertones.

He offers me one of the knives, and I take it gingerly while Orman returns to his seat and refills his tumbler. *What other contraband does he have tucked away in his private cabinet?*

The sharp blade of the knife slices easily through the noodles and pings as it contacts the porcelain dish. I raise it up and note that I'm the one bringing the knife up to my throat. It might be purposeful symbolism. Orman is just holding his knife and watching me.

"These are beautiful knives," I say, holding mine so that the pearls catch and diffuse the light from overhead. "How have you managed to collect such rare and valuable objects during your stay at the Northern Laboratories? Or is some of it from your assignments off site?"

"I am a collector of fine things, and if I come across something I want, I find a way to possess it," Orman replies with a thin smile. "As you may or may not know, I have a very critical and important position." He twirls the knife slowly between his thumb and index finger, peering at it studiously.

Suddenly he stops, and his eyes meet mine in a foreboding stare. "I use my position to obtain certain—advantages—for myself, as well as for others. You could benefit from a friend like me, Mason." Though he says it as an offer, it sounds like a threat.

"I don't really need—" I begin.

"You don't know what you need, Mason," Orman interrupts. His voice has finally broken with anger. He catches it and adjusts his tone. With fatherly concern and a sickly-sweet niceness, he says, "I want to ask you to reconsider your decision to work under Shelby. Give me a chance—just a while—you may find that you like working under me."

I swallow a bite and wash it down with some whiskey in an attempt to clear the lump in my throat. The lump remains. I think I understand. He wants to control me directly. "I'm not certain I want to remain permanently under the study of another scientist…"

"You want to try another area of independent research?" Orman asks in a dark voice.

"I suppose I may," I say weakly.

"Mason." Orman stands, tumbler in hand, and begins pacing his office floor. "Might I advise, as your elder and as your superior, that you really don't want to do that. Independent research here in the Northern Laboratories can be—dangerous."

This is definitely a threat. I stand and pace the floor with him. I carry my tumbler so I have something to occupy my hands. Orman paces nervously back and forth. I stand directly in front of him at the center of his office and attempt to make eye contact—desperate to diffuse his anger.

"Orman, will you at least let me consider my options before I make a final decision?" He stops directly in front of me, staring down into my eyes.

"Do you really need time? I can offer you more than any senior scientist at the laboratories. Sure, maybe Shelby has seniority, but she's jaded, she's been here too long. I'm still here!" He gestures toward himself. "I still care."

I think of what the volunteers say about him. *Orman's dead inside.* There must be some truth in that statement. There's something else inside of him too, and I'm just seeing it tonight. There's a hunger—a need—that lives in his hollow soul. The fine things he collects, the way he surrounds himself with sycophants who blindly admire him, and the way he spoke to the president's committee in the recording all lead to one conclusion. He needs to feel powerful. I think he'll do anything to ensure he does.

I stand very still in front of this dangerous man, uncertain what I should do or say next. If I agree to join Orman's team, I may be stuck working directly under him for the rest of my life. Working under him would make planning my next steps difficult, no matter what Shelby has planned. *How long could I hide my knowledge of the cure from him?*

If I reject Orman's offer, however, the rest of my life might be a lot shorter…

The silence persists a moment longer before Orman says, leaning down so that his hot, whiskey-tinted breath brushes against my ear and the side of my face, "I promise I'll make it worth your while."

Feeling the strings of his trap tighten like a noose around my neck, I relent.

"You make a persuasive argument, Orman. I see that there really is little other choice than to join your research team." I give a small smile and, thinking of Frances, bat my eyelashes to diffuse the obvious sting of my words.

I'll let him believe that he can control me.

I offer him my drink-free hand, but he brushes it aside and puts his arm around my shoulder, pulling me close. "I knew you would see things my way!"

I try to adjust so that my body isn't pressed up against his. He looks down on me with a radiant, triumphant smile. I look up at him, defeated.

He went for the kill and succeeded.

FIFTY-TWO

"I CAN'T BELIEVE you agreed to work on Orman's team," Simons puffs between haggard gasps of air. Redline exercises leave no man opportunity for victory. We're all humbled by the effort.

It's been weeks since I had the opportunity to talk with him. Weeks of feigned compliance on Orman's team, turning my back to the volunteers while carrying oversized, overpowered weapons. Weeks of mimicking the man I hate and isolating myself in painful loneliness day and night. I've had to avoid Simons and his team in the dining hall, and our schedules haven't aligned in the training field in so long.

I rest my hands on my quadriceps, holding myself up and resisting the urge to vomit. "Believe me," I say between breaths, "it wasn't like I had another choice."

Simons shakes his head and spits. I stand up and wince as my abdominal muscles protest, still suffering from the effort. "I suppose not," Simons relents.

I turn in response to the sound of Jorey vomiting enthusiastically into a trashcan on the side of the track. I squint at him through the sweat pouring into my eyes. Cain laughs and slaps Jorey on the back—his smile persisting even after ten repetitions of redlines. I follow Simons without thinking, like I always do, forgetting that I'm supposed to be distancing myself. We join the group.

"Look here, brother! We've got a true champion," Cain says to no one in particular.

"Whatever, man," Jorey whimpers, spitting to clean the vomit from his mouth. He rests one hand on either side of the large black can, leaning over it and panting still.

"I mean it! I truly do," Cain continues enthusiastically, standing by his side, waiting for him to finish his business. "Any man who pushes himself to the point of upchuck is a real champion in my book."

"Hardly," Jorey says, turning away from his vomit. "I'm just the guy who's going to get torn to pieces by the near-dead if we're ever in a redline-critical situation. You're welcome."

We all laugh as we walk away from the track. I pat Jorey on the shoulder and reassure him. "No worries, *brother*," I say, imitating Cain's voice. "In a redline-critical situation, there will be *some* slower, stockier fellow who will honorably offer his body as a sacrifice for your escape."

Jorey wraps his arm around my shoulder and pulls me in for a sweaty side-embrace, still delirious from his effort. I note the warmth of his embrace in stark contrast to the one I'd been unwillingly pulled into in Orman's office. "Mason, I'll take your rosy outlook on life any day ahead of Cain's. At least I believe in your perspective."

Cain pouts, trying to look dejected and garner sympathy. Simons, who towers over even Cain, places both of his hands on his shoulders. "I suspect, Cain, that we all share that sentiment. Mason here is a realist, and what she says goes."

I catch the implications of Simons' statement even if no one else does. With these words, he is indicating to me that while he disapproves of my decision to join Orman's team, he believes me when I say that I didn't have a choice. He's telling the others to trust in me as well. He's telling *Cain* that the team follows Simons, and Simons has chosen to follow me.

The weight of Jorey's sweaty body causes me to bump into him every couple of steps, but Jorey's arm does not relent in its grip. I pat him on his soaking-wet back as we continue down the hall. He responds by squeezing my shoulder. We're nearly through the exit of the training center when a cold voice calls out.

"Mason! Hold up, Mason." Orman's beckoning brings me back to reality. I shouldn't be here. I'm supposed to be back on the floor with him.

I drop my arm from Jorey's back and turn. Jorey, however, doesn't release his tight grip. Cain and Simons also turn to investigate Orman's unsolicited call.

"What's up, Orman?" I call out across the hall, trying to sound unworried.

"I need you over here. I want to look into some of the mechanics in these weapons, and I think you should be involved." Orman isn't suggesting—his tone is clear and commanding.

I sigh. "Alright. I'll be right over," I call back. "Sorry, guys," I say to Simons' team.

I bring my hand up to remove Jorey's arm from my shoulder, but he's holding on with a fierce grip. I look over at him, his thickset face very near mine, and ask, "Jorey, are you alright?"

Simons places his hand over Jorey's, causing him to release his hold as I move away. I turn and face Jorey, whose face is still bright red from exertion. "He's alright, Mason. You know he's no good at redlines. I'll get him to the showers and bed early. You go on and help Orman. We'll see you during morning dining hour tomorrow," Simons insists, taking the burden of Jorey for his own.

I nod at the group and give them a reassuring smile. "Alright then, see you guys bright and early," I say before turning and trotting over to greet Orman on the weapons field.

Once I'm at Orman's side, I turn to see the group exit the hall, Cain —in typical form—making some jest to egg them on. I hold back a smile. I can feel my body stiffen as much from being in Orman's presence as from the exertion of the night. Laughter echoes through the doorway as they fade from my sight.

"Why do you waste so much of your time with those clowns?" Orman says while he strips one of his pulsar guns. His voice brings my focus back.

"I wouldn't call it a waste of time. And," I add, recalling something Tucker said once, "Simons has the most capable group of volunteers here."

Orman finishes his stripping and shrugs as he meets my gaze. "I'll agree with you on that. I'm frequently pleased with their work. In fact, I've requested that they be permanently assigned to the kill labs."

I step back from Orman, anger swelling below the surface so hot that it bubbles over. "That's cruel!"

I know without a doubt that the assignment has nothing to do with their capabilities and is just one more line laid out in Orman's trap. He isn't leaving any avenue of control unchecked. He wants his power over me to be complete.

"Mason, they're volunteers," Orman says coldly. His emotionless smile sends chills through me, which are enhanced by the slick sweat.

"They're still people," I protest, forcing my body to still.

"The Northern Laboratories requires calculated decision-making in order to progress smoothly. I've made the decision that's most beneficial to the laboratories—the sort of decision I expect you'd make, when pressed."

"You got me," I lie, too angry to keep it up. "What are we looking at here?" I ask, changing the subject and playing the role of the diligent student.

"Here we have one of my favorite little pet projects." Orman smiles mischievously. He may be able to bait and trap me, but I'm able to play to his ego just as well.

"It's a pulsar gun," I say flatly.

"Again, Mason, you're so wrong. This *was* a regular pulsar gun… until—here—take this and take aim at that 200-meter target."

Orman hands me the weapon and moves to my side. The gun is significantly lighter than the regular field weapons. I bring it up to my shoulder and take aim, resting my cheek against the barrel and breathing out as I steady my grip and zero in on the target. I pull the trigger, expecting a direct hit, but the gun kicks violently. A thick ball of energy spurts out, moving slowly and growing in dimension as it travels across the field. The violent kick of the gun caused it to scrape across my face, leaving a deep gash.

"What the hell is that?" I yell as the energy ball contacts a force field at the edge of the weapons field with a loud explosion.

"That, Mason, is my latest creation," Orman says proudly. He reaches out and wipes the blood dripping from the gash on my cheek. "I didn't mean to surprise you."

I pull away from Orman's touch and wipe the blood away with my sleeve. "It's fine. I'm fine. I just wasn't expecting such a kick."

"Try again," Orman commands.

I shake out my arms and prepare to take aim again. This time, I rest my leg against the barrier on my right and settle in for the impact. As I reposition myself, I feel Orman move in behind me and place his hand on my arm. He repositions the gun, tucking it into the joint before reaching his arm out to steady my supporting arm. His face rests on my shoulder, pressed against mine. "Like this."

I repeat my original action and squeeze the trigger. This time, I pull the gun into my body as I fire and move with the impact, maintaining control. The energy ball emerges this time on target. In a matter of seconds, it contacts the 200-meter target, which smolders and fumes as it's consumed.

"Whoa." The target is reduced to ashes. I am authentically impressed.

"Indeed," Orman agrees. I can feel his smile against my cheek.

"I'm a little sweaty from redlines," I say, pulling away from him.

"Hmm?" Orman says, finally moving away from me.

"How did you make it so light?" I ask, changing the subject again. I swallow at the lump in my throat that refuses to leave and wonder if Orman can hear the ragged thump of my heart in my chest.

"The weapon receives energy by satellite," Orman says. "The only components of the gun are the barrel for aim, the capacitor for energy accumulation and the software for firing."

"Impressive," I offer, wondering if there will be more to tonight's exploration of weaponry.

"I knew I could count on you to understand the magnitude of this accomplishment," Orman says. He again reaches out and wipes the blood from my cheek. "It's why I picked you for my team."

I can't help but think that there's more to the words than just the weapon. *What accomplishment?* As I bring my hand up to wipe my cheek, Orman moves his face inward, and I inadvertently catch him in the nose with my thumb. He recoils in pain, and I blurt, "Oh! Sorry!"

Orman makes an angry, agonized noise while cursing under his breath. When he quits writhing to face me, he's pinching his nose.

"Are you bleeding?"

"I don't know, ab I?" Orman asks dramatically.

If I weren't so scared of him, I'd laugh. Instead, I lean in over his face to investigate his nose. "I detect no damage," I say.

I'm looking up his nose when, without warning, Orman moves forward and presses his lips against mine. His hands wrap around me like magnetic lashings. Before I have a chance to respond, his mouth opens and his tongue gently moves against my still-startled, still-open mouth. He pulls me in closer and breathes a strange, satisfied noise.

I jerk backward. "What was that?"

All thoughts of the danger—every thought of what I'm supposed to be pretending to be—are momentarily halted.

"Kara, it's alright, you don't have to pretend," Orman says, his voice still cocky, but softer. He brings a hand up to cup my face, but I lurch away automatically.

"What do you mean? What are you talking about?" My arms are crossed against my chest.

"Kara, you don't have to worry about what people will think. This wouldn't be the first time..." Orman continues, stepping toward me.

I step back in response. "I'm not worried about what people will think. I'm worried about what you're thinking!"

My mind races back to the laboratories, to the situation and to the danger personified by Orman standing right in front of me. I process this new realization in an instant. If I stop him, he'll retaliate. He'll know he doesn't have complete control.

If I let him… there's no going back from that.

Orman stops and studies me. A shadow crosses his face, and his countenance turns cold. He may as well have read my mind. "Is it because I'm older?" he demands.

"No, it's not like that." I don't know what to do.

"Who is it, then? Don't tell me it's a volunteer!"

"No! It's not a volunteer… It's nobody. It's *not you.*"

It comes out of my mouth before I can stop it, and I know it's over. He knows the truth now. He doesn't have me.

Orman stares at me cruelly. "Be careful, Mason."

"I am being careful!"

Orman smiles as though he's caught me. "Are you?" His expression turns harsh. "I warned you, Mason, that I have an important position. You don't want to cross me. You're in very dangerous territory…"

I swallow hard but keep my arms crossed. There is no good decision, so I make the one I can live with. "Orman, I don't mean anything by it—honestly I don't, but I can't—I won't do it."

"I'm a selfish man," Orman warns. "You have one opportunity to be successful in the Northern Laboratories."

One opportunity to survive. That's what he means.

"Orman, I'm happy working on your research team," I offer desperately, yet firmly.

"Very well, Mason," Orman sighs. "You can have it your way."

Without another word, he picks his weapon up and walks away from the training field. I stand, frozen in place while he departs. He doesn't look back.

CHAPTER
FIFTY-THREE

I'M OFFICIALLY out of time. Leaving the training floor, I storm toward the living quarters. When I first arrived at the Northern Laboratories, Shelby instructed me to grant her access to my room. Was it her way of telling me that I would have access to her room? I'm about to find out.

My heart is racing.

I'm so certain that the door won't open that I practically fall through it when I put my ID card to the scanner and it swings forward under my force. Shelby is sitting at her table, staring ahead into nothing particular and looking tired—looking old. She doesn't seem startled by my unannounced intrusion. She doesn't even look over.

"Did you kill them?" I demand as soon as the door shuts behind me.

She looks down at the metallic table surface before bringing her gaze up to meet mine. "Kill whom?"

It's hard to imagine that I'm looking at the face of a murderer.

"You know who," I say, stepping in to face her.

With a bare foot, Shelby pushes the chair across from her out and waits for me to sit before answering. "I don't know who, Mason. There are too many. And for all of them, the answer is complicated. Yes. No. Not really. I helped. I didn't *know*."

Fifty-two years in the Northern Laboratories. So many deaths.

"Did you kill my family?"

She looks relieved and pained at the same time. I have my answer before she speaks. "Did I create the technology that resulted in their deaths? Yes. I'm guilty of that. But I didn't know what they were doing until it was already happening."

"Did you try to stop it?" I ask, slumping lower in the chair across from her.

"Of course!" she snaps. "But in the end, I only had the power to save you."

"Why?" All of the suppressed anguish threatens to burst through. *Why?*

"Because sometimes saving someone is better than saving no one." Her answer makes me feel hollow. It was random. Sitting across from me, she looks just as defeated.

"Why not Hank?" I look away from Shelby into her dim, empty room and blink back the tears that are fighting to join his name.

"Because of the test."

"Hank passed it too, you know," I growl.

"Of course I know," she agrees, "but your results were unmatched. You were the one I could argue for."

From the corner of my eye, I watch Shelby's arms flop to the table. Her head is bowed. She looks ashamed.

"You chose the wrong one," I say, tasting my own bitterness.

"I don't think so."

I turn my head, forcing her to look at me. "Why? Because I'm smarter? On that one test. One test! Hank's better than me in every way. He's cleverer, more patient, he's braver and... and he's gone because of *you!*"

I can't stop the ache now. It spreads from somewhere deep inside of me and robs the air from my lungs. A terrible shudder takes over my body, and I think I'll wail, but all that comes out is a faint whimper.

Shelby reaches out a narrow hand and lifts my chin. There's a steely determination in her eyes. "I saved you because there's never been anyone like you. *You* got the perfect score. That means something—or at least I wanted it to mean something." The light dims at the end of her statement.

Blaming Shelby for Hank's death doesn't bring him back. Nothing can bring any of them back. I squeeze my eyes shut and clench my fists in my lap. If I don't stop now, I'll be suffocated by the weight of their deaths.

"What about the others?" I ask, forcing myself to set my family aside—to look at the bigger picture.

"Not all of them, but yes. It would've been too suspicious if I hadn't," Shelby answers.

"Miller? Tucker? Horne?" Their names roll off my tongue like a roll call. My name comes next.

"Miller wasn't me. I don't know who did that one. I submitted Tucker's name. I oversaw both incidents. That's how I knew what you did in the simulation. I knew Smith was an accident."

It feels strange, now that they're gone.

"Why Tucker?"

"A report came in that someone was looking into the archives for Miller's death. I had to choose. I couldn't save both of you. I chose you because I hated the idea of letting you die after I fought so hard to save you… So I gave them the wrong name."

"He died because of me."

She shakes her head. "Tucker was going to get himself killed one way or another. No one questioned it when I submitted his name."

I think of what Orman said. *You're always off-limits.* He didn't think of me as a threat at first. He just wanted what he was told he couldn't have.

"What do I do now?" I ask.

"The answer is simple." She braces her hands against her knees and uses the combined strength of her arms and legs to stand. Her body seems to creak, but there is a smoothness to her movement. She's both old and young—capable and infirm. Good and evil.

She faces me, standing between the table and her bed. "Stay alive. If you can do that long enough, then I'll get you out of here."

It's not so simple. I wonder if I can follow orders for once.

CHAPTER
FIFTY-FOUR

I REFRESH THE SCHEDULE AGAIN, hoping that it's just a glitch. The same list appears, taunting me. I pound my fist against my desk in frustration and refresh the schedule once more, but nothing changes. I groan in exasperation, pacing the floor in front of my workstation, and let myself scream in the safety of my dormitory.

"This can't be happening!"

I knew there would be consequences after last night's incident, but I didn't see this coming. Everything is about to change unless there's an error in the system, and I know there is no error. The schedule lists my experiment in one month. *One month!* The largest floor in the kill labs is reserved for hive communications experimentation. I select the icon for my experiment and read the details listed:

Objective: Investigate Hive Communication via Electromagnetic Frequencies

The hive communication in mass patient bodies has been well-documented. Previous experimentation has failed to identify communication pathways via pheromone messaging. Secondary pathway investigation measured on the electromagnetic spectrum on the following frequencies...[expand]

Design: 250 fully neurologically developed patients. Frequencies are measured to detect variation and search for indication of communication pathway...[expand]

> *Experiment termination: Patient incineration…[expand]*
>
> *Assigned scientists: Kara Mason, Lead. Rick Orman, Gretchen Shelby, James Dunn, Anton Altman, supporting. [expand]*

The design is laid out before me like a death sentence. I feel sick. I bury my face in my hands and groan again. The sound doesn't even begin to diffuse my agony. *This can't be happening.* I have to talk to Shelby and see if I'm missing something.

Turning my workstation to standby, I finish readying myself for the cure labs. After today, the next month is reserved to allow for training time. If my experiment is actually happening, then I'm responsible for preparing scientists and volunteers alike for execution.

As I leave my room and head for the dining hall, I'm filled with a hollow sensation of hopelessness. I suspect there's little I can do. Orman is likely the driving force behind this.

I'm a collector… His voice rattles in my head.

My thoughts carry me heedlessly into the dining hall. Scientists and volunteers acknowledge my passing with polite nods and pleasant greetings, but I ignore them all, brooding in my misery. I grab a tray and slam it aggressively onto the counter, filling it with various breakfast selections and not really looking. I'm in the middle of heaping a large spatula-full of some egg-like substance onto my already-overflowing plate when someone finally breaks through.

"Hungry much this morning?" Cain's voice—easy as ever—registers, jarring me from my dark thoughts.

"Haven't you heard?" I ask, scowling at my overfilled plate of morning confections. "I've been malnourished, and I've got to keep my strength up!" My voice is filled with sarcastic chipper.

"Indeed you do," Orman intrudes. "I would hate to hear of another trip to medical, Mason; you've got important research on the horizon."

With this droll and condemning statement, Orman confirms my worst fear—the appearance of my experiment on the schedule is not an accident.

"You mean our test of your latest creation? You're right, I really do think there are some exciting implications in this field of weaponry…"

I watch Cain wince behind Orman's back at my ass-kissing. I have to bite my lower lip to stifle a smile, but the moment passes too quickly as Orman dashes my offer of compliance. "No, no, Mason, your experiment design has been cleared," he says with marked enthusiasm.

"I hadn't realized," I lie. "I know there were some serious faults in the integrity of the science…"

"Mason," Orman says, placing his hand on my shoulder and steering me away from Cain and the breakfast line, "don't be so modest. Every senior scientist in the Northern Laboratories recognizes your abilities. You're well aware of the *integrity* of your scientific design."

I let Orman's words resonate in my mind, allowing the hidden message to sink in. I don't bother to respond, knowing that he's made his decision—since he can't control me, he's chosen to destroy me. Orman steers me with one hand on my shoulder to his table where Hersh and Fisher sit, munching and talking carelessly about what must have been the goriest kill experiment this century.

"I've seen them ooze before, but the smell of their boiling flesh—" Hersh begins.

"Say no more, please," Fisher interjects. "You'll just remind me of their melting flesh. It was like watching sped-up decay."

Their conversation is so overtly repulsive that I wonder if Orman put them up to it. I check his watchful gaze to find his smug smile. "Sit with us, Mason."

I set my tray at the table and squeeze in. Fisher doesn't budge, forcing me to press directly against him. Orman clears his throat, and the scientist to my left picks up his tray and walks away without a word. Orman places his tray next to mine and takes his seat, sealing me in as they continue their horror-show discussions.

"I don't understand what you're complaining about, men," Orman provokes. "Surely the scientific advantage of watching the death process of patients outweighs the slight discomfort of their stinking decay."

I stare down at my plate, repulsed. Orman catches my disgust and seizes the opportunity. "Mason, eat! You were just discussing your need for nourishment. Don't let a little squeamish conversation dissuade you. Eat!"

I pick up my fork and begin shuffling the contents of my plate from one end to the other. I bring a small bite to my mouth, knowing that Orman is delighting in my misery. He gives me a sort of "atta-girl" smile as I take the bite and chew, forcing myself not to grimace or register any disgust. Behind Orman's gloating countenance, I spy Cain straying away from Simons' table. He makes his way to a table of scientists, and I lose sight of his tall, lanky frame as he leans down to speak with someone.

I lean into my plate, feigning another bite, and spot Cain. His head is cocked to one side, and his arm rests easily on the table a few meters away. He looks over in my direction and gestures. When he moves his arm, I can see that he's talking to Shelby. She looks my way and nods slowly. Cain's body sways with laughter as he follows Shelby's line of sight. She places her frail hand on Cain's arm and says something. Cain nods in agreement and returns to Simons' table. I bring another forkful of breakfast to my mouth as Hersh describes a patient's head subject to a pressure burst akin to the rupture of a cyst.

The image comes to light for me as I squish the eggy mess between my cheeks. I gag, unable to get the bite down. Hersh and Fisher immediately commence in laughter at my reaction. Fisher slams a heavy hand on my back as I continue to choke on my breakfast mess. "Uh oh," he chides, "Miss Hive here can't handle a little gore."

Hersh caws at Fisher's harassment as I continue to cough and sputter, clearing my mouth of its contents. "There, there, now," Orman says in a mock parental tone. "Let's not let my top scientist choke to death on her breakfast."

Who will be his top scientist when he's gotten rid of me? There were no new scientists this year. Maybe there isn't a need for the Northern Laboratories any longer…

It fits—the decrease in resources, the lack of graduating recruits and the increased instances of deaths of resident scientists. All this information points in the same direction. The Northern Laboratories are reaching their expiration date.

But what about the manufacturing plans? Orman is meant to be transferred once his work here is complete. Maybe the manufacturing isn't happening at the Northern Laboratories.

Orman's hand squeezes my leg harshly, immediately ceasing the coughing and sputtering along with my line of thought. He loosens his grip but doesn't move his hand. I slip my own hand under the table to brush his away, but instead, he grabs it and holds on firmly. Frustrated and embarrassed, I look up at Orman's goons and smile politely. "Nonsense, gentlemen," I say with audible strain. "Your conversations don't bother me in the least. I've only had a weak appetite lately."

"Your appetite has seen marked improvement, Mason." Shelby's quick and certain voice silences the cruel play at Orman's table.

"Thank you," I say, looking up at Shelby with a pleading expression. "I've taken my health to heart since our meeting."

Orman releases his grip on my hand and waves his arm dismissively. "If you don't mind, Shelby, I'd hoped to discuss an upcoming project with my team over breakfast. You've got Mason all to yourself in the cure labs today."

"I'm afraid I do mind, Orman," Shelby replies sternly. She might be the only person in the world who can command him. "I have some business I need Mason to attend to regarding yesterday's data."

"Surely it can wait," Orman protests—the child in this encounter.

"It absolutely can't," Shelby insists. She turns to me. "Mason, if you would please follow me to my office. I need your analysis on the statistical significance of your high-end data points."

I immediately find my feet and squeeze myself free of my seated captors. Orman stares at his breakfast tray, sullen. "You would think she was on your team, the way you pry her from her director."

"I don't believe Mason is on a research team any longer," Shelby says. "According to our schedule, she's directing her own research again." She says this last part with a daggered glare that Orman can't miss.

"Indeed," he replies in his characteristically icy voice. "Very well, then. I look forward to our preparations for her experiment."

Orman directs a malicious sneer after us as I follow Shelby from the dining hall. I make one last glance at Simons' table and see his team in their typical stasis. Jorey looks up from his tray and catches my gaze. He smiles broadly, catching Cain's attention. Cain says something, and Jorey's face turns crimson. Cain lifts his hand in a sort of salute toward me, and I nod, losing sight of him as we turn the corner. That's two I owe him now.

CHAPTER
FIFTY-FIVE

"TELL ME EXACTLY WHAT WENT WRONG," Shelby repeats, scowling down at the schedule displayed on the workstation atop her office desk. She sits with her arms folded across her chest and a black look darkening her face.

I don't answer. Shelby sighs as she continues to glower over the workstation. She says what I'm thinking. "It doesn't matter."

"Can you submit a change? Can you override it?" I ask, knowing already that if she could change it, she would have already. I bury my face in my gloved hands, yearning for the feeling of my own skin.

"I can't," she says.

"Well then, can you get rid of Orman?" I raise my head, eyes wide. Why has it only just now occurred to me? Couldn't an accident happen to him?

"No. Orman is untouchable." Her answer is definitive.

"So I'm dead then."

"It looks like maybe we both are," she says.

"What do you mean?" I demand, launching onto my feet without really knowing what I intend to do.

"You're not the only one under investigation," Shelby says.

I slump back into my chair. She silently hands me a form with a letter addressed from the DDC in the Capital City.

This is an official notice of audit —

A complaint regarding the ethics of Senior Scientist Gretchen Shelby has been registered. This notice is to inform the recipient that all relevant documents and experimental archives, along with all personal documents and possessions deemed related or suspicious, will be under review by the internal bureau.

The recipient of this notice is given one month's preparation. Failure to comply will be deemed an act of treason and punished to the full extent of the law.

—Department of Disease Containment — Bureau of Intelligence

"Is this because you've been protecting me?" I ask, peering wide-eyed over the letter at Shelby.

Shelby nods. "Among other things." She tilts her head in the direction of the cure labs, where Sima's short hair bobs as she dances over her workstation.

"The experiment?"

She nods. I never would have suspected Sima.

"I suppose this has been a long time coming. You can't get away with clandestine experimentation forever around here," she says, gesturing to her top drawer.

"What's going to happen?" I ask.

"They're going to eliminate us," Shelby says bluntly.

"How?"

"I suppose there will be some sort of accident."

Shelby's words drive home the real purpose of my experiment on the schedule.

"What about the volunteers?" I ask.

"Collateral damage. Orman seems to have a specific vindictiveness when it comes to Simons' group."

The vindictiveness is because of me. They're my group. I belong to them. I don't belong to Orman.

"It's my fault. If I didn't spend so much time with them, they wouldn't be in danger!" I slam my hands against Shelby's workstation in frustration. The resounding thud offers little comfort.

"Mason..." Shelby starts.

"Oh, what?" I interrupt. "I did everything you told me to do. I feigned stupidity, I sucked up to Orman. I've kept my head down."

Shelby closes her mouth and looks at me. The deep lines of her wrinkled face are even more pronounced by the anguish etched there.

"Can we get them out of the kill labs?" I ask. I'd do any number of stupid things to try to save Simons' group.

Shelby shakes her head apologetically. "Orman is a vengeful man."

"Tell me about it." I let my words run loose. "A possessive, vengeful, controlling asshole."

She studies me again, her lips turning into a fine pale line. "You did everything you could."

"Not everything." I can't stop the single tear from making its way down my cheek. I thrust my arm violently across my face to dispose of it.

"I would never tell you that you should have done that." Her voice is almost a whisper. "I can hardly live with myself as it is."

I continue to aggressively brush away the traitor tears and look at her in the dim light. "This isn't the first time, is it?" I ask, nearly repeating Orman's words.

"No, it's not." Shelby keeps her voice just above a whisper.

A series of terrible thoughts rushes through my mind. I can see Shelby's hand in each one of them. I want to slap her. I know that none of it is her fault, but I hate her for it just the same. I clench my shaking hands into fists and stare steely-eyed at her.

"How could you let him get away with it? How could you let any of them? You were content to be an accomplice in exchange for your safety?"

"I had to protect the cure! It's our only hope," she says, blinking watery eyes.

It's not enough.

"A cure for how many lives? You deserve to die just as much as the rest of them!" I say, overwhelmed with anger and despair.

"I do." Her voice is calm.

"I suppose your time has finally come," I say, a stabbing irony dancing in my shaky voice. My fists clench and unclench in my lap as I fight to restrain their trembling.

"Mason, I never said I was proud of any of this. All I have is my life's work, and not even that will redeem me." Shelby reaches her arm across her desk, pleading with me. Pain and regret fill her voice.

"It's too late now. It's never going to see the light of day." So many lives for nothing.

"It's not too late," Shelby whispers.

"What are you going to do about it?" As angry as I am, I know she's my only hope. I don't have a next step.

"Anything I can," she promises, with some strength returning to her voice.

"Is the government shutting down the Northern Laboratories?" The question comes out more like an accusation.

"I suspect they might be."

"Fewer supplies, missing volunteers, no new scientists. It all makes sense if they're going to abandon the research up here." I present my evidence as though she's on trial.

"We need to get you and the cure out of the laboratories—at any cost."

"Don't let those volunteers get in your way. Especially the ones you've had working so hard for you this whole time," I snap again. This time, my voice breaks, and more tears escape. I won't let her pick me over someone else again.

"Keep it together, Mason." Shelby bursts suddenly from her chair. Her hands are pressed against her desk for support. "You can't fall apart now. People are depending on you!"

I bite my lip to contain my frustrations. "What can I do? I can't stop Orman. If you can't stop him, I can't do anything—" I'm the helpless child on top of the boulder all over again.

"We're going to leave the Northern Laboratories. All of us," Shelby says, immediately silencing me.

"We'll never make it." I look up at her, standing ramrod straight at her desk, hair braided back and skin wrinkled around every bend. Her eyes are filled with a fiery light that brings new life into her old frame.

"We leave or we die."

She says it with such conviction. It makes her young again. She's right, but I can't imagine leaving the Northern Laboratories. I have no idea even where to start. Disappearing from the laboratories is no small feat. We'll be hunted the moment we leave. It doesn't seem possible.

"How?" I ask quietly, hoping she has our escape sketched out in her notebook right behind the cure.

"We have to create a diversion—a disaster—and leave before it can be contained," Shelby explains as though she really has planned it out.

"What about Orman? What about the rest of the government? The DDC?"

"Orman will need to be a casualty. Otherwise he'll continue to be a problem. He could ruin an escape." We can't dispose of Orman in the regular function of the laboratories, but as part of our grand exit— that's different. Will Shelby add him to the list of things she regrets? I won't add him to mine.

"And the DDC?" I ask.

"One thing at a time," she implores.

"Okay," I say, swallowing my sense of panic and doom. I decide to reserve Shelby's judgment for her crimes in the Northern Laboratories for another time. I don't forgive her, but I trust her. "How do we do it?"

"That's the simple part," Shelby explains, her quick wit taking over. "Over the course of the next month, you are responsible for training in preparation for your experiment. Instead of preparing for the execution of your experiment, you'll prepare for escape."

"And Orman?" I ask, pointing out the obvious flaw in her plan.

"I can keep him distracted." Shelby's smile lights up her face so completely that she appears to shed every one of her weary and heartbreaking years. "I've got an audit to prepare for, and Orman's position will require him to offer me whatever assistance I request. I'm getting quite old, and I just don't seem to have the organization I used to..." She opens her eyes wide and places her hands across her desk, knocking papers askew and spilling a file box over the other edge. The contents—folders filled with loose papers—spill across the floor and under my seat.

"How long have you been planning this?" I ask.

"Years," Shelby says. "Call your first meeting tomorrow after breakfast. I have a hunch Orman won't be available." Shelby's sly smile informs me that she's got something in the works already. I leave her office to prepare for the last cure experiment I'll ever perform in the Northern Laboratories.

FIFTY-SIX

TRUE TO HER WORD, when the cure lab assignment rotates out and the time is slotted for training, Shelby manages to steer Orman far from the session. I enter the training field to see Simons' group at the ready. Frances and Cain no longer look the part of fresh blood. Their bodies are lean and tired, and their faces reveal a certain strain that is the signature of this place.

The volunteers huddle together, talking lightly amongst one another, making it painfully obvious that Dunn and Altman—my scientist support—don't belong. I haven't yet figured out what to do with them, and I don't dare hope that they'll go along with what Shelby and I have planned. The knowledge that Sima made a report on Shelby, whether her intentions were malicious or not, is far too fresh.

I stand several feet in front of the group and call their attention by clearing my throat. It only takes a moment for conversation to settle and all eyes to be on me. Lacing my black-gloved hands neatly behind my back, I lift my chin and say, "I'm glad to see everyone made this training session a priority."

"What do you mean, Mason?" Altman asks, squinting at me through thick glasses.

"Who can tell me what personnel are assigned to this experiment?" I address the whole group, but I rest my gaze on Dunn and Altman.

"You know who's assigned," Dunn retorts nonchalantly.

"Indeed," I reply, keeping the command in my voice. I picture Amos as she addressed the volunteers at the Institute. No one questions her because she does everything with purpose. "Would you mind enlightening the rest of us?"

"Dunn, myself, Shelby, Orman and the volunteers," Altman offers with his eyes cast down, ever eager to avoid conflict.

"That's correct," I continue, still addressing the scientists. "Does anyone know where Shelby and Orman are?"

Their response is silence—which I had predicted, well aware that Shelby and Orman are deep in the archive room pulling decades of research papers that Shelby insists she needs to find. I am, perhaps, the only individual in the Northern Laboratories aside from Shelby and Orman who knows this.

"Alright, then," I say with feigned annoyance. "Maybe you'd be so good as to find them and ensure that they prioritize this training along with the rest of us?"

Dunn and Altman stare at me blankly, still unresponsive.

Knowing I have their attention, I seize the opportunity to rush them out of the situation. "Come on, men, this is a kill lab experiment, and none of us want to hinge our safety on teammates who were too busy to learn the experiment!"

My words finally persuade Altman into motion. He situates his glasses and asks, "Where should I search for them, Mason?"

"I'm no scientist's keeper. You know just as well as I do."

Altman heads toward the training hall exit, and I call back to him, my eyes still focused on Dunn. "Altman, take Dunn with you. Spread out so you can locate and retrieve them as efficiently as possible."

Dunn begrudgingly relents and falls into step with Altman. I'm certain they both feel relatively put-out getting sent on a chase after two other scientists while the volunteers are held back, but I don't want to waste any time worrying about it.

Once Dunn and Altman leave the hall, I'm left facing Simons' team in silence. The subtle tension that's been building inside of me eases despite the news I'm about to share. Still standing in silence, I move my hands to stretch, feeling my joints expand as I force out the tension.

"Is there something you need to tell us, Mason?" Simons wastes no time in our privacy to extract the truth. There's so much I want to tell him.

I meet their anxious gazes with one of my own. I have to start somewhere. Simons is expecting something, and I'm sure he's communicated as much to the team.

"I wanted to take this moment to say that I've decided to retire early from Orman's mentorship."

My statement is met with beaming smiles and snickers. Simons' smirk coaxes a smile out of me, but I quickly dismiss it with the reminder of what lies ahead. "Obviously, it wasn't without consequences."

Again, the group is silent. The volunteers look toward Simons for response. I stand in quiet appreciation of the leadership he commands. Simons straightens his shoulders, towering above the group. "What are we up against, Mason?"

I take a deep breath, feeling suddenly too small for such a large task. "My experiment design was initially rejected in peer review— "

Faced with blank stares, I start again, this time from the beginning. "I've been investigating the involvement of the government in the spawning and manipulation of infected patients, obviously without their consent. It turns out I was right—the government is responsible for the second outbreak and the evolution of the modern Zoribiatus strain. Shelby has known this for years, and she, along with some help, has spent her spare time secretly developing a cure which she'd intended for me to bring out of the Northern Laboratories. Now that plan is at risk. The government, using Orman as their instrument, plans to eliminate us. This experiment is meant to be the disaster responsible for our demise, and you're meant to be collateral."

The words rush out of my mouth with a mixture of urgency and nervous energy. As I search for my next statement, Simons speaks up.

"So what are we going to do about it?"

I've never been more grateful for him. I wouldn't be here without him, and now I want to make sure to pay him back.

"We're going to leave."

The group exchanges nervous glances. Amidst their solemn

concern, Cain cracks a smile. Simons catches Cain's smile and says, "Boy, if you've got something to smile about, it would serve you well to share it with the group. This is not the time for fooling."

Cain's smile turns sheepish, and his eyes fall to the ground immediately in front of him. "I'm just happy to get out of here," he says. It sounds like the truth, but I don't think it's the whole truth.

Simons chuckles deeply and slaps Cain on the back. "I don't know what you've got to complain about. You've just barely settled in, and you're already talking about leaving?"

The rest of the group joins in nervous laughter, relieved that some of the tension has gone from the room. Simons refocuses their attention by continuing, "Alright, Mason, how are we getting the cure out of this place?"

"We aren't just going to leave," I reply. "We're going to destroy the Northern Laboratories."

"What do you mean, *destroy it*?" Frances asks, anxiety clearly marking her expression.

"The Northern Laboratories have been dedicated to creating a strain of weaponized Zoribiatus. There are plans to manufacture that strain, and we don't know if that's meant to happen here or somewhere else, but we're fairly certain that as of right now, that strain only exists here. We need to destroy it."

"No," Frances says, shaking her head in a frantic back-and-forth motion. "No, you can't do that."

"We have to," I respond, trying to get a read on her, suddenly afraid that I've miscalculated the loyalties of Simons' newest members.

She brings a hand up to stifle a sob. In that moment, I realize my error.

"No, no, Frances. We won't destroy your families. The cryogenic storage is on a different circuit than the rest of the facility. They'll be spared."

I rush to her side, but Richards is there first. He puts his arm around her shoulder and brings her into a comforting embrace as sobs wrack her body. She says something into the fabric of his suit that I can't understand.

"They'll be here for us, just like they've always been. Only this way, we'll be bringing them the cure," Simons says, joining Richards and placing a hand on her shoulder.

Jorey's there too, creating a circle that doesn't include me. This is their moment. No one waits for me in those halls. I glance at Cain, who's also outside of their circle. He lifts his hands toward me, and I wonder if he likewise has no one.

"I wouldn't agree to anything that could hurt my baby," Simons coos.

Frances sniffles, slowly regaining her composure. "It's just... I don't —I c-can't—"

"I know. We all know. But this is for the cure. This is for *them*," Jorey says.

After another few moments, Richards looks over to me, his brow furrowed. "If we're meant to get away with the cure, then we can't destroy the labs. We'll have the DDC after us straight away."

"It's true," I concede. "The government will send DDC agents the moment they realize we're missing. Destroying the laboratory is also meant to buy us time for an escape."

I don't harbor any delusions that we'll convince the government of our deaths. I can only trust Shelby and hope that this time, the escape will be complete.

Simons nods in understanding, but Richards shakes his head, still unconvinced. "Are we certain there's no other option?"

"Our other option is death. And if we die, so does the cure. I'll let you weigh the merits of those options yourself." I surprise myself with the harshness of the message.

"I guess we better get to training then," Richards concedes, moving his finger in a quick arc to adjust the frame of his glasses.

"What exactly will we be training for?" Cain asks.

"Our escape," I reply.

AFTER WEEKS of failed scenarios and botched disaster plans, things finally start to come together. Simons uses his expertise to organize our transportation, while Shelby handles the problem of other scientists. I focus on the changes to the experiment design that will create a suitable crisis and the computer systems we're depending upon to pull it off. I've broken into the surveillance system and installed a creeping delay in the stream. By the time the experiment starts, there will be more than an hour's delay. This should allow us to execute our plan without observation.

"During a hive-mind experiment, things are already nearly out of control, so it's not unbelievable for something to go terribly wrong. The government—or Orman—or whoever wants us dead is counting on that, but we're going to use it to our advantage. Our disaster is going to take effect first." I explain the basic premise of the current plan to the group, trying to sound positive and confident, but I'm only met by looks of nervous skepticism.

"It makes sense in theory," Cain says, chewing the side of his lip in contemplation, "but there aren't any guarantees if we don't know exactly what we're trying to beat. We're more likely to get ourselves killed with all this guessing."

He's not wrong. My own mind runs over the same issues on repeat, denying me any rest. This plan makes the most sense. I've run it through my predictive algorithm and come up with the highest chances of success thus far—forty percent.

"It's a better plan than the last one. I say we give it a shot," Richards offers.

"Forty percent is nothing!" Cain laments.

"It's ten percent higher than thirty, and your plan came up at fifteen percent, so shut it," Jorey snaps at him.

"Says a program!" Cain shoots back.

"We're going with this plan," Simons butts in, ending the argument. He turns the group's focus toward me and asks, "So what's our role?"

"I need one volunteer to be suspended above the hive as bait."

"A sacrificial lamb," Cain mumbles.

"A risk, but the goal is to get everyone to safety," I say, wishing he didn't make me so defensive.

"Alright, when you put it that way… Hey, how about I do it?" Cain suggests, cracking a brilliant smile.

"There isn't a more precarious assignment. Are you sure?" I meet Cain's eyes, ready for another fight.

"If anyone can survive, it'd be me. Either I can do it or I'll die trying."

"Cain, don't be a fool," Simons admonishes. "We need to decide this as a team."

Cain's smile vanishes. It's a rare sight even during our most serious sessions, even when he can't stop arguing. He stares Simons down with an intensity that makes me uncomfortable. Cain's not an intimidating person, but his anger is almost tangible, and I think misplaced. "You know damn well there isn't a better position for me. I only respect your leadership as much as you respect our talents."

Simons nods slowly. He addresses me, "Mason, you have any objections?"

I shake my head. "If you're happy with Cain, he's a good choice."

"Alright then. Cain is bait; how many assists does he get?" Simons moves the plan along.

Riding the wake of Simons' command, I add, "We'll need strength and speed at the top. Everyone else is going to already be in a safer position."

Frances volunteers, and Simons consents to be the second. Jorey shakes his head and scowls. Simons catches his rough demeanor and asks, "What's got you, Jorey?"

Jorey shakes his head and grimaces. "I just know in a breakout like this, we're going to be running for our lives…"

"It would take a fool to miss that," Cain interjects with his typical ill-timed humor.

"Right," Jorey continues defensively. "It's just that I've never been able to run for my life—no matter how hard I train."

"It's alright, Jorey," I offer. "We can place you at our point of exit; you only have to stay ahead until we've made it out to the loading docks. Once we break the weather hatch, the temperature drop will slow the hive down, and we can make our escape." *Theoretically.*

Simons nods at Jorey encouragingly before addressing the rest of the group. "Anybody else have concerns?"

Richards speaks up. "What are we doing about Orman?"

"I'm glad you asked," I respond. "Please put on your virtual simulators. I've programmed the kill lab layout so I can walk you through some of the logistics."

The simulator presents the laboratories to us all—pristine and clean. I stand in the control room at the main station. The room is otherwise vacant, and I suddenly feel Shelby's absence. I stare briefly at her position before snapping myself back into focus.

"Alright everyone, take your positions. Richards, I want you on the overhead walkway," I instruct as the team begins to move.

"Jorey—" I pause, at a loss for what to do with him. He's right—we will, in all likelihood, be running for our lives, and if anybody needs a head start… "I need you at the exit point."

Jorey moves to the exit point, eying me suspiciously. "Will I be armed?"

"No," I say, after another pause, "you're going to open the hatch for Cain and his assists—and run." I keep my voice instructional and positive, but I can see Jorey's disappointment. I'm asking him to save himself instead of saving the others.

I think about standing on the rock, watching my family die. Dad asked me to do nothing. I'm asking Jorey to do the hardest thing.

"Look," I try again, "every single one of us is going to head out that exit point, and we're dependent on you."

"Right," Jorey says without making eye contact.

"*I'm* depending on you," I beg him to understand.

"What do you do?"

"I'm going to kill Orman." The edge in my voice surprises me.

"How?" Richards blurts before he can stop himself. His eyes bulge behind his thick glasses, and he smiles bashfully. "I mean, will you need help? I'll be armed…"

"No, I've got it. If we're going to have half a chance, we all need to focus on our tasks," I say.

"How are you going to, um, destroy the facility?" Frances asks, rubbing her arm.

"Once there's a breach in the safety systems, there are only one hundred and sixty seconds before automatic incineration. From there, all we have to do is hit the manual breach key, and the chain reaction will begin. Any one of us can do it from the docks if something goes wrong."

No one acknowledges my reference to the possibility of casualties. What's there to say about it? We can't choose the priority of deaths—not in a disaster. I don't intend to endanger anyone else if I can help it.

"We're just destroying the kill labs, right?" Frances asks. The section of her arm that her hand runs across again and again is red from worry.

"The manual incineration sets off a chain reaction that will take out the whole facility," I explain, realizing that Frances has never been to disaster training. Though I don't suspect even that would calm her anxiety.

"Are you absolutely certain the cryo-rooms will be safe?" Frances presses.

"They're on a different system with different securities. The cryo-rooms should be spared," I say.

I want to promise her, but there aren't any guarantees.

Frances looks relieved but not entirely convinced. "I don't know if I can just leave them…"

"You don't have a choice," Simons reminds her. "We've got to get the cure out of here or it doesn't do anyone any kind of good. In the meantime, the best thing for your family is to sit in those cold boxes and wait."

"Simons is right. If you ever want to see your families again, we have to leave." I take a deep breath before asking, "Is everyone ready?"

A chorus of nods reminds me how much lower risk the simulations are than the actual experiment. *Is there any number of times we could run a successful trial and be confident when the day is finally here?* I know there isn't. The best we can do is fish out all the possible tripping points in the plan.

I initiate the pre-programmed sequence, and we dive in. Inside the simulation, all of the danger is programmed. I can only hope that it half-resembles reality.

After a grueling couple of hours and two failed attempts, the simulation ends. A flicker of sensory disturbance finds us sweaty and breathless at the end of the endurance track. Removing my helmet, I rejoin the others. "Alright, that's not a bad start."

The team looks to one another with tight grins hiding their apprehension.

"There will obviously be a few additional tasks when it comes to it, and we'll have another three people with us at the exit."

"What's the plan? When it comes to Dunn and Altman?" Simons asks, rubbing a crease on the side of his head where the simulation helmets always dig in.

"Shelby is looking into their personal files. We may have to take them as hostages," I say, still uncomfortable with their presence in this mess.

"What else are you leaving up to Shelby?" Cain asks.

"Shelby has contacts. We're following her plan."

"Is she trustworthy?" Cain presses.

I roll my eyes, frustrated. "If we can't trust Shelby, we're not making it out of here."

"That's a lot of faith to put in one person. When you're on the outside, there's a lot to worry about, and I'm not just talking about the DDC," Cain says, placing his hands on his hips and leaning toward me.

"You think I don't know that?" I snap back. "That's why we need to trust Shelby!"

Cain nods but keeps his position. "I just want to know. We can't have any loose ends on this. If we put our faith in the wrong people…"

"What did I just say?" I turn away from him, overwhelmed. Cain has no reason to distrust her—no reason to push me.

Cain follows after me, undeterred. "It's just that we don't have to trust her if we don't want to. She's not our only hope. I could—"

"Are you seriously questioning me right now?" I let my anxiety flow out onto Cain like hot, spewing lava. "This is a good plan, and it's our only plan."

"I trust Shelby," Simons chimes in. "If you can trust me, you can trust her." He stares directly at Cain.

Cain studies Simons before backing off. "Alright. That's all I needed to hear."

"Everybody break for now. We'll run the program again, then our next meet-up will be in the cryo-rooms to select patients." I add a hint of false cheer to my last statement, which makes Frances shudder. As I watch the group head out of the training room together, I wonder if I've become as detached and sadistic as Orman.

Alone with that thought and my own apprehension, I take great care to wipe the simulation drive clean. I erase the programming code, the sequence tracker and the memory replay. It's nearly time for training by the time I've cleaned everything up, and I'm exhausted— maybe more from worry than any physical or mental exertion, but still, tired.

I walk toward the exit, fully intent on getting a bite to eat, when Hersh pops into the training room. "Mason, Orman wants a word with you. He's waiting in his office."

I nod but don't say anything, walking out of the training room without giving Hersh a single glance. I feel his gaze follow me down the hall as a knot forms in the pit of my stomach.

FIFTY-EIGHT

"DO you think I'm a fool, Mason?" Orman is standing in front of his desk and sipping from his tumbler.

"No, sir," I respond automatically.

"Stop it with that sir business! That's exactly what I'm talking about." He turns toward me, a wicked glint in his eye.

Orman's office is dimmer than before and has a musty smell to it. Orman, too, has a slightly neglected look to him—his face is unshaved, and his salted facial hair makes him appear older than ever. Something has affected his typically meticulous housekeeping and grooming habits. Shelby can't hold him long enough to have this effect.

"Maybe I should be asking what you've been up to?" I suggest.

Orman glares at me, subconsciously brushing his hands over his unkempt hair. I've hit a nerve. "Feeling bold, Kara?" He sneers.

I stare at him and don't speak, refusing to apologize. I stare long enough that he relents.

"I believe I'm the one who gets to ask you questions. I'm still your superior, even if you're no longer on my research team." He takes a step toward me.

"I prefer it if you called me Mason—just like everyone else around here," I say, side-stepping his approach. I turn to his desk and open his decanter full of liquor, pouring a heavy-handed glass and holding it up. "Need a refill?"

"Do you know what happens when you swim with sharks, *Mason*?" Orman steps toward me and takes the glass. I let go of it, but not before his body blocks my path.

"Sharks?" I ask, offering an innocent smile. "I imagine if I were swimming with sharks, I could consider myself far from here and in no danger from patients. Their stench could drive sharks toward them from miles away. It's lucky the disease has never crossed species."

"Very funny," Orman says, smirking. "It's good to know you learned something before running away from school."

His comment makes my stomach lurch. "I never said I ran away."

Orman stares down at me, baring his teeth in a mean grin. "I never said you told me."

I don't break eye contact with him, refraining from biting my lower lip with every ounce of self-restraint I can muster. *He might not know anything—he might just be toying with me.* So maybe he saw me in the medical facility… That doesn't mean he knows the rest of the story.

"So why don't you tell me, Kara Mason? Why *did* you run away to join the Scientific Institute?" Orman presses. "Who are you trying to save?"

I breathe out before I can stop myself. *He doesn't know.*

Orman reads my reaction and smiles. "There's no one left to save," he whispers.

His words hit me like a punch to the gut, but I refuse to cry in front of him.

"I always suspected that you'd be a problem. I'm not certain how you managed a placement in the laboratories instead of getting tucked away in another program."

"I wanted to become a scientist and work at the Northern Laboratories. It's the most honorable position anyone could hold," I say, quoting the city rhetoric.

"Well, your aspirations must have begun before enrolling because you just couldn't wait to start your life as a scientist, could you?" He takes a long drink from his glass.

"I've always wanted to help research for a cure. Just like Henry

Endgal," I lie. "What kid doesn't?" I push it a step further and add, "What kind of person doesn't want a cure?"

"The ones that want to live," Orman responds flatly. He takes a step back from me and paces away from his desk.

"Is there a reason you wanted to see me this evening?" I ask, edging toward the door.

"Indeed there is." His voice is loaded with derisive cheer. "Why don't you have a seat? Make yourself comfortable."

Resigned, I sit.

"Why don't you recount today's training events to me?" Orman asks, sitting in the chair directly across from me.

"Why don't you just review the training records?" I rest my hands in my lap, trying to look comfortable.

"I can't," he says, running his finger along the rim of his glass. "They're missing."

"That seems to happen a lot up here." I shrug, forcing a straight face as I meet his gaze.

Orman tightens his lips into a fine, white line. There's a long, uncomfortable pause while he drinks. A lengthy exhale brings the stench of the alcohol to my nostrils. I shift uncomfortably, waiting for him to respond. At least I know what he wants now.

"Aren't you at all worried about the scientists' role in the experiment? Or would that be an oversight in a place like this—a place dedicated to the work of a few experts to explore the nature and future of a disease that threatens our world?"

"Today was dedicated to getting the volunteers comfortable with their roles. I'll dedicate another session to the cooperating scientific team," I offer nonchalantly.

"Indeed," Orman retorts before we return to silence.

After another uncomfortable pause comes and goes, I ask, "Was that all?"

"Not quite." Orman halts my exit.

I cringe, gripping the arms of my chair in mixed protest and resignation. "Alright, then. What else can I do for you tonight?" I hardly contain the exasperation in my voice.

"Oh, Mason," Orman muses, "you could do so much for me…"

I give him an incredulous look, which he returns with his typical smug smirk. "Alas," he continues, "I believe we've passed that point in our partnership."

"And where exactly have we arrived?"

Orman smiles again, a predator toying with his prey. "Where have we arrived? Oh, Mason, you make it sound as though I'm driving our future…"

"Aren't you?"

"Mason." He savors my name like a fine drink before revisiting the delight. "Mason, you are currently responsible for driving the future that you prefer. *You* are in control. I'm merely the mechanism for driving your will forward."

"What are you trying to say?"

He's quiet. I turn to leave.

"You could change your mind, you know," Orman suggests, moving to fill his tumbler with the last of the amber liquid from the decanter.

"Is that so?"

"I'll offer it to you one last time. Tonight."

"What exactly does this offer entail?"

"Everything can go back the way it was—you can continue under my supervision, developing weapons and furthering the greater geniuses of the laboratories—of the world! I'm certain Shelby could get through her investigation without significant damage. She may lose a few of her experimental leads, but I'm certain that her contributions won't be overlooked," Orman ventures.

Does he really think that putting Shelby on the offering block is enough?

"And the volunteers?" I ask, afraid that I might betray myself and everyone else depending on this precarious meeting. Would I do it if they were guaranteed safety?

"The volunteers?" Orman asks, as though he's never given them a second thought. "I suppose they can do as they wish. Or they can continue serving in the Northern Laboratories."

Orman's suggestion of freedom for the volunteers isn't lost on me —nor is his insinuation that Shelby's investigation hinges on our current discussion. *Could I possibly get the cure out with them?* I bite my lower lip.

"You'd make a lousy chess player," Orman says.

"What do you mean?"

"All you do is stall." He drains his glass.

I exhale slowly and silently.

Deep down, I know he would never let the volunteers walk away from the laboratories. He would win everything, and I would lose.

"Orman," I say, so quiet I'm not even certain I'm speaking out loud.

He leans in to listen, placing his face so near mine that I can barely stand his smell. He cocks his head so that he can hear my voice more clearly, and his lips are upturned in what I can only assume is a smug victory expression.

"I'm afraid I can't accept your offer." My voice is no longer a whisper. I say it as eloquently as though I actually had the confidence to do something.

I'll lose this game, but he'll go down with me.

Orman looks surprised, but mostly I notice the dark shadows that spread across his face. He places his empty glass on the table and stands, turning away from me. "If that's how you'd like things to be, then."

"I'd rather."

"Well then," Orman continues, walking to his desk as though I were interrupting very important business. "I look forward to working with you in this next experiment."

"Very well, then. Have a pleasant evening." I turn the handle and let myself out of his office.

Before the door shuts behind me, I hear him murmuring to himself, and I'm certain that I hear my name.

CHAPTER
FIFTY-NINE

"IT TAKES APPROXIMATELY twenty-four hours to fully develop a patient from any stage with an accelerant," I explain, walking the frozen halls of the cryo-storage area with the team.

During this session, we have the benefit of both supporting scientists and Shelby, but strangely, Orman volunteered to take a pass. I drive the group around the corner to the third level, where storage of neurologically developed patients begins.

"Even still," I continue, "I prefer to choose patients that are already developed to the appropriate level. There's no reason to further progress a patient, in my opinion. If our halls contain patients that are sufficiently developed already, those are my choices." My pace is quick, but the whole group stays right at my heels.

"I thought most of the patients were here waiting for treatment. Are there really two hundred and fifty neurologically developed patients?" Frances asks, looking somewhat bewildered as we travel through hall after hall of frozen specimens.

"There are tens of thousands of neurologically developed patients at the Northern Laboratories," I answer.

"Tens of thousands?" Cain questions.

"Those are just the developed patients," Dunn offers, trying to be helpful. "We have several hundred thousand awaiting treatment."

"It's true," I confirm. "The total number of frozen patients currently residing in our cryo-storage is nearly half of the population of the new City States."

"The very reason we take such care to maintain our cryo-areas," Shelby emphasizes sternly, yet reassuringly.

"Where do they all come from?" Frances asks.

I give her a sharp look. We can't speak freely with Dunn and Altman so near. She catches it and makes a small *oh* noise.

"From outbreaks. Mostly in communities outside the City State protection—people who don't know better or can't do any better," Dunn answers. His tone is so convincing that I want to think he believes it—that he won't be a liability.

"So how do we pick?" Cain asks, brushing some frost off of a nearby storage container. Behind the mist is the blurred image of a man.

"We want patients that can survive twenty-four to forty-eight hours before the experiment begins," I explain, "but be choosy, I don't want body parts flying around the lab."

"—but if they're too fresh…"

A chill sweeps down the hallway as we turn another corner.

"Also, remember that we want fewer than 50 percent of our population rated as 'aggressive' to avoid unnecessary complications."

Altman turns to the storage container on his left and brushes the frost from the patient's information chart. "Jonathan L. Grelish. Submitted 100 percent neurologically developed for seventy-two hours. Aggression level—moderate. He'll do," he says, scanning the patient into the database.

"Spare us the names, Altman," Shelby corrects. "These are patients, not people. Scan them into the database to make sure they don't have any personnel conflict, but don't humanize them."

Altman hangs his head. "I've never done patient experiment selection before. I always work on the cellular level. We give our cultures names like Frank and Hanna to remind us we're working with a human disease. I can see how it's different when you're working with the whole patient…"

I put my hand on his shoulder. "You didn't mean it. But these volunteers have family upstairs waiting for treatment. It's not right to compare hopeless specimens that'll be terminated with them."

Dunn watches me, eyebrow raised, before nodding and returning to the search. I catch him stealing a glance at Simons and the others as he works.

"The database will notify us when we've processed the maximum number, and I'll review the statistics of the herd. We'll meet up after selection is completed," I say, dispersing the group throughout the frozen halls.

I stand, watching them go about their collection, waiting for Dunn and Altman to wander too far to overhear anything. Shelby stands nearby, reading patient charts but not scanning any.

"Not in the mood to make any selections?" I ask.

"There's been so much death," Shelby says somberly.

"This is the last time. After this experiment, there won't be any more developing patients, no more experimental slaughters, no more harvesting of organs or working casualties."

"This experiment is going to be a working casualty," Shelby reminds me.

"The evacuation alarms will sound. People know what to do. We're only destroying the laboratories," I insist.

"That's the plan," Shelby says.

"Is there a problem with the plan?"

"Two problems," Shelby answers.

"Dunn and Altman." I nod toward them in the distance. "What have you been able to find out?"

"I've gone over their files. They're safe enough," Shelby begins.

"Safe enough?"

"They both have families. I suspect that they'll try to contact them. If they give any indication that there were survivors..." Shelby ventures.

"Then we'll have to keep a close watch on them. Nothing inhumane, but we have to be certain. We can't give the government any indication that we've survived."

Shelby nods. "Are you ready for this?"

"As ready as I can be," I reply.

Heavy footsteps vibrate from down the suspended hall. I look over to see Simons and Jorey rushing back toward me with Frances not far behind.

"Mason! Something's up," Simons says, stopping short of us.

"The hall's empty after the eighth row!" Jorey finishes for him.

"Empty?" Shelby asks, eyes widening.

"What do you mean?" I ask.

"Each hall is packed eight deep, then the storage shells are empty," Frances says.

"They were full just last month," I say in disbelief. Shelby pulls up her tablet to scroll through.

"There aren't any withdrawal entries in three months," she says, running her finger across the data.

"My babies," Frances gasps as Richards returns to report the same information.

I pull my own tablet out and quickly pull their locations. "Level two, halls three, eight, fourteen and twenty. Richards—hall one, row forty-six. Go check!"

They disappear into the elevator as a confused Dunn and Altman return to discuss the storage phenomenon.

"What on earth do you think happened to them?" Dunn asks, rubbing the back of his head.

"I always thought it was strange that we never ran out, all those years, you know? It was bound to happen with screening and the kill experiments—not to mention big hive ones like this," he says, gesturing toward me.

"It's something else," Shelby insists. "There's something that someone isn't telling us."

I send Dunn and Altman back out to finish selection, insisting that even with the missing specimens, there are more than enough patients.

"This has to be Orman's doing," I say once they're gone again.

"This is bigger than Orman," Shelby says, tucking her tablet under her arm. "But I'm sure he's involved. Somehow. He always is."

Long minutes pass before the volunteers make their way back down to the selection floors.

"She's still here," Simons says with a relieved edge in his voice.

"All accounted for?" I ask, running my eyes across the red-cheeked and downcast group.

"Still here," Jorey agrees.

Frances nods.

"I haven't been in so long," Richards whispers.

"It was past time for all of us," Simons says, sweeping his hand across the room. "We've been living like they're gone. It's good to get a reminder of what we're in this for."

"You're right," Jorey agrees. "For them."

"For them," Richards and Frances agree.

Shelby puts her hand on my shoulder. "For all of them."

CHAPTER
SIXTY

"ARE you sure you can do it?" Simons asks, leaning back in his chair.

"Yeah, I'm sure," I reply. "I'm almost looking forward to it."

"I'm not so sure about that. Killing a patient is one thing. This is something else entirely."

We're talking about murder. I'd like to call it something else, but that's what it is. Killing patients has been legal since the first outbreak.

"I know it's going to be hard," I say, "but I have to."

"What happens if you don't? What happens if you miss?" Simons ventures.

"Maybe the patients will get him," I suggest hopefully.

"Or maybe he'll get you."

I flinch. I'm a good aim, but Orman is better. He won't need more than one shot. I let silence fill the space between us while I put words to the thoughts swirling in my head.

"If he gets a shot, he'll take it—and if he takes that shot, he won't miss. There's nothing we can do about it."

"Give Jorey a gun," Simons suggests.

"Jorey needs to get everyone through the escape hatch. That's the most important thing he can do."

I don't want to admit that I'm already afraid he won't make it out, even if he starts running at the beginning.

"I'm just suggesting that you might need some support."

"Look," I say, exasperated. I stand and begin pacing in front of Simons. I've felt the tension mounting all week, and now, with the experiment only hours away, I can't hold it in. I let it leak out under the mask of late night. Like always, Simons is there to absorb it.

"If I die tomorrow, I die. There's no saving me, and there's no going back on the plan. If I go down, you have to follow through. Get Shelby out, destroy the laboratories. End this thing!" Reality's harsh words hang in the air like a bad stench that neither of us can breathe through.

"It doesn't have to be that way," Simons says.

I don't reply. I won't even turn to look at him—I can't. Though I've made my mind up about this, it isn't easy. I stare into an empty closet. I sit at the edge of his bed, listening to his approaching footsteps.

"Kara, there's almost nobody that I want to get out of here more than you. You're like family." He places his over-sized hand on my head, making me feel small and overwhelmed.

"You have a good group. You can get Shelby out of here without me. That's all that matters." I fight the tears in the back of my throat.

"Maybe we can get you out, too. That's the plan, after all," Simons says, sitting next to me.

I want to believe it, though everything's stacked against the possibility. The forty percent changes to sixty with one working casualty—me. But what's twenty percent?

"Maybe I can get myself out," I say.

"That's the spirit."

"But if I don't... If I don't make it, I need you to take this." I hand him the parcel I brought with me.

Simons takes the package and studies it, flipping it over a few times in his hand. "Do I need to know its contents?"

"Research," I explain. "All of my research, all of the information on the disease, the hive, and how it was manufactured."

It's so much smaller than the last bag I packed before running away. Tucked within the front zipper is my only personal item—the bundle of fiber-optic wires I never managed to transform into a night-light. It's not that I couldn't—the process seems so simple now that it's laughable that I ever struggled with the concept. But I never did. Things changed too much—I changed.

"When did you put it together?" Simons asks.

"What?" I ask, lost in my own thoughts.

"The research," Simons clarifies.

"Oh. After Shelby explained what she knew, I put the pieces together. I connected all of my research and compiled it like Shelby's—so we could take it with us. Maybe, just maybe, it'll help us take down the government once and for all."

Simons puts the parcel into his travel pack. "I'm dropping these in the escape tunnel just before the experiment. Nobody should see me do it, and that's too soon to get caught on video."

"It still doesn't make sense," I continue, nearly oblivious to Simons' remark.

"Should I drop them at the loading docks?" he asks, surprised at my critique.

"What?" I ask. I see him indicate the stack of everyone's travel goods and comprehend his question. "Oh, no, your plan is good. I was thinking about the research."

"Makes sense to me," Simons says. "Government made a lethal weapon."

"But why? We still don't know who they're planning to use it on."

"Cain has his theories, but I don't suspect we'll know the real answer until we're out of here."

"Do you still think it's..." I pause, wondering if it's still not safe to name us, even now. "...us?"

He shrugs. "Until the cure, I wouldn't have thought we were big enough, but now I'm not so sure. Maybe."

I nod, and we sit, staring at nothing together. It's too late to do anything else, but neither of us seems to be able to pull ourselves from this moment. We came together to the Institute, and now we're going to leave the laboratories together. The light in the room fades with our stillness until all I can see are the shadows cast by our hands. The calm is peaceful.

In the silence, I hear distant muffled footsteps approaching. The sounds of the other volunteers. I entertain thoughts of what others might be doing or thinking at this late hour.

What will life be like outside of the laboratories? Will the command and structure of Simons' team withstand the absence of these walls? If we succeed, what's next? Rebuilt families, new lives, maybe even romances? I've spent so many nights dreaming of the worlds and people on the outside, and now I'm on the cusp of making it a reality.

My musing is interrupted by a light tap on Simons' door. Light floods into the room as Simons moves to investigate. I blink a few times as my pupils dilate and my mind re-enters the present. Simons leans in close to the door, one muscled arm grasping the handle, his other stretched up to brace on the sill. I note the tension that lines his figure, thinking that none of us can relax for a while yet.

A muffled voice makes its way through the closed barrier. I can't hear what it says, but Simons responds by cracking open the door. The shadow of a figure blocks the light from the hall—shorter, but nearly as broad as Simons—Jorey.

I stand to join Simons at the door, curious about what Jorey might be looking for at this late hour. Their muffled voices become clearer as I approach, and I overhear a splice of their conversation.

"—knew you couldn't sleep tonight. I just can't stop thinking about her." Jorey's voice is uncharacteristically low and soft.

"I'm thinking about her too, but you just need to stop worrying. Worry does no good," Simons responds with an equally soft voice.

"Worry about whom?" I ask. My voice is frighteningly loud by comparison.

Simons whips around, startled by my approach. The door swings open to reveal Jorey's full figure, and he jumps. "Mason! What are you doing here?"

Simons gives him an apologetic look as Jorey steps back into the hall, looking helpless. I shake my head. "I'm going over some last-minute details for tomorrow with Simons. What's going on?"

Simons steps between the two of us and intervenes. "Calm down, both of you. We're all a little nutty with anxiety right now, under-standably."

Jorey opens his mouth, and Simons gives him a stern look that reverses his motion. I wave my hands in the air, indicating that I would like *somebody* to explain what's going on. Simons gives me the same look he gave Jorey, and I drop my arms to my side, dejected.

"C'mon on in, Jorey, you can sit and fret with us," Simons offers.

"Yeah," I add. "Nobody's getting any sleep tonight. We can not sleep together."

Jorey looks from Simons to me and back to Simons again. He runs his hand over the back of his neck and over his unshaven face. He's about to say something when another door in the hall creaks open. Cain's sleepy voice calls to us from across the hall. "What's going on? Is there a party out here I wasn't invited to?"

Simons answers, "Might as well be. We've got two, one more's a crowd."

Jorey gives Simons another helpless look but steps into the room. He turns to me and says in a softer voice, "Hey Mason, sorry I interrupted your meeting." He shuffles his feet nervously.

"No matter," I say. "I think I'm just here because I can't sleep." I sit in Simons' chair, and Jorey moves toward the bed. I raise my eyebrow as I watch him, still searching for an explanation to his clandestine communication.

"Mind if we join you?" Richards asks, appearing at the door behind Cain. "Frances and I could hear you down the hall. We figured it had to be you guys. Nobody else would be up at this hour."

"Frances?" I ask, wondering why she was visiting Richards in the middle of the night.

"Getting some last-minute tips on close-range firing before tomorrow," Frances rushes to explain.

"Any tips on being last-minute hive food?" Cain jests as he takes a seat on Simons' bed next to Jorey. His silly smile immediately lightens the mood.

"Speaking of snacks," Cain continues, "anybody got anything? I'm starving!"

Frances and Richards join the group in Simons' tiny room, and we all cozy in to spend our last night together at the Northern Laboratories. Simons rummages through some cabinets and pulls out a package. He tosses it across the room, and Cain catches it. The rustling of the package piques everyone's curiosity.

"Chocolate square cookies," Cain reads. "Fresh like Grandma used to make them!"

"A friend sent those up a while back. I've been saving them for a special occasion," Simons explains.

"No occasion could be more special than this," Cain says. "Our last night under the roof of tyranny!" He opens the package and takes a cookie before passing the treats around.

Simons joins us, sitting at the head of the bed. His weigh added to the four other bodies causes the center to bow and groan. He takes a cookie. "This calls for a toast."

"To escape?" I offer.

"To Mason!" Cain proclaims. "For pushing so hard that she's forced us to make a great escape!"

The group nods in agreement. Jorey gives Cain a look so harsh that he blushes under its oppression. "To Mason," Jorey grumbles.

"To Mason!" everyone agrees in unison.

I take a bite of my cookie. It crumbles over my tongue, flavorless.

CHAPTER
SIXTY-ONE

THE KILL LAB is quiet when I arrive—hours earlier than anybody else. Simons is at the loading docks, getting our escape gear organized. Everything's in order now. Shelby's and my research is tucked away in our escape bags. Our patients are fully developed and being held in the loading hall. The volunteers are in the ready room, suiting up.

I lay out the weaponry carefully. Orman will be stationed at the main pulsar gun, ready and willing to fire. There is no position—save, possibly, for one involving his drinking glass—that he's more comfortable in. Shelby will be armed with a close-range weapon. I leave it hidden under the counter of her station, like we previously agreed. I tuck my own gun behind my recording equipment. After situating the weapons, I wait an hour to check the camera system and ensure that nothing is visible.

After I've checked every system and reviewed each step of the plan, I review it again. When that's done, I pause, whispering to myself, "Ready or not..."

"Here I come," Orman's snide voice surprises me.

"You startled me; I didn't hear the doors," I stammer.

"You seemed distracted. Nervous for your own experiment?"

"Hive experiments are the most dangerous here or anywhere else," I say.

"Indeed, but you've planned so *thoroughly*. What could go wrong?" As usual, Orman's question sounds more like a threat.

What does he have planned for today? I can only trust that our plan will unfold before he has chance to unleash his own.

"I suppose you're right, Orman. We've planned well," I say, injecting false confidence into my voice.

"I'm certain it'll be a fine execution," Orman says, delighting obviously in his words.

The entrance lights up as Shelby makes her way quickly through the passageways. I hear the beeping of her key code as she flashes her ID card and the door whooshes open. She walks into the experiment control center without a word and starts cuing up her workstation, not bothering to look over.

"Good morning to you too, Shelby," Orman says sarcastically.

"Let's just get this over with," Shelby says, a hint of sadness in her voice.

"Let's," Orman says, this time his delight better restrained.

I take my place at my own workstation and cue up the communication system. Orman busies himself with his pulsar gun and his own communications. While I'm certain that he's distracted with his own preparations, I reach back to touch my gun, reassuring myself that it's ready. He pulls out a headset.

"What do you need a communication headset for?" I ask.

"Your experiment came under criticism. I'm taking initiative in maintaining control." He winks at me.

This can't be good. I'll have to make sure I disable his system after I take him down.

Though they don't appear on the cameras, I know the volunteers are waiting in their ready room. Simons should have joined them by now. I exhale to calm myself before depressing the speaker and instructing, "Everyone at ready, we're going to open the kill hall for places."

I listen for the whoosh of the door breaking the vacuum seal. They move forward and begin to take their places without communicating. Richards climbs onto the walkway above the hall and situates himself with a pulsar gun. Frances and Simons begin pulling down the bait harness while Cain waits patiently, and Jorey makes his way toward the exit, carrying his own pulsar gun.

I open my mouth to say something when the crackle of another speaker interrupts my thought process. Orman's voice comes over the speaker system. "Jorey, you're a lousy shot. Why don't you trade positions with Cain? His mark is much better."

"Bait?" Jorey asks, dumbfounded.

"Yes," Orman smiles, glancing over at me wickedly, "bait."

The volunteer team is frozen in their positions, uncertain what to do next. I compress my speaker button. "Jorey's a fine shot. Let's continue how we've rehearsed."

Orman retorts quickly over the speaker system. "No. We're doing it the way I say."

Altman and Dunn enter the experiment station and exchange confused glances. I look back to them, feeling the weight of responsibility. They're my burden to carry. "Altman, please take up the station nearest Shelby for secondary recording. Dunn, as at our last training, scout for Orman."

"Don't scouts usually get a gun?" Dunn asks, looking for another weapon.

"It's Orman," I reply. "We don't need another gun."

Dunn relents. I shake my head and ask Orman without initiating the speaker system, "What are you trying to do? We've rehearsed this!"

"I've reviewed the experiment setup," Orman says. "I know that you didn't rehearse with Jorey armed. I take it as a cue that the volunteers aren't secure in their tasks, so I'm taking it on my authority to adjust as necessary."

He compresses his speaker button. "Jorey in the bait harness. That's final."

Cain approaches Jorey, who begrudgingly hands him the pulsar gun. Frances and Simons help Jorey into the harness and look over at me nervously. His hands are shaking. Orman sees and smiles sadistically. Cain takes Jorey's position near the exit and leans back against the wall, resting his finger just above the trigger. He aims his body toward the patient entrance, but his gaze is fixed on Orman.

"Everyone at ready?" I ask over the speaker system. A subtle tone of panic rises within me.

Simons gives a thumbs-up. I nod back at him and tilt my head toward Jorey. Simons nods slowly in response. The plan has changed. We've got to get Jorey to safety.

"Alright then," Orman says. "Let's get this show on the road!" He claps his hands together.

I enter the sequence to open the back hall door and release the patients. Across the long hall, I watch it open. Bodies begin to appear, moving slowly at first, but as their numbers increase, they seem to move more quickly. At the back end of the hall, I predict that maybe two hundred patients have made their way into the room. The door should shut soon, and the first experimental barrier—the force field between the hive and the bait—will collapse.

But more bodies flood the hall—far more, by my prediction, than two hundred and fifty.

I glance over at Orman and notice that he's not in his usual position, eased into the large weapon. He's sitting back, hands folded across his chest and smiling. I return my focus to the onslaught of patients still pouring into the hall—five hundred, six hundred? Their numbers are unending, and I'm certain we're beyond the capacity of the hall.

Are these the missing patients? Orman has been busy.

The numbers don't change our plan. It's only more dangerous now. That could be a good thing.

Still, I hold off on dropping the first barrier. The patients make their way to the front of the large hall. A patient stands out toward the front of the pack, dark and fresh. There's something strangely unsettling about it.

"Trudy?" Simons voice comes across loud and terrible, and I realize why the patient seems familiar.

She's not the image of the girl I saw years ago. Her skin is grey and loose, and her eyes are blank, but she responds still to her father's calls.

"Tell me that's not you, baby," Simons cries. The desperation in his voice pierces me.

These aren't the missing patients.

Now I know what Orman has been up to and why he called me to his office. I only have to search a moment to see who they are. There are so many small figures amidst the sea of bodies. He's developed children. He's developed the volunteers' families.

My gut lurches. "No!"

Frances's shrieks join the mixed medley of horror as she picks out the two fire-haired children huddled near a man. They're all here—Richards' wife, Jorey's parents—anybody we've ever known who was sent to wait for a cure—they're all in there, daring us to fire.

"First barrier coming down in three... two... one," Orman announces over the speaker.

"Wait," I cry, desperate to stop this awful progression. Orman proceeds anyway.

"Is that Walker?" Altman asks in a weak voice, staring into the horrendous crowd.

Before anyone has time to react, a faint flicker indicates the removal of the force field. The first patient responds. Fixating on Jorey's dangling legs, it snaps into focus, and the cloudy eyes dilate. A low gurgling noise emanates from its throat as it moves toward him. The wave of attention spreads through the group as we witness the hive initiate. I forget myself and watch the nightmare unfold.

The hive approaches quickly, swarming the hall floor just below Jorey's feet. Nobody moves. Richards' stare is fixed on his wife—the patient whose hair has fallen out in clumps, her skin collecting in pools as far as gravity will pull it from her sad, swollen body. She works with the lead of the hive, leaping up toward Jorey's exposed feet. Jorey calls out to someone in the hive, forgetting they're already gone.

"Orman, what did you do?" Shelby whispers as she watches helplessly.

"My job," he replies. "The question is, what are you going to do now?" His voice is a victorious sneer.

All of my hatred for Orman amasses in this moment. I'm driven, finally, to do what I suspect I may not have otherwise been able to do. "Damn you, Orman," I say in a shockingly calm voice. "Those are their families! They can't fire on their own families."

"They can't?" Orman asks with false sympathy. "Then by all means, allow me!"

Trudy has scrambled over the amassing hive and is now standing atop a compliant patient's shoulders. She's reaching hungrily for Jorey's legs as he thrashes and attempts to pull himself higher up from the harness. Trudy's mouth hangs open in a too-wide smile. Simons watches her in disbelief, unable to act. Other patients follow her lead, climbing on top of one another and making ground toward Jorey. Brothers and sisters, friends and spouses, rabid with hunger and mindless with disease emerge and disappear within the hive.

An electric crackling accompanies the blast from Orman's pulsar gun. The shot is a direct hit. Trudy's head spatters charred flesh over the huddled masses below. Simons screams in agony as the outstretched arms of the hive pull the headless body into their sea and she's lost forever. The hive progresses, undeterred by the shot. Orman fires again and again. Each shot is a direct hit to someone somebody cares about. He gives a sadistic whoop each time.

"Easier than a simulation," he jabs.

Still they progress, gaining with every second on the volunteers trapped within. There are too many patients in the group to keep them at bay with gunfire. Orman knows this, so he continues to fire, enjoying his sick game.

I compress the speaker and call out to the group desperately, "They're not your family anymore! Your families are gone. Fire!"

Cain is the first to respond, spraying hot plasma over the top of the hive in quick pulses. A few patients fall back, but more appear. Richards' hands shake as he takes one very precise shot into the back of his wife's skull and tearfully watches her sink out of view. I can see him mouth "I love you" as she disappears.

"Mason, the hive is out of control. We're going to lose the volunteers." Shelby's warning comes nearly too late.

Simons is trying to pull Jorey out of the harness, but hands are closing in on his legs. Without distraction, they'll lose him. Before I can think, I remove the second barrier and scream, "Over here!"

The patients on the edge of the group respond immediately, fixing their attention on the new target and pulling others along with them.

Their movements cause Orman to realize the barrier is down. He reaches up to his headset and spins a dial above his ear.

My chance to move is slipping away. I reach for my concealed weapon just as Orman realizes what I'm up to. He swings his gun around and takes aim. I pull my weapon into position, but I'm too late. Orman's already fired. I hold my breath and wonder what it's like to die.

CHAPTER
SIXTY-TWO

SHOTS ARE GOING off all around me. Everyone with a weapon is firing. I've lost sight of Shelby and the other scientists. The shot I expected to drive through my skull misses.

Orman cries out.

I try to orient myself, but everything is spinning into chaos. Orman's weapon is smoldering. He's holding his shoulder. Behind him, Cain's resetting his weapon. I look up and see Richards moving down the suspended walkway with Frances, Simons and Jorey. Cain hasn't opened the escape hatch yet.

"Open the hatch!" I scream. He lowers his gun and presses the button. Orman follows my gaze to Cain and identifies him as the shooter. The hive has broken into a disorganized free-for-all. Patients funnel into the experiment hall, lunging toward the nearest victims. I'm nearly out of time to make an escape, Orman dead or not. I breathe a silent prayer that his injuries affect his aim.

I reach for the gun at my feet and can't find it. I have to go now. Even Dunn and Altman are making their way to the exit. I sweep the room for Shelby and spot her halfway up the walkway, making progress toward the volunteers. She turns periodically to fire at the clamoring patients that progress from every direction. Orman stands and moves toward me, holding his charred shoulder. I scramble to my station and compress the manual destruction button.

I run toward the exit as patients swarm the stations. If I can make it before Orman, there's a good chance he'll get taken out in the incineration. He'll have no way out—all other exits are blocked. If I don't make it... *at least I can watch him burn with me.*

I'm halfway across the floor when a cluster of patients cuts off my progress. They've got Altman cornered. Unlike the chaotic and unpredictable behavior of the others, this group is quiet and organized—it's hive. Before I can do anything, they're grasping at him with dead fingers and tearing at his flesh with hungry mouths. His cries only last a moment. The floor is stained with his blood, and the patients smear it further as they disperse, fighting with one another to devour their prey.

Something is disrupting the hive behavior...

I scramble on top of Shelby's station, searching for an escape. Not seeing a better option, I grab the channel of piping that stretches across the roof. I make my way, arm over arm, diagonally toward the exit, as quickly as I dare without losing my grip.

All around me, patients swarm, searching for another victim. Orman stands in their midst, shockingly unscathed. His blood drips to the ground below him and splatters with his every movement, but still the hive isn't drawn in his direction.

Impossible!

Everyone else has made their way to the exit. I steal another glance, narrowly keeping my grip along the tangled piping. He's holding my pulsar gun in his uninjured arm. He takes aim again. If I'm going to make it, I have to jump.

Patients' hands brush against my feet as they reach out for me. I swing to build momentum, tucking my knees to stay above them. The pulse from Orman's shot barely misses my legs. He's lost his aim firing with the other arm. I can't let him take another shot.

Just as I release my grip and reach for the ledge, Jorey emerges from the exit, holding Cain's weapon.

"Don't!" I call out.

He ignores me, grabbing my arm as I narrowly catch the ledge.

Simultaneously firing a shot toward Orman, he pulls me up. Patients are making their way through the exit. I find my feet. Jorey has my arm in a death grip. We narrowly dodge another of Orman's shots.

"Run!"

I hit the lock button as we move into the escape. A low repeating alarm sounds as the exit makes its seal. I can hear, with no uncertainty, that there are patients already in the hall. We run like we've never run before, but still I gasp, "Did everyone make it?"

"Not Altman," he says.

"Where are they?"

"Ahead," Jorey breathes, already labored. He hasn't let go of my hand, and I can feel him losing ground.

Jorey still has the gun. I reach across in full stride and grab it from him. It slides easily from his hand. I cycle the gun's power as we sprint and search the tunnel horizon, dimly lit by the floodlights scattered above. We're nearly there.

I slow my pace so that Jorey can recover. Behind us, the entire structure rumbles from the incineration blast on the kill lab floor. *Goodbye, Orman.*

The rumble lessens, and from it I hear a chilling sound—the low gurgling of a patient locked in on prey.

I can't tell where the sound is coming from. Too much echo from the blast makes it impossible. We only have a few moments before attack. "Get behind me," I say.

"No, go! You can make it," Jorey says, pushing me forward.

Then I see it—lanky but still intact, Diaz emerges from the shadows, bolting toward Jorey. He sees it too and knows it's too late. Recognition of his former teammate only makes impending death more tortured. I bring up my gun, but before I aim, there's a flash of plasma, and the patient falls at Jorey's feet.

Shelby steps out of the shadows, blood streaked across the left side of her face. "Get out of here!"

"Shelby," I breathe, relieved.

Her name spills out of my mouth before I can pull it back, but everything from there happens as though in slow motion. Jorey lunges for me, knocking me off my feet as Shelby leaps toward us. The crackling of electricity fills the air, and my hairs stand on end. There's a loud sizzle as Shelby lights up, then falls straight to the floor. Behind her slumped mass are Orman's smoking gun and grim smile.

"I suppose you thought I was dead already," he sneers, blood oozing from his charred shoulder. He brings the gun to his mouth with his good arm and sets the reload with his teeth. I scramble to take aim, but Jorey blocks me with his body. I fire anyway and miss. More shots come from behind us, lighting up the tunnel with blinding flashes. Before they get close, Orman retreats into the darkness.

Simons and Cain rush forward, still firing in Orman's direction. I crawl to Shelby's side and search for her pulse. In death, her old body is even more frail. There's a small electric discharge when I touch her skin.

"Shelby," I yell. But there's no response.

"Come on, Mason, she's gone. You can't do anything. We have to go." Jorey pulls at my shoulder.

"Shelby… I can't do this without you!" I whimper. Jorey picks me up and pulls, but I refuse to release her hand.

"Come on, Mason, you've got to let go," Jorey pleads.

"We can't leave without her! She's the only one that can get us out of here, don't you get it?" I scream at him, yanking my hand from his.

The world spins around me. *It wasn't supposed to go this way.*

I'd imagined going over every single detail of the plan with Shelby at the close of each day, but it never happened. I spoke with Shelby about the most critical plans I've ever had a hand in developing exactly one time.

One time!

I don't know what's supposed to happen next.

"Shelby, I can't do this without you," I whisper.

"She's gone. We're going to have to find a different way. I know you can."

He doesn't wait for me to respond. Instead, he leans over and hoists me up by the waist, dragging me against my will.

Simons and Cain run up from the shadows. "Was someone hit?" Simons demands, taking in the scene.

"She wasn't supposed to die. She wasn't supposed to pick me over anyone else," I say, finally letting her hand slip from mine. No one else was supposed to die.

A symphony of gurgles resonates in the hall. I can't tell how many there are, but it's enough. Simons grabs me from Jorey, tossing me roughly over his shoulder. I bounce uncomfortably as the group runs. A few dozen patients race toward us with uncanny speed.

"Did you start the chain reaction?" Cain asks.

"What?" I ask, not making sense of his question.

"The reaction? Are the laboratories going to go down?" he yells.

Reality slams into me. Before Shelby died—before Orman ducked into the shadows—we had a plan. I recall depressing the manual trigger.

"It's done," I say, still numb.

Cain calls out ahead. "Start the truck, we've gotta go now!"

A rush of frozen air greets me as we burst out onto the exposed loading docks. An icy gust of wind steals my breath, and I blink in the grey light of day. Over the roar of the tundra weather, the transport vehicle engine rumbles to life. Cain jumps into the back, and Simons tosses me like a ragdoll before heaving himself onto the vehicle along with Jorey.

Someone moans as the vehicle lurches into motion.

"Where's Shelby?" Richards asks in an uncharacteristically tight voice.

"She didn't make it," Simons says.

"He's bleeding out. I need my bag," Richards responds.

The vehicle speeds off just as the ground beneath us begins to rumble. Even the subzero wind gusts don't diminish the heat that emanates from the entirety of the Northern Laboratories going up in flames. The rumble is deafening.

Minutes after the blast, everything goes silent. The wind makes the vehicle shudder and sway as it pulses through the frozen valley like a metronome. Frances does what she can to keep it steady on the icy road. I keep my eyes fixed on the plume of smoke above the flames, not thinking.

"We have to get off the road," Cain says.

"Not in these conditions. Are you crazy?" Simons protests.

"The roads aren't safe. We'll be too easy to find," Cain insists.

"There's no way anybody could have survived that blast," Simons objects.

"Somebody survived, and they *will* be looking for us," Cain continues. "We need to get underground."

"Underground?" Jorey asks, yelling over the wind.

"Just trust me, okay? How do you think I got here?" Cain growls at them, then he shouts out to Frances, "Turn off over here. We'll wreck the vehicle and head underground."

Frances complies, and we all stare off into the frozen nothingness, hoping Cain hasn't gone mad.

ACKNOWLEDGMENTS

To Drew, your love and support made this possible. Thank you for letting me spend 20-mile runs dissecting minor plot points. Thank you for always listening, helping me with the massive emotional load of life and writing, and thank you for making me believe that I could do this.

To my editor, who made sure that I didn't get away with too much introspection. Thank you for helping me bring my world to life, and thanks for helping with the pacing. The book wouldn't be what it is without you.

To my sister, Anne, who helped me identify one of the earliest problems with the story, and get excited about making the necessary changes. You've really got an eye for this.

And to the rest of my family and friends, for supporting me, encouraging me to write and follow my dreams. I hope that by writing and sharing, I've made the world a slightly better place. You made me believe it's possible.

ABOUT THE AUTHOR

Jill N Davies started out as a chemist working for a pharmaceutical manufacturing company. After several years working in development she moved on to become... a high school science teacher. (You see where this is going, don't you?)

Before she went full *Breaking Bad,* she took a sharp left turn at Albuquerque and decided to dedicate her working time to creating stories. She now writes in the quiet moments of her life, squeezing novels into the nooks, crannies and nap times that act like the pauses between heartbeats.

Her debut series combines much of her acquired knowledge and experiences with the fascinating dystopia of a science-driven world.

When she's not writing, you may often find her running the trails near her home, hiking the national parks, or reading the same book over and over to her two daughters.

Find more at www.jillndavies.com

ALSO BY JILL N DAVIES

MORE BOOKS FROM THE KARA MASON SERIES

Into the Deadlands (Book 2) - Releasing October 13, 2023

The Darkling Project (Book 3) - Release date TBD

Extinction Event (Book 4) - Release date TBD

www.ingramcontent.com/pod-product-compliance
Lightning Source LLC
Chambersburg PA
CBHW030106310726
48970CB00004B/1173